Sherlock Holmes is dead. His body lies in a solitary grave on the Sussex Downs, England. But Dr. Watson survives, and is now given permission to release tales in Sherlock's 'classified dossier', those cases that are, dear reader, unbelievable – for their subject matter is of the most outré and grotesque nature.

In this thrilling first volume of the Classified Dossier, a Transylvanian nobleman called Count Dracula arrives at Baker Street seeking the help of Sherlock Holmes, for his beloved wife Mina has been kidnapped.

But Dracula is a client like no other and Holmes and Watson must confront – despite the wild, unbelievable notion – the existence of vampires. And before long, Holmes, Watson and their new vampire allies must work together to banish a powerful enemy growing in the shadows…

SHERLOCK HOLMES & COUNT DRACULA

CHRISTIAN KLAVER

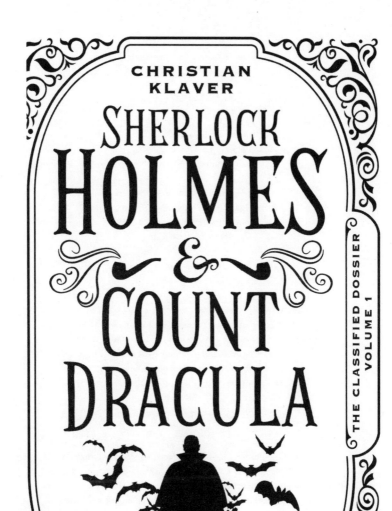

SHERLOCK HOLMES & COUNT DRACULA

THE CLASSIFIED DOSSIER
VOLUME 1

TITAN BOOKS

Sherlock Holmes and Count Dracula
Hardback edition ISBN: 9781789097122
E-book edition ISBN: 9781789097139

Published by Titan Books
A division of Titan Publishing Group Ltd
144 Southwark Street, London SE1 0UP
www.titanbooks.com

First Titan edition: September 2021
10 9 8 7 6 5 4 3 2 1

Case design by Julia Lloyd. Images © Shutterstock.

Printed and bound by CPI Group (UK) Ltd, Croydon CR0 4YY

To my wife, Kim, for all her love and support
for all these years.

INTRODUCTION

Astute readers will notice several discrepancies between this text, my previous stories, and the Stoker novel bearing Dracula's name.

On the Stoker text, I can only beg the reader's indulgence and state that there are several inaccuracies, not the least of which is the report of Dracula's untimely demise.

As to the inconsistencies in my own text, particularly surrounding Mary Watson née Morstan, I have been forced to change many dates and names in order to preserve the privacy and dignity of several of Holmes's original clients, muddling both the timeline in this tale as well as in my original stories. The particularly scholarly student of Holmes's cases will no doubt note that there are several instances chronologically after *The Sign of the Four* in which Mary does not appear, one of the many inconsistencies to which I refer. Again, I can only beg the reader's indulgence, but these small trivialities are necessary to preserve the secrecy under which Holmes and I have been sworn on many of his most delicate cases.

And some readers will already be familiar with Holmes's "black box", that depository of cases that included such wonders as "The Giant Rat of Sumatra", as well as the separate matters involving Mr James Phillimore, and the cutter *Alicia*. These accounts have yet to see publication, since their grotesque and outré nature would stretch the reader's sensibilities beyond any normal boundaries. They are, in a word, unbelievable, and I have held these cases in abeyance at Holmes's request to protect both his reputation and my own small credibility as narrator. But the time has come, finally, to reveal them, as per Holmes's instructions. I follow these instructions faithfully and humbly, and let my readers judge if we have done wrong to withhold them for as long as we did.

— JOHN H. WATSON, M.D.

Part One

COUNT DRACULA

Chapter 01

LESTRADE'S PACKAGE

It was late in 1902 when I found myself a resident once more in my quarters at Baker Street. My wife, Mary, was spending some months out in the country visiting the Forresters, and this gave me the opportunity to renew my acquaintance with Holmes to such a degree that I almost felt I had come back to bachelorhood on a permanent basis. On the third day, a tempestuous London storm howled through the chimney and tapped with wet fingers at the windows of our drawing room, making it a distinct comfort for us to be indoors.

But if the conditions appealed to me, they did not bring solace to Holmes. He had no active case at present and was quite beside himself with a hectic lassitude that had him twitching restlessly in his chair. I had tried, earlier in the afternoon, to regale him with a humorous anecdote from home, one with Mary packing up half of our domestic life to take with her into the country, but I let the story trail off when Holmes showed every sign of distraction.

Several times he cast a reckless glance at the door or the window, as if expecting some interruption.

"I am a little jumpy, at that, Doctor," Holmes said with a laugh, and I knew he had deduced my thoughts in that uncanny way of his. "It is only this dreaded inactivity, Watson. It exhausts me as work never does. It is doubly vexing when I know that trouble is brewing on the horizon, only I cannot get my hands on any of the threads, so that I have nothing with which to occupy my waiting hours."

"Trouble?" I said. I had been at Baker Street for nearly three days, and had the feeling that Holmes had been waiting for something all this time, but he had refused to be drawn out on the subject until now.

"You are unfamiliar with my cases of the past few months, Watson, so I cannot expect you to know my current state of affairs. Of late, I have been involved in several cases that seemed, on the surface, unrelated, but which, I have become convinced, all stem from a single source. I have been seeking them out exclusively, and turning all other unrelated cases away. The missing crews from the *Matilda Briggs* and the *Demeter*, certain tangential persons involved in the death of Radghast the booking agent, and the disappearance of Miss Violet Bell are all the work of one mastermind, Watson. It is all connected, and I am carefully drawing all the threads round me, feeling for the spider at the centre."

"Some new criminal mastermind? I thought you had rid London of any such pestilence."

Holmes reached out and picked up his briar pipe. He scraped

his pipe bowl clean and made ready for a fresh batch of tobacco by the expedient of rapping the bowl against the table leg, heedless of the shag bits on the carpet. He fired his pipe to the desired pitch before answering.

But his answer was interrupted by voices from below.

"At last," Holmes said, with no small amount of relief. "Let us see how Lestrade's come along with my little errand. If his urgency is any indicator, he may well have something of interest."

I did not know to what errand my friend might be referring, yet I could not help but feel a great sense of relief, for Lestrade's involvement meant a case of some sort. Holmes flashed me a wry smile, which was then gone in an instant. He'd noted my grateful exhalation and known the cause at once.

When Lestrade himself burst into our sitting room, the little detective wore the most solemn expression. In his hand he bore a small veneered case, such as a well-to-do gentleman might use to carry cards or cigarettes.

"Murder then," Holmes said. "And it took you somewhat out of your way, into the Farringdon district, I should say."

Lestrade started. "I'm familiar with your cunning ways, Mr Holmes, but how you could know all that without yet hearing or seeing any of the clues is quite beyond me."

"You brought the clues in with you, Lestrade," Holmes said with a wave of his hand. "It is no secret that they've torn up the pavement in order to begin construction in Farringdon, and in doing so thrown up a great deal of the red clay that I see about your shoes. I know your route was to Norwood, as I sent you there, and Farringdon is well out of the way. The fact that it is still wet and that you were in too much of a hurry to do more than a casual scraping at our doorstep increases the impression of great urgency. Also, your face and demeanour suggest something disturbing, despite your many years with Scotland Yard. What else but murder?"

"Well, I suppose my face does tell the tale plainly," Lestrade admitted. "I expect you remember Stross, the forger in Norwood that you turned us on to last week?"

"Yes, quite," said Holmes. "Did you find him at the address I gave to you?"

Lestrade nodded. "We did, and in the process of apprehending him we came upon something murkier than a simple forgery. When asked about it, the rascal would say nothing. This is a man who would send either of us to the bottom of the Thames without the slightest hesitation. To make matters stranger, this cool customer, who hadn't broken so much as a sweat during his arrest, actually broke down in tears when we questioned him about it!" The little detective held up the cigarette case. "We have been able to get nothing intelligible from him."

"And this is the item here?" Holmes asked. He gestured at the cigarette case.

"Yes," Lestrade said. "I've taken the liberty of bringing it with me."

"Let us see what we can make of it," Holmes said, rubbing his hands together as he warmed to his task. Lestrade handed the cigarette case over without further comment.

"Lacquered teak," Holmes said. "Expensive, but not otherwise extraordinary. It has seen some use by a man once wealthy who has since fallen on hard times. The clear markings of an amateurish repair applied to the hinge tell us that. Now then, let us look inside." He fell abruptly silent when he opened the box.

I shifted in my seat to get a closer look and gasped as the significance of what I saw struck home to me. "Good Lord, Holmes!" I said, for rarely had I seen a more shocking example of brutality and horror.

Inside, nestled neatly in red velvet like a rare jewel, lay a freshly severed human finger.

Holmes leaned closer, deeply affected not with shock or disgust, but with eager interest. He pulled his lens from a drawer and examined it all together first, then carefully removed the finger. He looked further into the box and made a satisfied noise. "This was originally used for cigarettes, as one might expect," he murmured. "Traces of them are still here." He carefully pulled a scrap of tobacco out and snuffed at it like a bloodhound. "An unusual and expensive brand. Made in India and not much seen in England. It has a very acrid taste that would not be popular."

Then he began a minute study of the finger itself. It was clearly a woman's finger, and showed no sign of decay that I could see. The hand it was taken from must once have been long and white, a beautiful sight before this horrible disfigurement had taken place. Holmes measured the length and width of the finger and even scraped underneath the fingernail, which was long and unpainted.

"The ring finger of the left hand," he murmured. "Very recently cut. It is difficult to be certain, since the cut has fallen very close to where a wedding ring would lay, but I would say that we are missing any sign of the indentation such a ring would make, so we can safely assume she was not married. The finger has no calluses, so we now have either a woman of the higher class or an invalid excused from menial labour. Very curious."

"What could anyone want with such a grisly trophy?" I asked. "Was it some kind of proof of kidnapping?"

Lestrade shook his head. "I have not yet had the chance to communicate with any other departments in the city, but there's no such missing person that we know of, and no ransom note was found. Nor do we have any idea who might receive one until we identify the victim."

Holmes shot an acute glance at Lestrade. "When did you get this?"

"We found it this morning, when the arrest was made. After finding this little bit of nastiness, we searched the house, but to no avail."

Holmes frowned, clearly displeased with this information. He sprang up and went over to the table in the corner that held his equipment for chemical experimentation, taking the box and finger with him. He rummaged among the retorts, test tubes, and little Bunsen lamps before extracting three empty tubes. He added a small amount of water to each, then carefully added a sample of blood taken from the finger to the first, and a sample from the box to the second. For the third, he jabbed a bodkin into his own finger to supply a few drops. He absently covered the self-inflicted scratch with a piece of sticking plaster, a habit I knew he performed in order to prevent accidentally poisoning himself while handling toxins. Then he measured a small amount of white crystals, dropping them into the waiting vessels. He followed this with a few drops of a transparent fluid from an angular green bottle.

He jerked upright as each and every test tube turned a dull mahogany colour. "I really must thank you, Lestrade," he said without lifting his eyes from the experiment on the table. "Already this case is showing an extraordinary number of interesting features. Some very interesting features indeed, including some I've never seen before. Perhaps a case unique in the annals of crime detection."

"Indeed," I said fervently. "I can hardly imagine a more cold-blooded act. What kind of monster could carry around such a thing the way another man carries cigarettes? It is barely imaginable."

Holmes waved a hand dismissively. "Oh, that is hardly exceptional. Recall, Watson, when the fifty-year-old spinster, Miss Susan Cushing, received a parcel in the post which turned out to contain two severed human ears packed in coarse salt and I think you will have to concede my point. No, it is the curious condition of the finger and the nature of the victim that interests me."

"We must help her, Holmes," I urged. The image of some poor woman maimed in such a fashion shook me to the core.

"I'm afraid," Holmes said, not unkindly, "it is all too likely that this particular woman is beyond our reach to help, but possibly we can be of some assistance in punishing the criminals involved."

"Begging your pardon, Mr Holmes," Lestrade said, "but the woman may still be alive. I would hardly call that wound fatal." He had taken his hat off and was currently worrying into a sorry shape in his idle hands while he watched Holmes.

"No," Holmes said. "You wouldn't, but I consider it the highest probability." He held up a hand to fend off further protests. "You have your methods, Lestrade, and I have mine. Be assured that I will send you a telegram with any advice or information that I have, as soon as I am sure of my facts." With that, he bent back over the gruesome piece of evidence, fishing out more test tubes for further experiments. Lestrade and I were clearly forgotten and dismissed from his thoughts.

Seeing it was no use to protest further, and that Holmes would not have any information coaxed out of him until he was ready, Lestrade gave a displeased grunt, crammed his hat forcefully back onto his head, and left.

Holmes spent the rest of the evening at work, completely ignoring the arrival of dinner. The parlour filled with an ever-increasing cloud of noxious smoke as he applied test upon test to his specimen. The miasma was augmented even further as he took more and more frequent breaks to sit and ponder, puffing away at his pipe until the haze became intolerable. It had gone past a three-pipe problem and well into a seventh when I finally gave up trying to read through the smoke and went to bed.

When I awoke in the morning, Holmes's chemical experiments were still underway, and the darkened room was dotted in that corner with the little blue flames of multiple Bunsen burners going at once. Holmes was not at the table, but wandered about our quarters with an air of extreme agitation. He smoked the old clay pipe, the foulest of his collection and the room was wreathed in blue smoke.

"Aha, Watson," he said at once. "Clearly this case goes deeper than I first suspected." He pointed with the pipe. "Take a look at our unique evidence and give me your thoughts on it."

Hardly knowing what to expect, I went to the table and bent over to look at the finger laid upon a Petri dish. The blood still glistened brightly at the severed joint without any sign of coagulation or clotting. Nor did it seem to show any signs of decomposition.

"Why, it looks as if it was freshly severed this morning!" I exclaimed.

"Exactly!" he said. "The blood has not dried or congealed, as we might expect. You may recall that I questioned Lestrade as to how long he'd had the finger in his possession. This was because it looked unusually fresh."

"A haemophiliac?" I asked.

"My thoughts precisely, though this kind of bleeding is exceptional even for such a patient. Female haemophiliacs are nearly unheard of, as I'm sure you know. Also the blood has several other irregularities. You yourself saw that it passed the Holmes blood test I perfected the day we first met, just before we became involved with the affair of Major Sholto, of Upper Norwood."

"I remember it well." How could I not, having also met my wife during those events?

"But the blood from this finger does not seem to correspond to most of the other characteristics of human blood, nor does the flesh of the finger precisely correspond to normal flesh. Whatever disease could change this person's chemistry rather thoroughly, so it must have been long-term, rather than something recently contracted. It is also curious that, though there is still some evidence of blood flow, the rest of the finger is quite desiccated, though it hardly looks it. I noticed this because the finger is much lighter than I should expect. It is also strangely resilient. There are indications that this may also be true in life, and that the disease dramatically alters the circulatory system as it progresses. This agrees with the differing characteristics of the blood. You will remember that I commented to Lestrade that the removal of a finger might, in this case, be fatal. Such is the nature of haemophilia."

"I do," I said. "To what characteristics of the blood do you refer?"

"Well," he said with a sly smile. "There are several. But this demonstration is the most striking." He took a small specimen knife and cut a portion of skin off the finger, adding this to a test tube that already had a clear liquid in it. He then sprinkled a small amount of a light grey powder into the solution and immediately a violent bubbling eruption occurred. In but a few moments' time, the reaction had ceased and I was able to see into the clear liquid that remained. The skin sample was gone, quite dissolved into the solution.

"What did you put in?" I asked. "Some destructive acid compound?"

Holmes went back to his pipe and got it going again before he answered. "Powdered silver," he finally answered. "Discovering this reaction was more accident than method, I must admit."

"Silver..." Nothing in my long medical history, nor in my unusual dealings alongside Sherlock Holmes, had prepared me for so extraordinary a statement.

"Yes, I quite understand your reaction," Holmes said. "All this leads us to infer the existence of a sufferer of an as yet unknown blood disease that leaves the victim so robust that a young woman is still capable of an active climb that would strain even an accomplished athlete."

"Climbing? But how on earth could you know that?"

"There are abrasions on the skin and, as well as traces of stone fragments both within the abrasions and underneath the fingernail. Not all of these are new, which suggests more than one such climb in the recent past. At first, I considered the possibility that she had been shut behind a stone door, or some other explanation for the abrasions, but the abrasions lead me to believe that the activity must have been climbing. You recall that I said there were no signs of the regular calluses that usually accompany the physical activity I would associate with a working woman. In addition, a professional climber would have specialized calluses, very hard and smooth, and there are no signs of these, either. This indicates either a woman of the higher class or an invalid excused from menial labour. Either answer seems at odds with our climbing theory, does it not? Or at the very least an unusual combination.

"Most blood diseases are debilitating to the victim," I said, incredulous. "I can hardly imagine such a person making a strenuous climb."

"Nor can I," Holmes said. "Yet I can find no other explanation which meets the facts that are presented to us."

"Good Lord," I said, remembering the prominence of haemophilia in the royal family. "You don't suppose that this woman could have been royalty."

"I consider it highly unlikely," Holmes said. "Remember, there was no sign of any jewellery, which makes it unlikely to be someone from court."

"What does this all mean?"

"We do not have enough data for a complete determination," Holmes said. "But I have several lines of inquiry. I believe that my next step is to visit West Sussex, where I know a man who deals exclusively in Indian cigarettes. One of the few places in England that carries this distinct tobacco."

"Then I shall come with you," I offered.

"That is by no means necessary. I think you would find this preliminary investigation very tedious, and there is not likely to be any danger at this stage. Also, I will send out several telegrams to other tobacconists, and I will need someone reliable to await their reply. But keep your revolver ready, Watson! With such a clue as this first one, I have no doubt that I shall have need of it, as well as your firm resolve, before this case is concluded."

Chapter 02

CARFAX ESTATE

I spent the rest of the day without further news, and the only break in the monotony came when a small package arrived for Holmes from the Ingerson Rifle Company. Having been given directions to intercept all of Holmes's mail for him, I opened the package with trembling hands, lest another severed body part should await me. Instead, I found a card from the company with a short note: "Per Your Instructions – Ralph Ingerson" and two small boxes. I opened these and found that they were laden with gun cartridges. But no ordinary cartridges. While the casing looked normal enough, the bullets themselves gleamed and shone, even in the moderately lit study. Silver. Of course, I made the connection between these and the unusual reaction to silver in Holmes's test, but I couldn't for the life of me imagine how that could make this kind of ammunition necessary. A bullet of lead would serve just as well, I should think, and besides I could hardly imagine an instance where we might need to shoot the *victim* of the case. Deciding that this portion of the matter was quite beyond me, I set the package aside and continued to wait.

No sign of Holmes came, and Baker Street received no further correspondence that night, but a telegram was waiting for me when I woke the next morning. It read thusly:

Come down to the Kensington Hotel near Kirby Cross train station in Essex County at once. Will send a cab. Come armed. Bring Ingerson package. SH.

I had Mrs Hudson send for a cab immediately. My old army habits stood me in good stead, and I was able to get my things together quickly enough to be ready for the driver when he pulled up to our kerb.

It was only a few hours later when I stepped out of the train and onto the platform at Kirby Cross. I hefted my luggage and found a cab waiting for me. The driver, a large fleshy man, grunted when I requested the Kensington Hotel and departed immediately. In just a few short minutes I saw a hotel sign, but was amazed when we rattled directly past it without pause or even any sign of slowing. I hammered my cane on the roof of the hansom, but the driver ignored me utterly. I was quite beside myself, particularly since we seemed to be entering a seedier and more disreputable part of the sleepy county. The hansom finally came to a halt underneath a huge yew tree. I burst out of the cab and shook my stick at the driver.

"See here, man!" I said. "What is the meaning of this?"

The driver was hunched over with his face in his hands, and I saw him pull something wet from the front of his mouth and then drag off a heavy wig. When he turned, I was astonished to see Sherlock Holmes smiling down at me.

"Forgive me, Watson," he said with a chuckle, "but I did think you would rather come to the heart of the investigation at once." He dropped the wig at his feet, and stuffed the cotton wads that he'd used to help change the shape of his face into his pocket.

"Good Lord!" I said, quite astonished.

Holmes next discarded the shabby outer garment he'd used as part of his driver's disguise and stepped down from the box only to usher me back inside the cab. When he followed me and shut the door behind him, his face had a deadly earnestness to it.

"I should warn you, Watson, that this case is possibly the murkiest, most sinister case in which we have ever been involved. My plan is for you to wait here and provide a rear guard while I investigate inside."

"Couldn't I be of far more assistance inside?"

"Perhaps," he admitted, "but this is one time that I fear the risks are far too great, and I haven't the time to explain them. It is already past noon, and we shall need every minute of the remaining day."

"If there is danger," I said stoutly, "then that is all the more reason for me to come with you. I quite insist!"

He gripped my arm in camaraderie. "I can always count on you, Watson. Very well. Did you bring the package from Ingerson?"

I wordlessly handed over the package of bizarre ammunition, quite at a loss as to why such elaborate precautions were necessary, but knowing that my friend would not order such a curiosity without good reason. Holmes pulled his own revolver from his jacket pocket and ejected the regular cartridges onto the cab seat and began replacing them with the silver bullet cartridges from the package. He gestured for me to do the same.

"Let me fill in the new details of this investigation," he said. "The case containing the finger was clearly used previously for the far more mundane purpose of holding cigarettes, yet Stross, our forger, does not smoke. So I theorized that the Indian tobacco found in the case might lead us to the finger's source. I resolved to trace the recent sale of the Indian tobacco, which led me to several unremarkable places, but also to here, the Carfax Estate. I have found a number of subtle and disturbing characteristics of this property, which belongs to the Lady Willingdon, an elderly widow who has been gone for some months visiting in Europe. She is unharmed and whole with all her fingers as of yesterday, according to the French officials that I telegraphed. Denied her inheritance because of her sex, she still has some wealth, but owns very little property in England. This is her sole estate, and she only has this because it was awarded back to her, after previously being sold to a foreign dignitary. Due to a legal miscalculation and the lack of said dignitary having any presence or legal representation, the sale was considered illegal, and came back to the lady some time ago. Neither she nor anyone in her employ has been here in many years. According to the officials, it has been abandoned and untenanted, but I have found tracks of more than one person at the entrance, so 'abandoned and untenanted' can hardly be accurate. We need to find out more about whatever clandestine activity is happening here. I urge you to the highest level of caution, Watson."

"Then whose finger..." I asked.

"That has yet to be determined," Holmes said quickly. I knew my friend well enough to guess that he suspected a great deal more than he told me, but also knew that he always had good reasons for revealing his deductions in the proper place and time. Following Holmes had never yet given me cause for regret, and I was far too old a campaigner to change my habits now. My gun now loaded, I indicated my readiness to follow wherever he should lead.

Not since the affair with Milverton had I felt so much that our roles in society had been twisted out of shape, as if we were now the criminals instead of upholders of the law. The gate may have been rusted, but we found the lock secure with signs of recent use. I had seen Holmes pick locks with the competence of a seasoned burglar, but after examining the gate he turned aside and walked the hansom around to the back part of the stone wall and used the simple expedient of pulling the carriage close to the wall and climbing over. Should any representative of the law have come by during this time we might have found ourselves in the novel and entirely unenviable position of being arrested, but luck was with us, and such was not the case.

Holmes lowered me down with a steely grip on my arm, then dropped down beside me with ease. It never ceased to amaze me, this change from a tweedy scholar in Baker Street to active bloodhound or even criminal, if the cause was just.

"Going in this way," he whispered into my ear, "we avoid any dogs, as well as those who might be watching the gate, since their activities are all concentrated there." And so it was. We made our way across the unkempt grounds so overgrown with bracken and gorse and so filled with dead foliage that it might not have been tended to for decades. The grounds had to be at least twenty acres, if not more, and included an immeasurable amount of overgrown foliage, a small stream and a dark, weedy pond. The house, when it came into view, was a very large, squared-off edifice, bulky against the grey sky. As we got closer, we could see that it was a haphazard affair, with some of it fairly modern, or at least of this century, while other portions of heavy stone looked positively medieval, with few windows, and those high up and barred with rusty iron. There was no difficulty gaining entrance, however, as many of the less substantial portions of the house were in poor repair and included several broken windows and doors falling nearly off their hinges. Holmes's fear regarding dogs proved to be unfounded, as there were none on the estate.

The inside of the house was in even worse repair than the outside garden. There was some torn and decrepit furniture, but mostly the place lay empty, as if much of what might once have been there had been carried off a long time ago. Old paint of a universally drab grey colour flaked off the walls and a smell of dust, mould and decay permeated every corner. Not a noise came to our ears except the whispering of the wind outside, and our every footsteps, which sent echoes through the apparently empty and abandoned structure.

We made our way through part of the house and found only more empty rooms until Holmes stopped me as we came upon the entrance to an old-fashioned courtyard. The doors were flung open and broken, one hanging only on a single hinge and swaying in the slight breeze. He pointed down at several sets of fresh tracks etched into the dust on the floorboards in front of us.

"Careful where you step, Watson," he said as he crouched to a nearly prostrate position to examine them. "Two different sets of workman's boots, one large, one even more so, both hobnailed. And an entirely different set of well-to-do gentleman's boots. Curious…"

"Holmes, look here," I said. From my removed position, close to the end of the hallway, I had nearly placed my hand on a crack in the wall without noticing the bullet lodged there.

"Excellent, Watson!" Holmes cried as he came back to look at my find. "Score one for you!" He pulled a penknife out and carefully pried the bullet free. "There is blood here." He wrapped the evidence in his handkerchief and placed it in his pocket as he went back to his work on the floor. "And more blood by your foot, here." The spot he indicated was just a few drops, but he used his knife to scrape up a sample of this, too.

"Give me a moment while I examine these markings." His path carried him closer to the entrance of the courtyard as he examined the area in minute detail. When he looked up from the doorway itself, a shadow passed over his face, followed by a look of grim determination.

"Whatever has gone on here," he said, "it seems that we are too late to prevent it. But perhaps not too late to deal with the villains responsible."

Seeing that Holmes's inspection of this portion of the floor was done, I entered the courtyard.

By the doorway lay the bodies of two men, so horribly battered and bent into unnatural angles that there could be no doubt about the nature of their death or the futility of my medical services. Their faces were twisted into a shocked rictus of horror. These were men who had seen their violent deaths coming. A six-shot revolver lay just inside the doorway. Holmes picked it up, sniffed at it, then opened the cylinder. All the bullets were still in place. He tucked it into his jacket pocket.

Then, in the centre of the courtyard, I caught sight of the third body, though it was nearly unrecognizable as such, being so badly charred. In an act of further barbarism, a stake had been driven completely through the unfortunate victim's torso, pinning it to a long plank that lay on the ground. Though I have seen many horrors in my career between Afghanistan and the innumerable cases in which I've assisted Sherlock Holmes, none of them chilled my soul in the same way that this scorched cadaver did.

"Holmes!" I said in a choked voice as I noticed something that increased my horror of the charred cadaver tenfold. "Look at this woman's hands!"

"Yes, Watson," he said. "I was wondering if you would pick out that detail."

"The left hand is missing the very same ring finger!" My

stomach and mind churned with the fearsome image of any woman being burned to death in this manner.

"Indeed it is, Watson," Holmes said. He picked a cigarette butt off one of the flagstones, sniffed at it, and gave a small cry of satisfaction. From there, he went through a search of the victims' pockets, finding, in very short order, several of the distinctive cigarettes loose in one of the men's pockets. "These are loose, but have at one time been in a cigarette case. You can see impressions from the clip used to keep the cigarettes in place. It seems very likely that this man provided that case for transport of the finger to Stross, who would then deliver it. But deliver it to whom?"

I had seen Holmes perform some thorough inspections before, but this one was exceedingly so. He took several more blood samples with his penknife, placing the contents in small tubes apparently brought for the purpose and labelling them as he went. His investigation included every flagstone and over-grown flower bed in the courtyard and even the bricks of the courtyard wall as high as he could reach. He poked, peered, and pored over every detail, even sniffing at the burnt corpse. He took longer going over this ghastly scene than I ever remembered him taking over similar scenes, muttering to himself as he went, though I could catch nothing of what he said and so was quite in the dark as to what he might have found out. It was several hours and well into the latter half of the afternoon before he completed his task.

"Well," he said, finally, "I believe that we can do no further good here, Watson, and it is well past time that we should be on our way. I wish to get back to Baker Street as quickly as possible."

"Have we learned nothing?" I asked. "Is there no clue to lead us to the villains that have done this monstrous thing?"

"Oh, I should say we've learned a great deal," he said, "but the conclusions are so fantastic that I do not dare entertain them until I have eliminated all other possibilities."

"You must clarify it for me, then," I said, "for it is all a muddle in my mind."

Holmes shook his head. "I have one further test before I can be sure." He grabbed my arm. "Come. It is vitally important that we spare no delay."

"Should we not at least summon the police?" I asked as we made our way out.

"That would be the worst action we could possibly take," he said without turning or breaking stride. "I believe the official force would be well out of their depths on this case, Watson. If what I suspect is true, then only harm can come from their involvement. Come, we may take a direct route, as the gate is clearly not watched as we feared."

He raised his hand to forestall any more questions, and we left as he had suggested without any further incident. I mounted the driver's box of the hansom and he wordlessly handed me the reins before sitting beside me. I could see that the day's investigations had troubled him deeply, as they certainly had me. But I had no doubt that Holmes's keen mind had penetrated far deeper into the mystery than my own and I could see my friend grow more and more agitated as he sifted the information around in his mind.

He fidgeted and frowned all the way back to the driver station near the train, where he wordlessly handed a number of sovereigns to a large black-bearded driver for use of his cab. The man tipped his hat low and murmured his thanks, which Holmes answered with a distracted air. Holmes let me handle the purchasing of tickets and luggage arrangements. All the way back to Baker Street I held my questions as he bit at his nails and lip, tapped his fingers, but would answer none of my questions.

When we finally arrived at our quarters, it was nearly six o'clock. Holmes rushed past Mrs Hudson's questions about supper, up the stairs and over to his chemical table.

He snatched up the case with the specimen finger in it and held it thoughtfully for a few seconds.

"There is no doubt," Holmes said, as if continuing a conversation from before, only I had not the foggiest notion of what he meant.

"No doubt about…" I prompted.

He gave a thin smile. "I've been far too timid with my deductions on this case, Watson. To begin with, while there have certainly been instances of variance from one finger to the next on the hand of any one individual, there is still no escaping the fact that when a great number of discrepancies mount up, there can be but one conclusion."

"I'm afraid you've lost me entirely, Holmes."

"This finger is not a match for the finger missing from the charred remains we found today."

"Not a match?" I said, surprised beyond reckoning. "Could there be a mistake, caused by the corpse having been burned as it was?"

"Come now, Watson," Holmes said, a little pained. "You cannot think me such a bumbler as to not account for that. But while the flame would, without a doubt, shrivel the skin and flesh and even, to a lesser extent, the bone, you cannot expect the process to *lengthen* the bones of the hand, can you? Our finger here is simply not a match."

"Then there are *two* severed fingers in this case?"

"So it would seem." He frowned. "And yet… yet, that is not the part of this case that perplexes me the most." His expression, usually so masterful while on a case, was filled with indecision.

"What, then?" I said.

But he shook his head and set the cigarette case down. Then he stalked over to the table and snatched up his Stradivarius. Falling into his chair, he began to pluck at the strings in the most desultory and, frankly, irritating manner. He turned away from me as he did so, watching the fading light out the window. I knew better than to press him for answers, so I opened the paper and began to browse for something to occupy my attention while I waited for Holmes to come around.

No sooner had I flipped the paper to the second page than Holmes jumped to his feet, dropped the violin unceremoniously back onto the table, and turned to face me with a dramatic air. The indecision had entirely left his face.

"Watson, what do you know about vampires?"

"Vampires?" I repeated. I'd been prepared for something unusual, but this was a staggering proposition coming from the logician. "Nothing more than fanciful stories. But why ask me such a question? You yourself have called the very notion rubbish!"

"True," he said, ruefully. "But now I am forced to revise my opinion in the light of overwhelming evidence. Consider the facts, Watson. You have already conceded the existence of a rare blood disease. We have samples, and have seen evidence of it."

"Quite true, but, Holmes... vampires?"

"Bear with me, Doctor," he said. "I have determined that the nature of this blood disease greatly affects the cell structure of its victims, replacing the chemical structure of the cell in such a way as to completely transfigure its makeup. You have already seen the violent reaction to silver."

"I am hardly in a position to argue," I said reluctantly.

"Agreed. Now... is it such a reach to suppose that such a victim might have entirely different dietary needs?"

"But, Holmes," I cried. "Drinking blood? Bats? Mist? Wolves? Frightened of the holy cross? Bursting into flame in sunlight? Surely this is madness!"

"Clearly we can't condone all these beliefs, Watson. Not in our orderly world. But let us take the last question first. I spent all night going over this sample of our haemophiliac, Watson. All night. I managed to discover the unusual reaction to silver, but there is one test I did not think of, and perhaps it may be the most conclusive."

With a swift motion, he picked up a scalpel and cut off a small portion of the finger and placed it on a small dish. He then placed the dish on the corner of his chemical table, near the window, where the last bit of daylight shone on it.

"We might have done this accidentally," Holmes murmured, "if not for the abysmal weather."

"What in the world?" I said, sitting bolt upright as a small curl of smoke puffed from the dish. The sample burst into low flame, then went up in a cloud of acrid smoke like a Chinese firework gone horribly awry. Smoke plumed up from the table, and we were both coughing uncontrollably before Holmes managed to cover it with a metal serving lid in order to smother the flame. Even so, we had to stumble around opening windows and waving sheaves of paper to drive out the smoke, and it took a great many minutes to clear our sitting room.

"Well, Watson," he said with a wry smile as we fell back into our chairs. "It seems my flair for a dramatic demonstration has somewhat backfired on me. Yet, clearly you will have to concede that there must be more to this vampire business than we at first believed. This also indicates, when you consider the details of the woman in the courtyard's death, that we have not one vampire, but two in this case. Each of them missing a finger."

"I don't know what to think," I said. "I cannot fathom how this could possibly be. If it were true, why has there been no outcry other than a collection of old fairy tales and that Polidori twaddle?"

"I'm inclined to think that this condition is rare, and the numbers of the afflicted must be very small," Holmes said.

"What you say must be true," I said, "but I still cannot bring myself to fully comprehend the undead. I simply cannot imagine how this could be, and yet I must."

"I think, perhaps, 'undead' is a term that is best discarded," Holmes said. "Vampires, or those infected with this blood disease, are remarkable, but still human and still fall in the purview of science rather than superstition."

"But what of the rest?" I said. "Turning into mist, or a bat, or being repelled by the holy cross?"

"I should think that we are not quite forced to accept all of the information that comes to us without some examination as to its merit. It occurs to me that some portions of these lurid tales are rife with more superstition than logic. The power of the cross to hold such a fiend, for example. Why should this be? But when you consider that many such crucifixes are made with silver, and that *this* material might well give such an assailant pause, this I can credit. But I am ahead of myself, Watson, and it is a mistake to theorize too heavily without all the data."

"But how did you know? How could you possibly have come to this impossible conclusion?"

"How indeed?" said a sonorous, cultured voice.

I sat bolt upright at this sudden intrusion, so startling was it. Holmes was even more galvanized, and leapt to his feet.

The man standing in our doorway was tall, taller even than Holmes, and equally gaunt. His features were sharp and strong as well, but there the similarities diverged. Instead of Holmes's lean, ascetic features, this man's bushy eyebrows, long black moustache and great mane of black hair combined to create an impression of fierce grandeur. Like a barbaric king he was, noble and proud without a trace of shame, and clad in a black cloak over a dark, sombre, expensive suit that looked many years out of date. The spatter of the rain and crash of thunder came loudly through the still-open window, which was curious in itself, as there had been little foreshadowing of such a storm.

"Be wary, Watson," Holmes said levelly. "We are in grave danger here. Consider the noise on the steps."

"But I heard nothing!" I said, quite taken aback at this unreal series of events.

"Precisely."

"You are an interesting man, Mr Holmes," the intruder said. "With a shocking clarity of perception." His English was excellent, but the intonation marked him clearly as foreign. He moved idly towards the window, as if unaware of his actions, and Holmes took several corresponding steps towards his desk. I was keenly reminded of two predators, the bloodhound and the wolf, stalking each other with deadly intent and malice.

"But, I assure you that your wariness is not necessary," the man said in a conciliatory tone. "Please sit, I mean you no harm."

Holmes moved behind his desk and picked up the revolver there. I made to follow suit. I still had the gun in my jacket pocket, and it would have been a moment's action to stand and draw it. When I tried, however, I found I could do nothing of the sort. I could not even take my eyes off the man's own, which burned like coals in the low flickering light of the small hearth fire we had burning. It was dark outside, which I hadn't noticed until now, and our comfortable sitting room in Baker Street felt transformed, a fragile and uncertain shelter in a dark and menacing world.

"That is quite enough," Holmes said, proving his own mobility by raising and cocking the gun in his hand.

"Guns mean little to one such as…" the man started, but his voice trailed off as Holmes calmly held up a bullet between thumb and forefinger. Even in the flickering and dim light, the gleam of silver was apparent.

"Most exceptional…" the man said. "A keen and disciplined mind, not to be distracted or diverted from its purpose." He smiled, and some tension in his eyes seemed to relax its grip. I found that I could move again. I sprang to my feet and yanked out my own revolver. Holmes held up a restraining hand, though, so I took no further action.

"You know my name, of course," the man said, still quite at ease.

"I do not know anything other than the fact that you are a foreign noble whose tastes run to extravagant means, but who has not been exposed to London society for some time. You are quite old, much older than you appear, and you are used to being obeyed implicitly. You have few servants, but the ones you have are fiercely dedicated. You travelled here without carriage or hansom, and have spent much time walking the London streets. You've had some recent distress, but that is not entirely what brings you here. I know that your disease has made you something both more and less than human."

"Ah… not so well informed as I thought," the man said. "I was sure that Van Helsing or Holmwood would have told you that much, at least."

"At this time three days ago I knew nothing of the matter," Holmes said. "And those names mean nothing to me. I have drawn my own conclusions as to your nature based on the evidence."

The man's face broke for just an instant, and a wild and feral look came over him. His mouth opened in the beginnings of a snarl, and the shocking white teeth sent gooseflesh down my back. But just as quickly, the man stopped, and his face resumed its look of caged civility again. There was a long moment's pause in which he seemed to have a great internal struggle.

"Forgive me," he said at last. "I thought you mocked me, and I am too old and proud to tolerate such a thing. But now I see that I was in error. I would have not thought such claims you make possible until today. I am familiar with your name, of course. It has appeared several times in my studies of the British Empire. Still, I assumed a certain amount of literary bravado to be present."

"I have often shared that opinion," Holmes said wryly. "Still, *I* do not make any false claims."

The man nodded slowly. "Very well, you do not know my name," he said. "I am Dracula. Count Dracula. And I... Forgive me – we are proud, we Székelys, and not often used to asking such things. The truth is... I have come for your help, Mr Sherlock Holmes."

My astonishment at this unforeseeable turn of events was enormous. If someone had barged into our sitting room and claimed to be Shakespeare's Puck or Don Quixote, I should not have been more surprised. To my even greater surprise, Holmes did not reject the proposition outright.

"I am selective when taking my cases," he said with icy tones. "Still, there are a great many details which I should like cleared up. I should warn you, however, that if you attempt another use of your powers I shall be forced to use this revolver. Surely you can see that this would be pointless and quite dangerous for you."

Dracula waved his hand dismissively. "I bear you no ill will. I have come to lay my matter before you, knowing full well that once you know the facts you will be unable to act except in a manner which will be beneficial to us both." If he was nervous at the firearm, he showed no sign. "You see, the matter that threatens me and my loved ones is perhaps an even greater threat to the city of London."

"Holmes!" I cried. "If this man is truly guilty of murder, surely you can't mean to allow this monster…"

My words trailed off as Holmes raised his hand in my direction. He leaned against the desk to make himself comfortable, still retaining his pistol. "Pray, Count," he said, "please continue your most interesting statement."

Chapter 03

VAMPIRES

The fire flickered low in the grate, throwing sombre tones over us all. The storm raged and dashed the windowsill with wet and errant flashes of light in an effect both haunting and hypnotic. Wind whipped through the open window.

"Very well," the Count said. "I will tell you everything." He sat with Old World dignity in the chair across from me. Holmes came from around the desk and sat in his customary chair, the pistol still in his hand. I took a moment to lower the window slightly in order to minimize the noise of the storm, but a pall of smoke and unpleasant stench lingered from the sliver of burning finger, so I was compelled to leave the window open a few inches, at least.

The Count was a man who spoke with careful consideration of his words, but whether this was an attempt to be circumspect or reflected some effort required to speak English I could not tell. I was also struck with how supernaturally still the Count sat, not reclining, not shifting in even the smallest, most human of ways and yet without evincing the slightest sign of discomfort. Even stranger, I could not detect any rising or falling of the chest, try as I might. I found the possibility of a walking man who did not breathe even more dramatic an idea than Holmes's shocking observations about vampires a few moments before. But I checked this line of thinking, as Holmes had impressed upon me the notion that there couldn't possibly be anything about the vampire that science could not explain, if a careful study were made. I vowed to devote my own humble powers to this endeavour once this fearsome investigation and campaign allowed it.

"You say you are unfamiliar with my name and do not know, perhaps, anything of my first trip to London," the Count said with a small and secret smile. "It may have a bearing on today's events, so I shall have to tell you something of it. You are perhaps familiar with Stoker's account of me?"

"You don't expect us to believe that nonsense!" I snapped. Though I hadn't read the novel, I knew enough from others to know it was filled with nothing but the fantastic and sensational.

"Nonsense indeed," the Count said, "for I tell you it is a pack of lies from beginning to end. However, the base fact that I found myself in opposition to Van Helsing and the others is, at least, true. As is, of course, the *existence* of vampires, though that bumbler Stoker has misunderstood our nature, particularly mine, most completely."

"I have not read Stoker's book," Holmes said, "but since you refer to it as a pack of lies, perhaps you could give us a true summary of events? Before you explain why you need my help."

Dracula frowned, but then nodded. "Harker did visit me, at my request, as Stoker describes, as part of a transaction when I purchased Carfax Estate."

"Carfax?" I said. "The property on Purfleet Street?"

"The same," Dracula said. "I believe it gave my enemy some amusement to make use of a property once belonging to me, but that is mere speculation."

"Harker visited you as part of the purchase?" Holmes said.

"Yes, but I give you my word I neither threatened nor imprisoned him. I took care to hide my vampiric nature, of course, particularly my longevity, but in this I was not entirely successful. While in my home, he broke through several locked doors and then, unfortunately, had an encounter with my three sisters that could have proven fatal had I not intervened. This event so terrified him that he returned to London, where I soon followed."

"You weren't worried about the exposure Mr Harker's story would bring?" Holmes asked.

"No," Dracula answered. "You will find that most such stories are rarely listened to. I had several firms to handle my business and resolved to do no more such business with Harker or his employer, Mr Hawkins, and considered the matter resolved. Harker himself was unharmed, if frightened, and returned directly to London.

"I then booked passage on a Russian ship, the *Demeter*, from Varna to London, but the voyage was mundane and dull. The need to drag about coffins filled with earth is another fabrication of Stoker's. I went as a regular passenger and the captain and crew arrived here unharmed. I played chess occasionally with the first mate, a man named Petrofsky. He asked few questions, spoke poor English, and played a very passable game, but I do not know any more about him. I cannot remember the captain's name or any of the other crew members. They were all Russian, like their ship, as far as I know. The ship may still be in service."

"It is not," Holmes said. "The damage while landing was too severe and it was considered more expedient to decommission her."

"Ah," Dracula said. He seemed a trifle sad about the news, then continued his tale. "Here, in London, I made several social acquaintances, including one Lord Holmwood. This man was a friend of Harker's, though I did not know that at the time. This is where I met Mina Murray, who later became my wife."

"Mina herself was infected with disease?" Holmes asked. "She is, too, a vampire?"

"Of course," Dracula said. "She would not have it any other way. Why should she suffer and die for no reason? Why should I wish her to?"

"Quite," Holmes said, though his dry tone indicated it wasn't so clear to his mind. He shifted topics. "Why Holmwood? It seems a curious coincidence."

"It was no coincidence," Dracula said. "I was not, however, pursuing Harker, as he was no longer of interest to me. But most of my social invitations came by way of my business connections and Harker, Hawkins, and Holmwood all moved in similar circles."

"I understand," Holmes said.

Dracula continued. "Mina. She had been engaged to, but never married, Jonathan Harker, as she had broken off the engagement shortly after his return."

"Why?" Holmes asked.

"She found him much changed," Dracula said. "His own unfortunate encounter at Castle Dracula and the recent death of Holmwood's betrothed had unhinged him. At least, that is how she explained it to me. Mina is a strong-willed woman and follows her own heart in such matters."

"How did Holmwood's betrothed die?"

"It happened before my arrival, so I know only what Mina has told me, but Mina's dear friend, Lucy Westenra, sickened and finally succumbed."

"Succumbed to what?" I asked.

Dracula smiled. "I had no involvement with her death, but I will admit freely that it has long been my suspicion that *some* vampire was part of it as the illness showed all the characteristics of a vampire attack. Van Helsing, a well-regarded doctor, was brought in on the case and he clearly knew something of vampires, though he had a very mistaken idea that it was more a matter of religion than science. Vampirism is an astonishing condition, to be certain, with many elements that no doubt seem supernatural, but it is not the bargain with Christianity's Satan that Van Helsing and Stoker seem to believe it is.

"Regardless, Van Helsing, Harker, Holmwood and two other men – Dr Seward and an American, Quincey Morris – confronted, then assaulted Mina and I, but I was able to extricate us without any loss of life. Unlike the novel, they did not pursue us out of London and I had thought that the end of the matter."

"John…"

I started, turning towards the open window. Mary? That had

been *Mary's* voice. Could she be here, in London? She should be miles away, with the Forresters, out in the country. I still sat in my chair, but I could see her in my mind's eye, standing out in the street, her blonde hair wet and uncovered, looking up towards our window. A wave of dizziness passed over me.

"Watson!"

I don't remember standing up, but there I was, at the window, shaken out of some kind of torpor by Holmes's sharp cry of admonition.

I turned to look back, feeling an expression of startled bewilderment on my own face that matched Holmes's. Dracula looked mildly curious.

I looked down in the street, expecting to see Mary there as I had in my mind's eye, but the street stood empty of pedestrians, only a solitary hansom clip-clopping slowly by.

Holmes appeared suddenly at my side, all solicitude, as he assisted me back to my chair. He sat me down and loomed over me, loosening my collar and then pouring me a large brandy.

"Here, good fellow," he said. "This should chase away the cobwebs." He shot an accusing glance at Dracula, clearly attributing my dizziness to some by-product of the vampire's effect on me. Dracula remained impassive under my friend's clear ire.

I took a long, careful sip of the brandy, accepting the warmth going down as a welcome tonic.

"Count," Holmes said, "you shall have to return tomorrow evening to finish this statement. Watson needs some time to recover his senses and I wish him to hear the entire story as well, for I may need his opinion on the matter."

Dracula did not answer, but when I looked up from my brandy, that side of the room was empty.

Holmes sniffed and closed the window and then he went out into the hall to look down the stairs. When he came back into the room, he closed the door quietly behind him.

"He is gone," Holmes said. "It may be just as well. I have facts to verify so I must leave you, Watson. But I have entirely underestimated the shock that the Count must have had on your system. Will you be all right for a time alone here? I shall not truly need your assistance until tomorrow evening."

"It's nothing," I said weakly. "Call the Count back now. I feel quite revived, thank you."

"It is late," Holmes replied. "I think you do us both a disservice to claim full recovery when your pulse and breathing indicate otherwise. Perhaps you had best retire for the night?"

"No," I said. "I shall be up a while. I couldn't possibly sleep now." On the contrary, I felt the need for fresh air more than anything else, but I did not voice this out loud.

"It has always seemed to me," Holmes said, "that the adage about doctors being the worst sort of patients is quite true, but still, I shall not object. Rest if you like, or stay up. I won't be long."

I couldn't imagine what Holmes could verify that couldn't wait until sunrise, but I was also aware that Holmes had many unorthodox sources of information. He had his top hat and coat on in an instant.

"It would be best for you to lock the door after me," he said, and departed.

I could not shake the need to get out for a bit, despite Holmes's warnings.

The night air was very cool when I left Baker Street, and the fog in the streets of London was as thick as I'd ever seen it. A hansom was immediately available, however, despite the extremely late hour, and I got into it at once thinking I might just ride around for a while. The driver, a man with a ratty top hat, bushy blond eyebrows and even bushier blond mutton chops, said nothing. What destination I gave him, I do not remember. I was too engrossed in consideration of the terrifying new information I'd been given this evening. The thought of a world with vampires in it boggled my very psyche and I did not notice at first when the hansom stopped.

Finally, the lack of movement caught my attention and I called to the driver, getting no answer. I stepped out onto the pavement and looked around, confused. This was no part of London I knew, but rather some narrow alleyway where the buildings stood thick and dark all around me. The driver's box was completely empty. How the man could have gotten off the hansom and away without my feeling the motion in the carriage or hearing footsteps was quite beyond me. Not to mention the fact I hadn't even paid the fellow.

Silence filled the air around me and even the normal noises of the city were muffled. I felt quite alone, stranded on an island in the fog. The alley ran for a great distance to either side. There were doorways to be seen, but they were all closed and unwelcoming.

I wished, not for the first time, that my cunning friend were here to examine the evidence with me.

A weight of lassitude fell on me then. Yet a small voice inside also grew deeply suspicious. Luring me out at this time was no accident. It couldn't possibly be my wife, not here in the city. Nor would she approach me in this manner. When I realized how neatly and easily I had been snared, I cursed myself for a fool. In my distracted state, I hadn't even thought that a cab waiting for me at this late hour was curious and I'd paid no notice of the route we took to get here.

"John…"

Impossibly, I saw Mary standing in the street behind me – my Mary! – in no more than a wisp of clothing despite the chill night air. Knowing that things were horribly wrong, but unable to prevent myself, I rushed over to my wife's side. I tore off my coat and flung it around her, but she seemed to have no interest in this, only clinging to me in a wanton manner I found most unlike the woman I had known these past years.

"What in the world are you doing in London?" I asked. "When did you come back and what are you doing here in the street, of all places? How did you even know I would be here?"

"Hush, John," she said, and nuzzled into my neck.

There was a sharp pain that lashed all through me. I struggled, for just an instant, before a heavy torpor seized me and I went limp in her arms. I could feel Mary's bite and the trickle of blood, but it did not alarm or surprise me; nothing could in that sleepy state. Feelings of confusion and surprise, that Mary should be here at all, still drifted around in the back of my trammelled brain, and then I knew nothing at all.

The next days are exceedingly hazy in my recollection, and I can only beg the reader's forgiveness for my lack of clarity. I would have no idea of the length of time missed by my narrative were it not for Holmes filling in the details later. It was nearly a week.

My own memories of that week are fragile and fragmented. They have the feel of an old mirror shattered and reconstructed with some of the pieces missing. I know that Mary was with me some of the time, which should have been a blessing, but was instead the purest form of shame and terror. I knew I lay insensate for at least several days, and that Mary came and went, leaving me for long periods by myself.

I do not know the precise location where she housed me during my convalescence, but I was familiar enough with the type of establishment from such adventures as "The Man with the Twisted Lip". The room was a long series of squalid cots, partitioned by thick, stained curtains. The air was heavy with brown smoke and the slightest taste of salt. That last told me that we were somewhat near the water, though the far-off cry of gulls would have done that on its own. The murmur of stuporous voices pooled all around me. I was in an opium den.

The hunger clawed at my stomach like a living thing, digging through the haze and deluge of scents and sounds. I knew that I had not eaten in days, but also knew that the days of rashers and kippers for breakfast were gone. Indeed, I could not even think of such things without a wave of nausea rising up inside of me. I felt so weak and feverish that I could barely lift my arms.

Mary appeared by pushing up one of the hanging cloths and sliding underneath. My senses were now frighteningly acute, particularly smell, and I could tell with certain accuracy how many people lay in this sinister place. A cloud of brown opium smoke came with her and the scandalous dress she wore carried on it the scent of an entirely different woman. I could guess all too well what had become of that woman. One curious thing penetrated even my febrile haze: Mary herself was an exception. Though odours clung to her stolen dress, she herself had a strangely subdued, earthy scent, much harder for me to detect than the rest.

She looked down at me with a small smile. "My poor dear," she said, in mockery of her previous concern for me. "I know what it is that you need, and nothing could be easier." She pulled up another cloth, revealing the berth of the man next to me. He was reclining in an awkward pose, lying with his head dangling off the side of his bunk and his limbs stiff at his side. His chin pointed straight up and his eyes hung open and glassy in an eerie testament to the power of opium to completely desensitize any man to any and all events around him.

"Mary," I pleaded. "Don't do this. You can't mean for me to…" I couldn't bring myself to finish the thought. This was Mary, *my* Mary, not some commonly cruel and banal criminal. I reached out for her, desperate to somehow reach the woman I'd married and loved all these years.

But the Mary looking down at me curiously wasn't the woman I'd known at all. She wore her face, but the expression of idle curiosity when confronted with someone else's pain was completely antithetical to everything I knew about her sensitive and caring nature. It wasn't something my wife could have done.

She seized me by the back of the neck and pulled me off the cot with prodigious strength, moving my not-inconsiderable weight as easily as if I were only a small kitten. She hauled me to an upright sitting position so that I was staring down at the pulsing neck of her proposed victim.

"You're hungry," she said, "and need to feed. But no problem could have a simpler solution, for all the nourishment you require is right in front of you. You have merely to *take* it. No one will miss this man. Arrangements have been made. If the opium in his system should concern you, have no fear of that. We have found that its qualities can be of great comfort during your transition."

Her hand was light and gentle and cool on my skin now, but I was not fooled. This creature was what the Count had made of my Mary, a demonic shell. Her eyes were wild, her expression sly, and I could still see, and smell, traces of blood around her mouth from where she had fed a short time ago. She was completely a creature of the night now, as I would be shortly, were I to succumb to the temptation before me. A further chilling thought went through me. She had said 'we'. She counted herself as one of Count Dracula's folk now, a vampire.

"No," I said, struggling to pull myself away from the unfortunate man in front of me. Mary held me there for a few seconds and then released me. I fell back, knocking over my cot with a crash.

"My dear, poor John," she said with a tinkling laugh, cruel

and expressive, that I'd never heard from her before. "You'll come around, John. Everyone does. You'll see." She left me. I could hear her feet delicately pad across the bare slats of the floor, a brief whispered conversation too faint to make out and finally the scrape of a door opening and closing as she left.

The profound weight of her words pressed down on me as I lay sprawled on the overturned cot. The hunger was scraping me hollow even now. If it got any worse, there would be no possible resistance. Escaping this prison was the only way to distance myself from the temptation that lay incoherently all around me. I had to escape now before I weakened any further.

I lurched unsteadily to my feet and found the strength to stand, after all. Pushing up the heavy curtain, however, caused me to slip and fall, and the curtain and part of the moulding came down with me in a raucous clatter. Inhumanly fast, a disreputable blonde man with mutton chops and bad teeth materialized at my elbow and laid his hands on me. Like Mary, he had very little scent, and so his sudden appearance surprised me beyond measure. Another vampire. When I got a good look at his face, I recognized the driver from the hansom that had taken me to Mary, and an anger at what had been done to me flushed through me.

With a strength I hardly expected, I pushed at him and he flew the length of the corridor and finally crashed through one of the curtained-off compartments at the end, tangling himself with the rug, cot, and the compartment's occupants.

Staggering out into the street, I moved at no great speed, but whether the attendant was seriously hurt or perhaps did not consider me worth chasing, I do not know. Mary was nowhere to be seen, which was a blessing. Having taken the time to find and trap me, I had to assume that she would want to finish her diabolical plan (no doubt, Dracula's plan) of infecting me with the same disease that had taken her soul. At any rate, no one at all pursued me.

The next few days are but a delusional blur. No opium addict's withdrawal ever taxed his system more than this ordeal taxed mine. I will spare the reader an endless recitation of the stumbling night of horror – not to spare myself indignities – but only because I remember nothing better than flashes of lucidity during that time.

I know that the light of day was far too painful to my eyes and skin, and I spent most of the daylight hours huddled in back alleys. It was on the first day of this that I lost my clothes when two immigrant workers rolled my unresisting form for all the material wealth that it could offer them. Miraculously, my watch and suit and wallet had not been lost in the opium den, but they were lost to me then. Like a character in a penny dreadful, I shuffled from alley to alley shaking as if from the ague, craving sustenance and finding nothing that I could eat. I was taken in at one of the soup houses, but I violently expelled the soup that a charitable soul gave to me. Everywhere all around me, walking temptation roamed in the form of the riff-raff and homeless of London and I was forced to avoid their company altogether, lest I submit to the cravings that howled inside of me.

A curious effect almost as predominant as the driving hunger was the transformation of my senses. I have already spoken of the heightening of my sense of smell, but I don't believe I have conveyed fully the effect that this had on my psyche, nor related what happened to my other senses. I thought that my vision had begun failing altogether when I tried to look at the moon overhead and found it lacking clarity. Or thought, briefly, that it was the London fog. Then I came to realize that my vision across long distances had become less keen. This did not inhibit me as I thought it might, partly because my vision was amazingly acute when it fell on things close at hand, certainly much more so than it had been previously.

But perhaps more importantly, the changes to my vision mattered less because my vision itself mattered less. My hearing and sense of smell had become so sharp that they had driven my sight into a strictly tertiary role. When coming into a new alley, I could detect the breathing and scent of any occupants immediately and place all their relative positions with unerring accuracy. Only as a second thought did I bother to pick them out with my eyesight as well. I didn't often understand this jumble in my head, but found that my first instincts were those of a predator on the hunt. A primal and burning core inside me would detect prey automatically and I would find myself stalking silently towards some hapless alley denizen before I forced myself to turn away. I felt more like a rabid automaton than a man of free will, and I was rather certain that I could kill with these new instincts without conscious decision on my part, a sheer horror to the thinking part of me. Instead, I used this new acuity to fastidiously avoid the other inhabitants of London, so that I should not fall prey to temptation.

I found other places to feed, but I am proud of none of these. I stole a butcher's shipment delivered to a kitchen in the dark hours of the earliest morning. I found that I could get some relief from hunger pangs by gnawing and sucking at the raw flesh for the juice, though I had to spit the worthless and spent meat into the street. This discarded bounty led me to my next source of nourishment. As the stray dogs of London fought over the scraps, I was able to snare one, God help me, and slake my thirst on the wretched creature like a savage beast. Once, I even stumbled into a charnel house and drank the cool blood from a puddle on the floor. I did what I must in order to survive, but still I vowed that I would take no human life, regardless of what kind of foul creature I had become. I felt that I moved through a disconnected landscape of haze and mist only remotely connected to the London I had known.

I could not bring myself to hunt more than the bare necessity to keep myself alive, and so I still felt weak, and found myself getting weaker as the nights went on. Even worse, I could not sleep. Each morning I slunk into the darkest corner that I could find – a coal cellar one day, the bottom of a dark stairwell on another – but these places did not bring any succour. I would lay all day, half conscious and groggy, swimming in the deluge of unfamiliar sounds and smells and certain that each scuffing noise in the street, possibly many houses away, would bring some fresh danger to my barely defendable position. There was no refuge, and after days without any sleep, I crawled into a drainage ditch and knew that I had not the strength to crawl out. Here I would perish.

When strong hands finally came to pull me out of the ditch, I did not have the strength to put up even token resistance, and it was then that I finally slipped into true unconsciousness.

Chapter 04

DRACULA'S STORY

I awoke in my own quarters in Baker Street and found myself in the curious position of immediately knowing where I was, without yet understanding how I came by that knowledge. With my eyes closed and my head upon the pillow of my own bed, a great many other things came to me. My rational mind could scarcely credit the information, but the predator inside me knew it all, and needed no proof.

I knew that it was barely night, and that the sun had set less than an hour past. I knew that Holmes was in the next room, despite the fact that he was quite still and made little sound. My brain had been collecting and analysing so many different scents that the conclusions popped into my head quite as if by magic. More remote scents called for my attention almost before I had identified the closer ones and all this information clamoured in my head like a roomful of talking people and I forced myself to go through the information carefully. I knew I must catalogue it if I were to control it. Otherwise, the massive flow of details would drive me to madness.

I picked them out one at a time. The bed had the smells of starch and a strange animalistic aroma. This lay over the top of every other scent in this room and I realized with a start that it was me, John Watson, M.D., or rather, it was the man I used to be. I did not emit this odour any longer and sweat was apparently a substance unknown to my transformed person. The impossibility of the science beleaguered me, but that did not matter as much to me as it might have a week ago. Also in this room was the smell of newsprint, the Arcadia mixture of tobacco that I favoured, various medicines from my doctor's bag in the corner, books and the soap and oils of my shaving kit. Even through the closed and draped window, I could also detect the air of London streets redolent with the sweat of man and woman and horses, and the droppings from those last, burning coal and the tang of strong drink.

In the next room, through what the air current told me was a partly open door, I could find even more, still just with the power of my new olfactory sense. There was Holmes's tobacco in the next room. I knew from memory that he kept it in a Persian slipper and could now tell you, within a foot, what part of the room it lay in. His revolver was out, and the scent of spent cartridges told me that it had been fired recently. Holmes's table of chemistry was a veritable barrage of smells. So strong were these that they might well have blotted all others out, but they were of such an artificial nature that it was quite easy to ignore these and concentrate on the rest. Holmes himself sat in a chair smoking; the sounds of his small motions and even his breathing were quite clear to me. I could even tell that it was the briarwood pipe. The rustling sound told me he read the paper. He was quite alone, I was certain. In the floor below us, I could hear the soft sounds of Mrs Hudson moving about and a faint whiff of the strong Scottish tea that she favoured. I was certain we were the only three in the building.

Which was why it was such a shock to me when I sat up and saw Count Dracula, the villain himself who had placed this horrible curse on me, standing in the shadows behind my opened door. My sense of smell had not registered his presence and somehow this frightened me horribly, as if he had materialized out of thin air.

"You monster!" I cried. Then I called out to the other room. "Holmes, beware! Danger most foul!" I surprised myself by snatching up a heavy oaken bookshelf with the intention of hurling it bodily at my tormentor. I still was not used to my tremendous vampire strength. It had taken several workmen to bring the heavy case up the steps when I purchased it, but I held it easily, unbothered by the shower of books and knick-knacks my manoeuvre caused.

Count Dracula stood immobile, without any expression of alarm. "I apologise, Doctor," he said mildly. "It was inconsiderate of me to startle you. I should have been more careful."

"You shall pay for what you've done to me, and for what you've done to Mary!" I took a step forward in order to hurl my makeshift weapon to maximum effect, but had to stop abruptly when Holmes entered the room and stepped directly between Dracula and me.

"No, Watson!" Holmes said quickly. "The Count is here at my request! Pray do not be hasty!"

"At your request?" I said, and felt, for the first time I can recall, a sharp betrayal at the actions of my constant companion. "You brought that butcher here? So he could see my misery first-hand?"

"He is not the villain that brought this fate upon you, nor upon Mary, my dear Watson."

"Oh, great mercy of Heaven, Mary…" I moaned, still holding the bookcase above me. In my first lucid moments in many days, the full weight of all that had happened to my Mary swept over me. Even if I could find a way to make Count Dracula pay for his crimes, how could I save her?

"I grieve for your loss, Watson," Holmes said, stepping close and laying a hand on my shoulder, which now shook with the effort of holding up the bookcase. "But Dracula has not wronged you. He is not the one who has done this to Mary. I give you my word."

"Holmes?" I said, amazed. "What can you possibly be saying? Who else?"

"That is a matter that bears some explaining. Believe me when I say that not only was Count Dracula *not* the perpetrator of the crime you accuse him of, but that he was also instrumental in helping me to locate you in time to prevent their final aim, no less than your eternal enslavement. And without Dracula's help, I should not have been able to prevent it."

I hesitantly lowered the bookcase to its former place. "And Mary? What can be done for her?"

Dracula stepped forward and spoke, "She is dead to you, Dr Watson, at least in the way that you knew her. She is in the power of an elder vampire now. She is no longer your wife. She is lost to you. Gone forever."

"Another vampire," I said. "How can this be?" I could feel the black weight of loss settle its talons deeper into my back. Mary, my own humanity. What nightmarish future awaited me like this?

"I am quite sorry," Holmes said, "that you did not have the opportunity to hear the Count's story to its full conclusion. It is most important that you do, I think. First we must attend to your health, for the Count assures me that this is quite a precarious time for you."

The Count himself did not speak, but watched the proceedings with an air of detached interest. Mrs Hudson was nowhere to be seen, and I could only assume that Holmes had forbidden her entrance to our quarters. He himself brought the tea service to my bedside.

Though a hunger consumed me, the thought of this once comforting ritual now caused a wave of nausea, until the aroma of something I *did* need came to me.

"Holmes!" I cried when I divined his strange joke. "Really, this has gone too far. I cannot go on with this charade as if nothing has happened to me!"

"Tut, tut," he said, pouring out the warm red fluid into a tea cup in front of me. "Of course you can't. But I also know that you need sustenance to survive, and is the consumption of flesh that every good British citizen partakes in really more cultured than this? Oh, I admit this is certainly very outré, to say the least, but I see no reason why you should have to descend to the level of a beast. This has come from the butcher's shop, the same as my breakfast sausage, and from the same source, I am sure."

My objections rose in my throat, but they were momentarily forgotten when Holmes set the tea cup of warm blood in front of me. It was the sheerest mockery in my mind to pour it from one of Mrs Hudson's best teapots. My hand shook as I picked it up and I felt a wave of deep emotion for this man who had done this for me, even though he acted as if it were nothing more uncommon than our usual breakfast. I finished the first cup. It was delicious. More than delicious. I could feel strength and life pour into me with every drop. I drained both a second and a third before I came to myself. Then I looked at the red stain in the cup. I wiped my mouth and moustache and my hand came away with an abhorrent red stain. Despair welled up in me again.

"Holmes," I said, my voice heavy. "I *am* a beast now. There can be no denying it. I am a danger to every citizen in London. Dear God, Holmes. I am an abomination and should be destroyed!"

"Nonsense!" Holmes said. "You are no more a danger to our fellow citizens than you were before your affliction. No, no, don't try and contradict me on this; the evidence is far too great against your position. You see, I have some knowledge of your wanderings before we picked you up. The hackney driver behind the paper factory, the butcher's boy on Windermere Road—" He ticked them off on his fingers, one by one. "—and the elderly gentleman last night, indisposed with drink underneath the floral display on Covington Way. In point of fact, you have gone to great lengths, despite your disorientation and starvation, to ensure that no other citizen suffered on account of your recent tragedy."

"It's true I have not hurt anyone yet... but how could you know?"

"Come, come, Watson, you know my methods. While the Count assisted in locating your person, I am not so great a bumbler that I didn't at least find traces of you."

"But... Mary..." I lifted my hands helplessly. "She was like a soulless monster when she had me in her power... Holmes, it looked like her, but it was *not* the woman that I married! I would swear to it. She was hardly a person at all!"

Holmes's face went very grave. "Ah... well there I am afraid that I am unable to provide any comfort, as much as I should like to. Our present conversation is enough to assure me that the Count's words are true about the nature of the transformation. The mental faculties, though muddled for a short while, do return, along with their memories. It is only the personality that is shattered."

I felt a blackness overtaking me at the thought of Mary's casual cruelty that I had witnessed. I could not even begin to compare it to the woman I had loved. How could her change be that complete? I certainly did not feel the same person as I once was, despite Holmes's assertions, but my thoughts remained intact. I could still understand right and wrong. Could Mary? There had been nothing but monster in her, behind that pretty and familiar mask. How much more could I lose?

"Evidence clearly suggests," Holmes went on, "that the primal need to feed is usually quite enough to overcome almost anyone's moral sense of right and wrong."

"Almost," the Count murmured, the first word he'd spoken in some time.

"Indeed," Holmes agreed. "In fact, Watson, if the Count and I were betting men, I should have won a great deal of money on you. I had no doubt that your character would come through the transformation intact, and I was right. You have risen over magnificent odds to do so. Far greater than I think you realize."

"A most impressive feat, Doctor," Dracula said. "Believe me when I say that most men do not do so well. The deprivation and madness of the change, followed by such a pure temptation to evil, breaks the soul of the transformed as surely as any bout of lunacy. It requires a great strength of character to survive it intact. A poet I'd known long ago once described the process as a 'shattering and reconstitution of the soul'. I've only known a handful of souls that could be said to be the same person afterwards. Call it one in a hundred. Most come out exactly the bloodthirsty monsters that Stoker accused me of being.

"But this," Dracula continued, "is a matter of semantics for the philosophers." He waved a hand dismissively, then came and sat down with us, helping himself to a cup of warm blood with no sign of self-consciousness. Even Holmes's usually unflappable composure was visibly unsettled, and his visage went taut.

"Thank you, gentlemen," Dracula said. "This will save time. I had not expected to find such a convenience. A product of modern thinking, no doubt." He smiled a predator's smile and the feeling of being unsettled deepened within me. I could see from a glance, however, that Holmes was quite resolute that we should have Dracula for an ally. I had always trusted in Holmes's judgement before this, and even in this time of my greatest confusion, I could not help but do so now.

"Now," Holmes said, his voice tight and full of forced bonhomie, "we shall have to give you that account of Count Dracula's tale that I promised and there are further details I should like clarified."

I hesitated. It seemed impossible that I should return to my old chair and listen to the beginning of another one of Holmes's cases, as I had done so many times before, as if nothing had happened to me. As if I were still the same person that I had been before. Doubts filled me as to whether the word 'person' should even apply to me still. Yet, even with all of my trepidations, many years of routine and habit had clearly left their marks, for I found myself settling into the sitting chair by the fire, just as I had so many times before, for all the world as if I was still Dr John Watson and not some bloodsucking creature of the night.

Dracula loitered near the window overlooking the street. When he started to speak, it was in a distant voice, almost as if he spoke to himself rather than to us.

"Before I speak of our trip here," the Count said, "my second trip, you understand, years later, with Mina – I should like to make you understand the signs of danger that came before, though I did not recognize them as such beforehand.

"My title is not an affectation for my ancestors were noblemen in my land, and though I was born to it, I earned it in battle against the Turks a hundred times over. 'Count' is not precisely correct, of course, being an English word. *Voivode*, I was called in my land long ago, though my legions have lessened in the last century. Be that as it may, the people of my land still pay me homage, particularly the Romany that make their home near Castle Dracula. It was through them that I came to discover a succession of foreign interlopers in my land, all of them focused on gathering intelligence on my homeland, my lands, and my person. Had Transylvania not been a remote place, much unused to strangers, it would likely have been far more difficult to realize what they were about, for they came in various disguises and with various stories. A few enterprising souls even managed to penetrate into the castle itself. But having been warned, I was able to… repel them."

I shuddered, imagining the dark stone corridors of some largely empty castle and the exact form that the Count's measures might have taken. He turned, a wistful and dangerous smile on his lips, one that didn't reach his glittering black eyes. His expression suggested he'd guessed my thoughts and was mildly amused by them.

"Even then," he went on, "I did not yet recognize the threat this represented to me. I had just brought Mina back to my home and there came a great deal of conflict between her and my sisters. Eventually, one of them, Dolengen, made an attempt on Mina's life and I was forced to expel all three of them."

"Excuse the interruption," Holmes said, "but when you refer to them as sisters…"

"I mean, by this, that they are also vampires," Dracula said. "We do not share mothers."

"Why cast all three of them out?" Holmes said, "if only one made the transgression?"

"Adaliene," Dracula said, "the eldest, felt that by protecting Mina, I was setting her above the three of them, and demanded Mina's blood. The other two follow her in all things. I refused, of course. Casting one out was the same as casting out all three."

"How long had they been with you at Castle Dracula before this?" Holmes asked.

Dracula seemed surprised, briefly, but whether it was at the question or simply the act of being questioned, I could not tell. "Centuries," he finally said.

"Thank you," Holmes said. "That is quite clear. When did this happen?"

Perhaps discerning one year from another was not a task the Count normally applied himself to, because he frowned, deep in thought. I shivered at the implications. Would I live so long? Would that kind of life, filled with pain and the faces of past victims, feel more a blessing or a curse?

"We are in the year of 1902 now?" the Count finally said.

"Indeed," Holmes said dryly.

Dracula nodded his regal head, paying no attention to Holmes's tone. "Then my first trip to London was in 1890, and Mina and I returned together to my home during that summer. Winter was just settling into the mountains when the sisters left, the very end of that same year."

Holmes had opened a small notebook and taken some quick notes. "When did the foreign interlopers, as you say, start coming to your country?"

"The year afterwards," Dracula said. "I became aware of the first in the spring of 1891."

"Did they give you no indication of who sent them?" Holmes asked.

"As I said," Dracula replied, "they came from a variety of countries and places, some as far as Germany or Switzerland. When questioned, they had little useful information except that all of them had the same mission – gather as much information as they could about my home and my own person. They were of various agencies. Banks and governments and other mercantile establishments."

"But all with the same goals and agenda," Holmes said with impatience. "Did you not consider how suggestive that was?"

Dracula looked regal and irritated and his eyes gleamed with dangerous anger, but Holmes did not seem to notice. "You believe," the Count finally said, "that this is the work of one agency or person?"

"I consider it very probable, yes," Holmes said.

"As do I," Dracula admitted. "But I did not realize it until very recently. It has to be Van Helsing. The other men involved, Holmwood and the others, are young, and it seems unlikely that they would have had the patience, insight, and subtlety required. Only I can find no trace of Van Helsing, or any of the other men that follow him, either here in London or elsewhere. Understand that my research in this endeavour was only idle curiosity until they took Mina."

"Tell us about that abduction and the events leading up to it," Holmes said.

"Very well. We came by ship, which landed three days ago in your Portsmouth. Since it landed by day, I was forced to remain below until nightfall, though Mina, of course, could still take to the deck."

"Why is that?" Holmes asked.

The Count looked suddenly very alert and cagey, but then his expression relaxed. "There is no point, I suppose, in dissembling, since I came to you for help. You and the Doctor will no doubt discover this in time on your own. Vampires become more stronger and more durable as we age, but also more vulnerable to sunlight, especially if we have not fed. The good doctor will find direct sunlight uncomfortable and a cause of great lethargy. A century from now, should he live so long, the benediction of the sun, if you have not recently fed, will cause you to burst into flame at the merest touch."

"A factor, no doubt," Holmes said, "of the ongoing influence of the blood disease. It gradually, over years, petrifies and ossifies the flesh, accounting for a great many features of the elder vampire. The great strength and resiliency, in addition to the vulnerability to sunlight, I should say. I should be very surprised if the elder vampire is not also much lighter than a comparable man, which goes a great way toward explaining the amazing climbing ability I've seen evidence of."

"I once had a passion for your modern science," Dracula said, "but discarded it when London became a sour place to me. Perhaps it may have some merit."

"Perhaps," Holmes said, a small smile playing for just an instant on his face.

Dracula's gaze flickered to the laboratory table with all the Bunsen burners and retorts and an echo of Holmes's ironic smile played around his own thin lips.

Holmes's face took on a note of concern. "One question: you say that it takes a century to develop such a susceptibility to sunlight, and Mina has not been a vampire for so long?"

"Yes?" Dracula said, clearly not understanding Holmes's question, though I did.

"The experiment with the finger!" I said.

"Precisely," Holmes said. "Forgive me, Count, but this may be extremely relevant. We have the finger that may have come from Mina's hand."

Dracula nodded, very seriously. "This is known to me. It is part of why I have come to you. You have, as you say, some of the threads of the case in your hand."

"Would you know her finger by sight?" Holmes asked.

"Most certainly," Count Dracula said.

Holmes got up and, with a small moment of hesitation, retrieved the cigarette case that still held the finger. He held it out to the Count, who took it carefully, as if it held something both very precious and very fragile. He opened the lid slowly and his face became like a thing of stone. His eyes blazed with a terrible, unholy wrath. But he said nothing. Finally, he closed the lid and returned the case to Holmes.

"It is the finger from her hand," he said.

"Help me understand, Count," Holmes said carefully. "You say that Mina would not have burst into flames herself, in the sunlight?"

Dracula nodded. "You are wise to question, but the explanation is no great mystery. A new vampire, transformed less than a decade ago, will feel the pain of the sun, but will not burst into flame. Starve that same vampire for a week, perhaps more, and that will change. Direct sunlight could then produce combustion. Also, our flesh, detached, develops the same vulnerability. Take a sample of the Doctor's flesh here. It need not be painful. A clipping of the nail will suffice. Take such a piece today and sunlight would not cause combustion. However, a week later, it would, since the blood has lost its potency.

He turned to me. "But know this. Blood is life to all things, even more so for you, now. A great deal will depend on how recently you have fed. Well-nourished, an elder vampire of sufficient will can brave even the full sunlight without fatal injury, though there is some pain. I myself have found your London streets during the daytime quite welcoming, since there are many days where the fog prevents anything like full sunlight. It is quite a natural harbour to vampires, in that sense."

Holmes again looked surprised. "You yourself have done this?"

The thin smile returned to Dracula's lips. "I have. Very recently, in fact."

I shivered at the fearsome and predatory look on Count Dracula's face, but Holmes was unfazed and merely made a note in his book. "Most interesting."

"So," Dracula continued, "when Mina and I came to London, our plan had been to wait until nightfall then leave the ship in order to seek out some of your London night life. But, again, I underestimated our enemy and overestimated the safety of your much lauded civilization. Your London police force was nowhere to be found when someone set fire to our ship. A burning alcohol bottle thrown into the rigging, I understand, though I did not know this at the time. All I knew was the sudden call of fire and the immediate smell."

"How did you come to know it?" Holmes asked.

"Conversation overheard from the gathering crowd," Dracula said. "I suspect a confederate among the crew of the ship, because a second fire started in the hold at the same time. I was in our quarters, resting, and slow to rouse, while Mina had gone on deck. By the time the fire had overtaken the ship, we were quite cut off from each other. At the same time, it was apparent that we must abandon the ship. I could hear her on the deck, you understand, and recognize her steps even among so many. I will tell you, gentlemen, that I have faced the Turkish hordes, but never did my heart quail as it did when I crouched at the bottom of the hatchway ladder, listening to Mina make her escape amid all that chaos. The stench of the smoke, the roar of the flames as her boot heels crossed the deck, and then a great crash as some part of the rigging came down and broke through the deck just as she gained the dock.

"Once she was safe, I tended to myself, acquiring a few things from our cabin and then making my way to the hold. As I said, this, too, was in flame, but not yet so fierce as the fire above, so I was able to pry up enough boards in the ship's hull for water to come in and allow me to escape that way. I swam through the relative darkness of the water and did not surface again until I was in the shade of the dock."

Dracula seemed a creature of inhuman stillness when he wanted, but traces of humanity clearly remained, because he started pacing back and forth between the short space from the chair to the darkened window.

"Having no need to breathe," Holmes said, "as normal men do, I would imagine this to be the safest route for both of you. Why did Mina not simply jump into the water?"

Dracula paused in his pacing and faced us. "You surprise me again, Mr Holmes, with your astuteness, but in this, you are only half correct. While you have no doubt observed that my lungs do not work as yours do, it is a mistake to think that water is our friend. You will discover this, too, on your own, Doctor. Rain is of no consequence, but do not cavalierly enter the water, as your new life depends on it. When waters close over the vampire's head, a stupor far worse than the sun clamps down upon him, followed shortly by the real death. Even a very brief time submerged is extremely dangerous for our kind. Mina might enter the waters and, having no experience with the water as a vampire, never come out again. She was well aware of this. I tell you that my short swim under the boat to the dock was a harrowing thing. It may have lasted two minutes, possibly three, and I almost did not make it before the darkness closed on me for good. It was as much as I could do to cling to the dock pylons and let life slowly return to my form."

Dracula started pacing again. "But it was then that true despair came to me, for I heard Mina cry out from the dock above me, and other voices, men's voices, calling to each other in such a way that I came to understand that they were dragging her away.

They did this by impersonating London policemen, though I did not realize that it was an impersonation until later. But the part that chilled me to the bone was that the voice commanding your policemen was one I recognized. Adaliene, the eldest of my banished sisters."

"Here?" I said. "In London?"

"Yes, Doctor," Dracula said. He turned back to Holmes. "I do not know how they managed this subterfuge or how Adaliene was able to move freely and unhindered in London, and under what guise she gave commands to your police. I was able, however, through questioning pedestrians in your city, to track Mina's abductors to a warehouse nearby. Both Mina and Adaliene are striking in appearance, making their passing somewhat notable. There, I found Adaliene, but not Mina, who had already been taken away in a carriage. I followed Adaliene, hoping she would lead me to Mina, but instead she led me to the Carfax Estate. There I made my presence known and, after dispatching men around her, questioned Adaliene. But other agents in her new master's employ had taken Mina, but Adaliene did not know where. My trail ended there."

"Adaliene could tell you nothing more?" I said, drawn into the Count's story despite my misgivings regarding having someone like Dracula as a client.

"She told me that Mina was lost to me," Dracula said, "unless I agreed to do her master's bidding. She had removed Mina's finger herself, though the order came from her master. Also that I would continue to receive trophies until I complied with his wishes and left London."

"Adaliene knew," Holmes said, "that this threat would have a significant impact on you?" At my incredulous look, he added, "While this may seem obvious to most of us, it is not a tactic an adversary would have faith in if they had only known Dracula from Stoker's book alone."

Dracula hesitated. "Yes."

"So," Holmes went on, "your adversary knew a great deal about vampires, knew a great deal about you and Mina, and your relationship, as well as your travel plans. Adaliene could not have been informed on the latter, at least."

"Not the precise details of our travel, no, though she could have easily guessed some of the particulars. I've made the trip by ship before."

Holmes tapped a finger on his forehead, pondering. "What else did she tell you?"

"She would not give me a name," Dracula said simply, "even unto her death. She told me a very small portion of the plans her master had, enough to concern both of us, I think. She did know a title for this master, but one that Adaliene swore would do me little good. It means nothing to me."

"What was it?" I asked, after the Count paused.

"They call him the 'Mariner Priest'".

"A man of God?" I said, astonished. "Dealing with vampires and kidnapping and severing the finger off an innocent woman? That hardly seems credible."

"I do not say it is true," Dracula admitted. "I say only that she believed it with all of her heart."

"We know that Mina's finger was delivered to Stross,"

Holmes said. "An intermediary who knew little of its story or significance, though his demeanour when Lestrade questioned him certainly indicates that he well knew how dangerous this affair was. This was directed by someone far above Stross, above Adaliene, even."

"Van Helsing," the Count said.

"Perhaps," Holmes said. "How he planned to locate the Count and deliver it is as yet unknown. Stross knows nothing. The Count had already interrogated him in prison before coming to us." Holmes shot a look of irritation at the Count, who ignored it.

"He knows nothing," the Count agreed. "Merely a hired intermediary awaiting instructions through courier. He did not know the name of Van Helsing or any of the other men that follow him. He knew very little, in fact."

"Our enemy seems to have a great many agents and resources," Holmes said. "None of them very well informed, the entire operation so compartmentalized that none of them can be followed to their source."

"This Adaliene knew no more?" I asked.

"She merely repeated that her new master knew everything," Dracula said. "Her threat, and the violence on Mina, naturally enraged me, and so I exacted an identical penalty upon her person, depriving her of the very same finger in recompense before leaving her to the sun's tender mercies."

"The very same scene of vengeance that we encountered at Carfax Estate," Holmes added. He looked significantly at the haughty and barbaric figure of Count Dracula, who looked hard at the two of us. Never in my life have I seen a look as imperious and uncompromising as the Count's, but Holmes's gaze was equally unflappable and after a long period of consideration, the Count nodded.

"I have been a prince and a soldier," he said, "long before I was as you see me now. But I am also a monarch, and they assaulted both my wife's person and my own. It is no less than war. You have yourself, Doctor, been a soldier."

I saw a very great difference between war on foreign soil and murder committed in the heart of London, but also knew that Holmes always had reasons for the choices he made. If he saw fit to assist Dracula, I would at least listen to the facts. I saw no reason, however, to pretend that I approved of the Count's murderous behaviour, so I said nothing.

"It is your belief that Van Helsing is responsible for this?" Holmes said.

"So my heart tells me," Dracula said, "for he has been the only significant opponent and danger to me for many centuries."

"I did not get the impression from your account that he presented a significant danger," Holmes said.

"Perhaps I have understated the case," Dracula said. "Nevertheless, it is true. However, there is a great deal that remains unexplained."

"The elder vampire that has taken Mary, for instance," Holmes said.

"Exactly," Dracula said.

"I assume that Van Helsing was not a vampire when you met him previously?"

"No," Dracula said.

"And you say it would take an elder vampire to transform Mary and hold her the way he has."

"Yes."

"If Van Helsing had become a vampire," Holmes said, "he would still be far too new to his vampiric powers, as you explain it, to have performed the feats we ascribe to Mary's capture and transformation."

Dracula frowned. "That is true."

"Would Van Helsing work with a vampire?" Holmes asked.

"I would not have thought so," Dracula admitted. "But I can think of no other explanation, other than that he has either colluded with a vampire or become one himself."

"Are either of these possibilities likely?" Holmes said.

Dracula shook his head. "I do not know the man well, but it was his devout, fervent belief that vampirism was not just a disease, but an unholy thing. An abomination, an affront against his Christian god. I cannot see him, in truth, doing either of these things. I am at a complete loss to explain it."

"Well," Holmes said. "Your case certainly does not lack for colour. When you questioned this Adaliene, did you ask about the other two sisters?"

"No," Dracula said. "Mina was my only concern. Possibly they are nearby or possibly they have parted ways. Vampires do not usually tolerate each other's company, but they have spent so many years together, that I cannot imagine them abandoning each other now."

"Had you any reason to expect them in London?" Holmes asked.

"None," Dracula said, resuming his pacing. "It is quite antithetical to their nature. They are like wild beasts, untrammelled by civilization, even more so than most vampires, which is saying something, Mr Holmes. I would have said that nothing was less likely, for while the teeming masses here in London make hunting plentiful, that advantage pales compared to the hindrance of your London society. The sisters, as I knew them, had absolutely no ability to blend or pass themselves off as anything less than clever animals, and should have been discovered and destroyed after their second day here. An orangutan would have an easier time hiding in…"

"In Paris?" I offered.

"Yes," Dracula said. "Just so."

"The dangers of inviting a literary man to any conversation," Holmes said, shooting me a glance that contained equal and conflicting portions of irritation and reluctant amusement. He turned back to the Count. "Do you have any explanation for this aberrant behaviour?"

"I do," the Count said, "though I suspect you know it already. Either the influence of this 'elder vampire', or Van Helsing, or both, if they are not one and the same. Perhaps they are two distinct threats, and not working together at all. It would certainly require a very old and powerful vampire to have commanded such loyalty from the sisters so quickly."

"How many vampires older than you do you know of?" I asked, the vision of these possibly plentiful monsters chilling my blood, inhuman though I now was.

"None," Dracula said.

"None?" Holmes asked.

Dracula gave us his thin, cruel smile. "Alive."

This forced an unusual train of thought upon me, since the Stoker book, as far as I knew, referred to vampires as 'undead'. Clearly this was not a view that either Holmes or Count Dracula shared. In light of what we now know of those afflicted by the disease, it is clear that 'dead' and 'alive' mean exactly the same things to a vampire as to the non-afflicted, and I will not make use of the 'undead' terminology here. It struck me that any of the afflicted, including Count Dracula, being dismissed as a non-person, as a thing bereft of life, was as personal and profound an attack as anyone could imagine.

"Holmes," I said, standing and pleading with him. "This has gone far enough. You cannot mean to align yourself with this bloodthirsty and savage creature!"

"There is this to consider, Watson," Holmes said, seemingly unruffled and unmoved by my impassioned plea. "I have gleaned a great deal from the Count here, but also from my own research." Holmes gave Dracula a wry look. "You will forgive me if I did not entirely take your information at face value."

Dracula nodded, composed now and looking every bit the Count he claimed to be.

"But now," Holmes said, "that I have done some considerable amount of my own research with both the various offices of law enforcement and also the caretakers of a great many cemeteries, not only here, but several other major cities – it helps to know what to look for, you see – I am convinced that the Count is correct when he says that this 'Mariner Priest' is a far, far greater threat to London than your average vampire and certainly more so than the Count."

My heart sank as Holmes went on, warming to his subject.

"While I will concede the point," he continued, "that the vampire represents quite a danger to the common man, it is not so great as one might think. First, the vampire under natural conditions is a solitary creature and no two vampires would work together or willingly share even quite vast territories. I have found indications that London has less than a dozen such mature, rogue and solitary vampires, for all her teeming millions. In addition, I have it on Count Dracula's word that he merely desires to rescue his bride and return with her to his estate near the Borgo Pass, and will present no further danger to Britain or any of her citizens."

"But why, Holmes, should we believe anything that he says? Why would you choose to assist this… monster!"

"Because, dear Watson," Holmes said, his voice growing very grave, "of the other claim regarding this Mariner Priest that Adaliene made to Dracula."

"Other claim?" I said.

"He is making," Dracula said, "more vampires."

"Does that fit Van Helsing as you know him?" Holmes asked. "You describe him as being on a campaign against vampires."

"I do not pretend to understand all the man's motivations," Dracula said. "But what other explanation is there?"

"I have no other explanation at the moment," admitted Holmes. "I have never met the man and need more data."

"It must be him," Dracula said. "He *is* making vampires. Many more vampires. Possibly as many as thirty or so already, with a goal of surpassing a hundred or so by the end of the year."

"A hundred vampires?" I said, astonished beyond all reckoning.

"By the end of the year," Dracula repeated. "This is the other reason I came to you. This proliferation is, perhaps, an even greater threat to my person than it is to London. You see, my kind, normally, has always been very careful about creating more vampires. My situation is unique in Transylvania and even that cannot last indefinitely. In the modern world, with your telegraphs and telephones, the need for secrecy is even greater. Unlike normal predators, our potential reign is centuries."

"Unless," Holmes said, "your modern vampire makes the capital mistake of advertising their own existence?"

"Precisely," Dracula said.

"The evidence," Holmes said, "supports the theory that this instinct is ingrained in all vampires, else we would shortly be overrun with teeming droves of them. Hardly likely to avoid notice."

"Now there could be hundreds!" I said. "All on account of this Mariner Priest that does not adhere to this conditioning? But you said that vampires would never work together!"

"They don't, normally," the Count said. "The occasional exception is the fledgling vampire kept in tow of its master, but rarely have I seen more than two vampires cohabitate this way."

"Like your sisters?" I asked.

"Indeed," Dracula said, "though I have never heard tell of any other vampire maintaining so many as three and they are a unique situation. It is always just the fledgling and the master and even that never lasts for long." There was a touch of smug pride in Dracula's voice at his accomplishment.

"And see how that turned out," Holmes said. Dracula frowned, but kept his silence.

I fell back into my chair. "A hundred…" Visions of a veritable horde tormented my brain, images of red eyes and snarling mouths filled with fangs. My Mary could be among them, too, and the idea haunted me worse than her death would have. It also meant that I might see her again, as she was now, and the idea made me shiver with horror and revulsion. But a small seed of hope grew within me at the thought of seeing her, mired as it was in Dracula's black predictions.

"Holmes," I said. "We can't let this Mariner Priest do this to more people. We can't. We must do everything in our power!"

"Just so," Holmes said. "Necessity makes for strange bed-fellows, to misquote the Bard. In this, Count Dracula is our greatest ally. His information on the woefully misunderstood subject of vampires has been paramount and his abilities are not inconsiderable."

"You have, Mr Holmes," Count Dracula said, "an almost insolent talent for understatement."

"Forgive me," Holmes said, not sounding very contrite at all. "In short, this Mariner Priest represents a new, more dangerous breed of vampire that has somehow transcended the bonds that hold all other vampires, even one as ancient as you. It is a peril unlike any London has ever faced, Watson. Can you see now why we must take our present course?"

"Good Lord, Holmes," I cried, "we cannot let this happen!"

"I thought you might see it our way," Holmes said. His tone was mild, but I could see that a certain tension in him lifted. "Now then, Count, I have some investigations to perform on my own and then, I think, we shall be very grateful for your assistance. Can you come back just after nightfall tomorrow evening?"

"Of course," Count Dracula said.

After the Count had silently departed, I asked, "What is our next move, Holmes?"

"I must beg your indulgence, Doctor," Holmes said, "but you have given me just the barest sketch of the events surrounding your abduction and forced transformation. I know that the events are painful to you, but I must hear the complete story."

I did so, giving him as much detail as I possibly could, though there were so many parts where my information was woefully inadequate. Even so, Holmes nodded thoughtfully during my description of the opium parlour.

"I believe I can find the place," Holmes said. "Or at least narrow it down to a few choices based on your description, and I should like to know more about our adversary in this case. But for obvious reasons, I should like to make my first investigations during the daytime. While you may not be a complete slave to the vampire's daylight torpor that Dracula speaks of, Watson, I do feel that you should test the limits before engaging in espionage in enemy territory." He spoke easily and naturally and his logic made sense, but we were both aware that such an expedition might very well involve another encounter with the vampire Mary. I was both strangely maddened and relieved that I should miss such an opportunity, but I could not muster up any coherent or lucid arguments to the contrary, so I deferred to his assessment of the situation. I thought I saw, too, a glimmer of relief in Holmes's demeanour that I had not voiced any objection.

"In the meantime," Holmes said, "this affair and our next actions require a great deal of thought." So saying, he abandoned his briar pipe and took up the clay one, filled it, and began to puff blue smoke into the room with such industry that the room was shortly intolerable to my sensitive nose.

It being late, habit carried me to the shelter of my room, but habit or no, I found that 'late' seemed to have a different meaning to my vampire flesh and blood. Did I even have blood, that is, a circulatory system, of my own anymore, or had I lost that, too, with Mary and my humanity? Feeling my own wrist, I could detect the faintest of pulses. Was that because I had just fed, thanks to Holmes's care and love of the grotesque? So many questions.

Those questions and many more rattled around in my brain while I lay in bed, far from even the slightest trace of slumber, but obstinately refusing to rise and lurk through the darkest hours like some kind of haunt. (The irony that these hours have always been favourites of Holmes did not escape me.) Still, I refused to rise, and lay there through a long and arduous vigil. Finally, after a waiting period longer than most ice ages, slumber came to me.

When I woke, there was but the barest glow of sunlight left to suffuse the outer pane of my window and I realized that I'd slept through the best part of the day, which probably indicated that I'd lain awake all night and fallen asleep just as dawn broke, despite all my best efforts. I rose in a foul mood as a result, and made my way down the stairs to the study and dining table. There, next to a more ordinary repast of cold meat and bread, I found Mrs Hudson's porcelain tea service. The meat held no appeal for me and I could already smell the intellectually repulsive but life-giving contents that lay within the teapot. Fortunate for my own person that Mrs Hudson did not go in for, or possibly could not afford to purchase, a silver tea service.

I stopped with my hand outstretched, looking at the teapot. Holmes was not present, had not been present for most of the day. The lack of recent scent in the room told me that as clearly as one of Holmes's own deductions. But the blood in the teapot was still warm, I felt sure. Placing my hand on the pot confirmed it.

Which meant that Holmes could not possibly have prepared this, but had instead given orders to Mrs Hudson to do so. How had he explained that? Even if he had come up with an easy and facile lie, how long would that story hold and how long before Mrs Hudson knew the truth about my condition? She was no dullard, and would make some deductions of her own as our sanguine ritual became routine. The woman already put up with a great deal of horror because of Holmes and I. Brawls and rifle shots, police and criminals, along with the accompanying theft, murder, blackmail, and espionage that all laid their sinister fingers on this doorstep, just because she chose to allow Holmes and I to stay at 221B Baker Street. Now she would have vampires, too, and that rested solely on my shoulders. How would she look at me once she understood what I had become? I was no longer a person and certainly not a doctor. How could I be, when blood now represented the greatest distraction possible?

How long I stood there, staring at the teapot, I do not now remember, but I heard the front door open and the scuff of a shoe on the bottom stair. This finally broke through my paralysis and I poured out a cup of the rich, warm blood and drained down the contents in one draught. I set the cup down and fumbled with a cloth napkin as Holmes, for surely it must be he, reached the top of the stairs. Some of the blood must have gotten on my moustache, because the napkin came away with the smallest of scarlet stains on it. I carefully folded the napkin to hide the evidence as best I could, not from the world's greatest detective, but from myself.

A stranger opened the door of our study.

My senses reeled, for it was Holmes, undoubtably Holmes, but also a complete stranger that faced me. He wore a beggar's outfit I hadn't seen before, all rags and tatters, and the changes Holmes had made to his stance, the way he walked, and even the way he breathed disguised him almost as well as the cast-off clothes and the small changes he'd made to his face. I detected, with tinges of both shock and admiration, that he'd even gone to a great deal of effort to alter his scent, though this measure failed him now in such close quarters as he'd undoubtably been wearing the disguise since this morning. I suspected that, knowing the nature of our new adversaries, he'd gone to a great deal more trouble to maintain his incognito than he'd ever been forced to before during his long and illustrious career.

Though Holmes had often enjoyed dragging out such subterfuges to the most dramatic effect in the past, he did not do so now. "I can see by your expression," he said in his normal voice, "that my disguises are going to have a much shorter duration than before if all of our future criminals possess the same noses that you and our current enemies do. I shall be glad to rid London of all vampires, excepting those here at Baker Street, if only to save pennies on second-hand clothes."

"Still," I admitted, "what you have done is astonishing!"

"Merely a necessity considering the circumstances of this case," Holmes said airily, though I could see that he was pleased at my praise. He walked across the study, flinging off his wig, coat, and other bits of disguise before he'd even gotten to his bedroom door.

He emerged a few short minutes later, looking, moving, and smelling like his own self again. "We have not a moment to lose, Watson. I should have much preferred to take our next steps during the hours of daylight, but I've reason to believe that our presence is needed to prevent the birth of several more vampires tonight. In the next few hours, in fact. Do you feel up for it, Watson?"

"A block and tackle should not hold me back," I said.

"Excellent," Holmes said. "I wanted to offer you a chance to strike back at the foul monster who has so wronged you, this Mariner Priest. I confess no small amount of personal guilt in this matter, since I'm quite certain that your fate was actually an indirect attack on myself, with the intention of distracting me from pursuing the Count's case." Holmes put a hand on my shoulder and I could see that my otherwise austere comrade was quite shaken with a deep emotion that I had always known lay underneath the cool exterior. "If not for me," he said, "your dear wife would still be with you, and not transformed as she was."

"It seems to me that this plague has come to all of London," I said, "and not just Baker Street, and that no husband and wife are safe until we defeat it."

"I knew I could count on you!" Holmes said. Then he turned to the open doorway. "Ah, Count Dracula, as punctual as I could have wished. That is well, for we shall have need of your help."

I shot to my feet, startled and nonplussed by the Count's sudden appearance. Seeing my reaction, the taller man gave me a thin, dark smile.

"Forgive me, Doctor," he said. "You will find, should you live as long as I have, that in addition to sensing the sounds and smells of those around you, that you will start getting a sense of the thoughts and emotions in those around you, as well, be they vampire or human. These thoughts are like sounds on an open sea, echoing and uncertain, but there, nonetheless. As this 'extra' sense of yours grows, you will find that clouding the perception of others will become almost second nature."

"The vaunted powers of the undead?" I said, unable to keep the scorn and despair out of my voice, for I was one of them now.

"Foolish!" Dracula hissed, his anger like a sudden storm. "Foolish to believe in fairy tales over your own senses. You are infected now. Tell me, do you feel like a death has come over you?"

"My life, as I know it, has certainly ended!" I shot back.

"Transformed!" the Count corrected. He took several steps

into the room, stepped forward, and urgently seized my arm, caught in an eager frenzy to drive home his point to me. "Smell the air around you, listen to the noises of the city. More of the world washes over you than ever before, and you are more a part of it than you ever were before the infection, more a piece of the teeming life that covers this globe. Does 'dead' or 'undead' seem the proper term to you?"

I paused, shocked and startled by his intensity. But he was not wrong. I could hear voices and movement in the street, in the shops and residences and other dwellings such as ours, and all the people and things there. Animals, even rodents, or something as comforting and civilized and completely human as the scent of Mrs Hudson's tea downstairs. As he said, this and many other things washed over me.

"No," I admitted. "I do not feel like one of the 'undead', however tragic and loathsome this transformation is to me."

"Nor should you," Dracula said. "I will not attempt to explain all of my powers, for I have never made a scientific study, but I believe these things exist in the real world. They do not come from superstition and I am certain that a scientist such as Mr Holmes will be able to explain them, given time. After all, starfish and other marine invertebrates can regrow limbs. This is known. There is a certain tree in Africa that displays extraordinary powers that in a man, you would call powers of the mind. It can call the proper kind of ant to itself, urging the ants to make colonies in its own bark and wood, through means unknown, and so create large colonies. It is a symbiotic relationship that benefits them both, but one the ants cannot refuse. Man does not yet know how all these things can happen, but they do. Is not superstition just science that we do not yet understand?"

"I suppose so," I admitted, perplexed and still a little frightened at his intensity.

The Count, seeing my fear, released me. "Forgive me. I did not mean to startle you, but it is a philosophical point that is very dear to me. I mean you no harm. We are allies in this endeavour, are we not?"

"I'm surprised," I said carefully, "that you'd willingly reveal your secrets to us."

"I have come for your help," Dracula said. "My research on you and Mr Holmes suggests that you are both men of your word. My original supposition, that we should only become adversaries should I prove a danger to England's laws or citizenry, and that you would both pit your full powers against any true threat to these things, still seems the strongest course. I have also seen for myself that your descriptions of your friend's reasoning powers are not exaggerated, so he would likely see through any falsehoods on my part. Therefore, truth, in this case, shall be my shield and dissembling only a hindrance. Is it not logical?"

"Descriptions of my reasoning powers?" Holmes said, with a short laugh. "Watson, I believe you have only yourself to blame for landing this particular client at our doorstep."

"You've read my stories?" I said. I could not, for the very life of me, imagine the Count engaged in such a mundane task as reading.

"Indeed," Count Dracula said. "You should be commended on your veracity, Doctor."

Holmes gave a short snort of derision. He'd made his own feelings on the 'sensational' nature of my stories clear enough many times in the past.

"It also had," Dracula said, "the distinct advantage of providing me with your address. Much more efficient than questioning one of your cabbies, I should think." Something that might, on another man, have been called the slightest trace of a grin, twisted the Count's aristocratic mouth. If anything, it made him more frightening than ever.

"Come," Holmes said, putting his revolver and several of the silver cartridges into his jacket pocket. "The rest of this discussion, including our destination, I shall have to explain en route, for we have lost too much time already."

Chapter 05

THE TOBACCONIST'S SHOP

"**32** Percy Street," Holmes called to the cabbie. "Off Tottenham Court Road, and time is of the essence!"

"You say that time is of the essence?" Count Dracula said with that odd, foreign formality of his.

"Lives are at stake," Holmes said flatly. "Possibly Mina's."

I held open the door, but Count Dracula, instead of climbing into the cab, paused before the horse in front, a tired-looking roan mare. Here he paused to stroke the mare's neck and whisper some words to her in his native tongue.

"'Ere now," the cabbie said from the driver's box.

Dracula ignored him, but kept on whispering in the horse's ear. A remarkable change came over the roan, who transformed from the dull creature she had been to a spirited marvel, quivering all over with barely suppressed excitement. The Count leapt with startling agility into the carriage and bodily lifted the driver out of the seat as if that robust man were nothing more than a small parcel. The driver picked himself up off the road and began to protest, but Dracula's wrathful countenance and Holmes's hastily produced sovereigns turned away any objections he might have had.

"You might have purchased a horse and hansom for half of what you've just thrown him," I said to Holmes.

"I fear we already have," Holmes said.

"We are ready," Dracula said. Holmes and I entered the cab as the Count watched us from the box above with his inscrutable dark gaze, a considerably unsettling situation.

"South," Holmes said as we sat down. Even before the word was finished, the Count clicked his tongue and the horse leapt like a creature on fire. I gripped Holmes's arm to keep him from tumbling out and it was all Holmes could do to get the door shut behind us before we were rattling down the cobbled street.

Dracula held the reins, but did not seem to be using them. Or else, he used such a light pressure as to be undetectable to my eye. But never did any horse on road or track run with the speed and unerring step as did our roan. Even more bizarrely, the other carriages and even people had an uncanny tendency to manoeuvre out of our way, so we flew through the streets like a veritable bullet.

Holmes had the window on his side open, so he could lean out and call out directions. With his unparalleled knowledge of London, Dracula's uncanny driving, and the roan's ceaseless efforts, we had reached and passed Regent's Park before I'd even realized it. Dracula led the horse briskly around obstacles with seemingly no regard for the safety of anyone, including ourselves.

A sudden torrential downpour struck us with unbelievable and terrible force, drenching Dracula and our horse at once, though neither took the slightest notice. Holmes and I were little better off, as enough slanted rain came through the open window that we might as well have been outdoors ourselves.

A curious thing occurred to me as we went: while the night around us was clearly quite cool, I was shocked to realize that the chill did not touch my skin in any sense. I should have been shivering and covered in gooseflesh under my wet clothes, as Holmes was, but those days were gone to me. Perversely, though I never once remember being grateful for the opportunity to shiver in the cold and wet before now, I found I missed the sensation once it was gone.

"Where are we going, Holmes?" I called out over the rain and noise.

"I visited several dens of the kind you described," Holmes said, "and believe I even found the man, the vampire, with the blond mutton chops that you reported as supervising your convalescence. There, I learned some very interesting facts."

"You spoke to him?"

"I didn't have to, Watson. Even had I not noticed the chalky dirt on his shoes, I should never have missed, even on my dullest day, the shovel he left carelessly leaning against the wall. It, too, had the same kind of earth on the blade. There is little by way of chalky dirt in the surrounding area, so a cellar was the logical answer, only the establishment didn't have one. I might have had a long search for the correct cellar if the man had not smoked many cigarettes in rapid succession."

"How on earth could that have possibly helped?" Even if I hadn't been in a carriage running at full tilt and had more time to ponder, I couldn't imagine how the two facts could be linked.

"It was the nature of the cigarette, Watson," Holmes said. Then, holding his hat on with one hand, he leaned partway out the window, shouting out his next direction to the Count, who turned the carriage with a suddenness that threatened to tip the entire vehicle over onto its side as well as plunging us heedless into a narrow street thoroughly choked with traffic. Another carriage suddenly appeared in our path, but the horses shied out of the way while our brave mare plunged through the sudden break in traffic with headlong abandon.

"It was another of our Indian cigarettes, Watson," Holmes said, falling back into his seat, but otherwise continuing his explanation as if we weren't about to cause and participate in a violent traffic accident, perhaps several. "I have mentioned their rarity, but another consideration is that they do not come cheaply. When I see a man, vampire or otherwise, with threadbare clothes and patchwork shoes, drinking the cheapest whiskey he can get but smoking expensive imported cigarettes, I begin to wonder if he might not have some connection to the same dealer we had reason to seek out the last time such an uncommon cigarette crossed our case. Sure enough, I returned to Govern's shop and found traces of the same earth on the doorstep, though none outside. I surmise that there is work in the cellar, but to what purpose?"

"I still don't understand."

Holmes rapped the ceiling of the carriage and called out again.

"Here, Count!" He pointed a long, lean arm through the window indicating a dark building ahead and to the right.

The Count must have tried to pull up the reins, or command the horse to stop in some other, more subtle means, but instead, our horse stumbled, ran a dozen more strides, and ran full tilt into a heavy stone wall next door to the shop. The hansom jolted off its wheels, slamming into horse and wall with a terrible jolt. Holmes and I were nearly thrown, but Dracula leapt easily and neatly off. Holmes and I were shaken, but otherwise unhurt.

I sprang out of the hansom and rushed to examine our faithful mare, but the Count was already there ahead of me.

His face was still as he knelt in the muddy street next to her inert form. "She is quite dead," he said. His voice was strangely sad, something I had not expected. He lay his hand on her neck for a moment, and then stood up. "Brave girl. She gave her life nobly. Let us hope that her sacrifice was not an empty one."

I stared, horrified beyond measure that this animal had died so suddenly and tragically.

"What did you do to her?" I whispered. "Did you cause her death?"

"I did not," Dracula said, and the man who had as much as openly admitted to hunting men and women in London sounded offended at my accusation. "Though I do bear some blame for it. I freed her of pain. She was old and lived a dreary existence pulling the cab around in this city. I underestimated the burdens on her. When I lifted all her aches and pains away, the sheer joy of running overtook her and this…" He gestured at the tragic form in front of us. "This was the result. I had not expected that. She felt no pain in the end. Her death was quite instantaneous."

I wondered how he could know that, but somehow believed him, and felt no small amount of gratitude that this was the case.

"Gentlemen!" Holmes called, striding to the front door of the shop.

Dracula remained a long moment, staring fiercely at the small crowd of a dozen or so men and women gathered near the dead horse and broken carriage. When they looked for driver or passengers, their gaze seemed to slide right past us. No one appeared to notice us or pay us any attention whatsoever.

Count Dracula, who had stood a moment to supervise the crowd, now turned, with the sternest of expressions, and followed Holmes. I marvelled at the impossibility of what had just happened and, not for the first or last time, found myself more than a little frightened by the Count.

The shop stood dark and empty. It was a two-storey building, with living quarters above the shop. A shiny, new-looking padlock hung from the front door.

Holmes had pulled out his leather case that held a selection of lock picks. It was remarkable to me that he might try such a blatantly illegal endeavour in full view of so many passers-by, but when I looked behind me, I saw that still, no one paid us any mind.

"You believe someone is buried in the cellar, yes?" Dracula said, and I realized that he must have clearly heard and followed our conversation in the hansom, despite the racket we'd made coming here.

"I do," Holmes said.

"Mina?"

"It's possible," Holmes said. "Another possibility is that this Mariner Priest is indeed making more vampires and needed a place for them to safely rest and then rise. This draws us towards the Count's elder vampire theory, but possibly away from Van Helsing as a subject if we cannot account for this activity in the light of his hatred of the vampire."

"It still seems the most likely explanation to me," I admitted.

"Who else?" Dracula asked. "It *must* be him."

"It is far too soon to tell, but there are several distinct possibilities and that one is almost as likely as the others. Come. Time is of the essence. Every vampire we allow the Mariner Priest to create is both another victim and another formidable enemy."

Dracula was no dullard, following Holmes's line of reasoning better than I had, despite my familiarity with my friend's deductions and methods. But now I saw the chain of reasoning from Holmes's observations in the opium den to their natural conclusion.

"I hear no one inside," I said, indicating the shop as Holmes selected one of his lock picks.

But he never used it, because Count Dracula stepped boldly forward and pulled lock and hasp both free of the wood with a sharp, splintery crack. He discarded the twisted metal with disdain and stepped inside.

Never had I felt such a pang of loneliness and desolation that threatened to unman me as I did at that place. It was not a matter of darkness, for my newly vampiric eyes could pick out details in the dark far better than they ever had before. No, this was an emptiness that touched the senses with a frightening chill that had little to do with physical temperature. There was a sharp smell from the left side of the house, where the shop with its many brands of tobacco lay, but no sense of any person in the entire place.

Dracula had gone a short way inside, where a set of narrow stairs led upstairs to the living quarters, while a door to our left led to the shop. He stood there, pale and isolated, quivering with repressed energy. Then he sagged, very slightly. It seemed a motion of the heart rather than the body, undetectable by the eye but powerfully felt nonetheless.

"She is not here," he said quietly. "If she were, I would feel it."

"Perhaps not," Holmes said. He strode three paces into the house and crouched, looking at the floor. "But I perceive that our friend with the dirty shoes and shovel has been. Let us see what work has been done in the cellar." His motion had somehow broken the subtle spell the house had cast over me, and I followed. Dracula, similarly galvanized, followed as well so that the two of us trailed Holmes, who lost no time locating the basement stairs in the kitchen and descending, with barely a moment taken to pull out his pocket lantern and light it.

Creaky wooden stairs led down into a dirt cellar. At the far end stood a pedestal of crates, all of them stacked together like an underground stage displaying a sordid theatre production. Standing in the centre of this makeshift stage was a black coffin, made with heavy, dark wood and wrapped all around with iron chains.

Dracula snarled. In half a heartbeat, he was at the chains, tearing them free as if they'd been constructed of mere cloth. They fell in a metallic clatter and Dracula tore at the box itself with fingernails like talons. Again, I felt a weight of fear fall on me regarding this man. It became clear at once that the Count was a man of powerful emotions held in check with an iron will, but that will had fallen away now. The wrath on his face was terrible to behold. His eyes blazed, his fangs protruded, and he looked more monster than he had ever before this.

When he hurled off the lid it split the side of the casket and something I'd been utterly unprepared for spilled out into the dirt. Water. Sea water by the scent of it. It poured out of the large, now broken coffin in a great gush.

"What in the world?" I said.

"What in the world, indeed," Holmes murmured. Clearly, he'd been just as surprised by the contents as I had.

The Count, however, paid little attention to the water and plunged his arms into the depths of the coffin, tenderly lifting out the frail form within. She was a pale woman with dark hair and a beatific face that must have shone with a radiant life when alive, either as a human woman or as a vampire. But vampire or woman, the figure once known as Mina Murray was demonstrably dead now. The Count fell to his knees, heedless of the several inches of water and mud, and he let loose with something partway between a sob and snarl.

I turned away. As much as the man still seemed a monster to me, I could not help but feel pangs of sympathy at the profoundly raw and naked grief that savaged the Count's face. I hadn't believed him capable of a deep, abiding and profound love. I did now.

"Why?" Holmes murmured behind me. He crouched, also heedless of the wet, and fingered a large splinter of broken wood that had come from the coffin. "There is pitch here. Dried. Someone prepared a coffin in advance specifically to hold and drown a vampire? Why, when there would be far easier ways to perform the same task?"

I looked back at the Count, horrified at Holmes's tactlessness in the face of such deep and debilitating sorrow. Dracula stood and carefully laid out the corpse of his great love. The final death.

"I foreswore all involvement with London," Dracula said, very softly. Even my vampire ears had to strain to make out the words.

"Because London meant nothing to me," the Count continued. "Only Mina. Only… Mina. Now, she is gone." He turned, then, a tragic figure with the sodden corpse of his truest love behind him on the oversized pedestal of crates. Mina's body looked wan and tired, inert, a physical shell bereft of anything that had given it importance. The important parts of Mina Dracula had all passed on.

"I am a man of my word," Dracula said, his voice still low, but throbbing with awful force. "I swore that once Mina and I were reunited, we would return to my homeland and London would have nothing to fear from either of us."

"I grieve for your loss," Holmes said.

So quickly did Count Dracula cross the intervening space that I had absolutely no time to react. Holmes had reached for his own revolver, but Dracula seized his wrist with one hand, easily immobilizing him. Dracula's eyes were wild, red, inhuman, his hair askew, his fangs protruding, the purely malevolent monster that I had feared him to be all along.

Dracula snarled. "But know this: London has taken Mina from me and London shall…"

"Vlad?" a soft voice said behind us.

"Mina?" The Count stopped. As quickly as he had come, he was gone, back on the other side of the room leaning over the body of his wife.

Mina, who, in some manner I could not begin to comprehend, was still alive.

"Mina, my love," Dracula said. He bowed his head, brushing his face against hers in a gesture I found oddly tender and submissive from so fearsome a man. A soft sob escaped his lips. It was a flash of the vulnerable emotion that he had not allowed to show itself at her death, but now slipped free.

Dracula's paralysing influence had evaporated its hold on me as quickly as it had come. I rushed to Holmes's side, helping him to his feet. He ruefully rubbed his neck, but seemed otherwise unhurt.

I turned, finally lifting my revolver, but Holmes wordlessly put a restraining hand on my arm.

"But, Holmes!" I said. He merely shook his head and I did nothing.

"Vlad," Mina said, listlessly trying to raise her hand to his face, but she was too weak. Dracula took her hand in his own and pressed his face to it, somehow seeming to come alive, to breathe, to exist, to thrive in a way he could not do alone, for all that Bram Stoker had wrongfully labelled him as one of the *undead*.

"I drowned," Mina said weakly. "Days ago. But somehow, I'm still here. How am I still here, Vlad?"

"I don't know," Dracula said. He spoke stiffly, even now gathering that mantle of aristocratic formality around him again, albeit slowly. "When I came into the house, I could not feel you, but you were down here just the same. I had not thought such a thing possible. I don't understand, but I thank all powers in the world that you are returned to me."

"It seems," Holmes murmured, "that vampires cannot drown, after all. You have greatly misunderstood the effect of water on your own kind, Count Dracula."

"But how?" Dracula said. Mina seemed to be recovering some of her strength and struggled to get up. Dracula solicitously assisted her, patiently helping her to a sitting position. He did not relinquish his grip even when she was upright, but remained with his hand supporting her.

"It feels," Mina said, "very much like death."

"Evidence suggests," Holmes said, "that drowning brings on a fit, not unlike a coma would do in a normal person. What do you remember, Mrs…" He seemed at a sudden loss, smiling ruefully. "I do not know your proper title, madam. Countess?"

"Just Mina," she said with a rueful smile of her own. "It's all I've ever needed. Mr…?" She looked at us curiously.

Holmes bowed deeply. "I am Sherlock Holmes, madam, and very much at your disposal. This is my esteemed colleague, Dr Watson."

Somewhat shamefully remembering my profession in the face of all the surprising events of the past few minutes, I made my way to Mina Dracula's side. For a moment, it looked as if Count Dracula might bar my way, but he did not. Mina's pulse was terrifyingly slow, even slower than my own had been last I tested it, and her skin was cold. Far colder than mine. I still had much data to gather before I had a full understanding of what constituted normal in a vampire, but my guess was that Mina was coming out of some kind of coma, just as Holmes surmised.

"Madam," Holmes said. "What do you remember?"

Mina was clearly made of stern stuff. She showed no sign of hysterics, merely a bone-deep weariness. But she furrowed her brow, her dark eyes pondering, as she considered my friend's question fully. "Very little. My abduction, of course, and when they put me in this horrible casket. Then they poured water in, water from the sea; I could taste the salt." She shuddered. "I don't think I shall ever enjoy being on a boat again, or even take a bath without remembering that. It was very much like drowning is all I can tell you. That, and the fact that I would do almost anything to avoid going through it again. I died. Or at least I thought I did." She looked at the Count. "I never thought I'd see you again." She touched the Count's hand and he gripped hers. Her tone was not overwrought, but a deep well of sadness lay behind it.

"If Van Helsing is behind this, we shall clearly have to revise our supposition that it is an elder vampire at work here, for he cannot have been a vampire long if he was fully human when last you saw him."

"Van Helsing?" Mina said. "He is involved in this?"

"We don't know," Dracula said.

"Whoever our opponent is," Holmes said, and there was a note of admonition in his voice as he caught Dracula's eye, "he clearly has a greater understanding of vampirism and the transformation than we do, despite your centuries of existence. Some experimentation may be required on our part."

"But not," Mina said with a rueful smile, "on me. That is another death I will avoid, thank you, gentlemen." Her voice was still filled with exhaustion, but there was a lightness to it. I found myself in deep admiration for one who could make light of such an ordeal.

"Never again," Count Dracula agreed. "On my life, I swear it." This caused Mina's smile to twitch, as if she again saw humour in the situation that everyone else had missed.

Dracula turned and looked at Holmes, but it seemed a difficult thing, as if tearing his gaze from Mina cost him something.

"Mr Holmes, forgive me," he said simply. "When I thought I had lost her…" He shook his head, then lifted it, his pride returning to him, though he still continued to support Mina. "I meant what I said. I am a man of my word. Now that Mina is returned to me, you shall have all my powers at your disposal to protect London. No Englander shall ever have cause to fear the name Dracula."

I could not help but find myself moved by this heartfelt statement, but Holmes seemed barely to have heard. He had moved to examine one of the crates that Mina's imprisoning coffin had rested on. There were far more than it required to hold the coffin but quite a few had been damaged during the deluge of water and Holmes pried one of these partway open.

"We shall have great need of your assistance, I think, Count," said Holmes, for he had indeed heard Dracula's words. "See here."

He yanked one of the lids off the rest of the way, revealing the contents. The crates were like coffins themselves, filled halfway with dirt.

The implications struck home at once. "Holmes," I said, "the Mariner Priest is indeed making more vampires here!"

"Many more vampires," Holmes said. "If the rest of these hold the same evidence." He reached in and pulled from the dirt a small object. He held it up in the light of his pocket lantern. A button, blue as a robin's egg. "Someone has been interred in here. There can be no doubt. There is evidence of a number of barrels having been here before, too. You can still see their impressions in the dirt."

Dracula assisted the still shaky Mina away as Holmes and I began to tear the remaining crates open. We found the same dirt in all of them. Most also had signs of previous occupation. Holmes had pocketed the blue button, and had also found an old, much tarnished pocket watch, a man's handkerchief, a pair of broken pince-nez, a train schedule, an apple core, wooden teeth, the scraps of a child's gingham frock, and no less than three pairs of heavily used dice.

"Eighteen," Holmes said. "Eighteen crates that most certainly held eighteen newly minted vampires." He shook the jacket pocket that now held our strange collection of discarded personal possessions. "We have a surplus of evidence that will give us insight into the previous lives of the tenants, but even a cursory examination cannot fail to suggest that they are from various walks of life. This may mean that the Mariner Priest is simply accosting whoever comes to hand. The handkerchief has stains from no less than three different brands of tobacco, so the shop owner, a man I spoke to only a few days ago, is likely among their number. His wife and child, too. The Mariner Priest constructed a veritable vampire factory in this cellar."

"But how?" Dracula said. "I tell you this thing cannot be done at such breakneck speed, even for a vampire willing to abandon every instinct and do such a thing. The process involves either being bitten repeatedly or drinking vampire blood, preferably both, before the infection is certain to be passed. It is long, painstaking, and highly individualistic. It cannot be reproduced with a factory-like mindset. It would require a vampire to perform it. Nor could you rely on a previous relationship or agreement to hold, since the vampire transformation is so destructive to both the personality and the intellect. Usually the elder vampire nurtures and can guide the fledgling vampire, but this is by no means certain."

"Destruction of the intellect?" I repeated. "Didn't that make transforming Mina a near-fatal proposition?"

"It did," Dracula agreed slowly, catching his wife's eye. "She convinced me to perform it anyway and I could not refuse her. She *knew* that she would come out intact, and she did."

"I believed in our love," she said simply. "Perhaps it takes a certain kind of person, emotionally, to survive the transformation, for I have always counted myself as one of great heart, and great passion, and disregarded those who deemed this a flaw of character, or fault of female temperament." She touched the Count's face tenderly.

I could feel the expression of astonishment on my own face, and saw Holmes's face take on one of irritation. I could almost hear his 'motives of women' tirade, which I had been subjected to more than once. 'Inscrutable' was the word he used, and he referred to it the way someone else might refer to a wrongful death.

Mina had clearly caught Holmes's look. "I think," she said, "that our Mr Holmes would become an absolute failure as a vampire." Her tone was gentle, light, her dark eyes bright, and she caught my gaze and gave a secret smile, as if she and I shared a secret between us about Holmes and Dracula that the other two could not fully comprehend. It seemed a completely illogical stance, but I could not fault the results, the almost tangible love that existed between Mina and Dracula, just as it must have before the transformation. I wondered if Mina did not, in fact, possess an understanding that even Holmes lacked.

"There is another thing," Dracula said. Here he gave me, and then Mina, a nod. "Humans may be creatures of passion over intellect, but I tell you that vampires are even more so. No vampire born in this century could do this thing, this cold and scientific experimentation, and no non-vampire would be capable. It must be someone very old, possibly older than I."

I put a hand to my own chest, wondering at what Dracula and

Mina had just said. Was, I, too, more a creature of passion than intellect? Had I been so before? But I had never possessed the icy intellect that Holmes could claim. I hardly knew how to measure the difference, but felt certain that the loves and passions of my life still beat in my stricken heart. Perhaps even more than they had before. Friendship, love, justice, *Mary*… all mattered to me deeply. Too deeply to measure, perhaps.

This gave rise to other thoughts. I knew that my circulatory system no longer worked the same way. My heartbeat now was so slight as to be virtually undetectable to a regular English doctor. I knew from my own experimentation that my heart still beat, albeit more slowly and quietly, distributing the blood I consumed much in the same way it had before.

"Our Mariner Priest must have a first-rate mind," Holmes mused. "Since he seems to have a much better working knowledge of the disease and the transformation. An expert in vampire biology, if you will, if his understanding of the effects of submersion on vampires is any indication. Also, it may be that this was discovered by accident if there is any truth to his nom de plume." He looked at Dracula. "You have heard of no such person in all the years?"

"I have not," Dracula admitted. "Though my country is an isolated one. I had thought, until now, that my isolation was a necessity, that no vampire could live long in the city for fear of exposure. Now, I begin to wonder. But, gentlemen, my lady, let us be free of this accursed hole."

"Why has there been no outcry?" Mina said as we mounted the stairs to the ground floor. "You would think that eighteen newly minted vampires, as you say, Mr Holmes, would cause quite a clamour. Have you seen no word in the papers?"

"None," Holmes said thoughtfully. We had reached the kitchen in the back of the house and started for the front door.

Holmes had taken the lead, followed by Dracula assisting Mina, while I brought up the rear. When Holmes opened the door that led out onto the street, he seemed to be struck by a thought and turned suddenly to ask a question of Mina or the Count.

A soft whooshing sound came to my ears, punctuated by a crack. Then a section of the wood panelling in the foyer exploded in a shower of wood chips. There, in the panelling, stood a large hole from a pistol or rifle shot.

Dracula immediately shielded Mina with his own body, pressing her against the opposite wall. Holmes staggered and I forced my way past Dracula and Mina in order to yank him back into the house. We both fell back against the same wall as Dracula and Mina, crouching down so as to present no target.

"Someone well-prepared," Holmes said tightly. "You can still see the shine from the bullet." He nodded at the place where the bullet had hit and I could, indeed, see the sheen of silver. Whoever shot at us, they knew something about vampires and how to kill them.

Holmes immediately bounced back up, peered out the still-open door for a brief moment, and then quickly dropped back down beside me.

"The park across the street," Holmes said, "judging from the angle of the shot. It is an air rifle, I should think, for I heard no loud shot and it is too long of a shot for a pistol, even in expert hands. Fool! I've led us right into a trap. It must be Dracula they are after if they're hunting with such specialized ammunition."

"Or Mina," Dracula said protectively.

Holmes shook his head. "They had Mina and left her as bait to lure us here. I should have known they'd anticipated our visit tonight when we discovered all their new vampires removed from the premises."

I tasted the blood in the air. "Holmes! You're injured!" The assassin had not completely missed after all.

"Yes," Holmes said. "One point for our assailant. But the wound is only minor, and we cannot pause to tend to it. I'm only grateful that I have no susceptibility to silver poisoning. It makes me a comparatively durable target. Such a scrape as this would be much more harmful to the three of you, I expect. There are a number of trees in the park. I suspect up among the lower branches of one is where our would-be assassin has made his home."

I risked a glance in the direction he indicated across the street, where a small copse of trees stood. The branches of several of them would all have made an excellent vantage point and the light was too poor to pick out his hiding place. I thought of the altered vampire eyesight. Sharper at close range and able to see in the dark, but not quite as good at long distances. I would need to get closer to try and find the villain.

Dracula had clearly been thinking the same thing. He stood. "Stay here with Mina," he said shortly. His eyes blazed and he spun, quick and feral, mounting the stairs up into the second floor of the house.

"Well then," Holmes said. "If Dracula is going to make his way across the street in secret and apprehend our assailant, it only remains for us to provide him some cover." He pulled his revolver from his coat pocket and stood, leaning quickly and suddenly out of the doorway in order to shoot his revolver twice.

He then ducked back into the foyer. "In addition to distracting our foe, that is very likely to summon the police, I should think, who ought to be a nuisance, but a welcome nuisance at this juncture all the same." His tone was jaunty but his face had become a rictus of pain. He'd moved freely enough so that I had thought the injury a small one, but now I thought again. It was clear that my friend had not been entirely truthful when he referred to his gunshot wound as 'minor'.

"Don't move," I said, kneeling next to him. "Let me have a look." His shirt and waistcoat were soaked with blood. I had earlier feared that the temptation of blood would forever make my doctor's profession impossible for me, but I did not even stop to consider it now. I tore open Holmes's vest and shirt, both of which were slick with red.

Holmes dropped his pistol and Mina scooped it up and moved to peer carefully into the street, ready to call out an alarm if the situation demanded it. Clearly this woman was no shrinking violet and I would wonder, later, if becoming a vampire had changed her in this fashion, or if it was this kind of spirit that had attracted Dracula in the first place. But now, I had only thought for Holmes and his injury.

A blood-curdling scream tore through the night from across the street, more inhuman than any sound I'd ever heard before.

I could not help but shudder and pity the poor wretch that might have cause to make that sound.

"The shooter," Mina breathed. "Vlad got to him." She sounded almost sad. Then she said, "Mr Holmes has passed out." Her face turned sympathetic as she watched my blood-drenched hands desperately performing the necessary field surgery to remove the bullet from his chest. It had not penetrated the lung, but was deep in the muscle, lodged against bone in such a way as to make me fear for my friend's life. For the first time since my transformation, I thanked providence for my new gifts. The feeble moonlight trickling through the open door was more than enough light for me to see clearly, and my fingers had a new sensitivity and deftness that astounded me. Before my change, I should have had to wait until light or transportation to a hospital. Still, I had only a small kit in my coat for tools and the wound was frighteningly dangerous.

"He will not survive," Mina said gently.

"Not without the transformation," Dracula said suddenly. He had come back into the house with that uncanny and disconcerting stealth of his. "You must infect him. It is the only way. Now."

I had thought Holmes unconscious from the pain, but his thin fingers closed weakly over mine.

"No," he said, his voice hoarse and low. It took all of my keen hearing to make out his words. "I will not be a blight to the world, not… undo all that I have done. I would not pass through the transformation intact the way you did. Even if I did, there would be an infinite amount of time for me to fall and become a menace to all that I hold dear. Promise me that *you will not allow it*."

"It will not come to that, Holmes," I said, fear rising up in me. I felt a desperate liar as I said it. "I can feel the bullet. I can get it. You shall survive this."

He did not answer me. Holmes passed out again, expending all his last strength on his plea to me.

Dracula and Mina said nothing, and I bent back to my task.

Chapter 06

DECISIONS

Sunlight streamed through the open window back at Baker Street. It would be many years, I now knew, before those rays would be a sure-fire death to me, but even now their light lanced to the back of my head any time I looked directly at them and I instinctively avoided their touch. At least the torpor of daylight had not taken me. Dracula had suggested that additional 'feedings' should bolster me against the need for sleep and I had found that this was true. Even more astonishing was that Holmes had clearly told Mrs Hudson a great deal of the truth, for she brought me a teapot filled with warm blood in the morning without demur or even my needing to request it. She patted my hand before she left the room in a gesture of sympathy and I found myself staring at the door she closed behind her for a long time after she'd departed.

I drank, and then picked up the morning newspaper, but it was a feeble distraction. I stared across the room at the sideboard, where Holmes had left the air rifle that Lestrade had brought yesterday for Holmes's inspection. It was the air rifle used by the assassin who had shot Holmes. Holmes had examined it with eagerness, then abandoned it with disappointment.

"You had thought it Colonel Moran's air gun?" I had asked.

"Well," Holmes had admitted. "Getting shot at with an air gun is not so commonplace an experience. However, this is not the same rifle and this…" here he pointed at the police sketch that Lestrade had brought us, "is clearly not our colonel. The man carried no means of identifying him and Scotland Yard currently has no leads."

The man in the sketch was clearly younger than Moran, with a strong jaw and a high forehead. He was also completely unfamiliar to me. Holmes had, of course, wanted to go down and examine the body, but I had forbidden it until he recovered a bit more. We knew this much already from Lestrade's report: the police had found him, his neck broken, against a large tree at least sixty feet from the dropped rifle. Dracula had apparently hurled the man a great distance.

"Of course," he said, favouring me with another glare, "tracking down the man's identity will likely be a trivial matter, easily accomplished once I am released."

I said nothing, confident that my course was the correct one and determined to be proof against Holmes's nettling.

"There is also this," Holmes said, pushing a piece of foolscap across the table to me. On it were scratched a dozen or so names, including a few that had been crossed out, followed by a list of professions and attributes, all of it listed in Holmes's own hand.

"What is this?"

"When we recovered Mina, you remember the crates we found? The vampire nursery, if you will?"

"Of course," I said, shuddering. "I should be hard-pressed to forget it."

"Just so," he said. "I think it would be foolish to assume that the Mariner Priest had just the one vampire nursery. In fact, since we know he has several vampires in his employ, we can reasonably surmise that there are also several nurseries, but he allowed us to locate this one easily."

"Easily?" I said.

"Undoubtedly," Holmes said. "On further consideration, I believe this was an operation that had several layers to it. The Mariner Priest had to anticipate that we might be able to track the place down. As such, I suspect that it served additional purposes, such as probing the strength of our relationship with Dracula, as well as keeping us occupied while he reaped the seeds of other, more deeply hidden such nurseries. There was also the opportunity for his assassin to take one of us out of the game."

"An objective he nearly accomplished!" I said.

"Yes," Holmes admitted. "But there is also a curious opportunity for us here. I was not able to find any common thread between the victims before, but now comparing them with a list of missing persons from Scotland Yard has suggested one."

"What is that?"

"We have on our new list," Holmes said, "a forger, a known gambler and rake, as well as one woman suspected of taking place in a confidence scam inflicted on several banks in our area.

There are many more possible names that would continue this thread."

"The Mariner Priest is recruiting criminals?" I said.

"Indeed," Holmes said. "Recruiting and transforming them, though not all fall into this category. There are no less than four sailors on this list, as well, which should incline us to think that his next moves would be something of a nautical vein."

"He is called the Mariner Priest," I pointed out.

"Precisely," Holmes agreed. "In addition, Scotland Yard has, as I suspected, two new murders, one in a cemetery and one in the morgue, that are almost certainly vampire attacks that require our attention. It is too soon to tell if this is an intentional threat or merely the Mariner Priest's discarded mistakes, meaning a vampire he cannot control, but either possibility bodes ill for London. All in all, it bodes for serious plans from our adversary. If we can only calculate what those might be!"

But Holmes had no more insights and shortly thereafter lapsed into an uncommunicative mood. He tried a few passes on his violin, but his injury would not let him continue and he was forced to lie down.

About mid-afternoon, we received a response to several telegrams Holmes had sent earlier. I took them into his room at once. Holmes was irritable, having been mostly bedridden for the past three days, but he was healing quickly and growing stronger each day. He snatched the envelopes from my hands and tore them open with shaking fingers. He read the contents of all three and then dropped them on the bedcovers with a disgusted sigh.

"Nothing! My only conclusion is that the Mariner Priest has withdrawn with his new squadron of vampires for I can find no sign of him. This convalescence has proved to be catastrophic, Watson! If only you could have handled that bullet without tearing so much tissue around it. This delay is intolerable!"

"The bullet had to be removed," I said mildly. I was privately very pleased with the result. The bullet had come out cleanly, and I thought the job a remarkably neat one considering the unfavourable conditions. Furthermore, I had been meticulous about the dressing and was very pleased to see no sign of infection. But I knew my friend could never rest easy with the Mariner Priest's continued freedom. No wound short of a fatal one could change that.

I longed to know the exact contents of the telegrams that had distressed him so, but, as ever, my friend divulged details only in his own time and fashion.

"Perhaps a late dinner would help?" I said. "Mrs Hudson has mentioned a brace of Cornish hens she might bring up for you. Mentioned it no less than seven times, in fact."

"Oh, very well," he said, waving his hands in dismissal. "If only to prevent further distracting inquiries. Any news from Count Dracula?"

"Not yet," I said. "It is still another few hours until the sun sets."

Dracula and Mina arrived a short time after dusk, using the bell and front door rather than the sudden and startling appearance that Dracula favoured by himself. Holmes was feeling strong enough to move about a little and I helped him into a chair by the fire so that we might receive company.

Fully recovered, the Countess Mina Dracula was a pale, exquisite creature with dark hair and an outwardly mild demeanour compared to her starkly proud and aristocratic husband. Still, every quietly enunciated word and polite smile the seemingly delicate woman made revealed signs of both a sardonic sense of humour and a very serious-minded intelligence.

"We have found the other two sisters," Dracula said without preamble. "They could provide no information as to the Mariner Priest, as it seems only Adaliene dealt with him. These two have been hiding in a nest under one of your parked railway trains for weeks. They will trouble London no further."

"You... destroyed them?" I asked. Even with the clear necessity, the image of the Count murdering his former consorts felt horrific and sordid.

"Not I," Dracula said, and his gaze flashed to Mina with some pride.

"That was my welcome burden," Mina said. "I felt I owed them something for this." She gestured slightly with her left hand, where underneath a black lace covering her hand still lacked the index finger.

"Have no concern, gentlemen," she added. "With proper care and feeding I shall have a new one to wear my wedding band on in five or six months."

"Indeed," Holmes said, raising his eyebrows. "That is good to know."

I have since confirmed this from my own experience. Surprisingly, vampire healing is a great deal slower than the human equivalent. A wound such as Holmes's would take much longer to close and heal. However, given enough time and an ample supply of blood, there is virtually nothing that cannot be regrown and eventually made whole in a way far surpassing human biology, as long as the heart and head remain intact.

Still, I shall not soon forget the burning light I saw in the eyes of Count Dracula's wife, and it made me uneasy. Partly this was because of what it displayed about her own soul, and possibly my own. Count Dracula was visibly proud of his terrible wife, and I believe their love was strong, despite the horrific nature of their, that is, *our*, nocturnal existence. Holmes, in assisting in her rescue, had won a great and terrible force over to his cause. I was forever humbled at how nations, sovereigns and now, even this vampire noble, found themselves indebted to the faculties of Sherlock Holmes.

"What of the other places I asked you to investigate?" Holmes asked. "Surely the Mariner Priest must have left some traces." He touched his bandaged side. "This inactivity, it's intolerable!" He cast another look of irritation in my direction. Quite unfairly, I thought, but I could at least understand his frustration.

"We found the man of Dr Watson's acquaintance," Dracula said. He favoured us with a grave smile. "Rupert Allens, the man with the blond mutton chops. He was getting ready for a long journey at sea, under orders from the Mariner Priest to abandon London. He was to board a ship to Portugal, draw no attention to himself, and await further instructions. He also told us that the Mariner Priest himself had already left London with a great many vampires. He does not know precisely when or on what ship."

"So the tobacco shop was not the entire catch," Holmes said. "I had feared as much."

"How do you know this?" I asked.

"He told me," Dracula said simply. "These individuals were easy enough to question."

"I should have thought," I said, "that vampires would be difficult to question, having less to fear."

"Then you would be incorrect, Doctor," Dracula said. "On both counts. My people are a superstitious lot. You have retained your civilization through the transformation, but this is not the usual case. For most, it is a movement away from reason, towards primal intuition. Examine the primitive hunters among your own people, and you will find no atheists. It may not be a religion that you recognize, but it is the same with us."

I found this to be a shocking statement, and had the sudden urge to ask the Count if he, too, had foresworn reason in this manner, but his forbidding expression warned me that such a question would not be welcome.

"Are they still alive?" I demanded.

Dracula gave me a flat stare by way of response. It was Mina who finally shifted in her seat and shook her head. "No, I'm afraid not."

"Would you have me release them to continue their murder spree?" Dracula said.

"You did what must be done," Holmes said, "for we cannot let them continue to murder in London, though I confess to some small pangs of guilt. The men on this list were all headed for the gallows, but still it might be a kinder fate than what befell them at your hands."

If Dracula was insulted by Holmes's judgement, he gave no sign. In fact, he gave the smallest of smiles that quite confirmed Holmes's statement and sent a cold chill into the pit of my stomach. "In any case," he said, "a gallows would not have sufficed." He turned his flat gaze onto me. "Console yourself, Doctor, with the fact that London's citizens are better off without them."

Mina carried a purse, which surprised me for some reason, from which she withdrew a newspaper and handed it to Holmes. "Here is the information for Allens's ship. I circled it for your attention." She turned then to me and said, "I'm sorry, Dr Watson. We did not find any sign of your wife."

"Not entirely true, my dear," Dracula said. His tone was gentle, but there was a note of admonition in it.

Mina made a rueful face. "We did find a number of her victims, I'm afraid," she admitted.

"Children," Dracula said remorselessly. "Three young boys, the youngest being only two, I should estimate. Very likely from the same family. She and the blonde man had been feeding on them for some time. Do you begin to see the purpose behind my methods, Doctor?"

I could see Mary's face, my Mary, and see blood on her lips, just as I had the last time I'd seen her. Children! The room swam briefly around me and a sudden creaking from underneath me made me realize that I was gripping the armrests of the chair so forcefully that I was in danger of tearing them completely free. I forced myself to let them go.

"My husband is harsh," Mina said, "as the wolf is hard. Stark and violent, just as the wolf, as life itself is. But he is never cruel for cruelty's sake. I wonder if most men can say the same." She shook her head to clear her thoughts. "But his point is well taken. I should not have referred to her as your wife."

"That woman," Dracula said coldly, "is dead."

Mina stretched out her gloved hand and laid it on my shoulder. "I'm very sorry, Dr Watson."

"Have you," I said, "ever killed children? To feed?" I was asking about her, but also, in the darkest parts of my heart, about what I was likely to become. I did not dare ask the same question of Dracula, for I felt all too certain that the answer would darken my heart. But with Mina, there was hope.

"I have not," she said firmly. "There is no need. There is plenty of blood, and plenty of willing victims, to make murder unnecessary. The death of murderers is one thing, but the innocent quite another, I assure you. The bodies of those poor children break my heart every bit as much as they break yours."

"Extreme measures must be taken, Watson," Holmes said to me gently. "Or else many more British citizens, children and otherwise, will suffer their fate." He turned back to Dracula. "What of the other addresses I suggested?" I could tell this sort of investigation by surrogate to be a continually frustrating experience for Holmes. In point of fact, I might have gone with them if not for the ever-present necessity of keeping Holmes interred here at Baker Street. I could see that he railed at the inconvenience his wound caused and would have gladly thrown his health to the winds of fortune had I not stayed at his side to prevent it.

"One had already fled," Dracula said. "The other, a back-alley cutthroat named Warner, was also readying to depart."

"On an entirely different ship," Mina added. She handed over another slip of paper, this one in her handwriting. "The information on the ship he'd planned to use, a different ship entirely than the one Allens had booked passage on. According to both Warner and Allens, the Mariner Priest has taken yet another ship, though neither knew any more." I could see as she handed the paper over that her writing was neat and precise, but also that the paper had a dark red smear on it, potentially blood.

"Warner's ship sails tomorrow night," Dracula said, "but Warner himself will not make an appearance."

"It is our theory," Mina said, "that the Mariner Priest, if he was ever in London at all, has withdrawn entirely and dismantled his organization here."

"That is as likely as any other explanation," Holmes admitted. "The Mariner Priest himself is the prize. Any machinations he has here can be abandoned and rebuilt, as long as the conductor of these events remains free. Seen in that light, his departure by sea makes perfect sense."

"But where does he go?" I asked.

To that, we had no answer.

"I know this man," Dracula said suddenly, crossing the room and picking up a piece of paper. He held it up for us to see.

"You ought to," I said. "You killed him." Dracula was holding the police sketch of the rifleman.

"And kept him from murdering us," Holmes added.

"Why, that's Jack!" Mina burst out.

Holmes and I looked at each other, surprise on both our faces.

"Jack?" Holmes said, turning to Mina.

"John 'Jack' Seward," Mina explained. "Once a dear friend."

"Ah," Dracula said, no visible emotion on his face. He was holding the sketch still and staring down at it. "I had not intended to end his life."

"But," I said, "you did not take care to preserve it, either." The Count's disregard for the lives of our enemies, his tendency to treat this investigation as a campaign of war, struck at the heart of my reservations about Holmes agreeing to work with him.

"No," Dracula admitted. "I did not. Nor did I take the time to get a good look at his face."

"Poor Jack," Mina said, bowing her head and folding her arms about her. She had taken a short step away from her husband. Now he moved towards her and she let him enfold her in his arms.

"I had promised you to spare their lives," Dracula said, speaking low. "There is no excuse. No forgiveness. My concern at the time had been simply to disable our would-be assassin and return to you as quickly as possible. I had not deliberately intended to end his life."

She shook her head. "No. Your word was exactly correct. He chose the role of assassin, to lie in wait and murder us from afar. He might have killed you, me, or Dr Watson. He nearly did murder Mr Holmes. He still thinks you responsible for Lucy's death, I'm sure. It is my foolishness at wanting to return here, to

London, that brought us into conflict with him and Van Helsing again." She touched his face, briefly, and he let her go.

"A strange choice," Holmes said. "To post a healer as assassin. I would have thought one of the others, the American, perhaps, as a better choice."

"Arthur," Mina said, "that is, Lord Holmwood, was an avid hunter and they all joined him regularly. All of them could shoot. I would not have thought Jack to possess the temperament of a cold-blooded murderer, but it has been a long time since I've known him, really. Too many great things have happened since.

"Have you any further questions, Mr Holmes?" Mina asked.

"Not at present," Holmes said. "I have a great deal to ponder."

"Yes," she said. "As do we. You know how to reach us now, I daresay?"

"Quite."

Mina held out her hand to her husband. "Shall we depart, my love?"

Count Dracula's expression was surprisingly tender as he took his wife's damaged hand in his own, but then he turned back to us. "Mr Holmes, I thank you and bid you farewell. I do not think it will be long before we meet again. This affair with the Mariner Priest, with Van Helsing, is far from concluded and I fear it is one that will affect both our homelands."

"Very likely," Holmes said.

Dracula turned to face me and nodded. "Doctor." Mina shot back one long look at me, as if she were challenging me again. *He is never cruel for cruelty's sake. I wonder if most men can say the same.* Then they were both gone.

Once Holmes recovered enough to leave the house, he spent the next few weeks attempting to read the traces of the Mariner Priest's organization, as it had existed, the way a fortune teller might read tea leaves. He came back from his last such expedition in a furious and dejected mood.

"I have done a great deal in the last few weeks to verify the Count's version of events over Stoker's fiction," he said. "The most striking of these, and the most compelling, is that there is not, nor has there ever been, an insane asylum next to the Carfax Estate, as Stoker's novel states. Seward did have employment at one, though it was in an entirely different district and his employment there has long since ended. The building is quite empty now."

"I had wondered about that point," I said. I was loath to admit that Dracula had been faithful to the truth, but Holmes pressed on.

"I have found documentation," he said, "for the Count and Mina's departure from the country in the time-frame he claimed and evidence that the men in question – Van Helsing, Holmwood, Seward, Harker, and Morris – did not leave London at all that year. Morris's return to America a year later is particularly damning to Stoker's version of events, since he is supposed to have died in Transylvania. Harker died the year after that, unmarried, in a traffic accident, and I have viewed the burial site myself and found it intact and unmolested. With Van Helsing, Seward, and Holmwood, we have a greater mystery than before as there is clear documentation that the three travelled together to Australia, immediately took an expedition to the wilderness there, and did not return. The authorities there are concerned, but do not find it surprising for three men to disappear in such an uncivilized place. It has caused a great deal of stir with the Holmwood family and estate."

"I should imagine," I said.

"There were some irregularities with that documentation such that I suspect a forgery. This is augmented by the fact that we know that Dr Seward *did* return to England, or perhaps never left. Our autopsy of Seward, as you know, gave us little information. Of Van Helsing and Holmwood, I can find no trace, either here or in Australia. None of this does much to either confirm or deny Van Helsing as the Mariner Priest. Even worse, the Mariner Priest has taken a measure that I can find no counter for."

"How so?"

"It is fiendishly simple," Holmes said bitterly. "It also accounts for his recruitment of so many sailors. Deucedly simple! Yet I can devise no stratagem to defeat it!"

"What do you mean?" I asked.

"His various agents have all landed and taken to sea once again. Now, I have reason to believe they are with the Mariner Priest on one ship." He collapsed into his armchair and despondently tapped on the armrest. I was deeply alarmed. Never had I seen him looking so defeated.

"We must give chase," I said. "Wherever he is heading, we must book passage at once. Have you discovered it?"

"His plans are quite known to me, yes," Holmes said, but the fact did not seem to cheer him.

"Then when do we depart? What is his destination?"

"That is just it, Watson. My theory is that he has no destination."

"No destination? But how?"

"He has taken a boat and gone to sea, but with no destination at all."

"What of the legend of running water?" I said. "We have seen ample evidence that water has a strange effect on the vampire."

"While they might be in some danger encountering a storm at sea, it would still be less than a human crew would face and British sailors have been braving those waters since the beginning of time. Also, the Mariner Priest has shown a certain ruthlessness with his personnel, as it were. Consider, Watson, he has ample resources to purchase a ship outright and now he also has a loyal and partly eternal crew. At sea, he has very little fear of discovery. Any ship that comes across them will play the victim and provide fresh blood and other supplies and is hardly any threat to a crew of vampires. They need only have enough of a human crew, in proper submission, to get them through the days and they can live indefinitely at sea. They can replenish crews and supplies as needed through piracy. This man's plans reveal a mind of the first order. They will be impossible to trace and will leave no clues except the occasional missing ship. And the Mariner Priest knows that I cannot take to life at sea and still guard England. So, the Mariner Priest, with this plan, need only wait."

"He has some plan coming to fruition here in London for his return?" I asked.

"You misunderstand me, Watson," Holmes said. "You forget, everything we know, every ploy or stratagem, must be cast in a new light based on the vampire's outlook. You yourself are too stolid of moral character to fully see the brilliance of his plan."

"But what are they waiting for?" I asked.

"For my death," Holmes said. "No, do not be alarmed, Watson. While there may be another assassination attempt, I do not believe that the Mariner Priest will gamble much on this. Not after the first one failed. But, don't you see, the Mariner Priest has only to *wait*. If there had been any doubt that the head of this vampire-ridden criminal empire was a vampire himself, this eradicates it. What is a few decades or more to one who is immortal? Time will remove the Mariner Priest's greatest obstacle, and there is no denying it."

I sat silent in thought while Holmes took his clay pipe out of the pipe rack and puffed furiously at it until the entire room was shrouded in smoke.

"Holmes," I said.

"Watson, Watson," he said with a rueful smile. "I thought you might come around to this suggestion again, but it will hardly serve. I cannot allow myself to contract vampirism, even to confront this nemesis. Come now, don't be so surprised. Your thoughts are apparent to any trained observer. You glance at the darkness outside, then at the specially filled teapot at your left elbow and back to the new painting you have acquired of the sunset and it is quite easy to follow the track of your thoughts.

At any rate, I have expected this suggestion for some time. But I'm afraid you do me rather too much credit with this one, Watson. I have all the makings of a terrible vampire; I would become a greater threat to London, over time, than the Mariner Priest would ever be. Oh, I know you have adapted rather admirably, but I'm afraid that I possess the antithesis of the qualities that preserve your outlook."

"Ridiculous," I said. "I have never met a man of stronger character!"

"Ah," Holmes said. "Again, I think we have fallen into unscientific language. Certainly I have an iron will in many important matters, but you are well aware of my black moods, the abyss that can entomb me during periods of inactivity. Perhaps strength and stability of character would be a better statement, or perhaps it is something that we do not fully understand yet. Suffice to say that I am not suitable."

"But, Holmes," I said, "if death is the only other option…"

"You know how I abhor boredom, Watson; it would be my undoing. You used to frown, with some justification, upon my use of cocaine, but imagine how much worse the addiction to *blood* would be. It would only be a matter of time before my need for stimulation brought about the worst results, and there would be nothing *but* time. Nothing but time. You see?"

I nodded miserably, as the horror of my new situation came down fully upon me once again. To sit idly by while the truest companion in the world suffered and died? I did not think I had it in me to do this. My affliction brought many gifts, but the curse of it lay heavy upon me, bringing with it a sense of impending doom.

Dear Mr Holmes and Dr Watson,

I hope you will permit my indulgence in writing to you in this manner, but there are some things here afoot, as Mr Holmes would say, in Transylvania that both of you should be aware of. Our castle is an isolated place, to say the least, and new ideas are slow to travel here. To say that these facts have formed and shaped my husband and his approach to outsiders, other lands and other peoples is an understatement almost to the point of falsehood.

But, it seems, our adventure in England with you has made a profound impression on him, in ways that I, and possibly Vlad himself, are just getting the measure of. He has never been a man, even in his previous life so long ago, to ask for help. He is far too proud. It was only my own abduction and the terrible circumstances that brought him to your doorstep. You gentlemen, for all your differences, dealt with my husband honourably and I believe the exposure has slightly mollified my husband's not overly generous viewpoint of the human race in general. Suffice to say that the past few centuries have left him, I'm afraid, with a very poor impression of humanity.

Under different circumstances, danger would encourage Vlad to simply reinforce his isolationist policies. While my husband is not a monarch such as you would ordinarily recognize, his wishes influence the Romany bands and Slovak villages occupying the countryside such that it is not too much to view the surrounding area as his dominion. Historically,

Vlad has concerned himself only with the health of these immediate peoples and shunned contact with all others.

Now, however, since our return he has extended his interest further into Romania, Bulgaria, Hungary, Galicia, Croatia-Slavonia, Austria, with a few tentative communications to the empires of Germany and Russia. There, for the first time in his living memory, which is a very long time, he has actively sought out other vampires and made some startling discoveries. It appears that our assessment of vampires as completely solitary and territorial creatures is a truism only in Transylvania and mostly due to Vlad's own dominance. While solitary vampires are still the normal state of affairs outside of my husband's homeland, they are not the only lifestyle. Vlad has been in contact with a nomadic tribe of horse-riding vampires several dozen strong in Hungary. A self-styled coven of vampire witches live near Krakow, in Poland. There are a group of Austrian nobles that rule in secrecy, unknown to their own monarch. Many more less cohesive groups also exist and Vlad has written and received a great deal of correspondence, as well as reports from his own agents, while I have filled pages and pages of ledgers recording names and places to help him try and keep account of them all. It has been very difficult to make contact with these various groups, since Vlad is known to be both powerful and unfriendly to rival vampires, but one recent change has made this far easier than before.

The Mariner Priest.

It is not only England where his name is whispered. His empire, unknown until a few years ago, is rapidly expanding.

Several of the groups above have lost members, either through violence or recruitment, to the Mariner Priest's organization, which honours no national or geographical boundaries. But for all the rumours, we have yet to unearth any substantial information on the man himself. However, I will forward to you such information as we do have in the hopes that more will be forthcoming.

Fondest wishes,

Mina

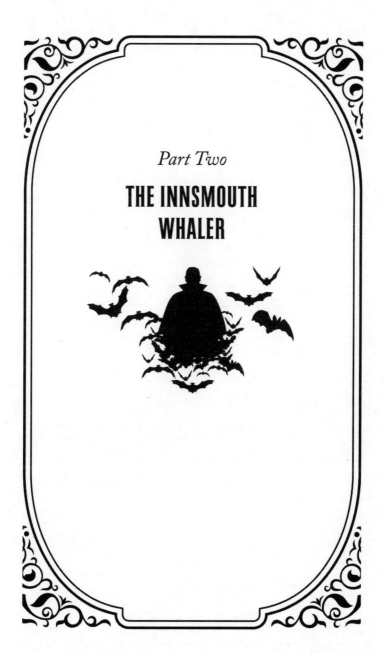

Part Two

THE INNSMOUTH
WHALER

Chapter 07

THE HÔTEL DU CHÂTEAU BLANC

"One would think," remarked Sherlock Holmes, "that the continual existence of vampires in London would at least provide some welcome distraction. Yet, I can only conclude that the average vampire is a dull creature indeed and shockingly predictable. It's intolerable!"

We were holed up in our rooms in Baker Street, trapped indoors by a storm of such fury that it had all of London under siege. Holmes, in one of his periods of dark lassitude after a successful conclusion to a recent forgery case, had already exhausted his patience on the filing of old cases. He stood now at the window, staring out at the confining storm as if he might banish it by pure force of will.

Though it was pleasurable beyond measure to be back in my rooms at Baker Street again, I dearly missed home. However, I could not even begin to imagine returning to the domicile that

Mary and I had shared. Living there in her absence would have been a dreary task. I missed her more than words could express. Unsurprisingly, the faux funeral that I'd been forced to hold in her honour had only deepened the sense of loss and conflict I had regarding the woman, still very much alive, who had once been my wife. Holmes was a noble friend, but he was poor company on the days when the world offered little to challenge or exercise his superior intellect.

"You once feared an army of vampires storming London," I said. "Surely the present situation is far preferable?"

"For the average resident, the state of affairs is certainly preferable," Holmes said, giving the window another look of disgust before giving up his vigil.

He sank restlessly into his lounging chair. "But the situation is quite trying for a specialist. Little did I imagine the mistake I made assigning Shinwell Johnson to patrol the morgues."

"Surely he's capable?"

"That is precisely the problem," Holmes said with a languid wave of his hand. "He's certainly capable enough to dispatch the commonplace problems. If only they weren't all commonplace!"

"I should hardly call it that," I said, a bit shocked at Holmes's dismissal of so gruesome and brutal a task, especially when I remembered my own disorienting and bestial transformation into a creature of the night. If I could emerge from such an experience and reassert my own humble personality and morals, certainly some of the other victims could, as well? However, our experience – and Shinwell Johnson's reports – did not offer much hope for this. Only a handful of new vampires appeared each month, but all of them demonstrated themselves as murderous beasts, without hope of rehabilitation.

"What of the Mariner Priest?" I asked.

Holmes sighed. "Nothing has changed. We've thoroughly broken his organization here in London and the Mariner Priest himself remains untouchable somewhere out at sea. I've been keeping track of any ships that have gone missing, but as you know, one missing ship, even if we could ascertain that the Mariner Priest was the cause, does very little to accurately pinpoint the fiend's position. It is possible that he is, at this time, somewhere west of Portugal. I fear pursuing him at sea for the mischief he could make here in London without our restraining hand. I fear that there are certainly vampires left in London, or else we would not need Shinwell Johnson's services, but I see no sign yet of any organization. Still, the Mariner Priest roams the seas unchecked. No, it is a hopeless tangle!"

Mrs Hudson's polite knock announced her. "Telegram for you, Mr Holmes."

Holmes leapt from his chair and snatched the envelope out of her hand. Mrs Hudson shook her head and left with an exasperated sigh as he tore the envelope open.

"A case, Watson," Holmes said. "We are saved! It comes from Gregson. A murder over at the Hôtel du Château Blanc. We'll need a cab. Mrs Hudson." He made a song of it, "Mrs Hudson!"

The Hôtel du Château Blanc, on the Chelsea Embankment, was a hotel made up to look like a castle, complete with an eccentric, if somewhat ill-smelling moat fed from the Thames and a working drawbridge. The architects had limited themselves to painting the portcullis on the front doors, however, and these were currently thrown open. I looked back briefly, but somewhat gratefully, at the torrential downpour. In a city like London, having to avoid the open glare of the sun wasn't much of a hardship.

Several constables waited for us in the lobby. One of them showed us directly up to one of the rooms where Gregson waited with the body.

Gregson came over as we entered the room, pulling out a small notebook. "Ah, there you are, Mr Holmes. Dr Watson, I was deeply sorry to hear of your loss. Tuberculosis. Such a bad business."

"Thank you," I said stiffly, thinking of the real fate that had befallen Mary. An actual case of tuberculosis seemed a kinder one. Gregson looked uncomfortable for a moment.

"What do you have for us, Gregson?" Holmes asked, eager to get to work.

"It's a pretty little puzzle of a case, all right. Let me show you."

I was something of an old campaigner, but could not suppress a shudder when I saw the waterlogged mass on the hotel floor that had once been a living man. He had been tall, possibly thin, but was now so puffed and bloated from being in the water as to be ponderously corpulent. An ugly fringe of lank hair clinging about the head and a dark, heavy moustache were the only features that remained to help with identification. The remains of a sodden dark suit and coat were still wrapped about him, and a similarly soaked hat lay on the floor beside him.

Holmes indicated the window where, even from here, we could see the ponderous passage of the Thames below. "What presents the difficulty? Surely it can't be too much for Scotland Yard to account for a drowning victim near the water?"

"It is the timing and nature of the drowning that is perplexing, Mr Holmes. I will explain. Yesterday evening, a Miss Lucja Nowak and her sister arrived at the hotel, alone. By all accounts of the hotel staff, Miss Nowak is a young American. Her younger sister is a child, somewhere in the neighbourhood of ten or twelve."

"How did they know she was an American?" Holmes said. "Her accent?"

"That," Gregson said, "and her luggage, which was marked as coming from New Bedford. There is a ticket stub among her items for the Atlantic steamer the *Lady Evelyn*, which arrived just yesterday. I sent a man down to confirm this, and Miss Nowak's name is on the passenger list. She must have come straight here from the ship."

"Excellent, Gregson. You quite surpass yourself. Do continue."

"The two of them kept to their room and saw no one all evening. You will have noticed that the main exit is directly past the front desk, which is always manned. There is a service entrance, but this area is populated by the staff around the clock, so we can be very sure on this point. Early this morning, while it was still dark, they received a visitor. This desk clerk says the man was quite belligerent, and did not give his name, but did show him this badge."

Here Gregson knelt by the dead man and used his pencil to lift the flap of the coat, showing us the tin star pinned to the man's waistcoat. "Though clearly a marshal from the Americas there is nothing to mark what territory or state he was marshal in, and no other identification on him. As such, he has yet to be fully identified. Though the face is hardly recognizable, the clothes here match, to the best of the clerk's recollection. It being so odd to receive a visitor at such an early hour and the surliness of the visitor both serve to cement the event in the mind of the night-time clerk, which he says happened at four o'clock.

"Shortly after four o'clock, the clerk was astonished when the woman and child dashed through the lobby and out the front door. Despite the night clerk's shouted objections, she found a cab waiting and disappeared into the night. She did not pay her bill, but even more astonishingly, she left all of her luggage here."

"Most curious," Holmes said. "What is your theory, then?"

"What can I think?" Gregson burst out. "We have accounts of a man coming into the room and the woman running out a short time later. Now the man is found, apparently drowned."

Holmes bent down for a closer look, turning the man's fleshy head to one side.

"I see no sign of a physical blow," I said.

"Which is precisely the difficulty," Gregson said. "How on earth could a woman overpower such a large man enough to push him out the window and into the Thames, let alone drag him back up? Why would they? Another person must have been present, but I can find no sign of him. And neither the woman nor anyone else could have slipped past the desk. But even if the two together could push a man into the Thames, why would they bring him back up, and how? The tide is higher now and would have been much lower at the time of the murder, but this being the second floor the water would not have been very close in any case. There has been no bath or other container of water on this hotel of the floor, according to the staff. Our murderers could not move the body up the stairs without being seen, assuming two people – one of them a woman – could even move such a heavy man, which I do not accept. Not even a monkey could climb the wall outside, and there is no ladder on the premises.

"I'm at a loss to explain how any of this could have happened in such a short time, for the entrance of the man and the escape of the woman could not have been separated by more than ten or fifteen minutes."

"It certainly presents some serious difficulties," Holmes agreed. He bent to look at the body, examining everything in that swift but minute way of his. The front of the dead man's coat, then his pockets, the collar, and the hands and face were all dealt with in a matter of minutes. "A large man," Holmes said, "with the curious calluses that show many years of handling rope."

"A marshal would ride a great deal," Gregson said. "Holding the reins as he rode."

"But not under such heavy pressure," Holmes said. "Nor do hands such as these suggest a gunman. No, this amount of roughening could only come from a life at sea. This badge, too, is curious. It is quite scratched and worn, and not particularly well cared for. The waistcoat is also far from new, but only two pinholes in it."

Gregson frowned. "I do not take your meaning."

"Perhaps not," Holmes said. "How do you account for the salt?"

"What's that?"

"You can smell it on the jacket," Holmes said, "and on the hair and skin."

"You just said the man was likely a sailor," Gregson said quickly, "and he was drowned."

"Yes, but certainly he did not wear this suit to work in. Moreover, being drowned in the Thames would leave mud stains and the like, certainly, but not such a strong scent of salt. Curious."

I smiled ruefully and shook my head, amazed as ever at my friend's sharp intellect. My keen sense of smell had immediately detected the salt that Holmes mentioned, even over the stench of the dead man, but being this close to the water, I had not thought much of it. But he was right, the Thames flowed down towards the ocean, not up, and while there is salt enough on the ships that come in from sea, it is not, in itself, a body of salt water.

"We know he walked into the hotel alive," said Gregson after some thought, "I fail to see why anyone should take him from this room, transport him to the Atlantic, drown him there and then bring him back. It's unfathomable."

"It is," Holmes said.

"You don't suggest that someone somehow smuggled a large amount of salt water up here for the express purpose of drowning him, and then disposed of it?"

"That does seem a little far-fetched, doesn't it?" Holmes said. "I don't suggest that, no." He left the body and went through the articles from the luggage, which Gregson had laid out on the polished wooden table. The first of these he pounced on with a tiny cry. Holmes held a small metal cylinder in his hand.

"I thought you might find that interesting," Gregson said, on firmer ground now.

"A bullet cartridge!" I said.

"Well," Holmes said. "This was not a pleasure trip for Miss Nowak, at any rate. I see no other bullets or cartridges, and no gun, so it is likely she has the gun with her. The size of the bullet indicates a small gun, such as a woman might use. Certainly no shots were fired in this room, or the hotel staff should have heard it. Possibly we should smell the discharge still in the room, too."

"I smell nothing of the sort," I said. Holmes nodded.

"Nor I," said Gregson. "Perhaps she was in some danger, to bring a weapon with her. It must have been frightening travelling without escort on a merchant vessel, and with a child."

"Perhaps it was to protect the child that she carried a gun," I said.

"Protect the child from whom?" Holmes said. I peered over his shoulder as he went back to the articles on the table. Here was the remainder of her ticket stub for the *Lady Evelyn*, several worn and plain articles of clothing, including several bonnets and frocks for the little girl, three worn American dime-store novels, the stubs of several spent candles, and a small leather case that held a delicate pair of silver pince-nez. Holmes gave this last item his particular attention for a full minute, then he examined the luggage itself, both inside and out.

"Well," he said at last. "Certainly this confirms her as an American."

"We have already questioned the captain and mates of the *Lady Evelyn*," Gregson said, "but we should question the rest of the crew and the other passengers, as well. They may know something of her story."

"It is as well that we should leave no stone unturned," Holmes said, "but I fear from the wax marks over these well-thumbed books that we shall find that these travellers kept pretty much to themselves during their voyage and likely did not spend much time with the crew or other passengers. Settling herself at a hotel near the Thames, which are generally less expensive, suggests that she did not have endless monetary resources. But there are certainly cheaper locations and this one boasts a bit more security than most. Most of her clothes show every sign of age and wear. A few articles are newly purchased, however, some of them quite well-made." He indicated a pure white shawl that did indeed look much finer than the rest. "So she did not have money for quite some time, but recently came into a sum. Possibly just before, or during her trip."

He indicated the pince-nez. "These were instructive, as well, so that we now know that Miss Lucja Nowak has a narrow face, is likely to be a careful and pretty woman, somewhat vain in appearance, and now seems to be loose in London without the pair of glasses that another person might want in a strange city."

"Holmes!" I said. "That is extraordinary!"

"Hardly," he said blandly. "The size and centre of the concavity indicates a narrow face, but somewhat larger eyes. The cork attached to these clips is far from new, but bears little sign of use. The same is true of the leather case. Both are of good, but not excellent quality, which again hints that her own prosperity was moderate before her recent windfall. If you will look through them, you will find that the prescription is quite strong and alters from top to bottom, so that we know she needed these for reading as well as for common use. Yet it seems she used these glasses remarkably little. Surely that implies some vanity? Very likely, they occupied a place at her bedside at home, and have only recently seen extra use during the long voyage from America. Do you follow?"

"Yes," I said. "I see all that now."

Holmes's inspection next covered the floor and walls, which went quickly until he reached the window, where he opened it and examined both sides of the windowsill. "What's this?" He pulled out a thread from the outside sill, then held it to the man's coat to show us that it matched precisely.

"Caught on the windowsill when he was pushed out the window!" Gregson said. "Perhaps he had leaned way over, giving her an opportunity to push him out. Which would account for no shots being fired."

"Perhaps," Holmes said, "though catching on the bottom of the outside ledge... I wonder." He lay on the ledge and leaned far out, applying his lens to both the bottom of the ledge and the outside wall. "Most singular," he called back. "Watson, tell me what you make of this windowsill."

Somewhat dubiously, since my sight in even clouded daylight was a poor substitute for Holmes's, I leaned out of the window and looked out. I mashed my hat down on my head as best I could to keep the rain off, and squinted down at the wall.

"There are… marks on the wall," I said. They were plain enough. Certainly Holmes had seen them just as easily as I.

Holmes stood next to me at the window, but even so, his whisper was so low that I nearly missed it.

"You're wrinkling your nose, Watson," he said.

I followed his example and spoke as quietly as I dared. "The Thames has a strong odour here, a particularly repugnant fish or frog smell."

"Ah…" he said, and turned toward the door. "We shall leave you now, Gregson, but I feel it likely that we may have something for you before too long."

Gregson was clearly unhappy with our departure. "I shall contact the American Embassy and see if they have any knowledge of a U.S. marshal here in England."

"I should do so," Holmes said, "but say nothing yet of his death."

"Why not?"

"I am not yet convinced that our dead man was a U.S. marshal."

"Well, that's as clear as day, Mr Holmes!" Gregson said. "Haven't we a body with his badge right on it?"

"Well," Holmes said, "I have given my advice."

"This is how *I* see it," Gregson said. "This Lucja Nowak is some kind of fugitive from America, followed by this U.S. marshal. He tracks her down and surprises her in this room. Clearly, if she's carrying a gun, she's quite on edge and ready to do anything to evade justice."

"But this man has no sign of gunshot wounds," I said.

"Perhaps she feared the retort of a gun would arouse suspicions and bring the police immediately. So she knocks the man unconscious, possibly with the aid of a male confederate that we have not detected, and throws him in the Thames. What could be simpler?"

"But this man is no recent drowning victim," Holmes said. "And you have not accounted for the salt, for the transportation of the body – either how it was done or why – or the single holes in his waistcoat."

"Perhaps there were two other confederates," Gregson said stoutly. "As to the salt and badge, these do not seem to be such difficult obstacles to me. However, I know how crafty and careful are your ways, Mr Holmes, and I shall follow your advice and say nothing yet about the marshal's possible death. But have you no idea where we should find this Lucja Nowak?"

"What should you do," Holmes asked, "if you did find her?"

"I should arrest her and take her down to the station so that I might hear an account of the events from her own lips. For I have a way with women, Mr Holmes, such that I could see through any lie she might wish to tell. If she's not an accomplice to murder, I'll lay odds that she knows a great deal about it."

"On that much," Holmes said, "we certainly agree. Well, you shall pursue your line of reasoning and I mine, and we shall meet later to pool our resources. I'll send you a telegram should I find anything of further interest."

I waited until we'd left the hotel and were getting into the hansom before speaking. "Holmes, could vampires have done this?" The thought of vampires at sea was still a haunting one to me. Surely the master criminal was not content merely to wait, especially when he had supernatural methods of revenge at his disposal? I kept my voice low, barely audible over the slushing of the hansom's wheels through rain. "Some are exceptional climbers, as you well know. Since vampires can't be scented as well by other vampires, perhaps…"

"I considered this, Watson," he said, "but it really won't do. None of the marks of vampire attack appear anywhere on our victim. Also, we know the difficulties that swimming present to a vampire. Hmm… I grant you, it is a pretty proposition for the logician. For now every problem we come across must be re-evaluated in the light of these new supernatural possibilities. But consider this: we know that vampires must feed and that even one bite has the potential to spread the blood disease that causes this condition. Since we monitor both the morgues and the hospitals, we know that this number is exceedingly small. I calculate that London can hardly hold more than a hundred vampires, possibly as little as twenty."

"Could not they drink animal's blood," I said, "as I do, and so ruin your calculations? Or take other steps to prevent the infections that would spread the disease?"

"We have Dracula's word that this kind of restraint is exceedingly rare. He himself leaves more than ample traces of his existence for the trained detective to find. No, Watson, you are a paragon of virtue and civility. There are over five million natives in this metropolis of ours. So, unless one should chance to visit Baker Street, the average Londoner's chances are greater of discovering an orangutan than a vampire."

"There is an unnatural pall on this case, Holmes," I said gravely. "I fear that we may find the Mariner Priest's foul hand on the far end of this affair."

"That is always possible," Holmes said. "But I have yet seen no sign of it."

"What then?" I said. "Is there a mundane explanation for these remarkable occurrences?"

"That is what we shall endeavour to find out. I trust you are not averse to running a little errand for me, say… this evening after the sun has gone down?"

"I should be delighted," I said.

"Then I shall draw a list of hotels I'd like you to visit." He drew out a notebook and started writing. "It is not as large as it might be. I shall assume from her previous choice that she chose a hotel with a moderate price and some security, if given the chance. We shall try this approach first, then widen our search if this list bears no fruit." He tore off the sheet of paper and handed it over. "It is best that you wait until evening for I perceive that the sun has quite taken its toll on you. When you do go, I would have you fresh and on your guard."

"What shall you be doing?" I asked.

"I have several inquiries of my own to perform," he said. "We shall meet in Baker Street before dawn and compare our findings."

Chapter 08

MISS LUCJA NOWAK

The list of hotels that Holmes had written out for me was not overly long.

Still, I worked my way through most of the list without any progress. I'd just received another negative inquiry from the night clerk at the Excelsior Hotel and turned to leave the desk, when a woman from the back room cried out, "Wait! Dr Watson!"

She burst out from the small room behind the counter, and came round the desk before the sallow-faced clerk could stop her.

"Shut your mouth, now, Effie," he said to her. "You don't know nothin' about this."

"Don't you know who that is?" the woman, Effie, snapped back at him, not at all daunted by his curt tone and flushed face. "'E ain't part of the regular force, is 'e? Why, that's Dr Watson! 'E's the one what works with Mr Sherlock 'Olmes! Don't mind me 'usband, Dr Watson. 'E don't know."

The man's face turned ashen. "Sherlock 'Olmes? I've 'eard of 'im. What's 'e doin' mixed up in this?"

"It's all right, Clem," the woman said. "This is a blessin', not a tragedy. If anyone can 'elp the poor woman, it's this man and 'is friend."

"They are here, then?" I said. "Lucja Nowak and her sister?"

"You're not part of the official police force?" the man said.

"Mr Sherlock Holmes has ever gone his own way," I said. "I cannot promise leniency if she was part of the gruesome murder at Hôtel du Château Blanc, but many a time someone has been under threat of law and Holmes has been able to help them by shedding light on the matter. If she is innocent, there is no better man to help her."

"Come on, then," the clerk said, waving a hand.

The Seaman's Port lobby contained oak panelling with nautical displays hung throughout, odds and ends that had clearly never been on an actual boat. Nor could your average seaman have afforded a glass of sherry in the restaurant there. We passed down a long panelled hallway. The clerk knocked softly at the last door.

"Miss Nowak?" he said. "It's all right. It's Clem, from the desk. There's a man 'ere to see you. Not from the police. I think 'e may be of some 'elp."

The door opened slowly, revealing a pretty young girl around twelve years of age, with a solemn white face, wide grey eyes and soft pale hair that floated about when she turned her head to look up at me. Her abstracted look reminded me of nothing so much as Holmes's when he was riddling out a complex puzzle.

I smiled down at the girl, who must have been frightened with recent events, but she stared back, showing no sign of alarm or any other concrete emotion.

"No fish," she said. "You can come in."

I looked at the clerk to see if this strange address held any meaning for him, but he shrugged, turned, and left.

I entered, closing the door behind me, for the child had wandered deeper into the apartment. Following her led me into a sitting room where her older sister waited. I would have known that they were sisters, even if I hadn't been told, with the fair skin, ash-blonde hair, and peculiarly solemn grey eyes. The young woman had none of the child's composure, however, and seemed somewhat broken. She sat half-facing a window, with red-rimmed and darkened eyes that spoke of more than one sleepless night.

"I beg your pardon, miss," I said, but got no response. Not entirely comfortable standing in a strange woman's personal compartment with only the silent child as a chaperone, I stood with my hat in my hand, waiting diffidently.

The woman stared out the window for many long seconds before she finally noticed me, and started.

"A man," the girl said. "Clem brought him." She looked back at me. "I like him." This surprised me a bit, as the girl had given no such sign, but, determined to put a brave face on things, I smiled down at the distraught woman.

"Miss Lucja Nowak?"

After a moment of consideration, she nodded.

"If it lies within my power," I said, "I should most like to be of assistance."

Her face looked up at me with the most curious series of expressions – startling in such a subdued person – bewilderment, exaltation, disappointment, and finally, bitter resignation.

"You can't," she said slowly. "No one can."

"If any man can help you," I said, "it is my friend, Mr Sherlock Holmes. What can you tell me about the murder at the Hôtel du Château Blanc?" After some silence, I added, "A man was murdered there, wearing a U.S. marshal badge. Did you see him?"

The woman seemed to have forgotten I was there, and only continued to stare out the window. I turned to the little girl. "What is your name, then?" Normally the subject of murder was far too loathsome to burden such a child with, but there seemed to be no other option.

"Elzbieta," she said. "He weren't no marshal."

My response was cut off by a terrific pounding at the hallway door.

"I know you're in there," a heavy, surly voice bellowed. "Don't make me break down the door!"

The reaction from the woman and the girl to this racket was only a knowing look, completely ignoring me. It was a terrible thing, that look. The unspoken communication between the two sisters held depths of lost hope and resignation. Hardened as I was to such things, it still sent a shudder through me. Written clearly on their faces was the verdict, long understood, that all plans to escape would be foredoomed to utter failure. Only the waiting remained for these two.

The door shook again, which sent a hot flare up inside of me.

I went back to the door, where the hinges already showed signs of coming free of the woodwork. It shuddered again under the heavy blows, and I yanked it violently open.

"Good God!" I said. "What is the meaning of this?"

The man facing me stopped short with his clenched fist still in the air and peered at me with bulging eyes barely held in check by a pair of small oval glasses. These, in turn, sat on a flat white nose. From under the brim of his squashed and dripping hat, unruly, greasy black hair stuck out in all directions. A similarly disreputable bushy moustache covered his mouth like a drowned Pekinese. A trace of scarring, mostly hidden by the moustache, lay on the top of the man's mouth. It was a pale, odious face, with a crafty and vicious expression.

More daunting than this was the terrible odour rolling off the man in nauseating waves. With my eyes closed, I might have mistaken him for a fishing trawler somehow crammed into the hotel hallway. His coat sleeves bulged with powerful arms and his chest and shoulders were like a hunched-over bear's. He thrust a beefy arm out to shove me rudely out of the way, but I stood my ground, blocking his way in. Fortunately, we were in the thick of the night, when I was at my full strength, for the force in this stout man was quite remarkable. When I proved immobile, however, he stepped back, surprise and suspicion showing behind the thick glasses in equal measure.

"Who are you?" he said, then waved his hand. "No, it doesn't matter. She thinks she can keep us from what's ours, but she can't! She knows she can't!"

"She does not wish to see you," I said coldly.

"But she will see me!" he sputtered. "She knows the futility of keeping me out, even if you don't."

Quiet, furtive steps came from the room behind me, and the soft scuffling sound of someone lifting a window. I could not believe that either of them had committed such a violent murder, and would offer them what protection I could. I would not let this violent, seething person past without some explanation.

"You'll regret this meddling!" he snarled. "I'll see that you regret it!" He spun his bulk around and stalked down the hallway without a further word.

I closed the cracked and abused door and went back into the room. As expected, the window was still partially open, the curtains dancing in the foul icy breeze. They were gone.

Staring with wonder, I reached out for the abandoned object they'd left precisely in the middle of the table. No wonder they were pursued from America. Placed in the precise centre of the table like a showpiece was a glittering tiara made of solid gold.

Following the escaped sisters proved to be impossible. While I could track them by scent down the fire escape and through the alley behind the hotel, despite the rain, the path onto the main thoroughfare, despite the late hour, had enough horse and foot traffic splashing through enormous puddles as to hopelessly confuse the trail.

When I returned to Baker Street, Holmes was not at home. I fair quivered with anticipation to tell him of my adventures and show him the circlet, but also with trepidation for the berating he was likely to give me for allowing a woman and girl to escape so easily and so ruin the entire evening's work.

The gold diadem glinted and shone, even in the dim light of our study, as if it caught a light not known to the normal world. The front of the tiara stood tall and curved. Crawling across the surface were cramped bas-reliefs of the most hideous nature, the images overlapping each other with maddening constancy so that one creature could hardly be distinguished from the other. The overwhelming mélange of amorphous shapes, with barely discernible bulbous eyes, hinted at monstrous combinations of aquatic or subterranean creatures without any clarity or reason.

Though I'd carried it here with no hesitation, a sudden reluctance fell over me to touch it now, for fear that some of the creatures might twist and fall off with any jostling, and so come into being. I covered the thing with my coat and tried to forget about it. Whatever it was, Holmes would fathom its deeper meaning.

Only after the breaking of dawn did I finally hear my friend's steps on the stairs. He entered the room wearing a scraggly beard, woollen cap, and worn pea jacket. He soon had this disguise off, however, and immediately fell to on the breakfast that Mrs Hudson had left. I brought the porcelain teapot with the scarlet ribbon around the handle from the sideboard, also left by our inestimable Mrs Hudson. I poured out some of the red liquid, still tolerably warm, so that I might try and shake off the lassitude of dawn.

"I found them, Holmes," I said. "I have seen them tonight, and they have left behind a—"

"The Nowak sisters," he said, "are hardly the centre of this case. Give me a moment to consider what I have seen, Watson, before you add fresh information. There are great depths to this case."

"But…" I said, and stopped when he waved me away.

"Great… depths," he said between mouthfuls. "Fiendish depths!" Though he'd fallen on the first dish with great vigour, he paused after lifting the lid off the second one, staring.

Holmes finally let the cover drop back on the food, then pushed away his half-full plate, and was now lighting a cigarette.

"What is the matter?" I said.

"Curried fish," he said. "There's no help for it; my appetite is quite gone just at the smell of it. I doubt I shall ever eat fish again without looking at it twice."

"Whatever are you talking about?" I said.

"Gregson was quick enough," he said, ignoring my question, "to track down the Nowaks' ship, but with a bit more ingenuity, he might have also found the one that brought Konrad Pawlitz, as well."

"Who is Konrad Pawlitz?"

"A businessman from Devonshire, come over some many years ago from Poland. My thought is that he may have been a distant relation to our Nowaks, but that is only one of many possibilities. The proximity to the harbour and a few other signs in the room at once suggested to me that she might have expected to meet someone coming in by boat. Checking for boats that arrived recently in nearby ports was the surest way to discover our victim's identity. The list of passengers matching our murdered man's description was small enough so that it was not difficult to narrow down that list to a single name. Pawlitz."

"Well done, Holmes!"

"But this discovery was commonplace compared to finding the *Bountiful Harvest*."

"Another ship?"

"Certainly, another ship, Watson, but not just any ship. *The* ship. A whaling ship out of the very same stretch of Massachusetts coastline from which our two refugee sisters have come. Or at least it pretends to be a whaler, but really the ship is too small for that purpose. At any rate, the sisters' ship has come from New Bedford, but this one sails from a much smaller harbour called Innsmouth. It arrived just after the *Lady Evelyn*, but secured itself at one of the little wharfs, so as to avoid notice. But I found her anyway, right where she sits in the harbour still like a bloated leech, waiting, waiting…"

He shook his head, reached over and pushed the covered curried fish plate another foot further away, and continued his narrative.

"I carried out my investigation in the guise of a dockworker, as you saw, confident that I might gather all the information that I needed as one of their own." He mashed his barely smoked cigarette into his breakfast plate and jumped to his feet. Rummaging among the desk he found the briar pipe. Finding this evidently more satisfactory, he packed some shag in and lit it from the gas.

"The *Bountiful Harvest*," he said, "has lain there less than forty-eight hours, but already dark myths spring up all around it. The sailors and dockworkers talk of nothing else. The swollen deformity of the hull, the odd sounds heard during the late hour from inside, the general disreputable look of the crew... but the most striking detail of all was the date, which the harbourmaster had just sent via telegram to America to confirm. I did not ask him to, mind; he'd already taken the expense upon himself. In another ship, the small detail might have been attributed to clerical error, but the *Bountiful Harvest* has caused such a commotion that all the details which do not match the expected are to be confirmed."

"What details?" I asked.

"As I said, Watson, the date of departure was the most striking of these," he said. "The *Lady Evelyn*, which the Nowaks took passage on, was a transatlantic steamer, and so took only a little over a week to cross the Atlantic, which is a fair but not unheard of time for a steamer. Quite the advancement over the three to six months it takes a sailing ship. Not only is this due to sustained greater speeds despite the wind conditions, but also to the fact that a steamer can take a straight line to its destination, whereas a sailing ship is often forced to track back and forth in a rather indirect course. Now, considering that the *Bountiful Harvest* is visibly a sailing ship, and not a terribly new one, how long would you expect it to take?"

"Three months?" I said.

"What would you say if I told you that the *Bountiful Harvest*, without the advantages of steam power, completed their journey in less than four days. The captain submitted a much more reasonable date to the harbourmaster, but a chance comment from one of the crew disclosed the actual departure date, which the harbourmaster confirmed with the American port. How would you account for that?"

"I really have no idea," I said.

"Nor I." He knocked out the still-burning embers of the pipe into the fire and proceeded to refill it. "The simplest assumption would be that the date is some error or fabrication, but certainly there is something very odd about this ship. Have you ever seen a ship with ports at the bottom of the hull, Watson?"

"Ports?" I said. "You mean an entrance of some kind?"

"That is exactly what I mean," he said. "I could see them quite clearly through the water, standing as I was on the docks. Permanent fixtures near the bottom of the boat. Keeping the copper hull clean on an older boat such as the *Bountiful Harvest* is no easy matter, and this task is a common obsession to any decent ship's captain. Barnacles and the like are scraped off any time she puts into harbour, for such protrusions affect the resistance of a hull moving through water and add unnecessary time to any voyage. But instead of a flat copper hull, this ship has huge, flat metal doors, with seals and handles required for their operation. In addition to this, there are a curious set of sealed holes high up in the hull. Though covered with clamped-on metal lids, they still presented themselves as great curiosities. No captain would allow such constructions, yet there they were, like an artificial mole on the face of a court beauty. Why?"

"I'm sure I have no idea," I said. I was intrigued by Holmes's story now, despite my previous urgency to relate my own.

"The crew, in general, is an unsavoury lot; dirty, sullen, and hunched over to a man. They watched me with unwavering expressions and took pains to drive me away from the boat when they saw that I had interest in it. Both of the other ships using the same wharf have made excuses and departed, so now the *Bountiful Harvest* is all by itself, sitting underneath the Blackfriars Bridge, like a poisonous reptile under a rock.

"My investigations after that were forced, by necessity, to be done from a distance. But before the afternoon, I chanced to see one of the sailors leaving in a most furtive manner, slipping down a rope near the bow rather than using the gangplank. He seemed different than his fellow shipmates, tall and blonde and without the open stare that seemed to characterize the rest of them. I took a chance and followed him and was quite rewarded for the trouble.

"He left the riverfront behind, moving at a brisk walk, as if all he wished were to put as much of the city as possible between him and the ship. When he seemed to feel that he had accomplished this and slowed his steps, his first destination was an alehouse near St Barts. I followed him in, made his acquaintance as if by accident, and with the application of a few more glasses of beer, drew his story from him. It was not difficult, for I don't think he could bring his mind around to anything else.

"'My name,' said he, 'is Winston Carson. I hail from America, as you can no doubt tell from my speech. I came over on a ship called the *Bountiful Harvest*, but I won't be going back on that queer vessel! In fact, I feel that I have just now thrown off an ill and monstrous fate having left it. My mam said never to have any truck with Innsmouth folk, and I should have listened.'"

Holmes paused. "When I asked him about the curiously swift

travel over the Atlantic, Watson, he was most anxious to tell me the tale."

"'Being a new hand,' said he, 'they did not give me access to all the ship, and there were curious doings onboard, with many secrets that the captain, chaplain and mates kept to themselves. Most of these were centred on the lower decks, where I was absolutely forbidden to go. My first assumption was that they were engaged in transporting some sort of contraband, which did not bother me.

"'Three days off the eastern coast of Massachusetts, the captain tells us to reef all the sails and batten down all the ports, as if to make ready for a storm. This was a cause for much curiosity, you see, as there was not a cloud in the sky. But Captain Waite was not the kind to tolerate questions, and we went about securing the ship as ordered. All while we members of the crew worked, the ship's chaplain and mates held some kind of heathen ritual.

"'I'd never seen the like. Certainly, it was no Christian ceremony, and the language – which the chaplain spoke and which all the mates and most of the crew answered in – was such an unintelligible and harsh warbling that it raised the hackles on me just to hear it. The chaplain, a broken-down, hunched-over fellow, with a great, misshapen head, wore a dirty fish-stained robe that I'd seen often enough, but also a striking golden tiara that I'd never seen before.'"

I was entranced at Holmes's rendition of the sailor's tale, but not so much that I failed to recognize a reference to my own strange experience, and I looked briefly across at the place where my coat was bundled around that same tiara, and wondered. Then Holmes continued.

"'At the conclusion of this ritual, they brought four unsavoury bundles out. I was coiling rope at this time, only a few feet away, and so got a good look as the chaplain's assistant heaved them over the port railing. The large and bulky bundles were wrapped in burlap, and coils and coils of cheap hemp rope. The first three seemed inert, lumpy things, and it was only their coffin-like shape that disturbed me, for no one had died during the voyage. But the last bundle clearly twitched, and a brief moan came from it, just before they flung it over the rail. I watched in horror as it disappeared beneath the ocean surface and fell back into our wake. The chaplain's assistant oversaw this operation. He was an odious man, though he had once been a U.S. marshal, I understand, or so some of the others told me. I cannot imagine the kind of justice such a man would hand out. When he wiped his hands unconsciously on his dirty canvas pants, I could see the unmistakable smear of blood.

"'"Cow carcasses," he said to me, for I'm sure my horror was written plainly on my face. "What did you think they were… *men*?" The man wheezed and laughed from merriment when he saw the shock that this statement produced in me.

"'Then four of the older hands, Innsmouth natives all of them, went down into the lowest part of the hold, where I was forbidden to go. A few minutes later, there was a strange racket, a curious metallic rattling that shook the entire deck. After a quarter of an hour of this, they came back up and the captain said that we were to wait. Well, that wait felt like hours, and the whole thing chilled me, even though I stood in the sun. At last, the ship lurched as if we'd just run aground. It near flung me overboard, but I could see from the expressions of the crew around me, and the easy way in which they all took grips in the rigging, that this was an expected event. This was what we'd been waiting for.

"'I heard a story of a whale that bumped a ship once, and I thought of that story right off as the hull gave a massive groan. For a moment I thought some force from below had seized us. Certainly the sea was dark and turbulent underneath the *Bountiful Harvest*, though there was no weather to account for it.

"'Then the ship lurched again, and the helmsman turned to bring the ship a bit to port. Spray pounded against the bow, dousing the deck while the ship bounced like a storm-tossed cork in the Atlantic rollers. I fair thought we were done for, then. The ship shuddered again, and we picked up speed as if entering a very strong current. Faster and faster we went as something unknown propelled our ship through the water at a frightening speed, faster than any ship I'd ever sailed on. The ship groaned and creaked under the strain, as if she would batter herself apart against the rising waves, but the Innsmouth hands have an uncanny way of the sea about them. Born fishermen, all of them, and they knew every trick there was to keep the ship afloat as we flew through the water.

"'You will scarce credit it, sitting here in London as we are, but we kept this up, night and day, doing double and sometimes triple watch for four gruelling days and nights. What nights! I got seasick for the first time, and I lost at least a dozen pounds what with being unable to hold any food. That, only with constant work and a bone-wearying fatigue, turned me into a wreck of a man. My own mam wouldn't recognize me now. That's how much weight I've lost.

"'At last, our navigator told us we were close to England. Four days to travel the whole Atlantic! Then the captain ordered most of the crew below. He thought at first to not include me, and there was an argument between him and the chaplain. There seemed to be some kind of problem with the numbers, and they would not have enough men to complete some mysterious task without me.

"''You are not from our little town," Captain Waite said to me, "and cannot be familiar with some of our trade secrets. I must command you, then, never to reveal what you are about to see below, for there are many fishing charters that would pay dearly for our secret. If you do tell our secret, I shall know of it. Such things have a way of getting back to us. Rest assured that we would have our revenge, should you not heed our warning."

"'Then the chaplain and assistant bade me to follow the rest of the crew down. As you can imagine, I was quite filled with curiosity and trepidation from all this.

"'You've almost certainly noticed the stench about the *Bountiful Harvest*. How could you not? It clings to me now so that I can barely stand to be among decent men. I shall have to take several baths and burn all my clothes if I'm to ever be rid of it. Well, the smell about the deck of the ship is nothing compared to the tangible reek below decks.

"'The space below is an open area with a vast beam that runs the entire length of the ship. To this support is affixed a series of great chains, massive chains with each link large as the span of my arms, but I could only guess at the length, because they ran up to hawseholes high in the hull, and then out into the water. They thrummed with a constant tension, and were clearly part of the cause for our maddening speed. It was our job to pull them back up, and to this, Eliot, the chaplain's assistant, and Marsh, the first mate, set us to work.

"I can only guess how far into the depths these chains dangled. Drawing them in was a Herculean task even with the forty or so men crammed into that hold. Whatever clung to the bottom ends, it would not release. We grappled with them for nearly an hour, trying to draw them back and all the time the ship seemed to be going faster and faster, and the beam the chains were attached to made a horrible groaning, and started to show cracks.

"'It's no use," the chaplain said. "They are held too tightly at the bottom, and we don't have enough men to effect their release!"

"'It seems to me," Eliot said, "that four was not quite enough. We should have had more men at the beginning, and so need less at the end!" He gave me a look then. He wears glasses, so I could not see his eyes properly, but I can well imagine the dark, cold look in them and I shuddered to the depths of my core and thought of the four bundles that went overboard.

"There is no help for it now," the chaplain said. "We shall have to release the chains here." Another groan from the ship and the first mate set us to battering and levering at the chains with a will.

"'Hammer, you dogs!" Marsh howled. "Release us, or we'll

all be dragged down and you'll be screaming from the depths and have Dagon's curse upon you all!"

"'The name of "Dagon" meant nothing to me, though the sound of it brought a coldness to my belly. But the name had a galvanizing effect on the men, more even than the threat of the ship breaking apart, and they howled and hacked and pried at the chains like madmen. There were eight sets of chains in all, and any one of them might pull the ship under. So panicked was everyone that our attack on the chains was disorganized, so that several of the men had gotten their arms between the links. When the first chain tore free, the length of it was yanked with terrible force and pulled two men with it out the hawseholes in the hull. These holes were not quite large enough for men to pass through unharmed, but the terrible force yanked them through anyway, and I have nightmares now about their mangled bodies. I do not know if they were killed there, but I hope they had that mercy, because both chains and men went into the water, lost.

"'This tragedy did not summon any caution whatsoever among the crew at the time, however, and we continued our frantic hammering and levering. I was just as mad with fear as the rest, mind you, caught in a fever I don't like to remember.

"'Before we'd got the rest of the chains off, we lost two more men. But finally we were free and the ship rested easy, with only the natural motion of the sea to affect her.

"'We returned to the deck, and Captain Waite and the chaplain congratulated us all, not with the grimness I might have expected, but with the levity and joy of a holy baptism. I tell you that it was a break from man's own world on that vessel, and I'm terribly glad to be free of it. You know the rest. I snuck off and now all I can think about is putting as much distance as I can between myself and the *Bountiful Harvest*. I shall have to learn both your English ways and a new trade, for I can't imagine sailing the Atlantic again, knowing what lies underneath.'"

With this extraordinary statement concluded, Holmes leaned back and puffed away on his pipe. The constant patter of rain tapped restlessly on the window. In fact, it had been raining since this case began.

"So what do you make of that, Watson?"

"I'm sure I don't know what to make of it," I said.

"An extraordinary tale," he said, "to be sure, and very difficult to credit. But backed as it is by the records… well, perhaps it is not all fancy. It also accounts for the hawseholes in the hull, though sheds very little light on the ports in the bottom, since they do not figure in his story."

"I can corroborate one thing about his tale," I said, and since Holmes's narrative seemed to have come to its end, I hurriedly supplied my own, finishing with a dramatic flourish worthy of Holmes himself as I unveiled the tiara.

"If this is the tiara worn by the priest in his story," I said, "at least that much of it must be true."

Holmes gave a soft cry and pulled the object closer, employing his magnifying glass and tape measure. He turned the tiara around in his hands, examining it from every possible vantage.

"Singular," he said. "I see no marks of moulding or etching, or any of the tell-tale signs that a British craftsman would leave."

An inexplicable thing happened to me then, one I should not

like to recall. I had the most overwhelming urge to dash the evil-looking thing from Holmes's hands, as if some ill fate waited for the man who dwelled too long on it. My hands fluttered on the table.

"A most curious shape," he said, and I reached out, too slowly, as he placed the tainted circlet on his head.

"Holmes, no!"

"I should hate to meet the person for whom this crown fit," he said, ignoring my outburst. He indicated where the front and rear portions curved out well past the limits of his own head, while the sides were far too narrow. "Only the grossest and most misshapen head would accommodate this rim, yet I can find no stress marks to indicate where it might have been bent."

A dark gloom lifted from me when he removed the tiara and covered it again with my coat, but even then a trace of that foul mood clung to me still.

Holmes, for his part, fell into an uncommunicative mood, giving every sign that he would be pondering all this new information for a considerable time. He merely shook his head when I hazarded a few questions, so I left him smoking and staring into space.

I retired to my room.

It was still raining when I awoke, having slept most of the day, and Holmes was still in his armchair and lost deeply in thought, so I busied myself with refreshment and the paper while I waited. We were both startled from our reverie at the sound of horses in the street, then the sound of Gregson's voice downstairs. It was almost midnight.

He burst into the room in a highly agitated state. "We had her, Mr Holmes," he said. "We had her and… well, you must come and see. Hurry!"

"The Nowak woman?" Holmes said.

"Yes, the Nowak woman!"

"Come, Gregson. You must really get a better hold of yourself and tell us what brings you at such an hour."

"They were at the Yard just this evening!" Gregson said, "the murderess and the little girl both, the woman ranting and raving like a lunatic."

"On what charge?" Holmes said. "Surely you didn't bring her in on the scanty evidence from the hotel?"

"Well, Mr Holmes," Gregson said, "I feel the evidence is a bit stronger than you do, which has turned out to be the correct theory, as proven by the fact that she turned herself in. Walked in and confessed the murder to the night watchmen before he could so much as question her. They sent for me at once, and I tried to wring an explanation from her, but other than confessing to the crime, she could give me no particulars. This is more a case for the asylum than for the police. Only now she's gone again!"

"Gone?" Holmes said. "You let her go?"

"I did nothing of the kind," Gregson said hotly. "A jailbreak, it was! And the cell they took her from is all a shambles. You must come see for yourself!"

❧

Bradstreet met us at the entrance, and he led the three of us past the offices and regular jail cells and descended down a winding and narrow stone staircase. I found no great difficulty with the darkness, but Bradstreet stopped on the next landing to acquire a lantern from a steel cabinet there.

"Surely you didn't put a woman and little girl down here?" I said, amazed.

"She insisted," Bradstreet said. "Screamed and hollered to beat the band until we really had no choice. She said it was the only place they might be safe, which makes little sense to me."

"Deeper and deeper," Holmes murmured, and though I knew he referred to the case itself, I couldn't help but reflect how accurately it also resembled the dim whitewashed staircase we now descended.

At the bottom of the stairs, a charcoal stove cast a lurid red glow onto the long stretch of cell doors.

"We housed her here," Bradstreet said. "I assure you, gentlemen, it sank my heart to leave a young woman and girl in this dark place. Still, that was as nothing to how I felt when I discovered them gone, and the cell in *this* condition. Never have I experienced the like."

Bradstreet produced an iron key and opened the nearest door, which let a nauseating odour roll out into the hallway. If something had crawled up from the darkest corner of the ocean and died on the spot, a few weeks later it would smell like this. I felt the gorge rise up in my throat, and from both Bradstreet and Gregson's faces, I could see they experienced the same.

Since my change, I'd often felt bludgeoned with London's

overwhelming attack on my olfactory senses, but never before had I felt it so keenly as standing outside that darkened cell. Atavistic urges to run, to flee this enclosed space, crawled through the hindmost regions of my brain and it was all I could do to keep my feet planted in place. I'd thought, up until now, that the discovery of vampires living in our midst, and then getting transformed into one, had shaken my faith to the core, but something about this place, this stench, hinted at something far more unnatural and sinister.

"Easy, Watson," Holmes murmured, putting a hand on my shoulder. His hand was steady, but even his stern face looked drawn and stretched, and in he went. Naming myself a fool and a coward inside for my hesitation, I followed.

The smell was even more overpowering in here, and my boots splashed in a shallow pool of foul sludge. The cold was enough to chill my skin, which was usually proof against even a London winter. Even the bare pallet against the wall was cold and waterlogged to the touch. An iron grate on the wall led to a boiler stove, but this, too, was cold to the touch. Traffic sounds came from outside through the window, but distantly.

"Surely this is unworthy of you!" I said, turning on Bradstreet. "No matter what the cause, I cannot believe you would put even a hardened criminal, let alone that poor woman, into such a dank and terrible place! No one could stay here very long without catching their death of cold."

"I give you my word," Bradstreet said in an outraged voice, "that this was not how I left her. You may inspect the other cells yourself and see that they are all dry and warm. Only here have the boiler pipes failed, and it was not this way when I left them. I am at a total loss to explain it."

"Look at this," Holmes said, drawing us over to the barred window, a narrow slit in the stone, too narrow for a full-grown person to fit through. Five of the six heavyweight iron bars had been torn out, seemingly by brute force. Even the stone around it was broken in places to so much rubble.

Holmes knelt, heedless of the water soaking into his trousers, to make as detailed an inspection as possible. The window was very high up in the wall, and all the furniture bolted into the stone, so that he could not reach the window. I allowed Holmes to climb on my shoulders so that he might get a closer look, but he was down again in an instant.

"I can make out no tracks," he said, "on account of the water. I should like to examine this place again after the water has been drained, though it may be that the water will leave none."

"Holmes," I said. "The odour is much more powerful, but it is the same as the stink of the man at the hotel."

"I thought it might be," he said. "For now, I should like to see the window from the other side. There is nothing further I can learn here."

This required us to go outside the prison and climb down from the street level to an aqueduct, flooded from the constant rain, that ran parallel to the street.

Holmes waved Bradstreet over in order to have better light from the lantern. "The bars have been torn out from the outside," Holmes said, "and not forced from the inside, which is hardly surprising considering the inaccessibility from inside." He ran his finger along the jagged patches of wet, broken stone, then dredged one of the discarded bars out of the channel of water. It was bent nearly in half.

Next he walked over to the window of the next cell, put his grip on one of the bars, and pulled, to no effect. Bradstreet and Gregson were debating the likelihood of someone attacking the bars without an inspector or constable hearing them, and were far too busy to overhear us.

"The bars are quite solid, Watson," Holmes murmured. "Put your hand to one of these and see if you don't agree."

I knelt down next to him and took a firm grip, exerting my full strength. Nothing. I took a deep breath, and after a concerted effort, thought I felt a shift in the mortar.

Holmes's sharp eye had picked out my slight success. "That's enough," he said quietly, "or we shall raise some questions best left unasked. If you wanted to free someone in this cell and were outside, could you do it?"

"I believe so," I said, "but it would take some time. Perhaps hours."

"And still you could not tear it so completely, as these other bars have been. This isn't just a loosening of the mortar here, but rather a savage destruction of the stonework all around. This, too, is where the water has come from, for they've broken through into this aqueduct."

"Certainly more damage than I could do."

"This smell," he said, "that reminds you of your adversary from the Excelsior Hotel. Does it not also remind you of Carson's story?"

"It certainly does."

"And the scent outside the window of the Hôtel du Château Blanc, next to the drowned man?"

"I'd forgotten that," I said, snapping my fingers. "Yes, it is the same."

"I think," Holmes said, standing up and speaking loud enough to interrupt the two arguing policemen, "that it is time to issue a warrant in order to search the *Bountiful Harvest*."

Chapter 09

THE BOUNTIFUL HARVEST

H olmes and I took a cab to Blackfriars Bridge alone, as Gregson would not be able to apply for a warrant until morning. The rain had broken for the first time in days, to be replaced by an equally dense, enshrouding fog.

"We cannot afford a delay," Holmes said, "or we will find the pigeon flown."

I hesitated. Any actions we took tonight would be without the benefit of the law behind us. "You think them responsible for Lucja Nowak's jail break?"

"Well," Holmes said, "they have pursued her across the Atlantic, and trailed her to two locations here in London. Having tracked her unerringly so far, who else should we look to first?"

"Do you still believe that there is nothing supernatural about this case?" I said. "Perhaps an elder, stronger vampire might have done this thing?"

"Those are two distinct questions," Holmes said. "If I do not see any sign of vampires, at least I am prepared to admit the existence of something else beyond the experience of your average Londoner. For is there not room enough in London for more than one creature of the night? You know my methods, Watson; I shall follow docilely wherever the evidence leads me. In this case, the evidence is certainly quite extraordinary. I have never known one with greater depths. But we shall have some answers tonight, if I'm not mistaken. It is well that you have brought your revolver. I will give credit to your vampire theory so far as to suggest you load it with some of these specially made cartridges from Ingerson, and I shall do the same. While I consider it the highest probability that vampires are not involved with this case, it *is* a matter of odds, and there is no reason to bet our lives on such odds when a silver bullet will do as well for any threats we might face as normal ones."

The cabbie let us off underneath Blackfriars Bridge, where the fog crawled slowly across the wharf, dampening even my heightened senses. The Thames was a murky expanse off to our left, sluggish and dark. The *Bountiful Harvest* bobbed on the water, only a bulky shape in the grey haze.

Holmes had worn a deerstalker hat out of deference to the weather, which made a strange spectacle in the city, but I could not fault the logic of needing greater protection against the cold and wet, which I did not feel as strongly. We moved slowly up the gangplank, our revolvers at the ready. Mine was a reassuring weight in my hand, on so grim an expedition. There were no workers or pedestrians there, an unusual sight on so busy a dock, such was the pall that dingy little ship cast about it. So overwhelming was my rage at the thought of that innocent woman and little girl at the hands of whatever horrid beast had left that savage destruction and malignant stench at Scotland Yard, that I might have stormed the ship like a buccaneer had not Holmes indicated the need for stealth.

But stealth or no, a burly figure stepped onto the top of the gangplank before we were halfway across. It was with no surprise that, with the light of Holmes's electric torch, I recognized the belligerent man who had pounded on the Nowaks' hotel door. The sound of shuffling on the deck made it clear he was not alone.

He bristled and put a forceful hand to Holmes's chest, his face stern. "You're not welcome here." Behind him on the deck, at least a dozen unsavoury sailors stood around. Cut from the same cloth as the man in front of us, they had a slouching and sinister manner. Never have I seen such a collection of unsettling gazes as the wall-eyed stares they gave us. Clearly, my revolver did not intimidate them in the slightest, and many held fishing knives or large hooks in plain evidence.

"You monsters!" I railed. "You have no right to hold women and children hostage!"

"We have every right," the man said hotly. "She is to stand trial for her theft in Innsmouth."

"You do have her then," Holmes said smoothly. "I thought as much, but this confirms it. No doubt you mean to arrest her in your role as U.S. marshal?"

The man gave a most insincere laugh. "Why whatever do you mean?"

"I also know that you attempted to use your role as U.S. marshal to intimidate the staff of the Hôtel du Château Blanc, for it was you that barged your way in there, and not Pawlitz. You left your badge, however, on the body you had delivered there, to confuse the police. But the body had no sign on the clothing to indicate a badge had ever been pinned there before, while I perceive that you have no less than fourteen holes in your somewhat worn and soiled waistcoat, holes precisely where a marshal's badge would be pinned.

"Damn your eyes," the man sputtered. "How could you see such a thing on a night like this?"

"I see such things because I *look* for them," Holmes said. "Come now, Eliot, this really will not do. You have the Nowak sisters, and we have the golden tiara. We might, perhaps, arrange a trade?"

"You're a clever fiend, aren't you? How do you know my name? I've told that to no one in England!"

"Tut, tut. If you haven't yet reasoned that you are dealing with someone a little sharper than the official force, let me advise you of the fact now."

"And you would give us the tiara, take the girl, and leave the matter without further meddling?"

"Leave it? I daresay not. If given the opportunity, I'll see you stand in the dock for the murder of Konrad Pawlitz, late of Devonshire. But it shall be some time before the Scotland Yarders are here, and I am inclined to take what measures I can in the meantime and secure the safety of the Nowak sisters. If the American authorities can succeed in putting a rope around your neck where the British ones have failed, I will count that a good day's work."

"Why should I deal with you?"

"Think this through, man. Shots fired would certainly draw the constables immediately, which, for the briefest of moments, goes against both our interests for it would put not only your liberty at risk, but also the lives of the Nowak sisters, unless I miss my guess."

"You do not."

"Exactly. Should we come to an agreement that does not involve summoning the constables, then we shall do what good we can, and you will have the chance, at least, to slip off your well-deserved fate."

"Very well," Eliot said, pointing at me. "But you shall fetch the tiara, and I shall hold your clever friend hostage here in the meantime, so that there are no tricks. At the first sight of the police, be assured that I shall cast him overboard. We may not be at sea, but there are deeper waters even in this domestic river than you can possibly know. And perhaps a hook or two might go with him, if you take my meaning. You would be well not to endanger your friend needlessly."

"I am not so easy a fish to hook," Holmes said. "However…" He pushed his way through the man and settled himself on the nearby rail, his revolver at the ready. "I shall wait right here while Watson retrieves the tiara and I'll thank you gentlemen to keep this most reasonable distance between us."

"Holmes!" I said. "How can you even think—" but my friend raised his hand and fixed me with his masterful gaze.

"It is a necessary evil, Watson," he said. "I shall be quite safe. Now you must hurry, for it would far behove us to have our transaction completed before sunrise, would it not?"

The thought of leaving my friend in this terrible predicament repelled me. I did not like the look of Eliot, or the relentless gaze of the Innsmouth sailors. I trusted in no bargain and considered trying my strength against the entire deck rather than leave my friend to their disreputable mercies, but Holmes called out to me softly, clearly divining my inner turmoil.

"Hurry, Watson. The night is slipping away." He tugged the deerstalker hat down further on his head as proof against the cold and wet weather.

I could see that he would not be dissuaded, and so left him, surrounded on three sides with foul assailants barely held at bay, with the water at his back. There were only six bullets in his gun, and more than a dozen men on deck, odds that worried me deeply, for all that Holmes was a formidable opponent. I hurried off into the fog, where our cab was still waiting.

The ride back to Baker Street was harrowing, despite the late hour, for I railed at the driver passionately, and had to assuage my conscience by offering him a gold sovereign if he made the trip in a timely fashion.

The golden tiara was waiting for me, and it was with some revulsion that I picked up the piece of inexplicably foreign jewellery. It shone like a brilliant spider and I could not help but feel that both Holmes and I, as well as the Nowak sisters, were but helpless victims caught in its glittering web. I was only too happy to shut the thing away in a leather bag. I breezed back out the door, past Mrs Hudson's querulous questions, and back into my cab.

I arrived back at Blackfriars wharf with at least two hours of the night left, but a storm shattered itself onto the Thames just as the cab approached, so that it was necessary to lean over and holler into the cabbie's ear in order to make him understand that he should wait again.

The wooden stairs down were slick with the sudden torrent, but I took them two at a time, only to come round the landing, stop, and cry out loud in anguish.

The *Bountiful Harvest* was gone.

I rushed to the edge of the dock, but the empty stretch of water the ship had sat in reflected the lightshow above with perfect and relentless clarity. There was no sign of them. In between the blinding pulses of light, darkness reigned above with the equally black surface of the Thames below and hapless London imprisoned between. No ships dared work the Thames in such weather, so only emptiness looked back at me, with no sign of the Innsmouth whaler.

My heart quailed inside of me. The Innsmouth sailors had given over reclaiming the tiara in order to make good their escape and had either succeeded in Eliot's threat of drowning Holmes in the Thames, or else had taken him with them as their prisoner. Probably they had never required the tiara, and it had all been a ruse on their part. Now I would never see Holmes again, for I had no doubt that if he had been taken prisoner, they would bundle him into one of the grisly packages destined to splash into the darkest waters they could find, one of their unwholesome cultist sacrifices.

The reader will not credit such speculation, but the unknown and blight-shadowed forces behind our enemies became suddenly clear to me, and despair came with the knowledge. The possibility that Eliot and his blasphemous god had somehow called forth this unnatural storm in order to foil any pursuit rose from the depths of my fevered brain as an absolute conviction.

Dagon. They had called to Dagon in Winston Carson's story, a story I now fervently believed, despite my early aversions to it. Dagon now seemed an unknowable but inevitable horror, an aggregate of malevolent urges and forces too potent for either Scotland Yard, myself, or even Sherlock Holmes to contend with.

I gnashed my teeth and scanned the water all along the wharf, hoping against all possibility that I might find Holmes, but only the opaque waters of the Thames stared back at me. I was quite alone.

Turning from the water with a sob, and clutching the sodden leather bag with their useless gold trinket in my hands, I raised it to the sky with a fitful cry of rage. There was no course of action left to me that could prevail. The police boats would be as fragile toys in this elemental fury, and any attempt to overtake the American ship would be madness.

Then I froze, and a cold chill descended down into the pit of my stomach.

A peculiar quality to the churning water of the Thames had changed, alerting some atavistic sense within me to the presence of furtive, hideous things beneath its surface. The stench from the savaged prison cell, abominably repellent, cut through the scents of the Thames and the rain. I think that the foul fishy odour had been growing for some time, but so stealthily that I had not noticed until just this very moment. I turned again to face the water, fully expecting some horror to come rising up. A churning in the water identified the spot, just a few feet away from where I stood on the dock.

My jacket pocket was empty, though my revolver had been there just moments ago. Vampire-enhanced strength or no, I did not relish grappling with any detestable minion Dagon might send forth, but I would not shirk to do so, if any action of mine might somehow alter this evil night.

The next events contain certain inexplicable elements, and even with the tangible outcome, I cannot say for certain that the next portion of my account is entirely factual. I shall have to represent the events precisely as I remember them, tinged perhaps by my current nightmares. This is as much veracity as I can honestly claim, and the readers shall have to judge for themselves if my tale is some fevered hallucination or a reference to an impending malfeasance that might someday come into its own, and until that day, is far better forgotten.

An inhuman hand reached out and gripped the dock, not quickly, but with a surreal slowness and inevitability that nevertheless took me completely by surprise. A face rose out of the water, not as a man might stand, but with a grotesque and horrid undulation that hinted at something far different than a man's legs still hidden underneath. Before my beleaguered senses could fully grasp the hideous features revealed to me in the flashing storm – part fish, part amphibian – another creature had joined the first, clinging to the wooden slats. Then another, then dozens.

I froze in revulsion, and by the time it might take to draw a breath, the long stretch of the wharf was lined with twisted and bestial faces.

No two creatures looked precisely the same, though certain hellish qualities prevailed. Their skin was shiny and slippery, of a greyish green hue, though I could see that some had only partly discernible white bellies and ridged backs. With their aberrant and inhuman features, an array of webbed fingers, palpitating gills, flippers, humped backs and those relentlessly bulging eyes, there should have been nothing of man about them, but there was. The traces of humanity, their vaguely humanoid shapes and knowing glances, made their existence an even greater abomination. They made no sound as they regarded me. Nothing moved but the lapping of the water, and the patter of the rain. Even the crash and rumble of the storm had slowed, as if by malignant command.

Gooseflesh crawled down my back, but I held firm and did not retreat. A feral growl tore free of my throat of its own accord and I'm sure that my predator's fangs were plainly bared, for all the change it made in that enigmatic, monstrous gallery.

They merely watched me… No! Not me, but the leather bag in my hand. "This?" I said, shaking the bag. Fifty or more ancient eyes followed the motion, confirming the guess.

"You want this?" I hollered. "I want my friends. If you have them, you shall release them to me!"

For the first time since their partial exit from the water, one of the fish-frog things moved, leaning down; it opened a saw-toothed jaw, and vomited an unmistakable slime-drenched object onto the rain-soaked wooden slats. My blood chilled to ocean temperatures to see it: Holmes's deerstalker hat.

"Does he live? You will return him... for this?" I yanked the shining diadem from the leather bag and shook it at them.

For answer, the creature that seemed to be their spokesman prodded the hat with a clawed flipper. Its gaze never left the tiara.

"Then you shall have it!" I cared nothing for the tiara, and would have gladly poured untold riches into the Thames for the barest chance of Holmes's safe return. I flung it in a far-out glittering arc, into the element of Dagon that no man – sailor or fisherman – can truly claim for his own. Before the object had disappeared into the water, the creatures around me had slid silently back into the depths.

The storm ceased with such amazing abruptness that I could still make out the ripples of the tiara's impact on the suddenly still waters. My eye followed the ripples further out, and revealed as if by a parting curtain of rain mist, was the dark prow of a police boat making directly for the wharf.

In the prow, the gaunt figure of Sherlock Holmes was clearly visible, unharmed. The golden hair of the young Nowak child was visible in the boat, as well, but of her older sister, there was no sign. While I was waiting for them to land, I found my revolver, which I had apparently dropped in my rush onto the wharf. I say 'dropped' but, in truth, the pocket out of which it had fallen was quite deep and I'd never had any problem of this sort before and I could not help but wonder at the possibility of some dark hand guiding the Innsmouth whaler and bringing misfortune upon its enemies.

I shook with an overpowering relief when the boat with Holmes and the others finally landed, and if there were tears of joy on my face, the rain was too recent for even the world's greatest detective to know the difference.

Chapter 10

THE DEPTHS

"Eliot and the Esoteric Order of Dagon," Holmes pontificated darkly, "as embodied by the crew of the *Bountiful Harvest*, have escaped, Watson. They had help, you see, help from *below*. Creatures from the depths." Unclamping the pipe from his mouth and pointing downward, he might have meant the bottom of the Thames, or some deeper, more infernal source.

"I know," I said with a deep and chilled shudder. "I have seen them."

"You have?" he said. "It sounds as if you have had altogether a more interesting time than I have. Perhaps you should tell your tale first this time."

This was easily done. We were both in dry clothes back at Baker Street. The young Nowak girl was with relatives – ones without any association to Innsmouth, or even America – that Bradstreet had discovered. Relatives, too, of Konrad Pawlitz, for Holmes's surmise that the murdered man was a relation of the

Nowak sisters had proven to be correct. The girl had been remarkably docile and self-possessed for one who had undergone what must have been a horrible ordeal, though I had not yet heard the details.

I hesitated during the telling of my confrontation with the fish-frog creatures, but finally told my entire story as quickly as possible.

Holmes shook his head when I told of flinging the tiara into the water, but held his comments until my conclusion.

"I really cannot congratulate you, Watson," Holmes said when I was finished. "You had only circumstantial evidence to believe that I was in their power, and no clear certainty that once your single leverage point was lost, that they should feel any compunction to honour your implied arrangement."

I stiffened with this rebuke. I felt this to be cold and callous treatment in the face of all that I had undergone for his sake.

"You are here, are you not?" I said.

"Well, that is hardly proof of anything," he said.

"Then how did you escape?"

"My recovery from the depths was never necessary, for the simple reason that I was never in them."

My irritation dissolved quickly, so eager was I to hear what had transpired after I had left.

"I knew the situation," he said. "I positioned myself in such a way that I should hear if they raised anchor and at the same time be able to protect myself with my revolver. It was a grim time, to be the one lone sentinel on a ship filled with murderous cultists. I consider my nerves fairly proof against shock, Watson, but it shall take me some weeks to shake the disconcerting vision of their combined unwavering gaze.

"A short time after your departure, Eliot issued orders to the crew in a harsh, guttural language that I have never heard before. Some of the noises he made were almost croaks or bleats, if you can credit it. I expected them to try for the anchor, but instead men were sent into the hold. A few minutes later the motion of the ship changed, and I realized that Eliot had somehow managed to free the ship from the anchor and moorings without using the capstan, and we were now adrift.

"You may not understand how unsettling this was, Watson, but consider the size and weight of your average ship's anchor. It typically takes four men to raise it using the capstan's mechanical apparatus, which is quite loud, and even then it is considered no easy task. Yet only by bringing up the anchor from below could someone affect the ship's release. Though we were close to the riverbank, I'd spent some time studying the area before, and the area underneath is both surprisingly deep and covered with a thick mud like a mire.

"You see? This was a shocking corroboration of Carson's fantastic story. Inhuman assistance from the depths, right here in English waters. This, too, accounts for the ports in the bottom of the ship, as these would allow swimmers to leave the ship unseen. The logic is sound, and inescapable. Your singular encounter further corroborates their existence.

"The storm fell even more fully upon us then, and while I am not quite so ready to attribute supernatural causes to its behaviour as you seem to be, my dear Watson, it certainly had the effect of sending the Innsmouth crew into a frightful whirlwind of activity. They were instantly caught up in the business of preventing the ship from being torn to pieces by the sudden gale. At any rate, so frantic was their plight that I was unattended to, and was able to make my way below decks in search of the missing Nowak sisters.

"Finding the cabin in which they were imprisoned required no great skill, for I'd noticed a woman's handkerchief covering one of the portholes when we boarded, and I found a corresponding door that was barred from the outside. When I forced the door with a broken-off length of spar, I found both of the Nowak sisters inside.

"This next part will pain your tender sensibilities, Watson, but I must impart it, for when I tried to pull both of the sisters from their cabin, Lucja, the eldest sister, refused to allow her own rescue.

"'Take Elzbieta,' she urged me, 'so that she shall never have to grow up in the blight-shadowed town of Innsmouth. But leave me! If you don't, the Esoteric Order of Dagon shall pursue me with means both foul and implacable, and so overtake us all. The only way I can secure her safety is to remain here. Refuse me, and I shall scream and fight you, making any hope of our escape impossible.'

"I could quite see her seriousness, and believed her to be sincere in her threat. The young girl, for her part, seemed to expect this decision from her sister, and while I cannot help but lament this horrible solution, I can also admire the intellectual calm with which Elzbieta viewed the situation. Most commendable."

Holmes had created enough smoke with his pipe that I was

obliged to open a window to relieve the poisonous atmosphere that had gathered during his tale.

"The rest is unremarkable," he went on. "Shouts came from the forward hatch by which I'd made my way down, so I made my way aft and up onto the deck by an alternate route, Elzbieta in tow.

"The Innsmouth sailors tried to prevent me, and I was forced to shoot two of them and throw another man overboard, before I managed to release the launch and lower myself and the girl into it."

"That poor, noble woman," I said. "To suffer herself such a fate at the hands of those beasts. Anyone unfortunate enough to dwell in such a town as this Innsmouth must be at the complete mercy of this omnipotent Dagon and his people."

"Tut, tut, Watson," Holmes said. "Surely there are enough mysteries of man and beast without bringing the occult into it."

"But, Holmes, I *saw* them!"

"I don't doubt it. In any event, we must accept the existence of something like your altered humanoids, creatures of some intelligence, who are both excellent swimmers and possessed of extreme strength. Even if not corroborated by your description, their presence was suggested by both the destruction of the jail cell and the lifted anchor.

"However, like your own medical condition, science is well capable of explaining all manner of inhuman creatures without accepting the tenets of some barbaric religion. An experimental extract, perhaps, may be the cause of such deformations. Or rampant inbreeding. Man carries enough darkness inside him to account for all the evils of the world. There is no need to attribute the phenomenon to the supernatural."

Though Holmes's logical approach was certainly the correct one, I did not feel the matter entirely accounted for in my own heart. His casual dismissal appeared to settle the matter entirely in his own mind, and I could not debate him. Certainly I had no tangible evidence to support my fears.

"I gather," I said, "that the Nowaks were to meet this Konrad Pawlitz in order find some place to live far away from America, and Innsmouth, but you have not told me the cause of his unusual condition. Also, what was the purpose of leaving his body in the hotel room?"

"Surely the motive is clear?" Holmes said. "Eliot needed to retrieve his two escapees, but he wanted even more to terrify them and put an end to their rebellion. So, when his visit wasn't enough, he went to great lengths to show them how totally in his power they were. They had placed their hopes on this distant relative, Pawlitz, who was supposed to meet them. You remember how Gregson had heard about the U.S. marshal visiting them in the morning, found the body with the badge, and was completely taken in. But it was actually Eliot that forced his way in, then threatened them, left, and then managed to present them with Pawlitz's body in as frightening and dramatic a manner as possible, thrown in through the window by, no doubt, the aquatic creatures you describe so colourfully, who are clearly at Eliot's beck and call. No doubt their involvement accounts for the salt water we discovered on the body. Probably he was drowned at sea and brought inland by way of the Thames. Eliot also must have returned, after the

Nowaks' flight, in order to pin the marshal's badge, his own, on the body so as to delay the police from easily identifying him. A ruse too clever by half, and one easily penetrated, since the dead man's shirt had no marks from the pin and Eliot himself, when we met him, had several.

I shuddered to think of the spectacle that Holmes referred to so casually, the bloated corpse of their dead relative flung in through the window. It chilled my heart. Certainly it must have had no small effect on the Nowaks, for all their courage.

"What of the *Bountiful Harvest*?" I asked.

"We must wait," Holmes said, clearly not looking forward to the prospect.

But it was only after a full day of waiting that the telegram that Holmes had been waiting for finally came. He pounced on the unfortunate Mrs Hudson when she came in with it. He tore it open with febrile eagerness while she fled our rooms with her hands thrown up.

"Ah," Holmes said. "There I'm afraid is more bad news. A telegram came a short time ago with a report forwarded to us by Bradstreet. Police boats followed the *Bountiful Harvest* clear out to the estuary. The storm had left London, as you know, but still raged to the east. The Innsmouth ship was seen to founder as they hit the North Sea and go down with all hands. A dark ending to a murky and unsatisfactory case."

"Lucja Nowak, Eliot, all the men… drowned?" The shock hit me as if I, too, was gripped in the frigid sea waters.

"Drowned," Holmes said testily, "depriving me of all data by which I might have completed this case."

"Holmes," I said, shocked at his coldness. "Such a statement is unworthy of you."

He flashed me a rueful smile. "Forgive me, Doctor. You are quite right. It is just the nature of this case has allowed me very little opportunity to exercise the powers which I might have brought to bear. With more information, I might have shed some light on the matter, and therefore the cult, and finally on that shadowed town of Innsmouth. Certainly there were more than just these two innocents and a handful of cultists at stake. I've sent telegrams to America, and the local authorities are willing to do very little for Innsmouth. The Esoteric Order of Dagon's hold is too firm, and I feel now that hundreds of residents shall suffer under their evil taint for many years before it is cleared up. I had hoped for better."

"It is a tragedy all around," I agreed.

"There is something else the woman said to me, Watson, that I have been pondering."

"What is that?"

"She said, before she forced me to take the child and leave her, that her original destination had been Australia and she cursed the luck that delayed her original ship, forcing her to take this one if she were to attempt an escape. She had not meant to come to England, but had had her destination chosen for her by circumstance."

"Ships do get delayed, from time to time."

"They do," he agreed, "and I did not think much of it at first, but now that I have had time to think it over, I wonder. I have been very busy as of late, what with vampires and sea monsters and golden tiaras, and I begin to suspect that some of these cases may have a single name behind them."

"Not the Mariner Priest?"

"The same, dear Watson," Holmes said. "There is a malicious subtlety at work that I am beginning to find familiar. Since I am also trying to keep watch on any possible activity he may be part of in London, he would have a vested interest in distracting me, and he has feelers and tendrils across most of Europe, make no mistake."

"But," I said, "America?"

"Well," Holmes admitted, "that is a stretch and thanks to a lack of data, I have precious little evidence to support such a theory. But I shall be on my guard, Watson. I recommend you do the same."

In an effort to unearth more of his precious data, Holmes developed a long correspondence with the authorities of Newburyport and Arkham, the two neighbouring towns to Innsmouth, and though the data coming back from America was always murky, it was enough to show that Holmes's conclusions were right at least about the foredoomed fate of that shrouded town.

Despite the police reports, another ship carrying the name *Bountiful Harvest* was reported sighted around reefs off the American Atlantic coast, though no ship with that name ever again entered any official registry.

Holmes's research also uncovered the dismissal of Marshal Eliot from the law enforcement service, two years after he was presumed by English authorities to have perished at sea. The names of many of the families in Innsmouth overlapped a great deal, however, and no substantial description was available, so this was far from conclusive.

Less than six months later, a man matching Eliot's description was killed in a bar fight in Newburyport. A claim ticket in his pocket led the Newburyport authorities to the discovery of a golden tiara at a local pawnshop, though if this was the very same as the one I had flung into the Thames, I could not guess. Last we heard, this now resides in a small museum in that same town, despite several well-funded attempts from well-to-do families in Innsmouth to purchase it.

Many months later, a Newburyport official responded to Holmes's continued telegrams by sending over a backdated marriage certificate between Brother Zachariah Eliot and one Lucja Nowak. A similarly backdated birth certificate for one Yosef Eliot, born of Zachariah and Lucja Eliot, came over a month after that. The actual date of birth was an estimate, but if taken at face value, suggested that the Lucja we had known – if this were the same woman – would have been at least two months pregnant on her arrival in England.

I think back to that evil-looking man, Eliot, shouting in the hall. *She thinks she can keep us from what's ours.* She'd left the tiara, and still they pursued her. It hadn't been the tiara that they'd been after at all. Holmes explained later that she must have known her own condition, and that this must have been the cause for her sudden and resolute sacrifice that prevented Holmes from rescuing her. The idea chills me as weather never could.

Certainly, as Holmes explained to me, Lucja Nowak knew something of what followed her, which explained the desperation of her theft. In addition to the tiara, Holmes's inquiries to the authorities at the American harbour of New Bedford found that she had sold several other, smaller gold items of similar quality to pay for her passage to England. Also, the nature of her pursuers was Holmes's only explanation for her bizarre demands for a deeper and more secure cell at the police station, though it did her little good.

Something else has preyed on my mind, as well, but I have dared not explain my fears to Holmes, and so engage his mathematical mind in my calculations. For even the numbers that revealed themselves to me does not entirely account for the four-day trip that the sailor, Carson, had described. I find myself thinking of the sacrifices to Dagon, and the chains to the depths, which leads my thoughts to something deeper than anything yet revealed. Something… larger, perhaps, out of man's sight. Lurking in the periphery of man's logic and reason.

I had requested that Holmes burn the fouled deerstalker's hat, but Holmes refused. He keeps it now in an oilskin bag, locked in a chest. He treats this artefact in much the same way as the picture of Irene Adler, and only during his blackest depression does he pull out this ill-stained token and refer to the Adventure of the Innsmouth Whaler.

Dear Dr Watson,

Thank you for your kind letter detailing ongoing events in London. I absolutely agree that it behoves both our causes to be as well informed on our enemy's movements as we can.

Vlad continues to increase our informational network, trading both information and supplies with the vampire clans in the surrounding countries to foster goodwill. It is a change in policy from the hostile one he has engendered for centuries, but one, I believe, that suits him better, though he is sometimes reluctant to admit it.

No definite news of the Mariner Priest's activities, but while we once believed that his activity was strongest in Switzerland or Germany, the focus of his attention, and possibly his physical location, seems to have moved further west, towards England. This cannot bode well for you and we recommend you keep on your strongest guard. Please pass our best wishes on to Mr Holmes.

Fondest wishes,
Mina

Part Three

THE ADVENTURE OF THE LUSTROUS PEARL

Chapter 11

THE PEARL

The following summer was an active time for London's only consulting detective, Mr Sherlock Holmes. In addition to the strange Adventure of the Blanched Soldier and the Tarlington Jewel Case, he also continued to delve into both the true identity and the activities of the Mariner Priest, but found little to satisfy him. Equally barren were his researches into Van Helsing, Lord Holmwood, or Quincey Morris, still missing in Australia. Dr John Seward and Jonathan Harker were, of course, dead, as well as Mina's friend, Lucy Westenra. Holmes had made a detailed study of the past lives of all the persons involved, including Mina's, but could find nothing illuminating there. Of the Mariner Priest, we heard nothing but rumours.

This past week, he'd done little on that front at all, instead maintaining an active correspondence with officials in France and Belgium regarding a series of international art thefts that buried our poor flat in diagrams, floor plans and maps so that paper covered every available surface. Holmes also had a habit of flinging records and notes in all directions when he was on a mad search for any one particular document, so that our problem elevated from inconvenience to organizational disaster. Mrs Hudson had absolutely refused to enter our rooms for days, and would only hand our meals across the threshold, for fear of further damaging some infinitely valuable yet woefully mistreated document.

As such, it was my beleaguered task when I rose in the evening to try and push enough papers around on the table to make room for the tea service left out for me.

"Take care, Watson," Holmes murmured without lifting his face from an article on the nature of pearls. Right next to him, precariously balanced and in danger of tipping over a nearby coffee cup, sat a microscope with a large pearl on the examination plate. "Those articles you cavalierly thrust aside may hold the key to over a score of burglaries." Holmes peered into the microscope and frowned. He'd presumably gotten the pearl from one of the victimized museums but he'd refused all evening to answer any question regarding it.

"Just as you have pushed aside the manuscript pages I tried to bring to your attention?" I said tartly.

"The write-up for the Kittredge abduction?" Holmes reached out a long arm and unerringly put his hand on the manuscript in question. He tilted it just enough to scan the title page before unceremoniously dropping it with an expression of distaste back onto the table. "Another of your overly romantic titles, I see. 'The Adventure of the Bloodthirsty Baron'. Really, Watson.

Terrible. It is just as well that you cannot publish this one for fear of exposing vampires to the rest of the world. Another of your classified dossiers, hidden from the world."

"It was the case itself that was terrible," I said. "Horrid business." It had been both thrilling and horrific to write, including as it did the murder of our associate, Shinwell Johnson, as well as the return and subsequent staking of the Baron Adelbert Gruner.

"On that, at least," Holmes said, "we agree. Poorly handled from start to finish. Bungled from the very moment I first met Baron Gruner over the De Merville case last year. A true reasoner would have recognized the supernatural nature of the threat the baron represented the *first* time around! His unusual influence over others, especially women, flying in the face of his sordid reputation. The appearance of Kitty Winter alone should have given me my first clue. That profound pallor, even for a woman of the streets. And those blazing eyes! Or the fact that our good baron made all his appointments after dark, had no fear of burglars, and possessed hearing keen enough to hear my intrusion into his rooms even when you were distracting him. Any one of these should have told me that something beyond the norm was afoot. I might as well have left it in the fumbling hands of Scotland Yard!"

"We did not yet know of the *existence* of vampires, Holmes," I said. "How could any man, even you, deduce such a thing on such flimsy evidence?" We'd encountered the Baron Adelbert Gruner during the series of incidents I later penned as 'The Adventure of the Illustrious Client' and come away from the affair without any knowledge of vampires and thinking the adventure quite concluded. This new story I'd written featuring the baron's return would never see the light of day, of course.

"If I'd listened to my own lectures, Watson," Holmes went on, "I'd have seen the truth of it at once, including the baron's recovery and return." He lit his pipe and drew morosely on the tip. "I begin to doubt myself and my powers, Watson. Had I seen the obvious signs, Shinwell Johnson might not have suffered the ultimate penalty for my gross incompetence."

"Unfair, Holmes!" I objected. "The baron has committed his last crime, thanks to your deductions. No man could have done more."

"Perhaps," he said. His expression was as phlegmatic as ever, but I, who knew him so well, could see he was still deeply affected by his doubts. "Though we may perhaps have a chance to do better over at Highgate, if you are not too busy to come? It is a short cab ride."

"Highgate Cemetery?" I said.

"Yes. We had a note from Miss Winter this afternoon." He strode over to the sideboard, pushed aside a stack of foolscap pinned down with an upside-down teacup and pulled the note out from the bottom.

"Here," he said, handing it over. The paper was stationery from Highgate itself, marked with a childish scrawl.

FUNNY MURDUR AT HIGHGATE. MAN BIT
AND STABBED. BIT MANY TIMES.

"Terrible command of the English language," I said, frowning.

"Funny murder, indeed. But there seems little doubt it must be serious."

"Indeed," Holmes said. "Written hastily, too, if I am any judge. She is quite right that it is urgent, too. Surely you see the significance of someone being bitten multiple times?"

"Multiple vampires?"

"That is one possibility," Holmes agreed. "Which is disturbing enough, considering how competently the two of them, overseeing the teams that you have rather fancifully named the 'Midnight Watch', have kept watch over the graveyards and dealt with such newly created vampires that arise. But what is far more likely – and more dangerous – is that one vampire has been feeding on this man for some time, meaning…"

"Meaning we have an elder vampire on our hands," I said, horrified. "Dracula said that only elder vampires are capable of that kind of strategy and planning."

"Well," Holmes said, "an older vampire, at least. Between you and me, I find Dracula's nomenclature a trifle imprecise. He is intelligent, but not, perhaps, scientific. I find some of the reasoning spurious. We know from experience that there is a period of nearly incoherent savagery at the very beginning. We have Dracula's assertion that this lasts only a few days, possibly weeks, but typically causes some destruction of the psyche and personality. But not the memory. I find that suggestive. I suggest the transformation, mentally, as a kind of brain fever. We also know that the Mariner Priest has found a way to alleviate or prevent that condition entirely."

"Van Helsing, you mean," I said.

"I am not yet convinced of that," Holmes said. "While it is certainly a possibility, we have not proved it. So, we have the feral *fledglings* that crawl out of the grave, hungry for blood and mindless in their pursuit of it. Miss Winter, Johnson, and the Midnight Watch deal exclusively with this sort."

I shuddered, remembering the timeless period when I'd been such a mindless beast, a fledgling vampire, mindless and savage.

"We have two exceptions to this rule," Holmes went on, following, as he so often did, my train of thought. "Yourself and Mina: transformed, but mentally intact. Then we have those that have recovered from this brain fever and have regained their reason, if not their personality or morals, such as Mary. Sorry, Doctor."

I had flinched at this casual mention of Mary, but nodded and waved for him to continue.

"Perhaps we should refer to these as *mature*?" He looked at me and frowned. "Not very scientific *or* poetic, is it? Well, I don't insist on this terminology, but clearly something is needed. Finally, we have Dracula himself, who boasts considerable powers that neither you nor any other vampire we know of share. The quintessential *elder* vampire, I should say."

"Yes," I said. I thought of how Dracula had paralysed me with his gaze the night we'd first met, though Holmes had not fallen under that same spell. Also, Dracula's control over the horse on that wild ride.

"Our Mariner Priest, of course, doesn't fall very neatly into any of these categories. If Dracula is correct and it is Van Helsing, either Dracula met him and did not realize the man was a vampire

– which is unlikely – or Van Helsing has not been a vampire that many years. Also, we have yet to reconcile his hatred of vampires with the Mariner Priest's use of them. Yet, whoever our Mariner Priest is, he seems to have an understanding of vampires that far surpasses Dracula's, especially in the nature of their transformation. How he has come by this knowledge is, I feel, at the very heart of the mystery. Dracula's other theory, that this must be the work of a mature vampire, one capable of reasoning and planning, has merit, too, but also some difficulties. Certainly whoever we face has no moral compunctions, such as you do, about feeding off their fellow man."

"Clearly this is of a most serious magnitude," I said. "You should have woken me. You say this body has lain all day?"

"It has," Holmes said, "but only because there is an even more pressing part of this case that required my attention before the body. This pearl came with the note." He handed over the pearl he'd been studying. "Does this strike you as remarkable?"

"Yes," I said, "quite. It is certainly one of the largest and most lustrous pearls I've ever seen."

"The very same description you gave it the last time," Holmes said grimly, "during the Sign of the Four."

"Surely you can't mean that?" I said, feeling suddenly very cold and hollow inside. "This is one of Mary's pearls?"

"Ah, we come immediately to the heart of the matter," Holmes said. "She never sold them, then?"

I shook my head. "No. We both agreed that such a memento of our first meeting should always be kept and we never had a serious need to part with them. They were more precious to us than our wedding rings. We kept them in the same box Mary had always used, but they disappeared when Mary..." I stopped, turning the pearl over and over again in my fingers. "That is... when she left." An ocean of darkness churned above me, pressing down with a crushing and destructive pressure I could hardly bear. Mary's laugh when I'd seen her last, just before she'd been party to murder, was like an icicle of blackest pitch. Dark and terrible in a way that was entirely unlike my own dear Mary.

Holmes's face was serious. "I *am* sorry, dear friend. I did not wish to bring up an unpleasant memory until I was sure."

"How can you be sure?" I said hoarsely. "One pearl looks much like another! Perhaps it is just a lookalike?"

"So I hoped," Holmes said. "Which is why this portentous sphere of calcium carbonate has been such an intense study for the past few hours. Jewellers categorize pearls into eight distinct shapes: round, semi-round, button, drop, pear, oval, baroque, and circled. Often, they will be crafted into pins and necklaces and the like to disguise the fact that they are *not* round. Perfectly round pearls of this lustre and size are exceedingly rare. In truth, I was half-convinced this was one of the same pearls at the start, but I needed to be sure. There are several other indicators, but that is the largest."

"But how could this be, Holmes?"

"Finding one in connection to a case with evidence of the equally rare 'mature vampire' must immediately make us look for the presence of the one vampire we know to be in possession of such a rare trinket. And if we look for Mary, we must also keep our most vigilant watch for the Mariner Priest. He created her and she is very likely his instrument. We have been waiting these long months for the Mariner Priest to make a bold move and I sense this may be it. I shall take just a moment to write out telegrams to my other agents of the Midnight Watch that keep our vigil over the city's cemeteries and morgues, to give them warning."

I drank my evening's breakfast quickly, the warm blood from the butcher's shop both appalling and intoxicating in equal measure. I set the still warm cup aside and made preparations with a sense of great foreboding. Seeing Holmes open the left drawer of his desk and pull out the black revolver that held his silver bullets, I retrieved my revolver, as well. I also added to our armaments my heavy silver-topped walking stick, which had a small bit of silver at the tip, but also a heavy weight of it at the head. I'd had a durable, leather cover especially made in order to hide my unusual and extravagant amount of silver, and also because handling it myself would be excruciating without it. Still, the cover could come off in an instant, when needed and the stick made a comforting weight. We had, of course, commissioned two of these weapons. The thought that these might be brought to bear against the woman who had once been my wife sent a horrible chill through me.

While Holmes dug out the dark lantern from behind a collection of books and monographs on poisons, I selected my gloves, my heaviest waterproof and my largest brimmed hat. I thought it unlikely for an excursion of this magnitude to come to a conclusion before the sun came up again.

Somersby met us near the southern entrance to Highgate, as had Shinwell Johnson so many times before. Our newest recruit to the Midnight Watch, Nigel Terrance Somersby was a dark-haired, bearded young man, stocky and well-groomed. He looked nervously at us through a pair of silver pince-nez, his heavy eyebrows drawn together. A light rain came down, further shadowing the already murky London around us.

"Mr Holmes," Somersby said as soon as we stepped out of the cab, "Dr Watson. This way, please. Most likely we'll have until morning before anyone else discovers the body. It's been hard enough keeping people away this long." Somersby was new to this work, inducted into our little organization to replace Johnson at Miss Winter's suggestion. I had my doubts, as he was visibly unnerved by the whole situation.

"The official force will have their chance soon enough," Holmes said. "Better to have a look at it now, even in the dark, than to wait for the Scotland Yarders to remove all traces."

Holmes looked at Somersby carefully, walking around him as if the man were a clue of the utmost importance himself. He was looking, I knew, at the man's face and neck for any signs of Somersby having been bitten. This strange examination didn't do much for Somersby's nerves, and his eyebrows shot up as Holmes prowled around him.

"I see no signs of infection," Holmes said. He shot me a glance for confirmation and I shook my head, indicating that I, too, detected nothing untoward. I could tell by Somersby's nervous scent that he was still very much human.

"Now, Mr Somersby," Holmes said, "if you would be so

good as to lead us to the crime scene."

"Of course, Mr Holmes. The body… that is… man…"

"Come now," Holmes chided him. "If the presence of a mere dead body is going to unnerve you, you'll be of no use to us when they start digging their way out and running around London trying to eat the citizenry."

"Don't worry, young man," I said. "I know it's unnerving to be dealing in such affairs, but it does get easier." I reached out to lay a hand on his shoulder.

"Don't touch me!" he yelled, flinching and drawing away.

"Have no concern," Holmes said to him. "I assure you that Dr Watson is one of the most morally steadfast men, afflicted or otherwise, that you are ever likely to meet."

"That may be," Somersby said, "but I don't want any of them to touch me." I let my hand drop, understanding all too clearly what he meant by 'them'.

"Take no offence, Watson," Holmes said. "His introduction to the affliction of vampirism was every bit as painful as your own, perhaps more so. Somersby was forced to retire his mother after she tried to murder the rest of the family."

"I understand," I said stiffly. "A horrible experience. My deepest condolences."

"My father and sister didn't see her," Somersby whispered. "Not the way I did."

"A horrible experience," Holmes agreed without any trace of sympathy, "which makes you the perfect recruit, Somersby. Miss Winter and I were in perfect agreement on that score. Where is she now?"

"Why…" the man started, then fell silent, looking back and forth between the two of us.

"What is it?" Holmes snapped.

"Why is it this man gets to live?" Somersby blurted out, "and Winter, too… while my mother got a stake in the chest? Why?" The man's voice was pained.

"I thought Miss Winter explained it to you," Holmes said impatiently. "Indeed, I should think the mere fact that Miss Winter bothered to explain anything to you at all instead of opening your throat would be an explanation enough for most people, wouldn't it? Most vampires wouldn't bother speaking. Your mother didn't."

"Holmes!" I said. I could see he was impatient with any delay to getting to the crime scene, and gave little to no consideration to what traumatic experiences might have brought this man to us.

"I should think," Holmes said, "that the distinction is obvious. Ninety-nine vampires out of a hundred come from the grave with a taste for human blood that, once indulged, can never be quenched. They feed on nothing else, and continue to feed on nothing else for as long as they live. Since there is no court of law that can touch them, it falls to us to apply the only effective solution. As it did with your mother. Vampires that do not murder have nothing to fear from us." He fixed the younger man with a steely gaze. "Is that clear enough for you?"

"Yes, sir," the man said miserably.

"Now," Holmes said. "Where is Miss Winter?"

"This way," Somersby said.

We were hidden from the entrance itself, and any attendants, by a slight curve in the stone wall. At this time of night, of course, the cemetery was closed. Somersby looked around circumspectly, and seeing no sign of anyone else on the street, led us over the four-foot wall. We dropped down onto a lawn of grass and walked round a row of poplar trees and onto one of the many wide lanes that ran through the carefully tended grounds of Highgate Cemetery. I could hear and smell the teeming life all around us. Highgate was as much a wildlife preserve as a burial site. A pair of foxes worrying at a fresh kill, a small bird of some sort, near a distant crypt, stopped and watched us warily as we passed.

As always, I was struck by the grandeur, the open beauty of the place, as we passed stone angels, scrollwork-etched crosses and even an obelisk with roses cut into the stone to match the garden of real rose bushes around it, the colours dimmed by the night. It must have been quite a blind and gloomy expedition for Holmes and Somersby, but darkness was no navigational obstacle to me. Even in the dark, everything jumped out into sharp relief as if cut out by an engraver's etching tool. When the moon broke from the clouds, the intermittent rain transformed everything into a shimmering wonder.

We walked through the West Cemetery, skirting around the Egyptian Avenue and Circle of Lebanon, though we could see the ancient cedar tree that sat in the centre. Somersby led us deeper into grounds, where there were fewer markers, and more of them dripping curtains of woven ivy. The decorative walls were made of brick, rather than stone.

A dark shape detached from a moon-shadowed row of beeches with a suddenness that made me start and pull my lips back from my teeth. I wasn't used to being taken by surprise, but vampires are reliant on scent, and give off very little scent themselves. This probably accounted for some of the disconcerting feelings that Miss Winter always stirred in me, if only some. We did not know all the details of how Miss Winter had come through the transformation, but clearly she had not come through untouched. I had Holmes's word that she no longer represented a danger to the citizenry of London, but I had my doubts.

"Finally!" Miss Winter said sharply. "Took your time, didn't you?" Then, without waiting for an answer, said, "You have it, then?" She was both paler and fiercer than ever, yet worn with the sorrow and sin that had made her bitter and fragile. She was an unsettling creature, ageless now, as I was, yet I could not imagine her lasting out the year. A dun coat, which had probably never been cleaned, hung from her restlessly moving gaunt frame. A matching hat, equally shapeless, covered her head, doing very little to restrain the wild mane of fiery hair beneath. I knew that Holmes paid both her and Somersby well, so the fact that she chose, still, to dress like a tramp of the streets was difficult to fathom. She carried a small, shapeless and colourless moleskin pouch in one hand that she worried at with her thumb.

"Miss Winter," Somersby said, "perhaps now isn't—"

"Just you hush!" Miss Winter said. "I'll have what he promised me, by cripes!"

"I have the second artefact here," Holmes said. "Just as we agreed." He took a packet out of his coat pocket, unwrapped the paper to reveal a shard of bone inside without touching it. He slowly held it out so that she might take the fragment herself.

She snatched it up eagerly, her eyes blazing. For a moment, the moon shone on her firebrand hair, and she looked alive, vibrant and beautiful in the way she must have before the streets of London and Adelbert Gruner had gotten a hold of her.

She undid the strings of the moleskin pouch and peered inside. "Oh, Porky," she said, her expression softening. "You deserved better, you fat, lovely, cunning, good-hearted devil. You deserved better than what you got." Then she turned a wicked grin on the shard Holmes had just given her. "And you... you cunning, dirty devil... well, now I have you both!" She tucked the fragment inside and tied the strings of her pouch up again.

She seemed a wild thing herself, and while I had Holmes's word that she had no human blood on her hands, it still seemed to me that she had a savage, ferocious core in her that would never be tamed, that would always be a danger, both to herself and those around her. Miss Winter, was, in my estimation, always one short step away from a life of violent murder. Still, she had not taken it as of yet.

"Come on, then," she said. "The body you're after is down the path this way. They left it in one of the unused graves." The expression of fierce anger reasserted itself on her face as she turned away from us.

Somersby watched her leave, looking even more unsettled than before. He leaned close to Holmes and whispered, "What was it that you gave her, Mr Holmes?"

Holmes's austere face betrayed a flicker of doubt and misgiving, but only for a second. "Miss Winter and I entered into an arrangement which involved several conditions on both our parts. One of my responsibilities was to procure her two keep-sakes from the two men in her life she wished to remember."

"I knew one man," Somersby said. "Porky – that is, Shinwell Johnson. But who, Mr Holmes, is the other?"

"The man responsible for Shinwell Johnson's death," Holmes said, "as well as shattering and twisting Miss Winter's own life, causing her imprisonment and then transformation. Baron Adelbert Gruner."

I shook my head. "One man she loved, and the other she hated."

"And possibly also loved," Holmes added. "And it may be anyone's guess as to which emotion runs the strongest, for I doubt that she herself knows. Vampire or not, Kitty Winter is still a woman first, which perhaps should give us some hope."

I shook my head. For a man of pure logic, his attitude towards women was never entirely logical, at least not to me.

"She scares me," Somersby admitted, "though I'd not have her know it."

"I'm afraid," I said to Somersby, "that you'll have to speak much quieter than that if you wish to be discreet. Miss Winter is vampire enough to hear you as clearly as if you'd whispered into her own ear. Indeed, I could have heard you from the other side of the wall."

"Then Miss Winter would have heard…" He went pale.

"I'm afraid so," I said, pitying the poor man.

"I didn't mean…" he started.

"Come!" Holmes said. "We have precious little time."

Somersby swallowed his fear and led us on. We caught up with Miss Winter down the path, near a swath of land sheltered on either side by fifty feet of towering trees. Graves were dug on both sides of the road, waiting with dark empty mouths for the tragedies that might fill them. The body lay in one of the closest graves, just as she'd said. Holmes waved everyone back, then crouched and lit the dark lantern so that he could get a better look at the ground, though the rain must have obliterated most traces.

"We don't know much about him," Somersby said. "But we have a little information. He had a wallet with some money, one pound fifteen, and a cheque issued from the Highgate Cemetery's bank to Victor Apligian, which we take to be the dead man. The cheque is issued for twenty pounds. He's also got correspondence that corroborates our theory as to his identity, an envelope addressed from Victor Apligian to Mason Hardweather, but there is no letter in it and the envelope has no postmark yet. The sender's address is a place on North Hill Street, not far from here. The destination is on Strait Road, near the Albert Dock."

"Likely the North Hill Street address is Apligian's home address, since there is no postmark."

"That was our thought as well, Mr Holmes. It's our guess that he was one of the groundskeepers here."

"I quite agree," Holmes said, still looking down. "You've handled that part adequately enough, but you've trampled all traces of evidence around the grave here. Usually wet earth is excellent for leaving impressions, but a pack of buffalo might have run through here."

"Didn't know it was a crime scene, did I?" Miss Winter said. "Not until after I found the body, anyway."

"I did take care during my approach," Somersby said quickly.

"Not enough," Holmes said.

"How did you discover it?" I said. "Surely you don't check all the graves every night?"

"Oh no," Somersby said. "It would take an army for that. But we do keep tabs, per Mr Holmes's instructions, on the doings in the local morgues, the hospitals, police stations and here in the cemeteries. At least in this section of London. I gather other agents or teams of the Midnight Watch do the same in other areas."

"Quite," Holmes agreed.

"A complete accident we discovered him at all," Somersby admitted. "We were walking past and Kitty smelled him. We could just as easily have missed him."

"And did you find any?" I asked.

"No, sir," Somersby said. "Only the body. Kitty says there are no signs of him rising."

"He stinks, he does," Miss Winter said.

Holmes finished his examination of the ground. "As I feared, the rain and other footprints have made it quite impossible to tell for certain, but I think it likely that this man died elsewhere and the body was brought here. Come, Watson, help me bring the body up into the light."

Victor Apligian had been a tall man, just short of six feet, but not overly burly, and no great burden. Handsome and boyish-looking, with black curly hair, wide mutton chops, and a face that might have been well-featured and affable, before death had drained it of expression. His clothes were somewhat more expensively cut than I expected from a gardener and workman, and I should have been surprised if his brown pinstripe suit did not turn out to be the most expensive ensemble he owned. There was no sign of hat, overcoat or umbrella. That he'd been bitten was evident enough: there were no less than three pairs of bite marks on the neck. But this paled in comparison to his bloodstained shirt front.

"Gunshot wound," Holmes murmured as he examined the body. "This much blood from the gunshot wound means he was certainly alive when shot, making the bullet, not the vampire, the cause of death… Curious. Still, there are multiple bites, with marks of lip rouge both on his mouth and on the bites. There are several more on the collar of his shirt, some of them quite faded. Please bring the light closer, Doctor; I do not have your eyes. There, yes. There are marks on his hands consistent with constant digging, which confirms his employment."

When Holmes had finished his careful examination with the swiftness that was particular to him, he said, "I agree with Miss Winter. Lividity and rigor are both normal. No signs of transformation or infection. Watson?"

"I concur," I said. "There will be no complications about a burial, at least." The catatonic state of an infected body, with the absence of both bloat and rot, would be a much milder smell in that case.

"Very good," Holmes said. "Perhaps the interior of the grave will still hold something of interest." Holmes took the lantern down into the grave to look at the ground where the man had lain.

"A funeral is bad enough, ain't it?" Kitty Winter said, appearing suddenly at my elbow. "But better that than a funeral where your dearly departed tries to open your throat and don't we both know it? Not that I wouldn't have liked to try and bury dear old Adelbert once and for all, only I ain't never got the chance." She caught my eye and I could not quite meet that feral, blazing gaze.

"You make me wonder anew," I said to her, "the wisdom of having vampires take part in a watch over their own."

"Do those doubts include yourself?" she said hotly. "Or just those of us from the gutter?"

"Of course they include my own person," I said. "How could they not?"

"Who else could you give a duty like this to?" she said with a bitter humour in her voice. "Who else better knows the dangers? Who else would stand for it? I don't mind, though. Least I got Somersby to get butcher's blood for me and a place to sleep during the day. Better than the poor sod that did this. Mr Holmes will give them a pretty ending, won't he? Rotter is as good as staked already."

"We will do what we must, of course," I said coldly.

"The pearl," Holmes said. "You found it in his pocket?"

"Yes," Somersby said. "The other items from his pockets I have here, including the cheque and letter I mentioned. The rest don't seem to be terribly significant, but knowing your methods, I have saved them here." He held out a heavy envelope.

"Excellent," Holmes said, taking it over near the lantern to examine the contents. "Hmm... a few coins in an otherwise unremarkable wallet... As you said, not much extraordinary here."

"No, sir," Somersby said.

"What is this? A sealskin pouch filled with... yes, ship's tobacco..."

"It was inside there that I found the pearl," Somersby said.

"Did you?" said Holmes. "There may be hope for you yet. Come, Watson. We have discovered all there is to learn here. Mr Somersby, Miss Winter, please continue your vigilance here in the graveyard and at the mortuaries, and alert me of any outbreaks."

I turned back to Miss Winter, still struggling to contain the helpless anger that her words had churned up within me, only to discover that she had slipped away.

Chapter 12

FAIRVIEW HOUSE

"If we are to continue having clandestine midnight meetings in the heart of cemeteries," Holmes said once we'd returned to Baker Street, "we shall have to locate those silk masks of yours from the Milverton affair." Holmes lit his pipe and puffed on it luxuriously.

"What are our next steps?" I asked.

"I shall need to check the docks," Holmes said, "to look for any sign that the Mariner Priest may have returned, possibly bringing Mary with him, which would be one explanation for the facts."

"And the other?"

"Why, that she never left England in the first place."

"Holmes! Surely that can't be true. We have kept careful tabs over all the vampire activity in London. The cemeteries, the morgues, even the butcher shops…"

"Yet we have not been entirely successful," Holmes said, "for while there have been few vampire incidents outside of the Baron

Gruner affair and those directly related to the Mariner Priest, that is not the same as having none. So there are at least a few vampires that continue to remain undiscovered in London. She might be one of those. Or she may have left London for the countryside and now returned. Even our Midnight Watch cannot keep tabs on all of England. It is a Herculean enough task to attempt to do so on bustling London. It is also possible that Mary did not depart on the Mariner Priest's ship at all. But I must make absolutely certain. The Mariner Priest has been guilty of more than a few subterfuges in his past, to say the least." He had his pipe going well now, and was staring out into the blackness of the night.

"But, Holmes, where is Mary, then? Can we say for certain that she was the one that committed this foul murder? Could it have been a random attack?"

"Watson, could it be that you don't see the significance of the lip rouge?"

"I'm sure that I am very slow."

He turned away from the window to face me. "It's the most suggestive detail we've yet encountered in this case."

"I see that it identifies the vampire as a woman, and one likely to have returned to an outwardly civilized, if risqué, appearance, if she wears lip rouge. That's how you knew it was a… what did you call it… mature vampire?"

"Precisely," Holmes said.

"I see. And also because of the repeated bites over time. A newly born vampire would have drained him dry in one feeding. The rareness of mature vampires and the pearl are what make you think it's my Mary."

"It pains me to say this, Watson, but she is hardly 'your Mary' anymore. But it's possible she's no longer the Mariner Priest's creature, either. We still know precious little about how he manages to create vampires in secret and accelerate them through the bestial stage, or what repercussions that process may have. There are many indications that he also has some method of controlling them that we don't understand, but that is mere conjecture now. I am getting ahead of myself. My first step shall be the docks. We've long known that the greatest part of the vampire population took ship with the Mariner Priest when Dracula started hunting them here. That, compounded with the presence of a tobacco smoked predominantly by sailors strikes me as rather too much to be a coincidence."

"Holmes," I said suddenly, "there was no pipe! What does he smoke the tobacco in?"

"I never get your limits, Watson. Yes, that struck me, as well. The missing pipe is one question. The other is why there is only one pearl. If we suppose that the pearl is some sort of payment…"

"Payment?"

"Why else part with just one pearl, when we know Mary had six? It seems unlikely that it could have been stolen, or it would be more likely that all six would be together. Also, Mary is now a quite formidable person, making theft even more unlikely. It *was* six originally?"

"Yes, the original six Mary showed us. There were six others in Sholto's story, still affixed to a chaplet, but that chaplet never resurfaced."

"Quite so. No, I read the single pearl as payment on Mary's

part, either for services rendered, or perhaps services to *be* rendered."

"If she could coerce him to let her feed, why would she need to buy anything? He would be putty in her hands."

"Yes," Holmes said thoughtfully, "the vaunted coercion of the vampire's bite. More addictive than opium and twice as deadly. We really do need more data on those particulars. Are you sure you wouldn't care to participate in a small experiment along those lines?"

"Holmes!"

"Well, perhaps not," Holmes said, waving a long, thin hand in dismissal. "But there is something I need you to do while I am gone."

"What is that?"

"I should like you to contact Apligian's family."

"What information am I to get?"

"The usual," Holmes said. "Everything you can. Perhaps when we know as much as there is to know of Victor Apligian, there will be something informative in it for us."

"You wish me to be the one to break the news to the family?"

"I will bow to your judgement and discretion on that score. What I wish is for you to get data. There is too much that is cloudy about this matter, and Victor Apligian is at the heart of it."

"We should notify the police, as well, Holmes."

"And have Scotland Yard tramping all over everything?"

"This is not just one risen corpse that we can make disappear without explanation or consideration," I said. "They have their duties, same as we do. They should know about the body, at least."

"Very well, Doctor," he said. "I bow to your conscience. Send them a note, if you wish."

We stared for a moment into the fire while Holmes worked his pipe. I lit a cigarette. Like so many other things, my transformation had changed the nature of smoking, since I barely needed to breathe. (I had also discovered that the idea of vampires not needing to breathe, like so much other vampire lore, was slightly mistaken. I'd done a little experimentation after our discovery that vampires could be forced into a catatonic state by submersion. The truth is that a vampire *barely* needs to breathe. I'd discovered that I was capable of holding my breath for nearly ten minutes at a time, which accounted for vampires being able to sleep whole nights in enclosed spaces, such as coffins. But I couldn't hold it indefinitely.) However, the thoughts swam so disturbingly in my head that I found after some minutes that my cigarette, unattended to, had burned out completely.

"Holmes," I said suddenly as a new thought occurred to me. "I don't suppose it could have been Kitty Winter herself?"

"I think it highly unlikely," Holmes said at last.

"It's Mary," I said, feeling a weight of misery settling more firmly upon me. "At the blasted Mariner Priest's direction, no doubt!" I hit the dining room table hard enough rattle all the china dangerously, and even prompt an outraged and perfectly audible "My word!" from Mrs Hudson downstairs.

"Watson," Holmes said gently. "Whatever can be done *will* be done, I assure you."

"And if we *do* find her, Holmes," I said. "What then? All the other vampires we've dealt with to date have been feral beasts, with little left of the human lives they once led, or else cunning monsters like the baron. What if she's still got some piece of my Mary left inside of her... only..." I lifted my hands, now cold, dangerous weapons in their own right.

Holmes put a warm hand on my shoulder in comfort. "We shall do," he said, "what our conscience dictates, as always."

"That's what I'm afraid of," I said miserably.

Holmes changed into his Captain Basil outfit – one of the few that did not require face make-up – and was out the door and into the London night before the hour was out. I was familiar enough with his methods to know that there would be no telling when he might return.

I could not imagine that the house's inhabitants would take kindly to a visit in the middle of the night, but neither did I wish to sit around in our empty lodgings without further information, when every possible bit of news was of such personal importance to me. I left without delay, but took my heavy daytime clothes with me. There seemed little reason to take a cab, and I covered the four miles or so from Baker Street with little difficulty.

The Apligian home was Fairview House, a great, dark house on North Hill Street close to Highgate Cemetery, where the dead man had tended the grounds. While not a manse, by any stretch of the word, it was a larger abode than I might have expected for a man with such a modest vocation. The place was by no means in excellent repair, however. With ramshackle boards and peeling paint, it had clearly fallen on ill times. Examining the outside and lawn yielded little of interest. I had managed to spend some time with both the walk and my examination, but there were still many hours before reasonable folk would be up and about. I found an alcove on the opposite side of the street where I could view the house and settled in to wait.

The night still held sway, covering the street and buildings with its sepia tones, when a figure shifted on the roof of a nearby surgery, and I realized that I was not the only one who kept vigil over the Apligian home. The man clambered down from the building, showing himself to be an absurdly tall, lanky man wearing an oversized beaver hat. He had a stern, reddish, weathered, and remorseless face, dominated by a huge, scarred beak of a nose. The long black hair that hung out from underneath the beaver cap was tightly braided, with beads and trinkets of bleached bone woven into it. He wore a black suit with much wear and dust on it, far too short for his oversized body so that four to five inches of wrist and ankle stuck out the ends. He landed easily in the street, despite the fact that his feet were unhampered by boot or shoe of any kind.

He stood for a moment further regarding the house that was also the subject of my interest, then turned and looked to the east where the shadowy bulk of the buildings could be made out against the sky. Not long until sunrise now. I remained motionless as he strode past my own hiding spot and disappeared into the alley behind a bathhouse. I could detect little scent off of him other than a slight whiff of dustiness. That the man must have been a vampire, I had no doubt.

That made two in this case already, straining to breaking point

Holmes's assertion that the average Londoner was more likely to discover an orangutan than a vampire. I slipped out of my doorway to follow him down the street, and then peered carefully around the corner of the bathhouse into the alley. Only to find… nothing. I moved silently into the alley. Of course there was no scent to follow, but there were also no marks in the soot and dirt of the alley, and no sound whatsoever of footsteps. I went down the next turn in the alley, looked at the walls for signs of ascent, but found nothing. The man had utterly vanished.

By the time I could approach the house and ring the front door bell, the baleful sun had been in ascension for hours. Its forceful presence was an uncomfortable hot pressure, even clouded as it was by the greyish London sky, and despite the protection of the heavy hat, gloves and great overcoat I had brought for just such an eventuality.

"Forgive my intrusion," I said to the woman who opened the door. "You are, perhaps, Mrs Apligian?"

"Miss," she snapped. "Who are you?"

The woman had even features, a dark complexion, and serious brown eyes that spoke of both hardship and the fortitude to endure such hardships, and more. Her hair was also dark, so dark that there was a sheen of blue in it like the raven's wing. She looked at me boldly. She had a fine, proud bearing and wore a simple dress, but cut from a finer cloth than most.

"You're not Victor Apligian's wife, then," I said, handing over my card. "His sister, then? "

"Sister," she agreed reluctantly, looking briefly down at the card, then back at my face. "Flora Apligian. Something has happened to Victor, hasn't it?" Her brown eyes clouded over and she was forced to look away.

There could be no dissembling in the face of such honesty and pain. "Yes, I'm afraid so."

"What's he done now?"

"Your brother's been shot and murdered, Miss Apligian. His body was discovered at the bottom of a grave in Highgate. I'm very sorry."

She sagged in the doorway for just a shadow of a moment, and then straightened again, the firm picture of English gentry. "Well," she said primly, "I suppose you'd better come in."

The solemn, once-grand interior of the house now matched the broken-down exterior. She led me across a worn and dirty parquet floor, through a hall lit only by a single gas lamp and some stained-glass skylights several storeys overhead that drenched everything in deepest blue. The place had a disused, musty scent to it. Dust lay everywhere, except for the trails shuffled through by the passage of just a very few people. I could see only three different sets of footprints, one clearly the lady's.

We passed through a stout oak door that swung silently shut behind us to leave us in a large vaulted study covered all over with shelves of books. On this side, the door was hidden, backed with more bookshelves, and I might have been hard-pressed to locate the door if it had not just shut behind me. The only sunlight in the place came from small stained-glass windows two storeys up, near the ceiling. It was something of an establishment made for my kind, dark and gloomy. I found it easy to avoid any trickle of light that came down, for the entire room seemed to be bordered in shadows.

There were signs the room had been cleaned recently, but not very well; only the spots within easy reach. I could see cobwebs and dust higher up in the room that would require a ladder to clean. It had once been a very nice room, cosy and warm, but was now very quiet and sorrowful. This was a fallen household, once great, and now struggling to keep something of its grandeur. But fallen as it was, it was not the house of a groundskeeper. Not, at least, any groundskeeper I'd ever known. There were several photographs of the family on the walls, showing Victor himself in life, as well as Miss Apligian, and a narrow-faced austere man that must have been their father.

An elderly butler tended to the fireplace – a job usually administered by a servant somewhat lower on the household hierarchy. He looked back once, briefly, showing a stiff, round, elderly face, and then kept on working. Since he showed no sign of coming to take my hat and coat, I hung them myself on a deserted coat rack in the corner. The rack had a thin patina of dust, as well.

"Tea, I think, Merton," Miss Apligian said. The butler got stiffly to his feet, then nodded with a facial expression that had nothing of cheer or animation, only a dreary heaviness that seemed to match the rest of the house. His footprints, when he left, were square-toed, of average size, precisely matching one set of tracks I'd seen in the dust. If Flora Apligian accounted for one, and the butler the other, that made Victor himself the likely match for the third set. The Apligians didn't seem to get many visitors.

"I always thought you might come here someday, Dr Watson," Miss Apligian said. "You and your celebrated friend. But I will candidly admit that I *never* thought it would be in Victor's defence. Tell me truthfully, Doctor, are your friend's powers exaggerated in all those stories of yours?"

"I've always found Holmes's feats unbelievable enough without adding anything of my own, Miss Apligian," I said gravely.

"Frankly, I do find them difficult to believe. We shall see. At any rate, I shall not try to deceive you. Indeed, why should I? I myself have done nothing wrong, and there is little you can do to add to the embarrassment that Victor has already brought upon this house, which is well-known to so many persons it would be hard to keep it secret at any rate. For I can tell you without exaggeration that Victor ran with a seedy crowd, and his untimely end does not surprise me. It saddens me, of course, but no... I can't say 'surprise' would be the appropriate word. How public is his murder likely to be?"

"I can offer what discretion as I may," I said, "but there is little I can do about the official police, which I must frankly warn you are likely to be here later today."

"Of course," she said. "Mr Sherlock Holmes is working on locating my brother's murderer, then?"

"Yes."

"Does he hope to find him? Or is this one of the cases that does not make it into *The Strand*?"

"We shall be the very souls of discretion, I assure you," I said.

"I have never used someone's name when they have requested otherwise. Our success is still a question, to be sure, but I have seen Holmes untangle cases far more complex than this."

Merton had returned with the tea, which he served. After this, he busied himself in a haphazard tidying of the other side of the room. Miss Apligian pretended not to notice, but her eyes flicked irresistibly over to watch the man occasionally. She took some time adding milk to her tea, which gave her something to do with her hands. "You're probably wondering what the heir to the Apligian name is doing planting flowers and digging graves."

"It is a curiosity." I sipped carefully at the tea, taking the smallest sip possible.

"It was an embarrassment is what it was." She sighed and met my gaze. "The truth is, Victor was… oh, I don't know. Touched, my father always said. We were sure that something could be done medically. My father had doctors from all over London here when Victor was a boy, but there was nothing they could do. Even after Victor had become fully grown, he was always a bit slower than anyone else around him. Even worse, in my father's eyes, Victor was never one for responsibility. Dealing with Victor has always been more like dealing with a young boy than a full grown man."

"That must have been difficult for you," I said.

"Yes, and rather more than that for Father. Victor was the only son, you see, but Father couldn't very well leave his business to someone with the mind of a boy, could he?"

"No, I suppose not. What is the family business?"

"Undertakers," Flora Apligian said. "Though now, after Father's death, most of the business has been handled by others."

"Your mother?"

"Mother is dead along with Father. It's just Victor and me now. Hmm." She hid her quivering lip with another sip of tea. "Just me, I suppose."

"How did your brother come to be a groundskeeper? That's not a very common occupation for someone with his background and means."

"No," she said, pursing her lips. Clearly, it wasn't something she'd been happy with. "He always liked Highgate. When he was younger, some of the current groundskeepers discovered Victor trimming some of the plants himself with a stolen pair of gardener's shears. They sort of adopted him, I guess you could say. Victor was actually good at that sort of work. It was one of the few things he *was* good at. The grounds manager was a friend of father's, and they let him stay on." She frowned. "Is there something wrong with the tea?"

"No. It's fine." I made myself take another sip from my still full cup. I'd always hoped that my taste for tea would return, somehow, after the change, but it never did. I didn't mind the sugar, but the tea itself was so strong and bitter to my palate now that I might have been drinking sewage.

"Tell me," I said slowly, "did your brother often do work for the cemetery after dark? Is that not somewhat unusual?"

"It is unusual," she said, "though not so much for my brother, who often used it as a place of business, but not what I would call cemetery business."

"I'm sorry," I said. "I don't follow you."

"Perhaps not," she said. "Victor fell in with a bad crowd among some of the other groundskeepers. They did not mind Victor being simple-minded, I guess. Rather the opposite, as they found it a useful trait in their criminal activities. Victor was unfailingly loyal to them, you see. Even when it wasn't in his best interests."

"Criminal, you say?"

"Your eyes light up!" Miss Apligian said. "More press for you and your glory-seeking friend, yes? Oh, Victor had a fine list of shocking habits for your stories, Doctor. Clandestine meetings in the middle of the night, sudden sums of money and great pains to avoid the police. And some of the characters that he'd do business with, well, none of them were from the gentry, that much is certain. None of them were welcome here, of course, and Father forbade Victor to associate with them, but Victor was quite beyond our control outside the house."

"These men who Victor fell in with," I said. "Can you tell me their names?"

"Only one, but he is the principal person you want," she said. "The ringleader. Mason Harweather. He's the first mate on the *Merry Widow*. He had achieved an influence over Victor that neither Father nor I ever managed. Victor would do anything for him. A perfectly odious man."

"Can you describe this Harweather?"

"Not well. I have only seen him once, out in the street while I looked down through an upper window. Somewhat stout, with thin, reddish hair."

"It was not here that he met them?"

"No. I always understood that he used the cemetery for that, or occasionally the alehouses. There is one just around the corner from here. These are all guesses, however. He did all his business away from the house."

"What do you know about Victor's role in these affairs?"

"He was the liaison between Harweather and whoever controls such affairs. A message boy, in essence. It did not call for much intelligence, only the loyalty that was Victor's strongest asset, and the unlikelihood of such an innocent-looking lad being involved."

"We found such a letter on his person, or at least the envelope for one," I said. "From Victor himself. Would such a letter be part of this?"

"I hardly think it likely. Victor's penmanship was atrocious. Such a task would only be a burden to him, and likely to anyone trying to read it. I understood that he carried letters from others only. Now, Doctor, I believe that I have been perfectly frank with you. Have I not?"

"Admirably so," I said.

"I am being so in part because I believe that to attempt to hide such things would only increase the length of your investigation here, and I wish for that to be as brief as possible. To be blunt, I consider both you and your press-seeking friend unwelcome here. It is already nuisance enough that I will have to repeat this information for the official police, for I surely will have to, won't I?"

"Yes," I said, "very likely."

"Very well, then," she said. "Is there any other information I can give you and so send you on your way?"

"Did Victor smoke?"

"Not that I'm aware of."

"Did he show any signs of illness these past few days? Reduced appetite, surliness or any reluctance to go out during the day?"

"Not that I'm aware of, though to be forthright with you, Doctor, we had become much like strangers to each other. This is quite a large house, and it is easy enough to avoid someone else living in it, if that is your desire. I know he went out to the docks yesterday morning. As far as I know, he was eating regularly."

"Would your butler know if his eating habits were normal?" I said, turning to look at the elderly servant.

He eyed his mistress, but at a nod from her he said, "He ate a full plate of rashers and kippers yesterday morning." His tone was icy and dry. "I cannot speak to his dinner, which he had out of the house. Likely it was something equally interesting, and well-pickled shortly after."

"Thank you, Merton," Miss Apligian said, standing up. "Now, if you will excuse me, Doctor?"

"There is one other thing, miss," Merton said. "That is…"

"Out with it," Miss Apligian snapped. "The sooner Dr Watson has all the information he needs, the sooner he is gone."

"Yes, miss. I only just discovered it myself this morning and all the other news quite drove it out of my head, but young Victor had his things packed."

"Packed, you say?" she said. "For a trip?"

"Yes, miss."

"Well," she said, "that is not so unusual. Harweather occasionally sent him with one of his other employees to the continent. It must be that."

"Of course, miss. I'm sure that was it."

"Thank you for your trouble," I said. "You have my card if there is anything else that you think Holmes or I should know."

"I have given you every information in order to be rid of you," she said. "I should not be likely to call you back. In the event that Sherlock Holmes does find the culprit of this murder, which I consider unlikely, do not expect our thanks for it. Such a thing will hardly bring Victor back. The two of you might have better spent your time honestly, on the police force, patrolling the streets as they do, and so prevent a crime rather than merely benefiting from it!"

There was little else I could discover here under such a hostile and intolerant countenance, so I rose and made ready to depart. Merton gracelessly handed over my coat and hat. I tried not to look suspicious putting on such heavy attire during a warm and sunlit day, but I needn't have concerned myself. They hardly paid me any attention as I left.

Chapter 13

RANDALL THORNE

North Hill Street is a busy thoroughfare, and already the pavement was choked with clerks and the like on their way to work. The torpor of the sunlit hours lay heavier on me than I expected, and I was eager to get back to the cool haven of my room in Baker Street before the sun climbed much higher. The weather was unseasonably clear and underneath the heavy burden of the sun, even with a coat and hat to avoid any direct contact, I felt exhaustion infuse my every step. Nor could I locate a cab, peering moleishly as I was through the sun's glare. I'd been too long a creature of the dark spaces between dusk and dawn and had foolishly underestimated the danger that daylight presented to those with my affliction. I crept along, keeping my hat brim low and my gaze down. Always before I'd gone out in the company of Holmes, who stood ready to prevent precisely the predicament that I was in now.

Once, I flinched as a passer-by in the busy thoroughfare

bumped into me and the glare of the sun off the street and buildings around me was like peering into a fully-stoked oven. Looking up was a blinding exercise in futility, revealing nothing but a burning haze. I had to get out of the street. The darkened doorway from the alehouse beckoned. I told myself that this was, likely as not, the same alehouse that Victor Apligian frequented. Holmes had often expounded on the virtues of such places as fonts of information. I pushed my way into the dim, cool interior with great relief.

The place, even in the morning, was already filled with a smattering of customers, the lowest dregs of the street that sought ale as soon as they recovered from the previous night's overindulgence. It was not a savoury crowd. Several narrow gazes picked out my well-made coat and stick, not overly welcoming. I walked unsteadily in the sudden silence to one of the empty tables. My lack of stability may well have worked in my favour. Certainly in their eyes, I was there for the same hair of the dog that they were, so at least I was of a kindred spirit, if disparate in class. The smell of the place was overpowering, stale beer and staler sweat, but at least it was out from underneath the pitiless glare of the sun.

The barkeep, a sour-looking and sour-smelling overweight man with a ginger beard, set a heavy wooden mug in front of me without speaking. Just tipping the glass enough to wet my moustache nearly made me gag with the foul stuff. It smelled nearly as bad as the man who served it, and with the same unsavoury character. He might have bathed in it. Still, I managed to put a little beer down my gullet and set the mug down without allowing my hands to shake overmuch. I nodded at him and took another draw.

The man guffawed, a reaction echoed by several of the patrons around me, but this seemed to be the reaction everyone had expected of me. I seemed to have passed some sort of unspoken test, and thereafter everyone ignored me. I sat in the welcome gloom unmolested, slowly marshalling my strength against another foray into the street.

The door opened again, and another patron stepped in. The murmur of the room, which had swelled after I'd taken my seat, now diminished again. If anything, this man was more out of place in this establishment than I was.

The newcomer was tall, with dark, hooded eyes, a sun-burnt face and a great hook nose that did not quite detract from his otherwise handsome appearance. He wore a rugged brown suit cut in the American style underneath a tan duster, and all of it topped with a ten-gallon black hat. He seemed the very figure of a penny dreadful novel, but whether he might be cast as hero or villain was any man's guess.

He turned that hooded gaze on me, unerringly. "You. Dr John H. Watson." He walked over to my table, his heavy boots thumping on the wooden slats of the floor, and sat. "We need to talk, you and I."

"Do I know you, sir?"

"That's the way of you Brits, isn't it?" he said. "Introductions and all that. We don't stand on that kind of ceremony in Kansas, I'll tell you. Well, I could get Mary to come introduce us, couldn't I? She won't be up until dusk, though. But then, I expect you know that."

I clenched my jaw, but said nothing.

His hand dug into a large pocket in the duster and came out with a heavy Colt pistol which he slammed flat onto the table with a thump loud enough to make the whole room jump, myself included. I gave a brief thought to my own revolver, but there was no opportunity to pull it out. He jabbed a finger at the silver inlay on the grip. "Just in case you think I don't know what I'm dealing with, I got silver in the bullets, too."

The patrons were starting to slip out the front and back doors, no doubt unnerved by the pistol used in this blatantly aggressive manner. Probably one of them would be back with the constables, although nothing was certain in this seedy establishment. Even the barkeep was slipping through a door behind the bar.

"Now see here…" I said indignantly.

"I'm here to talk about Maggie Oakenshot, who you call Mary," he said. "She's mine, and I want you *chaps* to stay away from her."

"Who are you?"

"My name's Randall Thorne, and Maggie, she's mine to take care of, not yours."

I stared at this strange interloper with keen distrust. The pistol looked new and well-cared for with silver inlay worked into the handle, but, from the smell of it, had clearly been used often. His hands, too, were large and sensitive, and I could well believe them to be gunfighter hands. Certainly he had not worked the railroads or the like with those hands.

"I'll take care of her, you mark my words," Thorne went on, seeming to enjoy the sound of his own voice. "She's a hard creature to track down, seeing as she likes the night life and a liquid diet, but I learned how to take care of her kind in Kansas and I'll not shirk things now."

"Good God, man, will you please lower your voice!" I said, shocked at what such open talk about vampires could mean in the daylight hours. He certainly wasn't one himself, handling silver and with that tan complexion, but he clearly knew plenty about them.

Thorne spread his hands. "No one here but us, Doc." I looked around again and found that was true. In fact, I'd known from the sounds alone. Thorne's belligerent manner and casual indifference to pointing firearms had cleared out the place entirely.

"Very well," I said. "How do you know Mary and what grievance do you hold against her?"

"Maggie now," Thorne said. "Not Mary."

"Of course she's not Mary!" I burst out, irritated and unnerved at the bluster of this American. I lowered my voice to a hiss, despite the empty room around us. "Not anymore. She's a monster. She's not the woman I married at all!"

Thorne said, leaning back with a satisfied look on his face, "There's some that would call her a monster, that's true enough. Ruthless as a hammer shark, that one. I've been called that myself, though I ain't infected." This man's narrative seemed inconsistent to me. He seemed to have a certain admiration in his voice when he spoke of 'Maggie', one completely at odds with his claim to be hunting her.

Thorne's grin turned cold and serious as he leaned closer. "I ain't infected… like you are."

My hands slammed the table of their own accord, and I shifted weight in order to jump to my feet before he lifted the pistol and pointed it at me again. "Ah ah," he said. "Sit back down, Doctor."

I reluctantly sat back in my chair.

He lay his pistol back on the table and went on as if there had been no interruption. "But if by 'monster' you mean she's no better than an unthinking beast, well there you're just dead wrong. She's as clever as they come. She's too much hellfire to play out the lady's life anymore. Won't be kept in the house by any man. But she ain't no beast. I want that part clear as day, now. Maybe vampires start out as animals and you're right to put them all down the way that you do before they slaughter any man, woman or child they get their hands on. I can't argue that. But when the fever dies down, the person emerges. The new person, that is. Murderers one and all, of course, but you get used to that. But you calling her a monster is why I'm here. I can see that Maggie had it right when she called you a bulldog of a man, and not likely to be thrown off our track, but I'm here to tell you that all you have to do is give it a day or so, and your problem goes away. I know where she's going to be, and I know how to put a vampire down. Less than eighteen hours from now, Maggie will have a silver bullet in her pretty little heart and I'll be on a boat off your tiny little island."

"The constables are, as likely as not, on their way," I said. "Wondering why the people of this establishment suddenly all spilled out into the street. They'll likely want to have words about brandishing that revolver."

"Maybe," Thorne said. His hand was still on the revolver, the barrel still pointing at my abdomen. "If you get in my way, Dr John Hamish Watson, I'll burn you, I'll expose you, I'll gun you down. I'll do anything in my power to hurt you and your toff detective friend. Besides, you know you can't send our girl to the gallows and still keep the secret about vampires. And I don't think you really want to put a stake to your own Mary, do you?"

"How many more murders will happen in this day or so that you mention?"

He shrugged. "Probably not more than one or two. London lowlifes. Nobody who'll be missed."

"Maybe it's as you say, and she's not my Mary anymore. Certainly, she didn't choose to be infected. But she *has* chosen what to do with her newfound strength, and what she's chosen is murder. Here in London, we don't allow murderers to wander the streets at liberty, whether it's with pistol or fang. I cannot let her continue just for purely selfish reasons, when we might be the only ones that can stop it. How could I allow it, knowing how many lives it will cost?"

Thorne let out a deep breath. "Well," he said. "I guess I should have expected that." His gaze flicked to something over my shoulder and he nodded.

I was half out of my chair, suddenly realizing that the American gunslinger in front of me wasn't my only threat. Another, more serious threat had stalked in behind me so quietly that even with my augmented hearing, I'd had no idea.

Now, enormous hands from behind me locked around my throat with a grip like a machine press. I had a brief glimpse of the rugged face of the man in the beaver cap before he lifted me bodily into the air and slammed me onto the table top with a crash that must have carried into the next building.

I was a man of twice the strength that I had once had, more fit now than I had been even in my youth during the action in Afghanistan, before I'd been wounded, but I was as helpless as a newborn kitten in the clutches of this towering vampiric savage. Furthermore, I knew that, as a vampire, my system was greatly less susceptible to the minor injuries that could bedevil other men. But major damage to the skull, neck, heart or spine could still end a vampire's life just as irrevocably as with other men, and the man clearly meant to break mine into splinters. His arms were like bands of iron as I flailed at them uselessly. His hands clamped down harder and I could feel a terrible, terrible pressure in my neck.

He lifted and smashed me back down on the table again, determined to smash the very life out of me, and the table collapsed like so much kindling underneath the onslaught. We crashed to the floor, with the man on top of me, his hands still attempting to break my neck. My hands groped blindly amidst the wreckage of the table and I clasped something heavy. The table leg, now free of the table entirely.

I swung it with all my determination, connecting with the man's temple. It seemed a feeble blow compared to the tornado of rage that throttled me, but the force of that throttling eased slightly, giving me a spark of hope. I swung again, and dealt a terrific blow across the side of his head. It didn't leave a mark on that oversized skull, indeed only seemed to make the man even angrier, but it did loosen his hold, as did the next one. When I finally managed to get my feet underneath me and shake off his grip, it also allowed me to finally get a full swing with all my weight behind it, and clout him across the face with such a magnificent blow as to send him sprawling among the chairs behind him.

"Good Lord almighty," Thorne said, with an air of wonder. "I've never seen any man, vampire or not, break Boucher's grip once he latched it on."

I finally got a good, close look at my assailant as he scrambled to his feet. He was tall, supremely so, as I'd seen this morning, with a huge axe blade of a face that glared out at me with dark, glittering eyes. All the time we'd struggled, he'd made no sound, a monstrous ghost. The beaver cap, still mashed onto his skull despite my pummelling, kept in place as if by supernatural forces.

"Boucher here," Thorne said, "hails from the rugged northern wildernesses of Canada, and has lived in country as hard as any I've ever seen. You're not likely to meet a stronger man, normal or otherwise. Best give in."

Whether he'd been a noble man in his previous life and vampirism had made him a bloodthirsty demon of a man, I did not know. But there was no mistaking his nature now, nor the malignant intent. He was magnificent in his own uncompromising way, but clearly, the life of any man, woman, or child would all come to evil ends in those oversized hands. Even now, as he climbed nimbly to his feet, those hands flexed and spasmed, as if eager to get themselves back around my throat of their own accord. I shot a brief glance at the wreckage of the table, looking for my silver-topped walking stick, but saw no sign of it. I would have to make do with the sturdy table leg in my hand, which had a decent heft to it.

Voices came from just outside the front door next to Thorne. He had thrown the bolt, locking it, but from the determined sounds and whistles, those measures wouldn't hold them forever.

"Seems I'll have to do it myself, then," Thorne said, raising the Colt.

I raised the table leg, the only shield I had. The Colt cracked and splinters flew off the end of the table leg and a hot needle flared in my shoulder. I dove behind another of the tables as a second shot rang out, and a second brand laid itself across my back.

I overturned the table to make it a better shield, then shot a quick glance over the top to make sure I hadn't lost track of Boucher. The towering man hadn't moved, but was still standing in the middle of the room, holding the battered beaver cap. My blows had torn a sizable hole into it. He shook the hat angrily at me and yelled an incomprehensible torrent of unknown words. It was French, I thought, but so thick an accent that it might have been another language altogether. The man was shaking with anger. He took a step towards me just as a stronger blow hit the front door behind him. Crouching behind the overturned table, I fished my own revolver out of my coat pocket.

"No time, Boucher," Thorne barked. "That's the police. Doctor, we'll have to take this up later."

Boucher shot a glance filled with fury at Thorne and then shook his hat at me again.

Thorne stalked over to the back door, opened it, and peered

out. "Do it your way, then," he snarled over his shoulder. "You can play the savage until they hang you from the gallows, for all I care. But I'd take warning, they usually do such things in the *sunlight*."

I cocked my revolver and stood up with the barrel pointed at him, but he paid no attention to my weapon or to the increased pounding on the front door. Boucher stood for a long moment looking woefully at the hat, then finally squashed it down on his head and followed Thorne out the back door. I could not bring myself to shoot an unarmed man in the back, no matter how much a villain he might be, but I was sorely tempted. I needed answers and they had just walked out. What grudge did Thorne hold against Mary, if any? Could I trust any of what he'd said? It seemed unlikely.

The police at the front door had increased their efforts to a frightful pounding by the time I lifted the bar off the door. The door smashed open and I had to step quickly back into the darkened interior as sunlight flooded in.

"Dr Watson!" Lestrade's face, with its eternally inquisitive stoat-like expression, peered in at me. "I hardly expected to find you here!"

"You got my note, then?"

"Yes, and was on the way to Fairview House when I was rerouted by this commotion. Thank you for the information, Doctor."

"I have always thought we two agencies must work together whenever possible," I said, with no small amount of guilt for the accumulating mountain of facts that we could not share, with Lestrade or anyone in an official capacity.

"You and Mr Holmes are an agency now, are you?" he said with a wry face as he took in the empty room and abused furniture. "Well, I suppose there's no denying that. What happened here, then?"

Two of the constables must have finally made their way around to the back door, because they now came thundering in on heavy boots with their billy clubs raised. I could imagine only too well the frightful impression the shots and crashing must have made to those in the street. The surprised looks from the constables on finding an empty room save for Lestrade and I was near comic.

"Did you see a wild man or American on the way in?" I said to them. "They were both tall men, and striking figures."

Both men shook their heads. "We saw no one," one of them added.

Lestrade pointed at the pistol in my hand, which I'd near forgotten about. "You don't have any bullet holes in you that I can see. Was it these two men you were shooting at?"

I shook my head. "They fired at me, but I never had the chance to shoot back."

"Get back out there, then," Lestrade snapped at the two constables. "Tell the others. Two men like that can't be hard to find." He looked at me and I expanded on my hasty descriptions for the constables' benefit.

"They can't have gotten far." Lestrade said, dismissing them. To me he said, "Mr Holmes isn't with you?"

"He was following another lead," I said, giving him a brief rundown of the encounter, omitting any connection to Mary.

That brought a deep flash of guilt, but I knew that we couldn't afford the exposure.

Lestrade eyed me with his dark gaze, and then sighed. "I think you are getting into Mr Holmes's bad habit of secrecy, Dr Watson, but I won't quibble. You've always done the Yard well in the past, and I wouldn't even be on the case yet if not for your tip. I take it you have already been to the Apligian home?"

"Yes," I said, and gave him a fuller rundown of the information I'd gotten there, such as it was.

He sniffed down at the notebook he'd filled with my information. "Not much yet to go on. I'll just see if we can't get a bit more out of the proprietor of this… establishment. If we can find him. I'll let you know what I get out of the Apligian woman, too. It may be more than you did. I have a way with such women."

"Yes," I said. "I'm sure."

He eyed me again, as if suspecting some joke at his expense, but my placid expression must have mollified him, because he nodded and put the notebook away. "When can I come by to Baker Street," he said, "to compare notes with you and Mr Holmes?"

"I have not yet had a chance to get Holmes's opinion," I said. "But I promise to send a telegram as soon as we know anything definitive. Excuse me, I just had a thought." I went back over to the broken table and fished up the table leg from the floor. The bullet was lodged neatly, as if it were a replica of some trick shooting demonstration. Also, Thorne had not been lying about the silver bullets. I let the table leg fall back into the wreckage.

"A nasty business," Lestrade said. "Pistols going off in a public place in the middle of the day. I don't blame you one bit for being shaken. I say, Doctor, you don't look well. Are you sure you're not hit?"

"Well," I said. "I *am* rather shaken. I had some trouble locating a cab back to Baker Street, too, which was the only reason I came in here in the first place."

"You can take mine," he said.

"Thank you, Lestrade," I said. "You have my gratitude."

I secured my hat and gloves and collected my stick while Lestrade called the cab over and started issuing orders to more constables.

"Doctor," Lestrade called out as I stepped out of the doorway towards the open door of the cab.

"Yes?" I stopped with the cab door in my hand, trying with all anxiety to hide the difficulty such placement held for me. The sun beat down on me through the fog with all the malice of an angry forge.

"Remember what I said about secrets, Doctor," he said seriously. "They weigh around a man's neck like quarry stones, if you let them."

"Quite so, Lestrade," I said, and stepped as unhurriedly as I could into the cab.

Chapter 14

SUSANA RICOLETTI

A lighting from the cab at Baker Street, I took one last look at the painful sun-shrouded haze above me, then entered gratefully into the cool interior. It was a lifted burden to mount the seventeen stairs up to our rooms, and an even greater one to find that Holmes had returned.

This fact was made readily apparent by the cloud of smoke that shrouded the ceiling of our room. The stench of Holmes's tobacco was overpowering, and I could barely see into the room. It seemed that I had left one offence upon the senses simply to walk into another.

The cloud parted briefly, revealing the painting I'd purchased several months ago from a shop on North Hill Street, coincidentally enough, not far from the Apligian home. It depicted a woman staring forlornly out from a tunnel underneath one of the bridges at a sun bleeding saffron and ember streamers into the sky over the Thames. I'd purchased it simply for the sunrise, a sight I knew

I would never see again. Even crawling around in the daylight, as I had today, I couldn't bear to actually look at the sun and wouldn't have seen anything through the burning haze. Now, however, it occurred to me how cut off from the rest of the world that lone figure in the painting was, and how very much like that figure Mary was. There was a hint of the forbidden in the yearning way the figure both kept to the shadows, and yet leaned toward the rising light.

Holmes sat by the window, smoking and thinking, silent as a Tibetan monk. I availed myself of some replenishment from the teapot with the scarlet ribbon that Mrs Hudson had left for me, drinking the first cup right down and taking the second with me to my chair. I noted with both astonishment and great pleasure that Mrs Hudson had finally decided to ignore Holmes's wrath, and had clearly beaten the document disaster overtaking our rooms into tentative submission, stacking most of them in boxes to one side of Holmes's chemical table. I sipped from my cup, pondering for the hundredth time what glib explanation Holmes could have given to that good woman to explain this grotesque new requirement of mine, and again could not hazard a guess, save that it could by no means be the complete truth. I finished the second cup and felt a great deal of my strength return. I'd poured a third before Holmes began to stir.

"Doctor," he said, "clearly something curious has occurred. Tell me everything. Leave out no detail."

I did, in great length, sharing everything that had occurred, including the depressing and faded grandeur of the Apligian home, to my assault from Randall Thorne and the French Canadian.

"I can still feel the man's fingers on my throat," I finished.

"A man who deals regularly with vampires without fear or harm, and carries silver bullets, is perhaps an even more impressive danger, I think," Holmes said. "I should never have sent you alone had I realized that such persons were on our trail. Tell me, did he have only the single pistol?"

"I only saw one, though he could well have had another. Why?"

"We have a man marked by a vampire bite and then murdered by gunshot, and only a short time later, this American obligingly comes along, knowing a great deal about vampires, and shows one of us both a pistol and the willingness to fire it, no matter the circumstances. We also have a known vampire linked to the pearl found on the murdered man's person, in addition to the bites. That much is all very clear, as are our likely culprits. It is only apprehending them that presents difficulty."

"Clearly he shot Victor Apligian," I said. "He must have. We have only to find the proof!"

"Tell me, Watson, did you notice anything unusual about the bullet in Victor Apligian?"

"No," I said. "I didn't."

"Neither did I, and certainly one of us would have noticed if it were silver, would we not?"

"Of course!"

"It wasn't silver. I pulled several of the fragments from the wound, and found only the sort of material one generally fires from revolvers. Which is why I ask about a second revolver. Does Thorne always carry silver bullets, in which case why wasn't

Apligian shot with one? Does Thorne, perhaps, swap bullets in and out, according to circumstances? This would indicate that he planned to shoot Apligian with the far less costly lead bullets, which is reasonable enough. From your description of the encounter, it seems that Thorne very likely followed you in and sent his murderous partner around the back to get the best of you. A plan constructed on the fly, as it were. This Thorne seems to me a rather impulsive character. No, something is not entirely cut-and-dried with that theory. At least not with a single pistol."

"What about your own investigations?" I said. "Did you find anything that would throw more light on the situation?"

"None quite so dramatic as your own, Doctor. I talked to a number of the dock workers, looking for any sign of strange doings in the night among the ships docked there, with nothing terribly untoward to report. I begin to doubt my original hypothesis that the Mariner Priest is involved, for I see no evidence that he's returned, and a great deal to indicate that he has not. I've sent telegrams to the police offices of some of the more likely counties for a refugee escaping London to attempt to corroborate the idea that Mary never went to sea. We shall see if anything develops along those lines.

"My first visit once the dawn broke was, of course, to the *Merry Widow*, where I was completely denied access by some very surly characters."

"But, Holmes!" I said. "How could you have known the ship's name? We only just discovered it."

"Well, you have only just discovered it. I, as I said, found it this morning. Come now, Watson, an addressed envelope with a missing letter is quite out of the ordinary. Enough to warrant our attention, I should think. Typically, a person only addresses the envelope after completing the letter, so it is unusual to see one without the other. Did someone take the letter? If so, why leave the envelope?"

"I didn't think much of it at the time," I said. "But now that you draw my attention to it, it does seem rather muddled. Have you a theory?"

"I had several," Holmes said, "but the one that turned out to be correct was simplicity itself. The remaining letter was mis-addressed, meaning he purchased one envelope, made some mistake or another…"

"Hardweather!" I said. "Whereas Miss Apligian distinctly said the man's name was Harweather, with no 'D'."

"Quite correct," Holmes said. "Our victim, by Miss Apligian's account, had not the most elevated of intellects, but he did not suffer for money or balk at this minor expense of buying a new envelope when your average letter writer would have simply penned in a correction. At any rate, I followed the address, and found the *Merry Widow*, with Mr Harweather on board where he serves as first mate. I was no welcome person on the *Merry Widow*, I assure you. But Mr Harweather himself was not averse to me buying him a drink or two at the nearby alehouse, which was money well spent. He avoided telling me anything he thought of as incriminating, but I gathered rather more than he realized, I should think. I noticed during my brief visual inspection that the captain has a rather expensive meerschaum pipe, while several of the mates have rather finer gear against the weather than one would expect. This causes me to suspect some additional income for the *Merry Widow* and her crew above and beyond legal cargo. Several details inadvertently dropped by our Mr Harweather convinced me of the fact."

"Smugglers, then?"

"Yes." He pulled out several telegraph forms from his desk. "Your story has, however, given us some valuable data. I think we might gather a bit more information with a few inquiries."

"What is our next step after the telegrams?"

"I think it may be time for us to come at this from a somewhat oblique angle," he said. He leapt to the door and bellowed down the stairway. "Mrs Hudson! A four-wheeler, if you please!"

He whirled back to face me, liberating his hat from the stand as he did so. "We're going to the East End Rookery. Perhaps I have mentioned the name Susana Ricoletti?"

"I don't believe so," I said.

"When Moriarty died, he left a large vacuum in the criminal element. It was a gap too large to be filled by any one person, and now London is plagued by no fewer than seven underground fraternities, each controlling their own piece of London. They are more direct and obvious organizations than Moriarty's intricate web was, and thus easier to trace."

"A woman?" I said. "Surely not!"

"A woman indeed," Holmes said, "and not one to be under-estimated. Both formidable and abominable, though she does have a code of honour, in her own ruthless sort of way. Which makes dealing with her preferable to some of the other feudal lords of crime."

"I begin to see," I said, grabbing my hat and coat. "This Ricoletti woman's organization spans the Albert Docks, and so she will have the information we need." I was weary, but Holmes's enthusiasm had reinvigorated me so that going out into the sun again did not seem as daunting as it had moments ago. "What makes you think that she will give that information to us?"

"She does *not* have control of Albert Docks, but has been fighting for control with the man who does," Holmes said with a twinkle in his eye. "The two of them have had the bitterest rivalry imaginable for years, but it has come to new prominence now that each of them has managed to entrench themselves into positions of power."

"Gentlemen," Mrs Hudson called out, and we heard the clatter as our carriage pulled up.

"Thank you, Mrs Hudson!" Holmes called back. "Also, please send a boy to the telegraph office for me. Three messages. They are on the table. Absolutely critical!"

"What is this other crime lord's name?" I asked as we swept our coats on and barrelled our way down the stairs.

Holmes had to fire his answer back over his shoulder. "Adamo Ricoletti. Her husband."

The rookery Holmes had in mind was along the Ratcliffe Highway in the East End of London. The stench of the city, always profound to my nose, rose to a prodigious reek that threatened to burn out my very skull, a testament to the poor drainage and worse sanitary conditions the squalor forced on its tenants. The babble of the city dwindled to a sibilant whisper as scruffy-clad street loiterers watched our four-wheeler pass. Men and women shouted off in the distance in a vehement strain that was sometimes violent, other times lewd, but always hidden or dimmed as we approached, the way chattering birds suddenly fall silent when sensing danger. A clamour rose up behind us after we had passed. As we rattled past the Tobacco Dock and the bronze sculpture of a boy and tiger outside of Jamrach's Wild Beast Emporium, the buildings became even leaner, taller and closer together so that it almost seemed as if we were descending into subterranean trenches that held the seediest and most unfortunate of London's tenants. The cabbie hadn't been happy about our destination and Holmes had already promised him extra payment as a result. The entire place seemed nothing but dark alleys filled with the stench of standing water and dilapidated tenements equally filled with desperation and whispers.

Holmes directed our cabbie to pull up to a kerb where several young men loitered with the insouciance only available to the young. Behind the young men loomed a row of adjoined buildings so cramped and narrow that it might have been one huge, dilapidated monstrosity. All the windows closest to us were broken and open to the elements.

"Blimey," one of the young men said as we stepped out into the street. Clearly, he recognized my austere friend's countenance. He smoothed back a magnificently bushy black moustache, trying with that habitual gesture – with not much success – to hide his amazement and perhaps just a trace of awe. Finally, he mastered himself, and his face once again resumed the expression of unconcerned hostility that seemed to be its default. "Almost a shame to see you two 'ere," he said. "I liked me a good story or two. Now we won't never get to read another. No way is the Lady goin' to let you two leave 'ere. Leastways not walkin', she ain't."

He hefted a heavy stick and the three others also produced similar weapons and stepped forward. I hurriedly raised my own stick, certain that we were mere seconds from a pitched street brawl.

"Save the banter, Hodges," Holmes said, unflappable to the last. "Tell Mrs Ricoletti that we're here straightaway. She'll be very interested to see me."

"'Ow do you know my name?" the youth said, surprised.

"It's my business to know your name," said Holmes. "Just as I know Laramie, Stoutworth and De Santos behind you. I also know, with tolerable certainty, what jobs Mrs Ricoletti has had you do this past month just as plainly as I know the blackcurrant pudding you had for lunch this morning, which, I might add, has no actual currants in it. Now hurry up and tell Mrs Ricoletti that we are here."

"Lord," the youth whispered. "You're 'avin' me watched, you is!"

Holmes, unperturbed, waved the boy away. To my astonishment the previously hostile youth dropped his threatening stick and hurried through the door behind him. The door, a ramshackle slat of wood without latch or handle, banged shut behind him after he went through.

"Blackcurrant pudding?" I asked quietly.

"We passed a sign," Holmes said, "not half a block back proclaiming the daily special as blackcurrant pudding for a mere farthing – surely not enough for real currants – and brown crumbs on both the moustache of our eager friend and the clothes of his comrades-in-arms. The deduction was a simple one."

"It always seems so simple after you explain it," I said.

"Perhaps I should stop," he replied with a touch of asperity. "No one ever admires the magician quite so much after his tricks are revealed."

"Hey!" the cabbie yelled behind us. "I didn't bargain for staying long in a place like this!"

"Here," I said, stepping over to hand a coin up. "Here's a half-sovereign for your trouble. There'll be another to rub against it after you take us out again. You'll be in no danger. Not as long as you're with Sherlock Holmes."

"Sherlock Holmes, is it?" the man said. "Well, that's different, then."

"Your efforts at work again, Watson," Holmes said with a grimace of satisfaction. "Your turn for romantic fiction does seem to have its uses."

"Thank you, Holmes."

The moustached youth burst through the doors, clearly in a rush. "Come on, then," he yelled, waving his hands at us. "*She* wants to see you."

"I rather thought she might," Holmes said with a bland smile.

We were led up the short flight of dirty limestone steps into the tenement building. The dingy landing had two open doorways on the left and right that led into what had once been separate lodgings and now stood open, since the doors had been torn off their hinges, probably to be used as firewood for one of the meagre fires that flickered within. Several figures of indeterminate age and sex wrapped in grey rags slept on the floors, as well as in the lobby and on the stairwell landing. The area smelled of mould and unwashed bodies and a cold breeze informed me that more than one window was broken or missing inside.

The youth led us up to the second floor to a heavy iron-shod door, on which he knocked. The door opened and we were led into a small and cosy room much at odds with the dilapidated squalor that lay without.

The room was as richly appointed as any prime minister's, with several well-cushioned divans, a sideboard with elegant scrollwork next to a glass cabinet with sherry and the like for discerning guests, and also a large mahogany desk. To one side, near the sideboard, stood a number of older men with the air of military advisors. Behind them was a second, smaller desk with another man sitting at it, taking notes.

Behind the larger desk, in a clear position of authority, sat a nondescript, middle-aged, dark-complexioned woman who watched us with a pair of wonderfully dark eyes and a smile playing around her thin lips. She wore an outfit of mousseline de soie, quite elegant, with a touch of fluffy crimson chiffon at her neck and wrists, as well as an enviable pendant adorned with blood-red rubies. The silence stretched out while she regarded us. Holmes said nothing.

"That will do," she said to her subordinates. "Better if you leave us alone, I think. These men don't mean me any harm."

The smile grew fuller. Her eyes sparked with a cunning malice and suddenly the woman didn't seem nondescript anymore. "Do you, Mr Holmes?"

Holmes scanned the room with an introspective gaze before meeting hers. "No. We do not."

"But Mrs Rico…" one of the men burst out, but his words died on his lips when she turned to regard him with a flat gaze, and then he, and all his fellows, trundled themselves wordlessly out. The last was the thin, reedy man at the desk, who put away several ledgers and papers into the rolltop section, which he then locked. When he left and closed the door silently behind him, all the sounds and scents from the other room disappeared, leaving only a comfortable silence and the smell of varnished wood.

"Well now, Mr Holmes," she said in a warm voice. "It *is* nice to see you again."

"And you, Mrs Ricoletti," Holmes answered. There seemed to be some tension hanging between the two of them, as if they were the only two persons in the room. She finally shifted her gaze to me and acknowledging my presence. "Dr Watson, Holmes's loyal and true biographer. I am touched. Would either of you care for a bit of claret, perhaps?" she said. "I was just about to pour myself some."

"A small glass, I'm sure," he said. "The pleasantries must be observed, mustn't they?"

"Yes," I said, somewhat taken aback. "Of course."

"Of course," Mrs Ricoletti repeated. She moved to the liquor cabinet and withdrew three glasses on a small black lacquer tray. When she turned her back to us, I could see that her hair, full in a lustrous curtain, was worn scandalously loose and free. Mrs Ricoletti was also one of those women that have an extreme poise to them, her every word and motion a carefully measured step.

"Clearly you two know each other," I said. I could feel the surprise still on my face. "You might have told me that part, Holmes."

"I was able to help Mrs Ricoletti out with a small matter some years ago," Holmes said. "I may have mentioned the case."

"I'm afraid," Mrs Ricoletti said while pouring, "that Adamo still hasn't forgiven you, even after he got out. He feels he owes you for those many years. The names he has called you! And myself, of course, but then, we are both used to that."

"Quite," Holmes said. "I have noted, in the passing years, that Mr Adamo's incarceration has been your freedom."

"It is not often such an opportunity comes along, and a woman must seize them when she can. But you're not here to reminisce. I rather sense that you are here to collect on the large favour you did me when you helped incriminate my husband, yes?"

"Yes," Holmes said. "I am looking for information on the operation at Albert Dock."

"That's Adamo's operation," she said.

"Yes."

"What makes you think I would have information on it?"

"Because you're currently contesting for control of it. A contest of which the outcome looks quite favourable for you, I might add."

Mrs Ricoletti laughed and took a sip of her claret. She leaned on her desk and regarded us, the picture of ease and comfort. "It seems I should come to *you* for information. Very well. It is a simple liquor smuggling business running supplies from the continent and landing them at various small inlets down the Thames. Not a terribly large endeavour, but lucrative. What else would you know?"

"The *Merry Widow* is one of these ships?"

"I believe so, yes. Unfortunate name and all."

"Just so. Is the captain of the *Merry Widow* known to you?"

"Not as such, though most of these men are cut from the same cloth. Rough sorts that don't mind taking a few risks. Familiar enough with the Thames to navigate in the dark and evade patrol boats and the like. Not terribly scrupulous, of course. I should have it here in a ledger – one moment." She moved to the smaller desk, produced a key of her own, unlocked it, and quickly located the ledger she wanted. "Yes, here it is. Horace Gunn is the man's name."

"No cargo other than liquor?"

"Liquor would be their usual cargo, but they're by no means an exclusive bunch. I know they would occasionally take passengers, if some important business of the Professor's needed doing, back when he still ran things."

"You surprise me, Mrs Ricoletti," Holmes said. "So few people had any knowledge of the Professor's existence or position. He was a man to work from the shadows."

"He was, Mr Holmes," Mrs Ricoletti said. "But it is *my* business to know things, too."

"A touch!" Holmes said. "A distinct touch, madam. Could you draw up a list of the *Merry Widow*'s usual routes?"

"I couldn't," she said, "but I'm sure one of my lieutenants

could." She went back around behind her desk, sat and laced her fingers, peering at us over them as she favoured us with a demure smile. "What we've spoken of so far was easy enough information to come by. Most of it, I daresay, you knew already. However, routes, definitive routes, are not so easy to come by and I am not a charitable organization, Mr Holmes, large favours notwithstanding."

"You haven't asked what I might do with such a list," Holmes replied.

"Very well," she said. "What *would* you do with such a list?"

"Almost certainly make a great deal of trouble for Mr Ricoletti's smuggling operation."

"That," she said, "is acceptable." She rang a small bell sitting on her desk and the door jerked open as if it had been connected to the bell by some hidden mechanical wire, and the thin, reedy man who had been in the room before stuck his head in.

"Joseph, can you draw up a list of the *Merry Widow*'s landing spots? Include any other information on their operations you think useful to Mr Holmes."

"Certainly, Mrs Ricoletti." He stepped into the door and moved over to the desk, carefully keeping his gaze away from the three of us.

"There will be some rough guesswork, of course," Mrs Ricoletti said. "There isn't anything like a regular schedule, except for the tides."

"Of course," Holmes said.

Joseph had pulled out pen and notebook and jotted down three entries from memory. He then pulled out a ledger, consulted it, and added several more entries to the list. He tore off the sheet and handed it first to Mrs Ricoletti. She nodded, looking at the list, and the man quietly replaced notebook and pen in the rolltop desk, locked it again, and left.

"This may be of interest," Mrs Ricoletti said. "Their most likely departure time is tonight. Or tomorrow morning, at any rate. Before first light. It goes without saying that they don't post a schedule, so that time is Joseph's best guess. But I find his guesses terribly helpful."

"Shocking habit," Holmes said automatically as he took the paper she offered.

"Of course," she said, that dangerous smile playing across her lips again. "You never guess. You... estimate the probabilities."

"Precisely," Holmes said. "It appears that the *Merry Widow* hasn't limited her travels to domestic shores, but has also visited America on several occasions."

"Yes. That's quite true."

"Thank you, Mrs Ricoletti, I believe this information will do quite nicely. We really have detained you long enough."

"But the Doctor hasn't even touched his claret," Mrs Ricoletti said.

"Forgive me," I said, carefully picking up the small glass. While I still enjoy a fine wine or claret, indeed more so than before my transformation, the woman's unnerving and formidable presence had made me forget all about the drink. It was a fine claret, bold, strong and sweet. "Thank you, Mrs Ricoletti," I said when I put down the empty glass.

"You're quite welcome, Dr Watson," she said.

"Quite an amazing woman," I said in the cab ride back to Baker Street. "Did she really take over her husband's criminal organization after your investigation incarcerated her husband? Remarkable!"

"Hmm?" Holmes said, pulling his gaze from the passing scenery. "Oh yes. Of the two Ricolettis, I consider her the far more dangerous."

"It was a shame she didn't have anything more useful for us," I said.

"Didn't she?" He then lost himself in thought again and would say no more.

It was with some relief that I noticed the greyish light getting darker. My watch told me it was now just past a normal supper time, which meant it was nearly time for my normal breakfast. I'd been going for nearly twenty-four hours now without rest, something that would certainly take its toll, especially if I didn't take in more nourishment. Just the little bit of claret made my head light and my stomach lurch, and the idea of blood left the same dark yearning and suppressed revulsion it invariably generated.

But it was very likely that I would need all my strength before this strange case was over.

Chapter 15

THE MERRY WIDOW

"A ha," Holmes said when we got back to Baker Street. He snatched up the envelope waiting for us on the table. "A reply to my American telegram."

"What does it say?" I asked.

"Let us work backwards," Holmes said, seeming not to hear my question. "Our original supposition that Mary had left England was clearly false. Let us suppose that she stayed behind in England. Would she stay in London? Probably not. So she retires to one of the more distant counties. This proves successful for a length of time, but then something changes, and she's forced from her self-banishment to London. Why?"

The tight knot in my chest that discussing Mary always brought on clamped down in full force. It was as much as I could do to focus my attention on Holmes's actual question.

"Perhaps she was discovered?" I said. "Or she's run short of victims she can safely feed from, or money, or shelter?"

"All excellent suppositions," Holmes said. "Another possibility is some outward stimuli. One of these drives her back to London."

"Victor Apligian simply had bad luck to encounter her, then? Perhaps the kind of establishments that he spent time in would facilitate that?"

"I don't think we need to rely on such random circumstances as those," Holmes said. "We know that Victor Apligian had a connection to this smuggling operation. It is possible the Mariner Priest had his own connection to this operation. We know also that Mary was with the Mariner Priest, if only for a short time. Is it not possible that she could have gleaned information about the smuggling operation through that association?"

"She was always clever that way," I admitted bitterly, galled that the attributes I had once been proud of in my wife were now turned to such dark purposes. "She'd listen to my stories of our adventures and gather far more from the clues than I first had."

"She approaches Apligian, then," Holmes went on. "One reason may be that she is looking for passage out of England, but there are better places, such as Portsmouth or Dover, so she must have something else in mind. Apligian also provides an opportunity for feeding, clearly, so Mary has achieved two goals with one person. However, there are certainly other places that would take the pearl as payment so, again, we have to ask ourselves: why London? However, she has been here for some days. We know this because of the many bites on Apligian's body.

The measurements of the bites confirm that we are talking about one vampire, not several. They also match the size of Mary's mouth, as best we can recollect, though we have no precise measurements. I don't suppose you have any?"

"Precise measurements of Mary's mouth?" I asked, surprised despite myself. "No, don't be absurd."

"Too much to ask," Holmes conceded. "In addition, I perceive that your incisors have changed markedly during your transformation, though possibly not enough to facilitate recognizing vampires in hiding on that characteristic alone. Also, I noted during Dracula's attack on my person that the incisors grew when he became angry, which warrants further study."

"Really?" I asked. Now that I recollected the Count's terrifying visage in my mind's eye, I could see the fangs, much more prominent than they normally were. I raised my own hand halfway to my mouth wonderingly, then let it drop again.

"Regardless," Holmes went on. "It still remains a mystery why she should choose London when there is danger for her here and other cities would suit a safe escape much more admirably. If she is leaving the country, it makes the *Merry Widow*'s departure tonight a very urgent part of our own timetable. Her destination is of interest, too, if the *Merry Widow* is abandoning her usual trips skirting around the isle in favour of the United States."

"What of Thorne?" I asked. "Is he not tracking her, too? He seemed to think her death at his hands a certainty."

"I am not so certain that I should rely on Thorne's testimony," Holmes said. "It was a long shot, but I thought someone of his description might have a military record and so I sent inquiries to several officials in Kansas. One of them spent a great deal in this loquacious reply." He waved a telegram paper at me. "They are familiar with the name. It seems Thorne's proficiency with the revolver is not to be underestimated. He's made something of a name for himself in Dodge City, Kansas as a lawman and gunslinger. His record was sterling until last year, when he abruptly ended his law enforcement career by staging a payroll theft from the very people he was supposed to be protecting. He struck gold in Apache territory, but he lost it all shortly thereafter to gambling debts. He hired himself out as a high-rate gun hand after that, often to criminal enterprises in the Americas, but had a habit of shooting his employers when there was enough profitable gain in it. A sudden shift in temperament and prospects, for someone that had been known only as a staunch lawman. His companion is known to them, too. A French Canadian known as Boucher, as you are already aware. They fell in together just as Thorne started his criminal career and have stuck to each other ever since."

"That fits remarkably well with the men I encountered," I said.

"There is one discrepancy," Holmes said. "You described Randall Thorne as 'very tall' to me." He stood up. "Think carefully – would you describe him as taller than me?"

"Well," I said, "he was wearing a large hat that added somewhat, but even so..." I thought back. "Yes. Yes, I would."

"That is interesting," Holmes said, sitting back down. "The Americans describe him as a few inches under six feet, whereas I am just over. The difference is slight, perhaps, and may be attributed to some error..."

"Heeled boots, perhaps?" I suggested.

"Very possibly, or a slight error on the part of you or the Americans, yes? But it does fuel the imagination, does it not?"

"How so?"

"I am not so sure that the lawman and the criminal are the same man," Holmes said.

"But you just said…"

"I said that Thorne committed a series of crimes, but it's possible someone else was also using his name. Then they both came here. They were looking for a way to escape the American authorities and I suspect the Mariner Priest assisted them for his own purposes."

"But how did Mary connect with these two scoundrels?"

"My working theory," Holmes said, "is that the Mariner Priest has somehow put them together for his own purposes. At least, it would not surprise me. I have felt his hand steering the helm of this troublesome ship that has come our way and the timing is suggestive. The man posing as Thorne needs an escape, and is provided one. He and Mary seem to be working some scheme together. Either they have thrown together such a plan overnight, or our American gunslinger had no sooner arrived than Mary chose to return here. It seems probable that these are related facts. It may be that Mary felt she needed protection and here is someone ready-made for the part, someone familiar with vampires and their ways, with a vampire companion himself, but not a vampire, so that he may move about and protect them during the day."

"That does seem logical," I said.

"There is also this to consider. Our Mariner Priest withdraws from England, taking with him the crew he has ready-made for the endeavour. But, it is my belief that he did not take Mary, suggesting that he has either discarded her, or he has left her here for some specific purpose which she can only fulfil here."

"What goal could that possibly be?" I asked, not quite keeping up with his rapid-fire chain of suppositions.

"Us, of course," he said. "She was transformed, and then you, as a uniquely venomous attack on our own persons, who stand opposed to his machinations. You have proved to be a tool unsuited for his hand, but perhaps Mary has not."

"Then Thorne's story of pursuing Mary in order to end her was pure fabrication? I suspected as much."

"And not a very good fabrication, at that," Holmes agreed.

"I nearly forgot," I said. "Lestrade may well be by soon. He'll want answers, if we have them."

"I think," Holmes said, "that while Lestrade certainly has his uses, I do not feel that giving him a full understanding of tonight's proceedings, or vampires in general, would be the wisest of choices."

"Perhaps not. What of Mary?"

"That is the very question I was about to put to you, dear fellow. You are the closest thing I have to a client in this case, and certainly the one most connected to our fugitive. The long chain of reasoning that we have laid out is not sound at every link. I am convinced that Thorne, whatever his real name, means us no good, and is linked to Mary. I do not believe his story. But it is also possible that Mary is no longer under the Mariner Priest's control. But she is *still here*, in London, which she knows to be hostile to her. However, let us for a second entertain the notion that she wants nothing more than to escape England in favour of the United States. If so, perhaps she is no longer *our* problem."

"You mean just let her go?" I said, stunned.

Holmes shrugged. "We have done so often enough before this. We know that she fed upon Victor, but we do not know for a certainty that she was directly responsible for Victor Apligian's death."

"Feeding is enough," I said. "I still cannot burn the images from the opium den out of my mind. You were not there, Holmes! You cannot possibly imagine the horror of my own wife urging me to feed – and kill! – when I was first turned. She wasn't my Mary anymore, but a bloodthirsty devil from my worst horrors. She saw the value of such men, of any men, of little importance. Also, what of the children that Dracula and Mina found?"

"The Count did seem to comport himself in a direct and truthful manner, for all that his motives are suspect," Holmes said. "Also, I have found myself impressed by Mina's character. However, it may be too far to call them impeccable sources of information. In addition, there is always the outside chance that they were mistaken."

"I *need* to find her, Holmes," I blurted out. Just speaking the words out loud brought a rush of understanding. I realized what it was that I yearned for out of this case. It wasn't entirely rational, but I suddenly burned with need to accomplish it anyway. "I need to see for myself. If she's still the monster that I remember, then we need – I need – to end her. So that no man, woman, or child has to suffer for what we allowed the Mariner Priest to create out of my sweet and dear wife." The words had all tumbled out, practically unbidden. "If she's changed, Holmes, if my Mary has somehow resurfaced from underneath the bloodthirsty vampire, then we need to help her." I looked at Holmes's austere face. "We need to help her… as you helped me."

"The Albert Dock, then," Holmes said, resolve coming back into his tone. "Tonight."

"Tonight," I agreed.

"There are," Holmes said, "some small arrangements to make before we encounter our good Mr Thorne again."

The portion of the Albert Dock where the *Merry Widow* sat was lined with shops, and we stationed ourselves on the roof of a run-down tailor's shop that dealt mostly in dungarees. The newly tarred roof two buildings over was an assault on the senses, the pungent, acrid fumes so strong that I felt my tongue to be coated with it by the time we'd sat ten minutes. By the end of the hour, I thought to be never rid of it, and three hours later, I felt certain it would forever command my sense of smell to the occlusion of all others. By comparison, the rich scent of the Thames, usually crowded with a veritable stew of foul stenches, became almost pleasant. Those same assaults, however, would shield any incidental scents of ours from Mary, Boucher, or any other vampires, which was much to our benefit.

Our famed London fog had rolled in with a vengeance as

night fell, putting hazy barriers of grey in all directions. The London docks never being entirely devoid of life, there were also the quiet murmuring sounds of a few sailors and dock watchmen, but none of them were close enough to interfere. These were all from neighbouring ships, however, for the *Merry Widow* itself was silent. Far off, someone was singing snatches of melody even I could barely make out, and which they, apparently, could barely remember. Even further off, the occasional foghorn lowed like ocean cattle, followed by the growl of an impending storm.

Our vigil commanded an excellent view not only of the *Merry Widow*, but also the long stretch of dock with ships clustered all about her like so many piglets squirming for position during feeding time. The surface of the Thames near the shore was such a thicket of stays, shrouds and mooring lines, bundled sail, swaying booms, and creaking spars that a person might have gone for miles in either direction without having to risk getting their feet wet. I saw no one on the *Merry Widow*, however.

I gripped Holmes's arm and pointed. "There!"

A figure had stepped stiffly out from the narrow space between two buildings, thin, and wrapped in a raggedy olive cloak. Her hands were held awkwardly behind her, bound. Over her head sat a rough cloth sack. Under the weak light of the single dock lamp post, it could have been nearly anybody, but I knew in my heart who it had to be.

"Mary," I whispered, trying to rise to my feet, but Holmes's grip kept me in a crouch.

Hands pushed her forward into the light so that she crossed the dock towards the *Merry Widow*. The hand wrapped as it was around her slender neck looked enormous, as did the towering figure of Boucher soon revealed behind. He looked around with a cagey fury, but kept a firm grasp of his prisoner so that she could not escape.

Thorne came right behind. The glint of metal identified the pistol in his hand, even so far as to hint at the silver that I knew was inlaid on the handle. A gunslinger's belt was wrapped around his narrow waist this time, gleaming softly with silver bullet tips that peeked out of belt loop and cartridge. Thorne's heavy-lidded gaze swept the docks, the other ships and the rooftops, but I do not think he picked us out in the darkness. He kept to one side of Mary and Boucher, always keeping the pistol trained at Mary's side. Lightning crackled in the sky behind them in dramatic arcs of light. Rain started falling in light drops.

"What sense does it make taking her hostage?" I whispered. "Surely if he meant to do her harm he could have done so by now."

"I do not think," Holmes said softly, "that Mary is the one under the hood. Thorne, you clever rascal."

"Who else, then?" I asked, but Holmes did not answer.

Thorne turned and spoke back into the darkness of the alley.

Another woman slipped out of the alleyway, wearing a dark, nearly operatic-looking costume of twill, narrow at the waist, with a fur-trimmed hood that hid most of the features except for the occasional strand of yellow hair. Though the fog alternately hid and then disclosed her, there was nothing surreptitious about her self-assured manner as she walked calmly to join Thorne. She stopped, looking around, and slowly drew back her hood.

Mary shook her blonde hair free, which was now far longer and wilder than I remembered it. Her expression was one of cruel amusement, almost alien to me, but still there was no doubt that this was my own Mary. Or, at least, this was the creature that my Mary had become. I had been very wrong about her being the prisoner, but whose face could it be under the sack?

"Holmes!" Thorne called out. "Watson! I know you're out there. Come out where I can see you, or your little accomplice gets it!" There were a few workers on the docks who stopped their work, but none of them were close to Thorne or the rest. One even took a step in their direction, but changed his mind after Thorne pointed the gun menacingly in his direction.

"It seems," Holmes said bitterly, standing up, "that Mrs Watson and Mr Thorne have not spent their time at Highgate idly. Our American gunslinger is mercurial and impulsive, but not entirely without some tactical acumen." I hurriedly stood up as well, looking down into the street at our quarry.

Thorne spat a word at Boucher, and the towering vampire nodded, a motion that jerked the enormous beaver hat in what might have been a comic gesture in other circumstances. He yanked the sack off their prisoner. Her hair was wet and tangled, and she looked far more feral and hostile than I'd ever seen her, but even at this distance, there was no mistaking the red-eyed, firebrand countenance of Miss Kitty Winter.

"Don't do it, Mr Holmes!" she shrieked. "That rotter already done for Somersby, or as good as! Shot him right in front of God and everyone and left him bleeding!"

"There is no God," Mary said. She spoke to Kitty, but pitched her voice for us to hear, as well. "I'd think you'd know that by now. We ourselves are the incontrovertible proof of that." She bared her teeth and moved closer to Thorne and Boucher so that the whole lot of them were in a tight bundle in the wet street below, the three of them gathered behind Kitty Winter.

I thought of that poor youth, Somersby. His family taken from him by the most violent means possible, so adamant that others should not suffer the same fate. It seemed a cruel injustice that he should be gunned down and left, dead or dying, in so cold-hearted a manner. I was shaking with anger.

"You villain," I started. "That young man had done nothing to you!"

"Give it up, Thorne," Holmes said. "The *Merry Widow* is a small sailboat and not a particularly swift one. Your escape relied on secrecy and that's gone now."

"Let me tell you how this is going to go," Thorne said, and his pistol never wavered from its place next to Miss Winter's side. "We're going to get onto that ship, and that ship is going to be allowed to cast off. You're a man famous for tricks, Mr Holmes, and I'm not having any of them. I see any sign of you, or a police boat following us, I shoot your little leech here. When I get sight of the open sea, then I'll put the girl into a boat."

"No boats!" Kitty moaned. "It'll tip and I can't hardly swim!"

"No?" Thorne said, surprised. "Isn't this here whole country an island? Well, no matter. Maybe you can't swim, but you can't drown, neither, the way I figure it. One way or another, you'll get back on dry land safe. Unless you press me! Don't press me, Holmes! None of us wants that!"

"Actually, Thorne, dear," Mary said, "that's not quite true. Our kind can drown. Somewhat more easily than the rest of you, as it happens. Don't ask me how, but it's true."

I glanced at Holmes's face, but he did not give anything away. Mina Dracula's incarceration had proved that vampires did not drown permanently, but the coma that immersion induced could be as good as death in this situation. I remembered Dracula fishing Mina out of her watery prison where she had lain, deathless but undying, and thought of what it might be like to fall into the Thames and be trapped there. I took one look at the dark water and shuddered. Pulling Mina out of a water-filled casket had been one thing; finding Kitty Winter's comatose body in the Thames would be quite another. It also seemed that whatever connection Mary had to the Mariner Priest, it had not included him sharing this information with her.

"No boats," Kitty moaned again. "I took a swim once, just after I got bit. The darkness! The darkness closing over me. I have dreams about the ocean swallowing me. Swallowing me and I don't never come out."

"We'll put her in a *big* boat, then," Thorne said in exasperation, for Kitty had begun to writhe in his grasp at the mention of drowning. "With a life preserver. As long as we're not interfered with!"

The gunslinger's reckless violence and brazen disregard for any law outraged and horrified me in equal measure. I cast my gaze up and down the docks, fearful that the local constabulary might catch sign of this spectacle and intervene. The workers were still looking on with consternation and alarm, but none interfered.

At least one man had run away, presumably to fetch an official, but there was no sign of any assistance yet.

"Come on down, Holmes," Thorne called out to us. "Down here into the street where I can see you!"

I looked at Holmes to see if he had any final stratagem, but Holmes's face was troubled. We climbed down the short drainpipe onto the lower roof of the nearby shed that we had used to make our ascent some hours ago. Moments later, we were in the street, facing Thorne, Mary, Boucher, and the captive Miss Winter across a dozen feet of dock.

"Fine," Thorne said, gesturing with the pistol toward a part of the dock well-lit by a hanging street lantern. "Over there, where I can see you plain."

After we complied, Thorne, Mary and the others moved around us to the part of the dock that was adjacent to the ship. There was still a good twenty feet between the gently bobbing deck of the ship and the dock, however. The Thames was riding high, so that the deck was some few feet over our heads, hiding the fog-enshrouded area even further from our view. The gangplank was down, but the deck was empty and the masts and spars lonely, dark skeletons in the storm-dimmed sky. There was, in fact, no sign of anyone aboard. Clearly the crew had gone into hiding.

"Ahoy there, you up on ship!" he bellowed. "We're coming up. Don't you worry about payment none, there's five more pearls like the one you saw. Five and you'll get them all. You have the word of Randall Thorne!"

There was no answer. The ship creaked as it lay slowly bobbing in the grip of the Thames, but nothing aboard her moved. Even if a crew had suddenly burst from hiding, it would take some time to prepare even a small ship like that for travel, but Thorne seemed ignorant or uncaring of such necessary trifles.

"I don't believe," Holmes said, "that the word of Randall Thorne is *entirely* relevant here."

"What's that?" Thorne said, his gaze suddenly sharp.

"Your name," Holmes said. "It isn't Randall Thorne. No doubt you're going to claim that every bit of your law career in Kansas City is true, but it simply won't do."

"I *was* a lawman in Kansas City!" Thorne screeched.

"Interesting," Holmes said, "since the records are quite clear that Randall Thorne built his career in Dodge City, though I imagine that distinction easy to miss for someone from Texas."

"Texas?" Thorne was nearly apoplectic by now.

"The drawl really is quite unmistakable," Holmes said. "Not thick enough for Kansas at all. I had some concern that Watson had simply underestimated your height, but I see that the Doctor was quite correct, which removes my last doubts, Mr Morris."

"Damn you!" Thorne said.

"Morris?" I said.

"Come now, Watson," Holmes said. "Who else do we know that has been connected to vampires, has extensive knowledge of the same, and is American?"

I snapped my fingers. "From Van Helsing's band of followers. Quincey Morris! The Texan!"

"Quite so," Holmes said. "I assume the real Randall Thorne is dead back in America?"

"Yes," Morris admitted, staring at Holmes as if he were the Devil himself.

"What I don't entirely understand is what the Mariner Priest offered you to make you come back here after you had quit England."

"An escape from the posse," Thorne, or rather, Quincey Morris, said. "And her." His gaze flicked to Mary. "You don't understand. Lucy haunted my dreams. Then Mina. Only I couldn't get either to look at me, except as an enemy. When I got the message from a strange party that Boucher and I could get quick and free passage out of America as long as I was willing to assist a certain *infected* woman that needed assistance, that didn't seem like a burden as much as an enticing opportunity." The euphemism was thinly veiled to anyone who knew better, but Morris's gun-waving theatrics had caused everyone on the docks to give us a wide berth and it was unlikely anyone could make out much more than every third word.

"His assistance must have seemed attractive to you," Holmes said to Mary, "for you to trust him so quickly."

"Quincey's bold," Mary said with a smile. "Brave, strong, decisive, and not afraid of a little blood. Plus he knows I have the protection of someone very powerful. He's too smart and self-serving for that. You can trust self-serving in a man."

"Mary!" I said, pleading now. "It doesn't have to be like this! You don't have to throw in with murderers and thieves."

"Oh, John," Mary said, "of course I do."

"We can assume that the subterfuge at the pub was a lie," Holmes said, "and a poor one at that, since you very clearly weren't a hunter of the infected. What purpose could that serve?"

"Your friend has the right of it," Morris said. "Sorry for the tall tale, Doctor, but I thought it would buy us more time than the truth. Mary told me it wouldn't do any good, that you would never back down, but I confess that I wanted to meet the man that Mary had attached herself to before me. How you held onto her, I admit, I cannot fathom. She's more woman than one man can hold without bloodshed, I'll tell you. Probably always has been underneath."

"Was Victor Apligian one of those casualties?" Holmes said.

"The Highgate boy?" Morris said. "I tell you, someone had already done him by the time I came across the scene. I won't lie to you. We've had too much subterfuge in this affair already, when I'd rather just come headlong at any problem. I'll admit, I had it in mind to kill the Apligian boy, the way he and Maggie were carrying on, but I didn't do it."

I ground my teeth. Somehow, Morris referring to Mary using her assumed name, and in such a familiar manner, added additional injury to that already volatile situation.

"She knows how that always maddens me," Morris continued. "But the boy was already dead when I found him. Seems someone else had it in for Victor, too."

"But you disposed of the body without ever bothering to search it?" Holmes said.

"All those graves about, it was an easy matter. Lord knows I've cleaned up after Maggie before." Morris shrugged, a strange gesture with both prisoner and pistol in his possession. "Figured the actual murderer would have taken any money."

"The important thing was to divert attention from the vampire bite, was it not?" Holmes said.

"Exactly," Morris agreed.

"A girl's got to eat," Mary said primly. "Victor was our contact for a fast ship, no questions, out of England. I knew however things turned out here with you that we'd likely need an escape route ready. It made sense to combine two goals."

"Then you came to London because of us?" Holmes asked.

"Of course I did," Mary snarled. "There's a bounty on you that would set us up in style for life. Besides, what better way to put my old life to rest, to put the pathetic name of 'Mary' behind me and embrace my new life as 'Maggie'? The world would be a better place for those of us among the blood if you were no longer in it."

I was stricken to the core by Mary's cruel words, spoken so matter-of-factly, but Holmes merely nodded as if she had already confirmed something he long suspected.

"You say it made sense to combine two goals with Victor Apligian," Holmes went on. "Just as it made sense to arrange passage for you and Victor alone, leaving your two erstwhile companions here in the law's tender mercy? At least, that's what you told Victor."

Mary's face was a sudden mask of anger. "Damnation on you and your deductions."

"Maggie?" Morris said. "What is this now?"

"How?" Mary snarled. "I told no one that! *How could you know?*"

"I didn't," Holmes said. "Not for a certainty. Until now. Thank you for confirming it. Victor Apligian did have his bags packed, and still had the pearl on his person, a trifle that Mr Morris clearly hadn't known, suggesting that some negotiation of Victor's own had drawn things out."

"You have to know that's just a story I told the boy, Quincey," Mary said quickly.

"Harlot," Boucher rumbled. "I said we should never trust harlots." He flung a gasping Miss Winter to one side and turned a murderous countenance on Mary. Kitty Winter stumbled towards the edge of the dock. With her hands tied, she couldn't get her balance and teetered near the edge, her face a perfect vision of horror.

"Lord, Mr Holmes, don't let me drown!" she wailed.

I sprang and caught her just before she stumbled her way into the Thames.

"Not the river," she sobbed. "Sweet Lord, not the river. I can't swim."

"You don't have to swim, Kitty," I said. "You're safe now." I pulled her away from the edge and she sobbed into my shoulder.

Boucher had spun to face Mary, his great hands flexing eagerly. He stalked her now.

"Kill you, harlot," he grated. "Kill you like I should have months ago, when Morris first found your worthless harlot carcass back in Herefordshire."

"I don't think so," Mary said, her eyes flashing as she lifted the barrel of a snub-nosed revolver. "That's far enough."

"That little pop-gun?" Boucher said. "You're going to need—"

The crack of a gun went off, but it wasn't Mary's gun. In fact, Mary looked a little surprised.

It was Morris's Colt. The gun discharged thunder and smoke, not once, but twice, then again and again until Morris had emptied the entire cylinder into Boucher's huge back. Boucher staggered with each shot, gasping, but did not fall. He turned disbelieving eyes back onto the face of his comrade and assassin.

"Quincey?" he said. "You'd do this... for her? For *her*?" Tendrils of foul, acrid smoke curled off his back, the silver burning with horrific ferocity through the vampire's skin and flesh.

"Afraid so," Morris said, calmly opening the cylinder and letting the spent casings fall onto the deck. He fed fresh ones into the cylinder, even as he gauged the amount of life left in the smouldering vampire in front of him. The crowd of onlookers started to back away, milling about in terrified confusion, but were too far away to interfere in any case. The weather had started to pick up, a thin wind tearing at the fog, but not yet dispersing it entirely.

"Keep your hands empty, Holmes," Mary snapped, pointing her own pistol at us.

Boucher groaned and stumbled, still refusing to fall despite the wounds from half a dozen silver bullets. His hands clasped loosely at the air. He moved shakily closer to Morris just as the gunslinger snapped his reloaded cylinder shut. But there was no need to fire again as Boucher stopped suddenly near the edge of the dock. He swayed one last time, then collapsed bonelessly into a heap. It took only a gentle nudge from the heel of Morris's cowboy boot to send Boucher's newly made corpse into the brown water of the Thames.

"Come, Maggie," Morris said, holding out his hand. "We have

a ship to catch." A deep roll of thunder came in from the north behind him and the wind picked up again, the brewing of a new storm.

"You're not angry?" Mary said, looking at him sideways. The barrel of her pistol still kept the three of us covered.

"Angrier than a hornet's nest," Morris said, "even though I know you wouldn't have gone through with it. But some things are worth fighting for. Worth killing for, too." He reached out his hand. "Come on, Maggie." The American's reaction was inexplicable to me, but there was no doubting his sincerity.

Mary looked down at the spot where Boucher had gone down into the water. "It wasn't much of a life anyway," she said, and that secret smile was back on her face. "We've killed better for less, haven't we?"

"That," Morris said, "would have a lot to do with why we *both* need to get out of London. Come on!" He reached again.

She took his hand and they both stepped onto the gangplank and ascended up into the ship. All the while, both pistols remained pointed in our direction. Rain sprinkled onto my face. We had yet to see any sign of crew on the vessel and I began to wonder if they were all in hiding or inexplicably absent. Either way, I could not imagine Mary and Morris crewing the ship by themselves, but that thought didn't seem to have occurred to either of them.

Morris kicked away the gangplank as soon as they reached the deck, and it fell with a heavy splash. Only two lines held the *Merry Widow* in place, which Morris untied, so it seemed some preparations had been made for departure, but none of the sails were furled. They wouldn't go far just drifting away with the tide, but the ship slowly pulled away from the dock, scraping briefly against one of the nearby docked boats before pulling free and moving deeper into the Thames.

"Come, Watson!" Holmes said. "Quickly!" He dashed across the dock, towards one of the boats alongside the *Merry Widow*, jumping across the narrow gap between dock and deck.

I glanced down briefly to make certain Miss Winter was in no further danger.

"Don't worry about me," Kitty Winter said. "I'll be up in a moment. It'll be more than some rough handling that does for Kitty Winter. Just don't ask me to go on no boat. And, Doctor… thank you." She lifted her tied wrists to her mouth and bit down. She'd have herself free in a moment or two.

I touched the brim of my hat and spun on my heels.

The jump from the dock to the first boat was a paltry thing, four or five feet at most, but by the time I spied Holmes's figure already leaping from the railing of the moored boat, the distance between the two vessels was already eight or nine feet, and growing. Holmes's leap wasn't quite long enough, and he fell grasping the *Merry Widow*'s rain-slick deck rail, just barely getting hold. I saw him dangling there awkwardly as the bow heaved. The wind whipped at his coat as if it meant to pluck him free with malicious intent and lightning streaked across the sky, painfully and briefly lighting the entire tableau.

"Holmes!"

I ran across the deck without any pause for thought, safety, or balance, and flung myself across the growing distance between the two ships. It was too far to jump, much too far, but I leapt anyway. Only after my feet had left the railing did the thought of drowning occur to me. The Thames was a brown, angry abyss underneath me, the sky an angry tumult above.

I'd underestimated the growing strength my vampiric affliction afforded me as compensation for becoming a creature solely of the night. My leap carried me easily over the gulf, and I landed as neatly as I could have wished on the rolling deck of the *Merry Widow*.

I spun, spied Holmes's hand still gripping the railing, and got a hold of it.

"Watson!" he said, gratefully.

"I have you, Holmes." I slipped on the wet deck, but then got my footing and hauled on his wrist. He scrambled aboard, then cast his gaze about. I'd barely paid attention to my surroundings until now.

There was still no evidence of a crew and this was a ship badly in need of one. It drifted idly as the wind picked up, floundering helpless. None of the sails were deployed, but any decent trick of the wind could well be enough to push on the naked masts enough to tip her over. The Thames was crowded with other ships, of course, and nearly always was, but none of them looked in any position to help us, all of them too busy with their own problems.

For the storm was no longer brewing, but fell on us with full fury. The *Merry Widow* was heeling dangerously now to port and quite in danger of spilling Holmes and I back the way we'd just come. The mainsail boom swung around with a great crash, catching the full wind in a way that made the entire boat lurch and groan. Water flowed up the scuppers and onto the deck while several lines and spars snapped.

The ship was in danger of capsizing at any moment. Even so, we'd already made it out some distance from the dock and into the larger waters of the Thames proper. It could have been the expansive stretch of Gallions Reach, but the storm made it impossible to tell, and there was nothing but grey curtains of rain in all directions. The elemental fury blanketed all my senses, and I thought wildly that I would never complain about the mere din of London again. The stench alone of salt and refuse that came with the Thames clogged my nostrils. There was a bulky darkness above us that suggested one of the bridges, but it was impossible to tell which. Likely, we were within a hundred yards of shore on either side with ships that could affect a rescue, if only they'd known of its existence, but the storm obscured everything more than a dozen yards away. If the *Merry Widow* heeled completely over, which seemed likely to happen at any moment, there would be no hope of rescue or assistance until the storm abated.

"We can't stay here long!" Holmes shouted over the sudden downpour.

"Where is the crew?" I shouted back, for I was now quite sure that Holmes had something to do with their absence.

"Gone!" Morris's voice said behind us. "That's right, isn't it, Mr Holmes? Somehow you did something with the entire crew." He was behind us on the deck, gripping onto the mainstays to keep from slipping. The other hand still held his revolver, but the ship was getting too rocky for him to keep it trained on us and maintain his balance. The tilt of the deck made it so that he looked down at us from a height. Holmes and I had managed to get our feet braced against the railing, but further movement risked slipping, and disappearing forever into the water behind and below us.

The doors to the captain's cabin flew open and Mary struggled up the short flight of steps to the deck. "Empty!" she said. "There's no one on board at all!" The port-side railing dipped at frightening intervals into the water as the ship pitched back and forth. Each time it seemed less likely to ever rise out again. The sole light, a covered deck lantern hanging from the main mast, pitched crazily with the ship's motion, throwing eerie, glimmering shadows. Splashes and plumes from the bucking aft of the ship threw up spray that hissed on the hot iron of the lantern, perpetually threatening to put it out, but never quite accomplishing the task.

"What did you do with them?" Morris raged.

"Lestrade had the crew seized this afternoon. They are all languishing at Scotland Yard. Now, there is no one here to help you and no place for you to escape to."

"Lestrade," Mary spat. "But on your orders." She still had her gun and had it pointed at us now.

"Yes," Holmes said. "You might as well give up, there's nowhere for you to go."

"The invincible Mr Sherlock Holmes," Mary sneered, "who knows everything because it is his business to know it! Mr Sherlock Holmes." She spat the name like a curse.

Then she turned on me. "Has he even explained the game to

you, dear John? The stakes, the moves, the *real* players? How the dangers that have fallen on you these past months, including my transformation, the sea monsters, and even Morris here, are all the work of your one true enemy?"

"The Mariner Priest!" I said.

"How predictable," Mary said. "Poor John, ever the slowest person in the room. But has he told you who the Mariner Priest *is*? No? I see by your face that he has not. Poor John, stumbling around in the dark, even now, as a creature of the night! The irony is delicious, is it not?" She seemed to be entering a crazed fit, as if her words had been locked inside of her for so long that they virtually battered their way out of her without any conscious decision on her part. The gun seemed all but forgotten now. Even Morris seemed entranced by Mary's sudden explosion of anger.

"Of course he hasn't told you," Mary yelled at me, "because if he had, then you'd know that my transformation, *your* transformation, the vampire plague and so much more besides, are all because Holmes has refused to bow before the one superior intellect that has crossed his path. All this has happened to you, to me, to assuage Mr Sherlock Holmes's injured pride! Do you not know, *really* not know, who transformed me, John?"

"Holmes?" I said, turning to look at my companion. The rocking of the ship and the thunder and rain crashed, but distantly, as if the world around us held its breath, waiting.

"I suspected," Holmes said, his face a tortured mask, "suspected from the start, but could not be sure. The cunning, the plans within plans, it all pointed to the same conclusion."

"Say it!" Mary screamed. "Say his name!"

A shadow had passed over Holmes's face, but he stood taller and shouldered whatever burden that shadow brought with it. When he did speak, it was with a clear voice, easily audible over the storm.

"Professor James Moriarty," Holmes said. A thrill of astonished realization ran through me. Moriarty? Could it possibly be?

"Holmes!" I said, bitter at him keeping this vital piece of information from me.

"Yes!" Mary said, still focused on Holmes. "Moriarty is the one man you've never beaten, regardless of what you believed. The one man you never *can* beat! He is a better strategist than you and a far, far better vampire than Count Dracula could ever be, and he is coming for you both! Mark my words!"

She lifted the gun again. "The irony is that you're not actually going to live long enough for Moriarty's revenge to fall on you, because you die. Here. Now!"

I readied myself to jump in the way of the bullet, but the rocking ship made such an action impossible. The storm had swelled again and thunder boomed up in the grey sky.

Then a feral grunt, shockingly loud and out of place even over the storm, caused Mary and Morris to glance to our right. Mary's mouth dropped open and Morris's eyes went wide. I turned to look.

A large brown hand gripped the railing near the bow of the ship which dipped briefly under the water, then, as it rose, the railing and its occupant were revealed together. I heard Morris gasp.

Boucher dragged his bleeding and half-drowned body onto

the deck. The ruin of his back, briefly visible as he dropped awkwardly to the deck, was a horror to behold, roiling and smoking like a bubbling cauldron from the silver lodged within. His eyes, when he stood, bulged horrifically, and he seemed more animated corpse than man.

"For... a... woman," he spat at Morris. "For... a... *woman!*" The words he flung at Morris seemed not to come from his mouth, but rather dredged up from both the depths of his chest and from infernal domains unknown and unspoken. He lurched across the deck. Both Morris and Mary fired, not at Holmes and I, but at this new danger. But Boucher kept coming.

We were mere feet from their target, too close. Both Holmes and I scrambled out of the line of fire. I felt a hot furrow of fire plough its way across my shoulder.

"Watson!" Holmes's voice cried out. The silver bullet seared me to the bone. The pain had thrown me into shock, I knew. I fell to the deck as more shots tore through the air, followed by the smell of cordite, more powerful than I'd ever remembered it.

Hands dragged me away from the shooting. Then I was wedged with my back against the quarterdeck wall. "Watson!" Holmes said again, his face a stretched mask of concern above me.

I tore myself free of the pain. The storm and ship snapped back into focus just as a horrible grinding noise came from below. It thrummed through my feet and rattled my skull, and the deck swayed. The motion flung both of us to one side, and it was only Holmes's iron grip that kept us from tumbling right off the ship's deck.

Wood splintered, and the world screamed and tilted impossibly underneath us. The *Merry Widow* had ground up against something, something that was tearing her hull out.

Morris and Mary were both better braced, and kept shooting despite the lurching deck. It seemed both absurd and impossible that anyone could shoot a man, vampire or otherwise, so many times and not kill him. But Boucher was still on his feet, looming between the two of them and the two of us.

Holmes started skirting around the combat, just as the world lurched again. The enormous support of one of the Thames' bridges could be seen through the curtain of rain. The deck was nearly level now, but buckling like so much thin ice. I dragged myself to my feet.

Somehow Holmes had gotten across the deck, and had his hands on both of Morris's wrists. They struggled now along the slippery deck, wrestling for control of Morris's pistol.

The ship lurched again. The sudden motion flung me against the half-dead Boucher and he spun and tried to grapple with me. The huge hands reached for my throat, this time, to finish the job. He seemed mad and insensible, but determined to rip asunder anyone unfortunate enough to fall into his hands. He pressed me back against the railing, and the wood ground against the bones in my back. Then, the rail cracked, and I could feel it giving way.

I groped for the swaying lantern, meaning to use it as a weapon. I got a hold of it with my right hand while jamming my left into the crazed vampire's chest in a near-futile effort to fend him off. Boucher's spectral face leered at me.

But past that face, amazingly, I picked out another face.

Mary. She'd gotten her footing and was aiming, very carefully, so that she could put a bullet into the back of Sherlock Holmes's head. I had not a moment to lose.

I thrust the lantern into Boucher's face, smashing glass and mangling the thin metal with the force of my blow. Oil splattered and Boucher's head went up in an instant bonfire.

He screamed, a horrible wail like a wounded hound. His hands lashed at his own face, scrabbling at it as if he meant to flense away fire and flesh together. I shoved him further away, ignoring the railing that threatened to finally snap behind me, and kicked out. My foot took Boucher full in the chest, and he flew, a flaming missile that went, gratefully, precisely where I'd aimed him.

He crashed into Mary.

Her shot went wild. Boucher grappled at her, now, and the two of them were covered in burning oil. Not just Boucher's head now, but both their bodies, the mizzenmast that they crashed into, and the sail above it all blazed. In a world of pitch, tar and sail, sailors live in constant fear of fire for good reason. The fire ran in all directions, in no way impeded by the rain. In instants, the entire bow of the ship was a conflagration that enveloped them both. They screamed and thrashed, becoming small infernos in their own right. Boucher's figure finally collapsed to the deck, immobile, gone at last. Mary survived some further twenty or thirty seconds, a harrowing and haunting vision wreathed in agony and flame and writhing in pain. Her screams still haunt me now, many years later. Finally, it was cut short as the burning deck collapsed and both of them fell into the fiery hold, where gouts of more flame and a great shower of sparks showed that the fire down there was even more terrible. I had to turn away.

"There!" Holmes shouted, and pointed with Morris's pistol, which Holmes had wrested from Morris. Holmes had his other hand on the scruff of Morris's neck and the defeated American looked to be an entirely broken man. I looked to where Holmes pointed and saw the welcome twin lights of the police boat through sheets of rain behind us.

"Lestrade!" I breathed.

"As dogged as ever!" Holmes agreed.

The backs of my own hands were smoking from where some of the oil had splashed on them and I only just now thought to smother them with the wet sleeves of my coat.

The *Merry Widow*'s entire main deck was engulfed in flame now, too, along with most of the sail, and the sulphurous blast of hot air battered and singed us in equal measure. Holmes dragged Morris's limp body over to me at the railing. As if in sudden irony, the railing which had kept me from falling under Boucher's assault, under no visible pressure whatsoever, shook itself loose under our gaze and tumbled into the Thames.

"Can you make it?" I shouted at him, nodding my head to indicate the somewhat daunting swim between us and the approaching police boat.

"We'll have to!" Holmes shouted. "We haven't a moment to lose!" He flipped Morris's pistol casually into the water and grabbed hold of my shoulder. We jumped and tumbled into the Thames. Only after I hit the water did I remember that the *Merry Widow* had been a liquor smuggling operation.

The towering pillar of flame when the fire got to the hold was, I'm told, nothing short of spectacular.

"Tell me again," Lestrade said some hours later back at Baker Street, "what the *actual* plan was? Or was it your intention to nearly get braised and poached with high-proof grain whiskey?"

"I'm just grateful you were there to pick us up!" I said.

"Those were Mr Holmes's instructions," Lestrade said pointedly. "As if I'd do any less. Might have warned me about the whiskey, though."

Never had my old chair felt so comfortable than it had now, with the danger of drowning so close behind me. It had fallen on me hard, the coma-like torpor, a black, spinning, spiralling suffocation of sensation that terrified me far more than death ever could. I remember Dracula claiming that the vampire's transformation brought out the deep-rooted superstitions of the psyche, making vampires more prone to the baser emotions than before. I hadn't believed him then, but I did now.

"Well," Holmes said. "Things did get rather out of hand. I knew Morris was reckless, but not that he was suicidal enough to board a ship and cast off without any visible crew." He lounged, fully at ease in his purple dressing gown, which had seen much better days.

"Those suicidal instincts," Lestrade said. "Nearly got us all killed. Bad enough for us on the police boat, but you and Dr Watson were even closer. You took an awful chance, Mr Holmes!"

"One we'll not take again," I said heartily. "I assure you."

"You took the worst of it, Doctor," Lestrade said. "Are you sure you're all right?"

"My hands are remarkably well recovered," I said. "But my shoulder still hurts. Makes me feel as if I've come full circle, somehow."

"One wound on top of another is poor luck," Lestrade said.

I nodded, though the truth of it was that the Afghan wound hadn't bothered me for months, not since my transformation. Given a proper supply of blood, I could heal more thoroughly, if not as quickly, than I ever had before. Now, however, it seemed that Morris's silver bullet had inflicted an identical wound and the poisonous wound throbbed more painfully than the Jezail bullet ever had. Still, it should heal again, if excruciatingly slowly.

"Well anyway," Lestrade said. "Afterwards we picked up Captain Gunn and Harweather, per your instructions, Mr Holmes, and charged them with murder, to boot."

"Murder?" I said.

"Oh," Holmes said languidly. "Didn't I tell you? Harweather killed Victor Apligian. Considering the gunpowder on his clothes and the neck injury that precisely matched the very unique weapon in Maggie Oakenshot's possession…" He trailed off and gave me a look filled with meaning to ensure the oblique reference to Mary's fangs, a reference obscured for Lestrade's benefit, as it would have necessitated an explanation of vampirism.

"At any rate," Holmes went on, "Maggie did injure the boy, but that was not the cause of death. We have Morris's confession that he found and hid the body, and no reason to doubt it, so I had Lestrade question Harweather on the matter directly."

"There was no need," Lestrade said with a chuckle. "Mr Holmes had already led me to detain Harweather and the crew of his ship on a smuggling charge, and also to delay the escape of your fugitive couple. After the arrest, Harweather told us everything before Mr Holmes's message to question him even arrived. His account corresponds with Thorne's, that is Morris's, account in every way."

"Harweather shot the boy for the pearl," Holmes said, "because Apligian had shown it to him, but Morris, also looking for Apligian, stumbled onto the scene almost before the body hit the dirt and Harweather, who does not seem to have the nerves for murder, ran off."

"What doesn't track for me, Mr Holmes," Lestrade said, "was why, when Thorne, or rather Morris, stumbled onto a corpse that had been clearly shot and was still warm, he should be so keen to hide the body. He could hardly think that the knife wound would land his lady in jail since it was clearly the gunshot wound that had killed the man."

"Well," Holmes said, "I am not entirely certain that Morris was in his right mind by that time. It seems that he has had to cover for her before and no doubt that strain took a toll on his sanity."

"If you say so, Mr Holmes," Lestrade said doubtfully.

"Not every criminal is a mastermind," I said helpfully, knowing that we could not possibly explain Morris's need to hide the evidence of a vampire wound. No more than we could explain that Maggie was actually Mary.

"Morris didn't think to search the body," Holmes said, "being too concerned with hiding the evidence."

"You say," Lestrade said, "that the Apligian boy showed Harweather the pearl as part of a negotiation to have Harweather give Apligian and Maggie Oakenshot passage out of England?"

"Just so," Holmes said, "though whether she would have gone with Apligian or Morris in the end given the full range of options is anyone's guess."

"I rather think," I said reluctantly, "that she had no intention of leaving Morris. I believe it may have been some kind of capricious game between the two of them."

"Perhaps," Holmes said. "Who can fathom the motives of women?"

Maggie Oakenshot, Mary's name in her new life. A life she seemed quite taken with, it seemed to me. She was dead now, truly dead, not living a violent, murderous, soulless existence and not dead from illness as I'd been telling everyone. It had been my hand, in the end, that had brought it about, a fact which sorrowed me greatly. I could not feel the full weight of guilt, however. *Maggie's* life after she left me had been one foul deed after another, culminating in her attempt to murder Holmes. Death would have come for her in any circumstance, I told myself, my actions notwithstanding.

Holmes went on without noticing my silence. "Harweather had once smoked ship's tobacco, of course, which made Victor bringing monetary payments to Harweather inside of such a pouch the perfect cover. The fact that Victor himself carried tobacco and no pipe was, of course, the first clue. Nor did he smoke.

"It then became clear that Harweather and Apligian had been arguing. Apligian wanted to book passage for him and Maggie

Oakenshot, and showed them the pearl to secure the bargain, which proved to be his undoing. Harweather murdered him for it."

"Miss Apligian will have to eat her words," I said without much relish. "She was certain her brother's killer would never be found."

"Then Morris," Lestrade said, with satisfaction, "came on the scene immediately thereafter, possibly drawn at a run by the shot. But why would he be in the graveyard in the first place?"

"For precisely the same purpose," Holmes said. "Morris as much as confessed to it. He'd gotten wind of Victor and Maggie's involvement and was determined to eliminate the competition. Only Harweather beat him to it. Harweather had no time to get the pearl on account of Morris's arrival and Morris did not take the pearl because he did not know to look for it. It is the most likely series of events. Pity we didn't get a chance to verify it."

"But why would Morris hide the body?" Lestrade asked. I looked at my companion.

"Maggie," Holmes said with no trace of deception, "was a habitual poisoner. Morris had gotten used to disposing of such bodies. This, to him, was merely one more."

"A poisoner, you say?" Lestrade said wonderingly. "Do you have any evidence for such a claim?"

Holmes shook his head. "None whatsoever."

"Well," Lestrade said. "With her body in the Thames, and Morris to stand trial on multiple counts of murder, I guess it doesn't matter that the woman's guilt will likely be overlooked at the inquest."

"Most likely," Holmes said.

"Best be off," Lestrade said. "I have more paperwork down at the station to do. Not like you unofficial persons that get to put your feet up at the end of a case."

"In that," Holmes said, "you might be in error. I suspect the good doctor's paperwork is just beginning."

"And they'll probably get five shillings apiece for them down at *The Strand*," Lestrade said morosely. "No such luck with my reports, I'm afraid."

"Bad luck," I agreed.

"No accolades back at the station, either," Holmes said dryly, "for another job well done?"

"Holmes," I said. "Really."

"Well," Lestrade said, draining off the rest of his brandy and giving me a broad wink. "At least I have no complaints about the way you share your spoils."

"Any time," I said. "The least we can do in our gratitude."

He put on his coat, but lingered a moment at the door. "This portrait," he said, pointing with the still-smouldering cigar tip. "Good to see you put this up. What was here before? Bridge or sunset or something?"

"Nothing important," I said. Lestrade was pointing to a portrait that Mrs Forrester had had commissioned as a wedding gift. In it, Mary was standing in the Forresters' sun room with a brilliant panorama of windows behind her and the sun on her face. She looked as sweet and compassionate as ever any woman could have been. In a word, beautiful. *Death would have come for her in any circumstance*, I told myself, *my actions notwithstanding*.

"You've got the right of it, Doctor," Lestrade said seriously.

"Nothing more important than family. I wonder why you did not put it up before?"

"I just…" I said, then paused, feeling yet another welling up of emotion. "I just wasn't ready."

"She was a lovely woman, Doctor, and no mistake," Lestrade said. "My condolences again." He gave me a curious look, and while I knew Lestrade would most likely never uncover the full truth, it was clear he knew that some irregularities were going on here at 221B Baker Street. He shrugged and stepped out, closing the door softly behind him, leaving Holmes and I to ponder the events of the past few days.

Suddenly, the full weight of loss fell on me again. Death would have come for her in any circumstance… only it had been my hand, *my hand*, that had ended her life. I had come through the transformation intact. Why couldn't she have? Holmes, and even Dracula, had spoken of this feat of mine as if there had been something extraordinary that I had *done*, but I knew that statement couldn't be further from the truth. If I had a blessing, it was the associations of my friends and loved ones. I went through that transformation, that great tunnel of darkness not unlike death, and came out the other side still John H. Watson because of the strength that my association with Mary and Holmes had given me. Even the implication of special moral character on my part left a bitter taste in my mouth, for I knew it for the kind-hearted lie that it was.

Because I had failed Mary. Failed her unutterably and completely. Her love had been enough to bring me through, but my love hadn't been anywhere near enough to save her. She hadn't forgotten her life as Mrs Watson after her transformation into a vampire, she simply hadn't felt any compelling, burning moral need to adhere to it. She'd cast aside her life with me with no regrets. Then, when she'd threatened Holmes, I had ended her without a moment's hesitation. My love had failed one test after another, had failed *her*, again and again. Now she was gone from me, twice damned by my own actions, while I was doomed to a cursed and immortal existence, wearing the same suits, the same hats, drinking blood out of china that had once been used for the commendable practice of drinking English tea while everyone around carried on as if I'd not done something horrible, as if I hadn't done horrible things and failed everyone around me utterly.

"There there, old man," Holmes said, standing next to me and laying his hand on my shoulder. I'd been so lost in grief, sitting with my head in my hands. My dear friend, usually so masterful in every situation, suddenly seemed awkward and uncertain standing next to me and the contrast forced an ironic smile onto my lips, for all the weight of my grief.

"Here," Holmes said, plucking a handkerchief out of the pocket of his dressing gown and handing it down to me.

I nodded my thanks, taking the handkerchief while he made himself busy ringing for tea. After that, he seemed momentarily at a loss. Then he picked up his violin.

He began to play a mournful and melancholy tune. His face, so often stern, took on an expression of sublime sadness as the melody wrung itself into something infinitely beautiful and also infinitely sad. It was nothing less than a lament for Mary Watson, and for the loss that it inflicted on those of us that had known her best.

Mrs Hudson, when she came, displayed her uncanny intuition and slipped unobtrusively in and out so as not to interrupt. I closed my eyes as the music somehow conjured, within me, the lonely scent of a moor at night, then the near-silent sounds of clouds covering the moon just before the storm, and finally, Mary's face and the image from my painting of the woman in darkness yearning for the sun, which were, of course, one and the same. The last note had faded for at least a minute before I took a deep, ragged breath, and opened my eyes.

Holmes wordlessly set down the violin. Put his hand companionably on my shoulder again as he passed, then went to the table. Mrs Hudson had laid out the service most completely, but Holmes found some trifles to correct and then poured out a portion first for myself, from the red-ribboned teapot, and then actual tea for himself from the other pot.

I sat and took up my cup. "Miss Winter is recovering from her ordeal?" I asked. "That was quite a fright, I'm sure."

"Yes," Holmes said. "She may be of sterner stuff than you give her credit for."

"And Somersby?"

"Also healing admirably," he said. "Miss Winter is taking exceptional care of him, I should think. She was quite distraught after watching Morris shoot him and being so sure he was dead. If help hadn't come to them so swiftly, or if the bullet had not ricocheted off the ribcage, or if Morris hadn't been in so much of a hurry, Somersby might well have died. It was a near miracle he survived as it is. I think it's given both of them a new perspective."

There was a long stretch of silence while we both drank before Holmes said, "What did prompt you to put Mary's painting back up?"

"I simply feel," I said, trying to dredge up the tangle of my hollowed emotions, "that I can grieve now. I couldn't before, you know." Strangely, thoughts of her were painful, but not quite as much as they had been before. Something else that was healing.

"Ah…" Holmes said. "The bliss of matrimony. You miss it, I gather. Certainly this last case is not a very strong recommendation for the institution. I cannot say that I have ever understood its appeal."

"Likely not, Holmes," I said. "Likely not."

I finished the sustenance in my cup, took care to wipe my mouth carefully, and lit a cigarette while Holmes filled his pipe. It was still a strange sensation to work my lungs, but the change had, if anything, increased the pleasure of smoking. The same was true of brandy, and so I poured us each a small glass. Outside, the city of London boiled and bubbled with human activity while we sat in comfortable silence.

"So," I said, taking a deep breath. "This implacable and cunning new enemy of ours isn't a new enemy after all, but an old one. Moriarty."

"Yes," Holmes said. "I'm afraid so."

"How long have you known?"

"I have suspected from the start," Holmes admitted. "But there has always been an incompatibility between my suspicions and the Mariner Priest's methods such that I doubted myself. Nothing I could always put my finger on, you understand. The Moriarty of old always played a careful and cunning game, ever trying to improve his position. While the Mariner Priest, his new persona, if you will, is reckless and destructive. Moriarty extended his control carefully, like a spider extending his web, while the Mariner Priest's methods are anything but careful. How can one preside over a criminal empire in England, or anywhere else, if you burn the city to the ground? Similarly, where is the secrecy that characterized Moriarty's every move before this? Now, our opponent holds the secret of the vampire and suddenly he abandons all secrecy? He produces vampires with careless abandon, and how can that fit his agenda, for if the world at large understands the nature of vampirism, his own existence is in just as much jeopardy as anyone else's. Also, we had Dracula's opinion that Van Helsing was a likely culprit or the entirely contradictory theory that an elder vampire had to be the answer. While it seems our good doctor Van Helsing has taken some curious actions, I find no reason to believe it is connected to our current danger. Also, I think we must discard Dracula's elder vampire theory. Clearly Moriarty has brought a level of experimentation and discovery to the condition that Dracula cannot match."

"His tactic of staying out at sea seems shrewd enough," I observed.

"Yes," Holmes admitted, "but he could be drifting in relative obscurity and isolation, but is instead engaging in gambits aimed at us that require his interaction with shore when he might lie entirely in wait and succeed that way."

"Perhaps," I said, "you have underestimated the personality change that the transformation brought about? Perhaps it pushed Moriarty over the edge of reason?"

"Yes," Holmes said. "It may be as simple as that. With your sterling example sitting in the chair across from me, as your staunch personality has remained intact, perhaps I can be forgiven an error in judgement for not understanding how it has changed him."

Holmes had put a peculiar emphasis on the word 'forgiven' and I saw a flicker of uncertainty in his masterful expression. His brown eyes watched me carefully and with, I thought, a nearly imperceptible question in them.

"Yes, Holmes," I said, with a small smile. "I think you can be forgiven a small error in judgement."

"Capital!" Holmes said. His tone was light, but I could see that his burden had been lightened.

"But what of Moriarty?" I asked. "Do you believe Mary? Has he abandoned his tactic of staying safely out to sea? Is he coming to England?"

"I do believe her," Holmes said. "In fact, I'd guessed as much and have written to Count Dracula to call in our favour, as it were."

"They are coming here?"

"I cannot tell," Holmes said. "They have not responded and I fear the worst. But one thing is certain: Moriarty is coming and we had best be prepared."

Dear Dr Watson,

I am afraid that we cannot depart at once for London as you and Mr Holmes request, for reasons that I believe the rest of this letter should make abundantly clear.

We also have been weathering strange occurrences, and while they might not be as bizarre as the affair you described involving the Innsmouth whaler, they have been a bit more direct in their hostile intent towards us. Knowing what we know about the Mariner Priest, we cannot help but think that this assault came from him.

This is what we know: some intrepid soul, a man of iron courage, I should think, made their way secretly into Transylvania, avoiding notice and detection as a stranger, evaded the villages and roving Romany bands that would have no doubt alerted Vlad to his presence, and penetrated into the castle during the day while we slept. Not just into the castle grounds, but past the few servants that might have been about during daylight and down into the foundations of the castle, placing a great deal of explosive there. Neither of us is well-versed in such things, but it must have been a great deal, perhaps involving more than one trip. It was cunningly done, Vlad says, and indicates at least a rough survey of the castle and great stealth.

All we know is that we woke to an upheaval of the earth as if the very land was split asunder. We did not know it at the time, but have since discovered that several storeys of the western side of the castle were broken by the blast and several tons of mountain collapsed onto our resting place. The collapse could easily have crushed us where we rested but though our resting places were breached, the heavy stone above us broke in such a way as to provide a small amount of shelter. You are familiar enough, Dr Watson, with the nature of our existence to understand how close to death such a situation could bring us. Though we did not need air in the same way as we would have in our previous lives, we had neither strength to shift the rubble or any sustenance. A vampire may be able to do without food for much longer than a non-vampire, but that also made starvation a very real possibility considering how thoroughly we were trapped, a much more frightening prospect.

However, given some few days, we were able to shift the stones enough to effect a passage out. Even then, it was a very close thing and we emerged weakened and emaciated. Were it not for the assistance of Vlad's faithful servants that sought us out, we should not have survived.

It may be some time before we can journey to London. However, before this disaster befell our home, I was able to acquire a steamer ship, the King's Ransom, *which now lies in wait for us in Varna. Vlad was not keen on trusting this particular modern device, but I have convinced him that speed would be of the essence. When we come, it shall be by that route.*

The Mariner Priest is getting bolder and more powerful. If he is willing to strike at us in this manner, it cannot be long before a similar blow falls on the two of you. Please be on your most vigilant guard, for I should hate to lose either of the few friends I have left in the world.

Fondest wishes,

Mina

Part Four

OLD ENEMIES

Chapter 16

NEW FRIENDS

"Holmes!" I said with some exasperation at our table in Baker Street. "My breakfast might not be what it once was, but I hardly think it will be improved by this!" I held up the bloodstained corner of some paper that Holmes had strewn all over the table. "Nor do I think you want your documents tainted in this manner."

"There you would be wrong, Doctor," Holmes said tartly. "For that document was tainted long before it came in contact with your repast. Forgery is too kind a word for it! A complete fabrication would be a better expression, and one that would have hindered our battle with Moriarty in no uncertain terms, for all that it is steeped in tedium and monotony. To say nothing of Mrs Hudson's fate! Even worse, for all that I have pledged to remain on my most vigilant guard, this oblique attack would have landed a telling blow, except for the timely intervention of Watson's Irregulars."

"What on earth are you talking about, Holmes?" I asked, getting more perplexed by the moment.

"An agent of Moriarty's," Holmes said, "for it must be one of his, though I have not as yet begun to trace the trail, set into motion a complicated swindle involving forged tax documents and a false claim by the crown threatening to seize the property."

"The property?" I said. "Baker Street?"

"None other," Holmes said. "Agents of the crown, likely innocent themselves, but working on the falsified information, issued a warrant to seize the property only yesterday. Fortunately, our good Samaritan, one Beatrice Gladstone, or one of your Irregulars, intervened on our behalf. Spending a not-inconsiderable sum to clear the matter up."

"My Irregulars?" I said, "I'm sure I have no idea to whom you refer."

"A reader, dear boy," Holmes said, and his irritated expression split into a rueful smile. "One of Watson's Irregulars. No? I thought it a catchy term but I see you do not. At any rate, she is an avid fan, by the sound of it. She works in the government office where the false papers landed and, recognizing the address from your lurid tales in *The Strand*, immediately set about to rectify the situation from her own pocket. I tried to send a cheque to recompensate her this very morning, but she's already replied and refused. It seems that Mrs Gladstone has won the argument for you regarding your literary talents. At least this round, anyway."

"Holmes," I said, "that's remarkable!" I took a sip from my cup and then frowned, finding the taste stale and slightly bitter.

"Yes," Holmes said, "another of Moriarty's attacks, I'm afraid.

I had to discard the fresh blood delivered this morning from the butcher's shop and make arrangements to substitute another. Far less fresh, I'm afraid."

"But why?"

"Because the first batch was poisoned, Watson, with silver."

I set my cup down, suddenly feeling a chill. "Poisoned? How could you possibly have known that?"

"Because I've been on guard against it," Holmes said, "and have tested your supply after each arrival to make certain that only livestock contributed to it, and not any agent of the Mariner Priest's, that is to say, of Moriarty's. Having unique knowledge of your needs and weaknesses, it seemed a likely angle of attack. At least I did not need Mrs Gladstone to safeguard us on this front!" He sighed. "But have no fear – I have a confederate, with secrets of his own that I have promised to keep, that very likely has a line on a fresher source of repast for you that should be more secure against contamination without asking too many questions. The need for one gallon of chicken or cow's blood is easy enough to explain away, but asking for the same on a continual basis is quite another thing. Fortunately, Raffles—"

"Raffles?" I said. "The burglar from your last case? I think I must sit. This is a great wealth of information coming very quickly."

"Things are coming to a head, Doctor," Holmes said. "They are not likely to slow down until this affair is quite finished, one way or another."

That had an ominous ring to it, but I knew that Holmes did not exaggerate. If anything, he understated the case. The fact that Moriarty had already taken the pains to come at us from the flanks, as it were, did not in any way assuage me. Holmes was right. This was a campaign that could only end with our downfall or his.

"This Raffles," I said, "can he be trusted?"

"Well," Holmes said, "like I said, I have in my pocket a secret of his that he considers quite outrageous. It is not every man that occupies the finest gentlemen's clubs by day and commits burglaries by night. Even then, I would not have acquiesced even that far, except that he has limited his victims to those that have come by their monies through illegal means and has even passed along a great deal of information that has brought more serious and immoral criminals to the dock. Little does he imagine that we hold a considerably more outré secret."

Holmes's tone was jocular, but now that I looked for it, I could see that being on guard against Moriarty's constant schemes was starting to tell on even his iron constitution. His lean, ascetic face was haggard and his dark eyes sunken.

"Holmes?" I said. "When did you last sleep? You cannot bear the burden of this all on your own shoulders."

"I'm afraid," he said by way of reply, "that we have rather more to worry about than just food sources and economic matters." He pushed a letter, already opened and no doubt examined, across the table to me. I recognized Mina's handwriting at once and snatched it up. Inside, she detailed an attack on their own person right in Dracula's ancestral home.

"Holmes," I said in wonder. "Moriarty brought part of the castle down!"

"So it would seem."

"It's… it's unbelievable!"

"I'm afraid it is all too believable," Holmes contradicted. "Count Dracula and I represent the very greatest threats to Moriarty's dominion. Moriarty continues to be more aggressive. If this is the measure he's taken for Dracula, I do not think it egoism to expect an equally fatal plan for ourselves."

"It seems that Moriarty is no longer willing to wait until our… that is, your eventual demise through old age. What has changed?"

"What indeed?" Holmes asked by way of agreement. "It seems we shall have no help from the Carpathian Mountains. They have their own war to deal with and it is a defensive battle at best. I'm afraid that this may put a possible dampener on your medical activities."

I had, indeed, resumed practice in the medical field and had been very successful at it, despite the necessity of keeping mostly night-time hours. It made house calls problematic, as no one is very impressed by an overly lethargic doctor, but with my newly enhanced senses and far steadier hand, I had created quite a name for myself.

"I had some cases this week," I said, "but these are finished and I have nothing very absorbing now."

"That is well," Holmes said. "I will send a note for Somersby and Kitty Winter and have them speak to our other operatives of the Midnight Watch so that everyone is on their highest guard. It would be just as well to send one to Lestrade and Gregson at the Yard, though I will have to take some care with my words so that I can elevate their alertness without letting the cat out of the bag, as it were."

"You may not have to," I said. "I can hear Mrs Hudson talking to a delivery boy from the Yard now. They've sent you a telegram."

"Really?"

"Mrs Hudson is a lovely woman," I said, "but her voice does rather carry."

"Excellent!" Holmes said. "Your ears are getting keener all the time. Soon enough I shall just instruct the Yarders to shout messages out of their window; what it lacks in secrecy it will more than make up in convenience." He shot up from his chair and was at the door the very instant it was opened. No sooner had Mrs Hudson taken her first step into the room than Holmes had snatched the telegram out of her hand.

"Thank you, Mrs Hudson," he sang, as he steered her gently but inexorably back out of the room. "You are quite correct that messages from the Yard are worth our immediate attention!"

Poor Mrs Hudson, long-suffering personage that she was, was still taken aback by this strange and abrupt behaviour. "Mr Holmes! You and your deduct—" But the door slamming behind her quite drowned out the rest of her words.

"My deductions indeed," Holmes said. "Soon I shall be riding on your coat tails, Doctor, instead of Scotland Yard riding on ours! Ah, Lestrade has an unusual body in the morgue that he would like us to look at, just the kind of thing I have asked him to keep watch for. Excellent! How quickly can you be ready to depart, Doctor?"

"Smell the night air, Doctor!" Holmes said in the cab. His face was animated and flushed with excitement. "Can you not sense the imminent possibilities?"

The night air was very strong in my nostrils already, as London always was now. I shook my head at Holmes's excitement, knowing full well the source. It never ceased to amaze me how contrary to all human experience my comrade could be. Having just discovered that imminent death was rushing across the world towards us and London, another man would have certainly felt fear or anguish, but not Holmes. He was truly at his happiest when grappling with a dangerous problem that was too much for the talents of others. Moriarty's return might have been a curse for England and the world at large, but there was no hiding the fact that it was a pure gift to Sherlock Holmes.

Even the cold night air and then the grey and even colder tunnels of the morgue did not diminish my friend's whetted appetite. He eagerly rubbed his hands together as Lestrade led us to the body and removed the covering sheet. The deceased was a smallish man, Caucasian, perhaps twenty to thirty years of age.

"Washed up to the shore near Brighton," the sallow-faced little detective said. "Which wouldn't have caused the local authorities to send it so far up to us, except for the wound. I'd like to know what makes that kind of wound in a man. Sickens my stomach, I don't mind telling you."

There could be no question as to the cause of death, for the wound in the centre of the man's chest was terrible to look upon. Nor was it caused by any conventional weapon, but rather a horrific burn of some sort, causing the skin to char and flake all around the chest.

"How long ago did this happen?" Holmes asked.

"They discovered the body yesterday morning and brought it to us last night," Lestrade said. "We have no information from Brighton about how long it lay in the water for they do not know, but they suspect body was dead at least two days before it was found. Hardly any rigor left, see?" He seized the hand and wiggled it back and forth, showing how loose the muscles of the arm were. "I know that water can alter the conditions, but there's hardly any bloat to this man at all."

"Thank you, Lestrade," Holmes said without looking up from the body. "We shall meet you back upstairs after we've finished the examination."

Lestrade rolled his eyes at me, but left without further demur. He was far too familiar with Holmes's often icy demeanour when on a case to take too much umbrage now, and well aware that my friend routinely made discoveries that Lestrade could hope to get nowhere else.

Holmes looked the body over in that quick but minute way he had, checking the hands, feet, and clothing in addition to the wound.

"Watson," he said. "Come give me your opinion, if you would be so kind."

Lestrade had been right on one account, for the man's body was certainly not showing any signs of the decay or rigor mortis that one would expect from a corpse so long at sea, and very little sign of being attacked by fish or other marine life. There was some of the bloat, but again, Lestrade had also been perfectly correct in saying that it was far less than expected if the story were accurate.

I would have normally expected a great deal of blood for a wound like this, but the water had washed it all away. Still, little blood was not quite the same as no blood at all, and I examined the curiously vicious droplets I found near the edges of the wound, rubbing them along the tips of my rubber gloves.

"Holmes!" I whispered urgently. "The man's blood, it is not normal. I think our victim may have been a vampire!"

"So I surmised as well," Holmes said. He had retrieved a scalpel while I was examining the body and handed it to me now. "If you will probe the centre of the wound I think you may find a confirmation of our hypothesis as well as some clarification as to the nature of the wound. It is just as well that you are wearing gloves."

I had followed his deductions to have a fair idea of what he meant by that part. Thinking of the horrible and violent reaction that silver had caused to Boucher, the likeliest cause of this particular wound became obvious. So, it was with some newly learned revulsion, if not surprise, that I cut into the centre of the wound and found the glint of silver waiting for me.

"A silver bullet," I said, "and certainly the cause of death."

"Clearly," Holmes said. "What of the face? Does he not look familiar?"

There *was* something familiar about the face, now that Holmes had brought my attention to it. A young man's face, handsome, blonde, but I could not place it.

"Imagine, perhaps," Holmes said, "a superior sneer across those lips?"

"John Clay!" I said. It all came rushing back now, including the long, underground vigil in a vault not unlike a tomb, and one of the more daring bank robberies ever conceived. The Adventure of the Red-Headed League! Clay had dug a long tunnel from a nearby pawnbroker's shop to the vault in question. I remembered, too, the condescension that he'd shown the arresting officers when taken into custody. One of the more dangerous men that Holmes and I had dealt with in the past.

"It seems as if Moriarty," Holmes said, "has decided that he no longer needs his star pupil."

"You think there is a connection, then?" I asked.

"Well," Holmes said, "I had long surmised a connection between the two based on Moriarty's role in criminal society as a criminal consultant and the outrageous nature of Clay's robbery attempt, but I'd never had the opportunity to confirm it. The mere fact that Clay is here, instead of in prison, suggests he had outside help. This, however, is a rather intriguing development."

"What can it mean?"

"Clearly," Holmes said, "this man had been transformed. The most likely source is our Mariner Priest. That is to say Moriarty himself. Had we any doubt about Moriarty returning to England, I would say this would tip the balance of probability in that direction, making it more than likely that Clay and Moriarty came back here on the same ship. We can take that as a working hypothesis, at any rate."

"Is there someone else hunting vampires?" I ventured. "Someone that knows their vulnerability to silver? Someone hunting Moriarty's ship, perhaps?"

"I should think," Holmes said, "that if there had been an organization aware of vampires to the extent that they've armed men with silver cartridges and outfitted a ship with the purpose of hunting Moriarty at sea, that they'd have also involved themselves in watching over the vampire problem in London and we should have encountered some sign of them ourselves. Since we have not, I conclude it highly unlikely."

"Who then?"

"The most likely choice is Moriarty himself."

"Shoot his own agent?"

"We know John Clay to have been a highly ambitious man," Holmes said, "and Moriarty to be even more so, as well as being extremely ruthless. I can only surmise a falling-out between the two men. It must have been a truly serious one for Moriarty to abandon his investment in Clay's education, but it is the theory that best fits the facts." He straightened up and turned about from John Clay's cadaver. "In the meantime, we shall let Lestrade know the identity of the body, but breathe no word regarding the unusual nature of the disease, nor any explanation of the wound, as we understand it."

"Of course not," I said, a little hurt that Holmes should have to tell me, of all people, that.

"Very good," Holmes said. "In the meantime, we shall need to try and locate any bolt holes where Moriarty could safely bring in a ship with a vampire crew and hide them."

"Could Lestrade not help with that?" I asked.

"I have a better idea," Holmes said.

Chapter 17

THE NEW BAKER STREET IRREGULARS

Holmes's concept of a 'better idea' became clear when we returned to Baker Street and he dispatched a telegram to Kitty Winter to mobilize the Baker Street Irregulars and send their spokesman to us for instructions.

While we waited, Mrs Hudson brought up a letter. Holmes, standing pensively by the window, violin dangling listlessly from his hand, bounded over to snatch the paper from her. He gave her the violin in trade and tore it open. Mrs Hudson made a tsk-tsk noise, shook her head with fond dismissal of Holmes's typically cavalier manners and crossed the room to put the violin down on the desk near the window Holmes had just left. She then beat a hasty retreat.

"Some excellent news, Watson," Holmes murmured. "Count Dracula and Mina are indeed coming to England after all. It seems they already departed Varna some two weeks ago and are expecting to land in London inside of a week. If Varna had not had broken telegraph wires, we should have gotten this news much sooner."

"That is good news," I said dutifully, although I had mixed feelings about their arrival. Still, with Moriarty in England, we should need all the allies we could get.

"Now," Holmes said, looking with irritation at his watch, "if our emissary from the Baker Street Irregulars would only arrive!"

The Irregulars were a key group of informants for our operations, keeping their eyes peeled for unusual disappearances, especially among the lower classes, where such things are more easily overlooked by the official police force. Normally, the Irregulars and the Midnight Watch needed to work closely together, and Holmes often relayed direction through Kitty Winter, but in this instance, Holmes was keen to relate his instructions directly to Holly Hoskins himself. As such, he paced in irritation, looking at the window often and several times picking up his violin to play only to set it down again. The last time he did this, the position of the violin was so precarious, wedged against the side of the window, that I was forced to jump up and rescue it. He smoked several cigarettes and two pipes as we whiled away the hours, always loitering by the window. I tried to engage myself in the paper, but it was a dreary time and all I could think about was the danger coming to us in the form of Moriarty. I'd never seen him except for a brief glimpse from afar, but the vulturous image of the man had begun to haunt my dreams as well as my waking hours. All in all, it was a tedious vigil for both of us.

Three hours passed before the doorbell rang and Mrs Hudson

allowed the ragamuffin form of Holly Hoskins to come up. (Young Wiggins, no longer quite so young, had long since aged out of the Baker Street Irregulars and was now, due to Holmes's patronage, a police inspector out in the country with a young, pretty wife and his second child on the way.)

The dirty little urchin announced herself with an insolent, "Must be a bit of a carriwitchet, eh, to 'ave Mr Sherlock 'Olmes call me in direct like."

"Quite," Holmes agreed.

She lounged into the centre of the room, a wisp of a girl, with coffee-coloured skin and dark curled hair underneath a black-and-white checked boy's hat, but confident and certain despite her size. Holmes had originally attempted to install a young boy named Doherty as their new leader, but Holly Hoskins had effortlessly bullied Doherty out of the position and taken over herself, much to Holmes's surprise and chagrin. However, she'd proved herself during the Adventure of the Bloodthirsty Baron and had been so instrumental in locating the baron's missing carriage that even Holmes had been forced to admit defeat on this particular front and accept her as the new leader of the Baker Street Irregulars. He'd told me in confidence that she was by far the sharpest of a sharp lot and had something of his admiration, but there was little to show that in his expression now.

"We are looking," Holmes said, "for a ship that may have docked in the past two days or will dock shortly with a crew of sailors that take pains to keep below decks during the daylight. It would be a large ship capable of holding at least twenty men, possibly more. They may be a merchant vessel, but would have armaments to allow them to defend themselves at sea. They may dock at night and keep to themselves or may dock during the day with a skeleton crew. Above all, I am looking for any rash of disappearances near the docks."

"What are the wages, governor?"

"There's a shilling each in it for you," Holmes said, "but you must promise to exercise caution, Holly. I would not see you or your charges added to the list of the disappeared for all the world. If you find anything that matches this description, you must report it to me or Watson here. You stay well clear of any ship that matches that description and avoid any areas demonstrating any disappearances you uncover. We shall pick up the investigation at that juncture. Is this all quite clear?"

His solemn tone must have made an impression, for Holly nodded carefully.

"Very good," Holmes said.

We kept vigil throughout the rest of the night. I was no longer such an early riser, and as such it was nearly noon when Holmes bounded up the bedroom stairs and pounded on my door. He'd made so much noise coming up the stairs that the latter action had hardly been necessary. Even so, the daylight torpor was difficult to shake out of my head until Holmes shouted out: "The reports are in, Doctor, and we are bound for Gravesend!"

I completed my toilette and came down the stairs as fast as I could.

"Gravesend is a far cry from London proper," I said as Holmes slid a teapot towards me. It reeked with the savoury aroma I craved and I poured out a cup full of the dark red liquid and drank it off without a second thought, giving no more consideration to the chicken that had given his life for this meal than I did for the pig that had donated Holmes's bacon. Peculiar the things you can get used to.

"Holly has quite outdone herself," Holmes said, standing up and abandoning his breakfast, untouched, in order to pace around the room. "She has ambition, that one has. Better even than Wiggins was. She passed my request and some of my shillings down the Thames and information trickled back up. One of the ships near Royal Terrace Pier has reported several missing sailors. I didn't tell Holly to keep watch for missing sailors specifically, but I should have. It is sound thinking on her part. You'll soon have to leave Baker Street and start writing up her cases next, mark my word!"

"That bothers you?" I asked, noting his agitation.

Holmes waved off my comment. "No, that is all to the good."

I lifted a piece of bacon out of the serving platter and tried a small nibble, out of nostalgia, but found that I could taste only charred flesh. I hastily bundled the rest of the piece into a napkin and discarded it onto an unused plate with a sigh. "What then?"

"Things are coming to a head. Miss Winter and Somersby are coming here in a carriage to take us to Gravesend. Moriarty is very possibly waiting for us there and Dracula's ship is due to land tomorrow night. I shall send a telegram to the Count to give him and Mina all the particulars. The pieces are all hurtling themselves across the board to meet in the middle and it shall be a strange thing indeed if events do not have a serious impact on London and possibly, just possibly, the rest of Europe. Except…"

"Except what?"

He reached the shelves at the end of the room and spun, elevating a finger like an excitable schoolmaster. "There is a piece of this equation we do not have in our hands, Watson. You remember my outrage and despair when I discovered that Moriarty had fled to sea to patiently await my demise?"

"Yes, of course."

"It was an elegantly simple solution, remember, and I was not willing to abandon London in order to pursue him and so could devise no strategy to beat it."

"Quite so."

He stalked back in my direction. "So then, what has changed? Something is driving Moriarty to bring things to a head rather sooner than he had planned."

"But what?" I said. "We have so little information. How could we possibly fathom his reasons for doing anything?"

"There is little enough information, it is true," Holmes mused. "But little is not the same as none. We have our deceased John Clay in the morgue, do we not? What can we infer from that?" Plucking up my doctor's bag from its resting place near my chair, he casually dumped out the contents onto the floor and started stuffing some of the cardboard boxes filled with Ingerson's silver bullets into it.

"Holmes!" I said, picking up my stethoscope, bandages, and several other odds and ends, and putting them in a little pile on the table.

"For Gravesend, Doctor," he said. "Come now, what can we infer?"

"I am sure that I am very stupid," I said, wishing, as I often did, that Holmes would simply come to the point.

"Moriarty has pitted himself against both London," Holmes said, "and Transylvania, or rather against the protectors of both those places." He opened another drawer in his desk and pulled out a heavy mallet and several wooden stakes. After a quick moment's thought, he opened another drawer and pulled out a large deerskin pouch and dumped that in, too. Leaving my bag on the sofa, he dashed back into his room, raising his voice as he rummaged among his things in there. Overtaken by curiosity, I went over to the bag and pulled out the pouch. I tried to open it, but the cords were knotted shut.

"Dracula assured us that controlling other vampires was no easy task," Holmes called out from the other room, "and also of the fracturing of personality that almost always comes with the transformation to vampirehood. We have seen that Moriarty seems to have found a way around that, to be able to transform his victims and still retain control, building a vampire horde that neither I, nor Dracula, nor any other agency in the world, could hope to contend with. His entire enterprise has been built on this threat and our need to counteract it or perish."

I stopped working momentarily on the pouch cord, and shivered again, as I always did, at the thought of teeming hordes of vampires in Moriarty's thrall running rampant in the London streets.

"But," Holmes said, stepping back into the room, "what if his method of control has failed him? What if there is one, or more than one, convert that threatens his newly formed nocturnal criminal organization from the inside?" He held a silver dagger in his hand that glinted brightly.

"That would change things a great deal," I said. "Has that happened?"

Holmes came over to me, took the pouch from my hand, severed the cords in an easy flick from the silver knife, and handed the pouch back to me. He dumped the knife into the bag with the rest, then went and yanked open the door.

"Mrs Hudson," he called down the stairs in a sing-song cadence. "We are awaiting a four-wheeler with Somersby and Miss Winter in it. Please keep a watchful eye on the door!"

I could hear the outrage in Mrs Hudson's voice from here. "As if I'd let them stand on the doorstep when they arrived, Mr Holmes. I can hear a doorbell as well as anyone else. I never!"

I sniffed at the deerskin pouch, but really, there was no need. In fact, there had barely been a need to open it if I'd been less distracted. The scent of strong tobacco filled the room.

Holmes spun, shutting the door behind him, then sank into a chair. He waved at the tobacco pouch. "It is a long train ride to Gravesend. There are other possibilities," Holmes said, returning to the question of Moriarty's motives, "but I rather favour internal strife as the most likely one. Why else would he suddenly abandon his perfect stratagem? Moriarty was ever a careful and cunning foe. Moriarty driven to haste is even more dangerous."

"More dangerous?"

"Don't you see?" Holmes said. "We no longer have just Moriarty to worry about, but his possible rivals. In short, the rest of his vampiric empire. Moriarty's recklessness with making more vampires still prevails, only his control over them is suddenly in question. Unless I am very much mistaken, the situation is rather like a raging river now and my fear is that if we do not find and defeat Moriarty in very short order, possibly days, the river will drown Moriarty, ourselves, and possibly all of Europe."

"Mr Holmes!" Mrs Hudson called from the bottom of the stairs. She kept calling as she came up the stairs as fast as she could, finally bursting into our sitting room with an out-of-breath: "The *King's Ransom!* That was the steamer you were waiting for, wasn't it? That was what you told me, I'm sure of it!"

"Dracula's ship," I said.

"Slow down, Mrs Hudson," Holmes said, bracing her in the doorway with both hands on her shoulders. It was a good thing, too, for she looked near spent from her dash up the stairs and he eased her into the nearest chair. "What is it?"

"The *King's Ransom,*" Mrs Hudson panted. "It's been sunk!"

Chapter 18

GRAVESEND

olmes fell into a dark mood immediately after the news regarding Dracula's steamer and did not speak at all while we were waiting. He sat near the window, looking out at the dreary rain and clutching the special edition that detailed the sinking of the *King's Ransom*. He sent off a telegram to his brother in the British government, Mycroft, explaining the importance of the Royal Navy apprehending the ship that had committed this foul crime in the very lee of English waters and explaining, in carefully coded language that Holmes said Mycroft would understand completely, the unique danger that a boarding action would involve. The ship must be sunk at a distance, then divers could be sent to finish the job.

But once that communication had been sent, Holmes's energy seemed to be spent and he fell back into a foul funk. Even when Kitty Winter and Somersby arrived, he left Baker Street in silence and entered the cab with Miss Winter and Somersby without a word of greeting. He continued to stare sullenly out the window, while I explained that we had had a setback unrelated to our current mission, for Holmes had not even told Miss Winter or Somersby about the existence of Dracula or his possible intervention.

It was a sombre and dreary drive through the rain to the Victoria train station. Kitty Winter was agitated to the extreme, since the train station represented the greatest exposure to human society she'd had in months. It was all Somersby could do to convince her that she would not be found out and staked by one of the porters before we ever got on board.

Fortunately, the heavy rain minimalized our contact with others and gave us cover from the daylight as well as an excuse to cover our heads and faces. It approached the level of farce, with me verbally prodding Holmes to get him out of the cab and Somersby physically guiding Miss Winter in an equally overt manner. I paid the cabbie, purchased the tickets, and made arrangements with the porters for our luggage, all while herding our eclectic little flock up into the train. Despite not needing to breathe anymore, I gave a sigh of relief once I'd gotten everybody safe in the compartment of the passenger car. Holmes settled into the corner without a word and stared morosely out of the soot-stained window.

It was only after the train had chuff-chuffed its cumbersome and weighty way out of the station and built up a full head of steam that he finally broke his silence.

"There is more danger here than you realize, I think," Holmes said suddenly. "I really am not doing any of you favours by bringing you along on this excursion. Moriarty has been ahead of us all the way and there is every likelihood that he will anticipate our coming, as he has anticipated everything else, and be waiting for us."

"If Moriarty has prepared a trap for us," I said, "then all the more reason for us to be along, for you shall need our help."

Holmes's smile was heartfelt, but also a little sad. "Good old Watson," he said. "The transformation really has not changed you at all. It is quite as remarkable as any little talent I may possess for the detection of crimes. Perhaps more so, if I am not quite mistaken." He was still lounging with his head pressed back against the compartment wall, but his eyes shifted to the other two on the bench across from us. "And you?"

Somersby looked uncertain but Kitty Winter did not hesitate. "This Moriarty fellow seems cut from the same cloth as Baron Gruner was, to hear you tell it." She straightened her hat, a small lavender concoction that had seen far better days. It was clear that, like me, the fatigue that weighed on both of us always during the daylight hours was no trivial burden. Her eyes were sunken hollows, but a fierce passion burned in them, too. "By cripes!" she said. "The Gruners of the world have had their way with the rest of us for far too long, if you ask me. I'm yours to the end, Mr Holmes."

"Well," Somersby said, looking over at Miss Winter uncertainly. "I'm in, too, then, if the rest of you are. It wouldn't be... uh... manly to give in to trepidation now, would it?" The movement of the train jostled him and he sat up straighter and looked back and forth from Holmes and I as if looking for confirmation, or perhaps a possible escape. A small smile tinged the fierce look on Miss Winter's face, but she turned it slightly away from her companion by pretending to look out the train window and so he did not see.

"Indeed," Holmes said dryly. "What are we, as men, to do but press on regardless of the danger. Quite right." He, too, sat up straight, making a visible effort to throw off some of the gloom that had overtaken him.

"Where, precisely, in Gravesend, are we going?" Somersby asked Holmes.

"We shall start in the docks and the warehouse districts," said Holmes, "looking for signs."

"Signs?" I asked.

"Well," Holmes said, "it is rather too much to hope that Moriarty will be clumsy enough to leave us a trail of bloody corpses, freshly turned earth, or victims stumbling around with holes in their necks and far-fetched stories. However, I am assured by Holly that several sailors have gone missing in this area, so it may be that the Baker Street Irregulars will turn up something in the streets, bars and taverns of Gravesend, but I have instructed them to concentrate on the areas a short distance away from the docks, since that is where the greatest danger lies. The places directly adjacent to the docks will be our assignment. It may be that Moriarty and his forces still remain on the ship that brought them. I should much prefer to locate their ship or other den while the sun is still up, but we shall be under the same burdens as Moriarty's forces, since half of our search party will be struggling with the torpor, so it is just as well that each of you has a human companion that can assist you.

"What is far more likely," Holmes continued, "is that we shall have to wait for nightfall for their increased activity to reveal them."

"But, Holmes," I said, "might not Moriarty have made arrangements? Shipments of pig's blood waiting for them, or crates to transport them during the day? Human servants could handle these arrangements. Why should they have to reveal themselves at all?"

"They shouldn't have to," Holmes said. "If Moriarty has full control of his forces, then we play a losing hand. He has superior numbers and the cunning to hide them until they can strike with the fullest effect at a place of his choosing. We can only dog his trail and hope that he makes a mistake that we shall be able to capitalize on."

"That's if he doesn't play wolf to our dog," Miss Winter said, "and turn on us long enough to tear us to pieces."

"Quite right," Holmes said. His smile was thin and ghastly and very quick, then it was gone and his face grew serious. "As I said, a losing game. That would be the danger I referred to earlier and it is quite serious."

In the end, it went much as Holmes had feared. We split up into two teams and canvassed the docks as best we might without seeing any sign of where Moriarty might be hiding vampires, or even any sign to confirm that he *was* hiding them. It was a bright and sunny day, which lay a heavy weight upon me, and twice Holmes left me in the cool interior of a dockside pub to question the inhabitants and recover my strength while he covered more ground.

"Do not engage Moriarty or his minions without me," I said on the second occasion.

"Fear not, Doctor," he said, "for we are running out of daylight and I shall need your sharpened senses for what comes next."

However, he had turned to leave and then spotted Kitty Winter and Somersby coming in the door. He'd taken no more than half a step when a beefy patron of the bar took a long step backwards into Holmes's path, knocking the detective backwards.

"'Ere now!" the bruiser said, turning and baring his stained and not entirely intact set of teeth. "I ought to teach you a lesson, I ought!" It seemed that this man had a penchant for altercations, perhaps in this very establishment, if the two missing teeth, cauliflower ears, and puffiness around the eyes were any indication. I moved to intervene. Holmes was a formidable fighter in his own right, but there was no sense in taking that risk now, when we had Moriarty to worry about. When I got to Holmes's side, I noticed the layers of scarring on the bruiser's knuckles and my estimation of the man's pugilistic experience went up several notches. Perhaps a prize fighter or the like.

"I'm gonna teach you a good lesson," the man snarled and reared back.

Holmes had his hands up, ready for anything, but then the bruiser made an anguished face, clapped his hand to the small of his back and collapsed on the spot, revealing Kitty Winter directly behind him.

"Come on!" Miss Winter snapped. "We haven't the time

for that sort of nonsense! We found it, Mr Holmes, or at least we found something that doesn't smell right. If your man's not behind it, I'll eat my hat!" She unclenched the smallish fist that had felled the prize fighter so easily and straightened the tiny hat in question. Her face was still pinched and tight. Likely, mine was the same, for fighting the torpor of daylight took a strain. My struggle came with an ache behind my eyes that made every movement a trifle painful.

"Found it!" Holmes said to Miss Winter, excitement and relief in his voice. "Very good, Miss Winter. Score one for your team." He glanced down at the ruffian still groaning at his feet. "Or rather, two."

"Come on!" Miss Winter said again and we followed her out into the street.

A cool wind cut through the street and one didn't require enhanced senses to taste the salt on it. The sun hung low and heavy in the sky, wreathed in vapour trails of clouds. It was perhaps two hours until nightfall, if that. I could see Holmes's and Somersby's breath and had to remind myself to work my lungs a little so as to present a natural appearance. We had exchanged our planned search patterns, so I already had a good idea of where we were heading as Miss Winter led us a short distance along a serpentine path towards the docks.

She stopped suddenly, peering down a dimly lit alleyway in a half-crouch. Ahead of us, two men stood in the gloom under a sign that listed the owners of the warehouse behind them as the Wilson Haberdashery.

"There," she hissed, so low that I almost couldn't hear the

words. Holmes was immediately behind Miss Winter, with me and then Somersby bringing up the rear carrying a wrapped bundle of shovels and other equipment. We all followed her example and pressed ourselves against the rain-slick brick wall to our right.

"There," Miss Winter said again. "Posted sentries or I'm a spring chicken and sailors to boot!"

"Wait," Somersby said from behind me. "How can one person be a spring chicken and sailors?"

"Ssh!" Holmes hissed back at him.

I looked back; the young man looked both horrified and confused.

"The sentries are sailors," I whispered, taking pity on him.

"Ah," he said.

"Holmes," I said, leaning forward. "You said that Moriarty is almost certainly expecting us."

"Yes," Holmes said, "of course."

"Then this is almost certainly a trap," I said.

"Of course."

"Perhaps we should think about—"

"We haven't time for that sort of patience, Dr Watson," Miss Winter said sharply. "Have we now?" So saying, she stood, brushed down the front of her dress, and started towards the sailors, her boot heels making audible thumps on the cobblestones. Miss Winter normally had a penchant for moving silently, so this time her noise had to be intentional.

"Here now!" she called out. "What's a couple of rum blokes such as yourself doing out in the cold?"

"Keep walkin', sister," the nearest man growled at her. "This is private property."

"It's a haberdashery, ain't it?" Miss Winter said, adjusting her hat on top of her head.

"Not open to the public," the man said, putting a hand out to stop her, but it never landed. With blinding speed, even to my eye, Miss Winter slipped past the man's arm and seized a fistful of his coat. One sharp push and the man, who had to weigh at least fourteen stone, flew a dozen feet and crashed into the other guard so that they both went down in a confused tumble.

Then Kitty Winter leapt with a low, feral, and unfettered growl that chilled me as the night air no longer could. She landed on the nearest man in a crouch and I heard a strangled cry and the tearing of clothes and flesh.

My revolver in my hand, I rushed to Miss Winter's side, horrified at her actions. "Miss Winter!" I shouted as I grabbed at her shoulder to pull her off her helpless victim.

She turned at my touch, still crouching, fangs bared and prominent, pale eyes wild and dangerous, and raised her hands like a predator's claws.

"Kitty! No!" Somersby shouted.

I raised my own hands, sure that she might leap at me and tear my throat out. I had my pistol, but couldn't bring myself to fire.

Then the moment passed and she took a deep breath and straightened up. "Aye, I knows what you thinks of me now, don't I? Plain as day." She stepped away from the two crumpled bodies and I could see with relief and growing shame that both men lay unconscious, but clearly unharmed. I could even, now that I listened for it, hear their breathing. Still uncomprehending, I looked at where the one man's shirt was torn wide open.

"I heard…" I stammered, "a tearing."

"He had the key under his shirt," Miss Winter said, holding up a cord with a single key on it.

Holmes stepped forward and took the key from her. "If a herd of antelope stumbled through here," he said bitterly, glaring at the lot of us, "they could not have made more noise." Holmes, still glaring, stepped over to fit it to the lock. "If Moriarty did not know we were coming before, he certainly does now."

Miss Winter delivered her own withering stare and Somersby and I exchanged guilty glances.

"Come on," Holmes said. "There's no help for it now." He stepped in, followed by Miss Winter and then, belatedly, Somersby and me.

My nerves had worked themselves up to a fever pitch so that I half-expected the warehouse we stepped into to be teeming with hordes of fanged and hostile sailors, but nothing could have been further from the truth. Instead the dimly lit interior showed only aisles and aisles of tall shelves filled with round boxes. It was plenty for me and Miss Winter to see by, but Holmes had brought his pocket lantern and lit it now. I kept waiting for some outcry to come from further in the building, but the place seemed to be deserted. I listened as hard as I could, but though I picked up distant sounds from outside – the sounds of people and the occasional hoofbeats – I could hear nothing in the dark, cool interior of the building but us.

The shelving units were wood, some of it makeshift and in very poor repair, but I scented nothing more sinister than wood rot in the air. The men outside, the guards, had been very human. Perhaps we'd made a terrible mistake. We only had Kitty Winter's hunch that this place housed anything unusual, and after all, was it so remarkable to find sailors outside a warehouse in the dock districts?

"Holmes," I said, whispering. "Could we have the wrong place?"

Miss Winter looked sideways at me, chewing her lip.

"It's possible," Holmes said to me, "but here, look at this." He held his pocket lantern over a small clump of dirt on the cobble-stone floor. "This is not from outside and is still moist, so has been left here rather recently, for the air is dry. The men outside did not have any earth like this on their shoes. The balance of probability is that this has come from a basement and been left here recently."

"How in the name of all that is holy," Somersby said, "did you see that particular bit of earth on this dirty floor?" He would have been echoing my exact thoughts if I had not seen Holmes display this particular talent before, so I was also prepared for Holmes's answer.

"Because I *looked* for it," he said, simply. "Now, let us see if we can get a look at that basement."

We started to spread out slightly, moving carefully and quietly, taking care to keep each in sight as we looked for a way down.

"Balance of probability?" Somersby whispered. "You mean

you're guessing? I thought that you never guess. A shocking habit, you called it."

"Another victim of the Doctor's literary crimes, I see," Holmes said, but he spoke so quietly that Somersby could not have possibly heard him, though I certainly did.

"You did say those very words," I said.

"Here!" Miss Winter said from further in. "A door!"

We all gathered around the door she'd found, a heavy, ominous wooden door of indeterminate age, bound with iron bands and set in a doorway of arched fieldstone. It had a latch and a heavy padlock, which hung incongruously open.

"A disturbing sign," Holmes said. "The feeling that we are expected grows and grows." Nonetheless, he unhooked the lock and swung the door open. A slight and stale breeze, cold and fetid, caused me to shiver and carried with it the smell of fresh-turned earth and the slight but unmistakable mustiness of vampire. Since vampires were usually hard to detect for other vampires, the wave of scent gave me gooseflesh. It wasn't just one vampire down there, but many. Possibly dozens. I hastily fumbled my pistol out of my jacket pocket. We'd found our horde, just as Moriarty clearly intended. Now it only remained to put our foot into the trap the rest of the way.

"Gonna regret this," Miss Winter said, echoing my thoughts. Her voice was steady, but her face was a mask of fear. Somersby's was even worse and he swayed briefly so that I thought the man might faint on the spot, but Miss Winter grabbed his arm and he gave her a tight, weak smile.

"Easy in," Holmes whispered, "but not easy out." His jaw was clenched as he raised the pocket lantern so that the light fell on cobblestone walls and a set of wooden slats leading down. He started down and I behind him, but Kitty Winter pushed her way in front of me, which startled me enough to make me hesitate half a moment before I followed. Somersby came after me, bearing a pistol that gleamed in the half-light. He'd come prepared, too.

Holmes drew his own pistol and then stopped and turned slightly to address Miss Winter behind him. "Only three of us have revolvers – perhaps it would be better if you waited upstairs?" I knew that Holmes had supplied all of his Midnight Watch operatives with pistols and silver cartridges, including Miss Winter, but she apparently did not carry one.

"Shove off," Miss Winter said. "You think Somersby takes care of the fledgling vampires we find? Not hardly."

"You have no pistol," I said, keeping my voice very low.

Miss Winter shook her head, clearly distressed at our stupidity. "You might have remained the same, Dr Watson, with your dainty manners and spending all your time reading and the like, but that's not how most of us come out of it. Men or women, don't make no difference. I may be human enough to stop me from going on a killing spree, but that don't make me *human*. Now we've already woken half of our reception party, I'm sure. Best we keep moving and not stand here whispering loud enough and long enough to wake the other half!"

Holmes caught my eye over the top of her small decorative hat and shrugged helplessly. We continued to descend, trying to be as silent as we could manage. There was a chill moisture in the air and somewhere water drip, drip, dripped, very slowly. Somersby slipped on one of the shaky slats partway down and fell against me, nearly dropping his pistol. The canvas-wrapped bundle of shovels came loose from his back and clattered down the wooden stairs, making a horrific racket that made me cringe.

"Sorry," he whimpered. "Sorry, sorry." His silver pince-nez fell off his nose as he crouched to try and close the bag tighter, a move far too late to do any good.

A particularly large shovel banged off the bottom few steps and landed right at the feet of a shadowy figure lurching out of the shadows. Feral eyes, lank brown hair, and a mouthful of fangs were shown in the light of Holmes's pocket lantern. The creature sank into a crouch, preparing to leap up at us, but Holmes's pistol went off with a crack and the vampire spun and fell in a heap.

Kitty Winter sprang down the steps with a snarl and another vampire, a ham-fisted man with a shopkeeper's apron still on, seized her by the arm. Her fangs had grown with her surge of adrenaline, as well as her fingernails, transforming her in an instant to an apparition out of Hell. She swung her sharpened talons, tearing her assailant's throat out with one brutal motion. The man gurgled black blood in a sickening spray and fell to his knees. He tried to rise again, but by then I was there to put a silver bullet into his brain. The crack of my pistol and the smell of cordite was an assault on the senses in this underground setting, but the man tumbled lifelessly to the dirt. The burning smell of silver coming into contact with vampire flesh made my nostrils itch.

A woman stepped into the light, looking from her once-white

dress and blonde curls like she'd been on her way to get her photograph when Moriarty and his minions had gotten a hold of her. She *oozed*, stalking towards us with a boneless, liquid, inhuman grace that could not possibly have been hers during her previous life. She laughed, baring her fangs which already had blood stains on them, though I could not imagine from what source. Behind her, shuffling in unnatural and haunting imitation of what had once been her mother, a young girl in a matching dress, hair also in blonde curls, leered and stalked monstrously behind.

Thinking of the single worst moment in my entire life, the night Mary had tried to shoot Holmes, forcing *me* to shoot *her*, I pulled the trigger. I had to wipe the moisture out of my eyes, but my hand was steady.

The little girl didn't even seem to notice as her mother fell, but only licked her lips and shuffled towards us. Another shot rang out, this time from Holmes's gun, and she, too, fell.

"Element of surprise *indeed*," Holmes said as he and Somersby joined us on the dirt floor. His tone was jocular, but the delivery came through clenched teeth. The greatest detective in the world had warned us that we were going to step, in all likelihood, precisely into Moriarty's trap and so we had. All around us, the trap was springing, springing and springing.

Vampires toiled from rough mounds of earth in all directions. The ceiling of the basement was low enough for Holmes to have to duck the individual beams, and six or seven vertical support beams loomed in all directions, blocking some of the view. But I could feel the openness of the place. The cellar was large, probably larger than the building above, stretching back into the darkness like a warren of tunnels. A small theatre could have been housed in this space and Moriarty had filled the whole bloody thing with vampires, it seemed. Groans and snarls and the sounds of digging came from all directions and Holmes's lantern showed dozens of the figures struggling from the dirt. Perhaps more. We formed a rough semicircle with the staircase at our backs and prepared for an assault from the very depths of Hell.

I had my revolver in one hand and my silver-topped stick in the other. I pulled the cover off and the silver gleamed in the wan light. Holmes spun and quickly moved to hang the lantern on a nail convenient for the purpose hammered into a beam next to the stairs. He snatched a folded sheet of paper that had been hung on the same nail, quickly stuffed it into his jacket pocket, and hung the lantern up. When he rejoined our defensive semicircle, he had his own revolver back out and the stick similar to my own, also now uncovered. Somersby had abandoned the pack of shovels, but pulled a wooden mallet and stake out. He promptly put the mallet between his teeth so that he could hold a pistol in one hand and his stake in the other.

Miss Winter was between Holmes and I, with me on the right-hand side and Holmes on the left. I aimed and took careful shot, dropping two of the vampires on my side before they even freed themselves from their shallow graves. Holmes's revolver went off and I imagined he was doing much the same.

Miss Winter, clearly not content to hold her ground in a defensive action, bounded into the fray. She wrestled the nearest vampire, a young woman in a nun's habit, to the ground with a sharp, twisting motion. Somersby, who seemed to have left his terror behind now that he was in the thick of the action, stepped up and fired one precise shot into the back of the vampire woman's head. His pince-nez were back on his face and gleamed in the lantern light. Miss Winter leapt again and tore out another throat and was on the next vampire before the first one fell. Somersby followed, clearly falling into a battle rhythm they'd developed working together, though unlikely practised on multiple vampires before.

Holmes and I moved forward more slowly, guarding the flanks and moving deeper into the huge cellar.

"Don't let them circle around behind us, Doctor!" Holmes called out. A vampire rushed him and Holmes hooked the man under the arm and performed an adroit throw, one of his Baritsu moves. The vampire twisted and fell and Holmes used the silver-tipped cane, which like mine, had a heavy bludgeoning weight of silver on one end, and a small silver spike on the other. We may have walked into the trap, but we had not come blindly. The silver tip pieced the vampire's chest with ease and the man sagged and died on the spot. The horrible, bubbling chemical reaction that silver generated in vampire flesh filled my nostrils with an acrid stink.

We certainly had experience with the Midnight Watch in handling the monstrous fledgling vampires, which were terrifying even in small numbers. There was no sign of Moriarty's method to preserve the personality here. These were monsters. Bestial screams and savage growls rang out all around us. None of them had any trace of humanity left and they were still crawling out of the earth further into the darkness. Even my night vision could not see to the far end of the cellar walls and I now revised my estimate of their count. More than a dozen, surely. More like *dozens*, in fact.

Our offensive wedge formation held for nearly a full minute. That is to say, for as long as our silver bullet cartridges held out. I pointed my gun to fire at a sallow youth only to have the hammer snap down on an empty cylinder. He rushed me and I clubbed him with my walking stick, but it was only a glancing blow and we both went down in a tangle of limbs with him on top of me. He snarled and tried to get his teeth into my throat, but I was able to rap him soundly on the side of the head with the heavy end of my stick and his grip loosened. Another blow from the stick and I was able to push him off, get to my feet and sink the sharpened tip of my stick into his chest. It sank all the way in with surprisingly little effort and I could feel it hit dirt. The boy screamed, spasmed once, and went still. A cold fury swept through me, not at this poor victim of a boy, but for Moriarty, who had made him into a slavering monster and then put him into harm's way. If ever a man deserved retribution, it was Moriarty.

I crouched there for half an instant against my better judgement. Another vampire was wrenching itself free of the dirt half a dozen feet away.

Kitty Winter was her own kind of slavering monster, screaming and lashing at the vampires around her with blinding speed. A much larger female vampire seized her by the collar and hauled her around, but Miss Winter spun and lashed out with so quick a motion that it could not be seen and the larger woman clutched her throat and fell to her knees. Miss Winter kicked her over and Somersby was there with hammer and stake to finish the job.

I felt a moment of pure envy at her power and freedom and at the same time, fear that the transformation changed her so irrevocably that it was just a matter of time before her savage nature would break free and make her a danger to all. Perhaps this foray into violence would relieve those symptoms and give her more time, or perhaps it would exacerbate the animal nature within her. Holmes had claimed once that Miss Winter had a firm grip on her wicked nature, and relied upon it in her work. I envied her that, for I knew it was something I could never do.

I yanked the walking stick free of the corpse I had made and picked up the empty revolver. Our defensive battalion had fallen apart as quickly as it had formed. I was still only a dozen feet from the bottom of the stairs and the flickering lantern, while Miss Winter and Somersby had penetrated a good forty or fifty feet into the cellar's interior. Vampires were crawling out of the earth in all directions, including between us.

"Holmes?" I said, twisting around.

"Here," Holmes said, materializing from behind me. His face was tight and streaked with dirt. He'd lost his hat and overcoat and there was a gash on his brow, but his steely gaze remained. He took my pistol from my hand and replaced it with his own. "It's loaded." He nodded at the vampire nearest to us, newly free of its grave, and I shot it.

"The lantern is running low," Holmes said. "We'll have to rely on your eyes in the darkness." He was loading my revolver with silver cartridges. By the time I had emptied his weapon, shooting carefully to make each bullet count and dropping the nearest six vampires, Holmes had loaded my own revolver and we switched again.

Miss Winter and Somersby were too far away, sixty feet, at least, when a bald-headed vampire stepped in between them, separating them. Miss Winter had her hands full with a pair of monsters of her own and they were all too jumbled together for me to get a clear shot, especially at this distance. Somersby pointed his revolver and fired, blowing the vampire's hand off at the wrist, but the vampire simply used his other hand to slap the gun contemptuously away. I could hear it thump in the dirt some yards distant. The vampire used its good hand to grab Somersby by the throat. Somersby gurgled as he was lifted in the air, scrabbling desperately at the clawed hand on his throat.

"Somersby!" I shouted, lifting my revolver. Holmes had his own weapon ready and aimed, but I could see by the way he squinted and looked uncertain that the darkness was too absolute for Holmes to have any chance of seeing and hitting his target.

Never in my life did I feel the weight of someone else's life in my own hands the way I did then, cocking the pistol, taking careful aim, just as the vampire bent to tear into Somersby's throat.

The pocket lantern hanging on the nail at the bottom of the staircase chose that moment to flicker and die, leaving us in complete and total darkness.

I took the shot anyway, knowing that it was Somersby's only chance. The muzzle flare was bright in the darkness and I heard something hit and a grunt, but then the chaos descended again as vampires rose up all around me. I could not see them, for even vampire eyes are no good in the absence of all light, and my usually keen scent was of little use with the muted scent of other vampires. There was little use for the pistol in such conditions so I dropped it into my jacket pocket and shifted the walking stick into my right hand.

There was nothing wrong with my hearing. I had only to focus it to hear Holmes's breathing behind me. I put a hand on his shoulder.

"Back, quickly, to the staircase," I said, nudging him in the right direction. Holmes complied and we shuffled our way backward, slowly, carefully, listening, listening…

The first shuffling step came from my left and I lashed out with the stick. A snarl and a body fell to the floor. I could smell a fresh burst of a silver burn on vampire skin. The relief was short-lived, as Somersby and Miss Winter both screamed at the same moment. Somersby's scream was one of pain and horror. Miss Winter's one of rage. Both cut out suddenly.

Holmes squeezed my shoulder. "I can make my way back to the lantern from memory," he breathed. "Do what you can for them!" He nudged me briefly in that direction and stumbled off. There were vampires in all directions now, including between us and the staircase, but Holmes was right. Miss Winter and Somersby needed my help the most. I heard Holmes's revolver go off twice as I stumbled further into the cellar.

The rest is a jumble of darkness, sounds, fury and pain and battle in that lightless cellar. I heard Miss Winter snarl and made my way to her, calling out when I got close so that we should not strike each other. I lost count of how many opponents I grappled with in the darkness. A dozen? More? Less? I cannot, to this day, say how many. I know Holmes's revolver went off five more times and then went silent. Empty.

I felled another opponent with the stick and called out. "Miss Winter?" She was close. I'd heard her grunt only moments ago.

"Here," she said. "Help me up." I found her hand in the blackness and pulled her to her feet. We instinctively turned, back to back, to ready ourselves for assault from all directions.

A sudden light flared in front of me. Holmes had gotten to the lantern and I could see his haggard face as he held it up. Vampire corpses lay at his feet.

I looked at the ground around Miss Winter and I. More corpses. Nothing moved except for us. We seemed to have survived the onslaught. How many vampires lay dead around us, I still could not say for certain, but it seemed a veritable army of them, at least fifty by my rough count.

"Somersby," Miss Winter breathed. She took two steps and pushed aside two vampire bodies to reveal Somersby's pale face.

"Oh," Somersby said weakly. "Hello. Are you a sight for sore eyes." He looked sad and lonely without his pince-nez.

"Oh, Somersby," Miss Winter breathed as she pushed the rest of the bodies away. There was an enormous amount of blood covering the young man's waistcoat and shirt. His clothes were torn away and the neck and the upper part of his chest, and I could see the great lacerations and blood all over him. His neck was one large wound and bubbled every time he breathed.

"I can't feel my legs," he said.

I knelt down next to him. I had to move another corpse out of the way to do so and saw it was the bald-headed vampire with a terrible bullet wound in his head.

"You hit your target admirably, Doctor," Holmes said softly just behind me. So I'd hit my target after all, only it hadn't saved Somersby. At least, not for very long.

"Here now," I said, using some of his shirt to sponge away the wound. There was so much blood. The wound looked worse and worse the more I could see of it.

"Oh, Nigel!" Miss Winter gasped. She looked at me. I opened my mouth to try and say something encouraging, but she must have read the despair in my face, for she looked away and bowed her head. A sob caught in her throat. "Oh, Nigel."

"No," I said, "I've seen worse than this in Afghanistan on soldiers that were walking cheerfully around just days later." I tried to put all the hope I could into my voice, but it sounded false and flat, even to my own ears.

"Where are my glasses?" Somersby asked.

"Here," Holmes said, handing them to me so that I could put them carefully on Somersby's face. Miss Winter had Somersby's hand gripped in her own, though I noticed his fingers didn't grip her back. He seemed immobile from the neck down.

"You are an honest man, Dr Watson," Somersby said softly. "You mean… well, I'm sure… but falsehood ill becomes you. I can tell when I feel my life… slipping away."

"The vampire's bite!" Miss Winter said. "Vampires heal marvellously! Why, I had a vicious cut from a broken glass on my hand here and see!" She held up her palm. "Nothing! No sign of

it! Healed as good as new! We'll have you up and walking in…"
She brushed her hair back in preparation to lean over him.

"No," Somersby said. "I don't… I don't want that. Besides,
what kind of life would it be? Are you… are you happy… as a
vampire?"

Miss Winter shook her head in defeat. Her hat had come
loose at the beginning of the fight and her long red hair hung
down, covering her face. "No." Her voice throbbed with emotion
and was so low that I had to strain even my hearing to make out
the words.

"No," she said again. "I ain't happy. It's a living torment. Better
than death, I imagine, but only just barely."

"And that's," Somersby said, "if I can heal a spinal injury.
Otherwise, I might have eternity lying on my back, sipping
blood through tubes, if I'm lucky. Correct, Doctor? It's my spine,
isn't it?"

"It's possible," I admitted, "but not a certainty."

Somersby shook his head, the only part of his body he could
still move. "It doesn't matter. I'd make the same decision without…
the spinal injury. I don't want to go on…" His gaze flickered over
at the bald-headed vampire corpse. "…as one of *them*."

"Oh, Nigel," Miss Winter said. "Nigel… we can beat this.
Perhaps being a vampire doesn't have to be a living torment, if
we did it together! Or Dr Watson can save you without turning
you into a vampire! He saved Mr Holmes when he got shot,
didn't he, in conditions no worse than this, I'm sure! Didn't you,
Dr Watson?"

"I'm sorry, Miss Winter," I said.

Somersby had been struck by prescience in his last minutes and had known better than we that his life was slipping away, and I could see without a doubt that he was gone. He'd sagged slightly and the silver pince-nez slipped from his nose, revealing that his eyes were now vacant. There could be no mistaking that his breathing had stopped.

"Hellfire and damnation," Holmes said. I rarely, in our many years of acquaintance, even in the most stressful and gruelling of cases, remember seeing him so distraught. His top hat had been lost long ago in the struggle and his hair was out of place with one long lock dangling over his forehead. His face was dirty and damp with sweat.

Holmes stumbled back to the stairs and fell to a sitting position on the bottom step. He, almost absently, reached into his jacket pocket and withdrew the piece of paper there. I remembered now, he'd snatched it off the nail on the beam nearest the stairs in order to hang the lantern. Now, his gaze drifted down to the paper and I heard him mutter the same "Hellfire and damnation" again.

"What is it, Holmes?" I asked.

"A note," Holmes said. "From Moriarty." He thrust the letter at me. "Read it aloud, Watson. I haven't the strength or the eyesight just now."

Dear Mr Holmes,

Please take it as the highest compliment that I can bestow when I tell you that I write this letter having absolutely no doubt that you will show both the insight and the perseverance to follow my trail of breadcrumbs and come upon this little hideaway, and so, this letter. I will also pay you the compliment of assuming that you both braved the dangers that lie buried here and have also survived, for it would give me a pang of regret, I assure you, to hear of your death, however much it might simplify matters.

May I also offer my deepest sympathies, for the balance of probability is that not everyone you have brought into the basement with you has survived the experience.

You may wonder at my return to England, and well you might, but really, you should have deduced most of the reasons by now. If not, I shall elucidate.

You are already aware that the transformation from human to vampire is not an easy one. (How is Dr Watson, by the way?) While the memories remain intact, it also releases such animalistic urges in a man's interior self such that he is hardly human anymore. If a man is the sum total of all his experiences then I suggest that a few weeks or more living as an animal, exsanguinating any creature unlucky enough to stumble into your path, is quite enough to unmake your previous personality. The sanctity of life becomes meaningless when everyone around you is reduced to 'food' and the morals of society become an altogether different, and more laughable series of meaningless restrictions. (Again, pass my regards to both Dr Watson and, of course, his loving wife, of dearest memory.)

The procedure for skipping this phase of the transformation is absurdly simple. If you have not deduced it yet, then I make *a gift to you now. Forcibly submerging a vampire has the effect of rendering them into a coma-like state. During this time, it is simplicity itself to keep the vampire alive, fed, and docile while the initial stage of the transformation runs its course. This does not prevent the shattering of the soul, for they are still monsters, but tractable ones. The submersion method, as I call it, has the advantages of keeping your recruits from running amok at inconvenient times. You will also discover that starving a vampire, as these have been, will revert your average vampire to the mindless state you find them in now.*

However, some ambition is not entirely affected by the transformation. I am certain that you remember a young associate of mine, one John Clay, that I was forced to dispose of. (I understand you were able to examine his body, yes?) Not only did he harbour grand dreams of replacing my position of power among our coterie of newly recruited vampires, but he managed to convert nearly all of them to his cause. As such, I found myself on a ship at sea with a nearly rebellious crew all around me. It was as much as I could do to convince them that you had gone and that London now presented itself as ripe for plunder. This is the method, the lie, I dare say, that I used to bring them to you, my solution. I thank you for disposing of them for me.

In return, I give you England, as I take a steamer to distant lands. Now that the near-rebellion has been quelled by your most capable hands, I shall have no trouble taking my remaining forces out of your reach, adhering to my original plan to stay as such until time has finally taken care of you.

I tell you in all confidence that the new senses that come from life as a vampire quite make up for the enforced diet restrictions. My new love of the sea has been born out of just such a change in temperament and I shall quite enjoy spending the next few decades roaming it.

I regret, truly, that we shall not meet again in your lifetime.

Warmest regards,

Professor James Moriarty

Chapter 19

GUESTS BOTH WELCOME AND UNWELCOME

In the end, Kitty Winter sent us home.

We tried to be solicitous after her devastating loss of Somersby, but after her initial bout of weeping ended, she angrily rebuked us and started taking matters into her own hands. She instructed us to hail a cab and send messages to summon more of the Midnight Watch to assist her in both Somersby's collection as well as the respectful disposal of the many other corpses there that deserved the dignity of burial, however discreet they were required to be. Her grief seemed to have burned itself into such a smouldering passion for these arrangements that it became clear that she would allow neither Holmes's assistance nor mine, and we were summarily dismissed.

"You have to handle the bastard that's done this," she said to Holmes hotly. "I can't find him, but you can, and I can do this. Best we each get to it, I should think." She fixed us with an angry stare and I got the distinct sense that she would prefer to be alone with Somersby's body for a short period so that she might say goodbye in private.

"Quite right," Holmes said deferentially and, raising his eyebrows to catch my gaze, indicated that we should beat a hasty retreat out into the road in order to hail a cab, as instructed.

"For as long as I live," I said, when we'd stepped out into the street, "I shall never completely understand women."

"That is unfortunate," Holmes said idly, "for of the two of us, your experience with women is far greater than mine, I dare say. Well, you shall have ample time to test your theory, for it is probable that you shall outlive most of the women you encounter."

He dropped this thunderbolt into the conversation without seeming to give any real importance to the words, for he was already stepping out into the cobbled street in search of our cab. I stood near the door, suddenly struggling with a fact I'd known for some time, but had refused to put into words. Any chance I had at a life like the one I'd had with Mary was certainly shattered. Similarly, the bachelor existence I currently maintained with my friend and confidant would also come to an end. Everything and everyone I knew would die while I remained. Outliving Holmes, in particular, was still a fate that my mind refused to encompass, and the idea made my flesh crawl. My future seemed a dark and bleak road and these few little adventures that I shared with my good friend were a bright flare in the darkness that would go out altogether too soon. Only I would remain, with only the likes of Kitty Winter among my acquaintances rather than my dearest friends. It was a sobering thought.

It was short train ride and then another quiet cab ride back to Baker Street, for both of us were very much lost in thought. Holmes's face was pensive and introspective and he bore several visible contusions and cuts around his neck and temple that he had not bothered to attend to. I knew that I looked much the same, despite my more durable nature, now. One gash on my right cheek, in particular, felt serious, though my handkerchief, when I carefully applied it, came away with very little blood. I only noticed that I still held the handkerchief after some long minutes of riding, so stricken was I with Holmes's casual insight and prediction of doom.

So much lost in thought, in fact, that I barely paid any attention to our surroundings and it was something of a surprise when we pulled up outside of Baker Street. The cabbie had to call out to get his fare, for we both stumbled from the four-wheeler and would have both walked away from the cab without paying if not reminded.

I had just put my foot on the step leading to our front door when a hand like iron gripped my wrist and hauled me off balance. Out of the corner of my eye, I saw another figure accosting Holmes. The horrific night and underground battle that we'd just endured had frayed any last shred of my nerves down to their last threadbare existence and I turned and faced the shadowy apparition that had my wrist. I heard a bestial snarl tear from my own lips. The apparition had me in its grip, else I would have drawn my revolver, not caring that we were in full view of the street. As it was, I raised my left fist and unleashed the most terrible blow I could muster.

The figure surprised me by letting go and stepping back, so my swing encountered only empty air. It was another few precious seconds before I could regain my balance and claw the revolver out of my jacket pocket. There could be no doubt. Whoever this was, with that awful strength, it had to be a vampire.

But when I raised the pistol, it was Holmes's hand that caught my wrist.

"Watson!" he hissed.

"Your forbearance, Doctor," the apparition said in a familiar voice.

"Count Dracula?" I was astonished.

And so it was. Count Dracula himself stood before me. Mina, too, I saw. She had been the figure 'accosting' Holmes, who had clearly identified the two of them much quicker than I had.

"But your steamer sank!" I said.

"Yes," Dracula said. "Very inconvenient, all things considered." He had bent to a slight crouch during our physical altercation, but now stood to his full height. "But come, let us step away from prying eyes, shall we?" He had dragged me into the middle space between the two street lights and most of the way toward an alley, but this was hardly a full measure and we were still all exposed to any prying eyes. I couldn't take my eyes off the Count, whose very existence seemed a virtual impossibility in the face of the news we had gotten about their ship.

"Why not retire up into Baker Street?" I said. "Surely that is the safest place."

"Because, Doctor," Mina said, not without a touch of impatience but speaking low, "*that* is where your Professor

Moriarty, is waiting, almost certainly to murder the both of you the moment of your arrival. Can you please draw further away from the building where we can confer without concern for unwelcome ears?"

I belatedly dropped my pistol into my coat pocket. We were very fortunate that few people had remarked our little display, but that fortune would not last if I kept waving firearms about. Holmes, who seemed very much recovered from his dark mood on the sight of the Draculas, seemed not at all distressed about the news of Moriarty hiding away in our rooms, and had a reinvigorated twinkle to his eye now. It disturbed me somewhat, the favour that Holmes shone on the considerably dubious person of Count Dracula, but even I had to admit that if we had to enter into a confrontation with Moriarty, I much preferred the Count's additional forces on our side, rather than against.

"Mrs Hudson?" I asked quickly. "If Moriarty has breached our rooms…"

"She is quite unharmed, I assure you, and completely unaware of Moriarty's presence," Mina said. She drew the rest of us further into the alley and then around the bend of another building before we gauged the distance to be a safe one.

"How did you escape a sinking ship?" Holmes asked.

"I took a great many precautions to preserve our secrecy," Dracula said. "I sent several caskets and even a few imposters on other ships to throw him off the scent. These, however, clearly did not serve their function and Moriarty was able to penetrate my ruses. Mina, however…" Here he shot a glance of pride and something that, on another man, might have been contrition, toward his raven-haired wife, "took the additional measure of acquiring an influence over the ship's captain."

"You fed on him?" I said, astonished. Yet again, I could not countenance the Faustian bargain we'd made combining our efforts with these two dangerous persons, but Holmes said nothing.

"I did not injure him," Mina said, somewhat dismissively. "But Moriarty's pirates cannot say the same. I offered our good captain a chance to escape with us, but he refused. We used a small boat in the darkness, you see, while the ship, and the captain, kept the pirates busy. Your merchant navy lost a good man that night, which is deeply regrettable."

"Moriarty claims to have left the country," Holmes said, patting the waistcoat pocket where he had stored Moriarty's letter, though he did not proffer an explanation to either of the Draculas. "While I do not necessarily believe this, it is uncharacteristically blunt and forward of Moriarty to attempt an ambush with his own hands."

"It took us some time to get to the English coast," Dracula said. "We then made our way here, though not in time to catch you leaving today…"

"More's the pity!" I said with feeling. "For we could have sorely used your assistance."

A flicker of surprise crossed his face at my words, possibly unprepared for my desire to have him accompany us. "So I gather," Dracula said, his gaze flickering to the many cuts and abrasions visible on our faces, and I could see him visibly acknowledge the level of danger that we must have gone through.

"We thought it best to watch your home," Mina said, "and await your return."

"I would have waited in your home," Dracula said, "but Mina insisted it would be disrespectful."

"If we had," Mina said primly, "we would have lost our opportunity to observe their *other* intruder, whom we saw entering through the second-storey window. Moriarty, without a doubt, or someone sent by him."

"There cannot be many people left to send," Holmes said. "With one portion of his forces waiting for us under the warehouse in Gravesend and his more loyal minions carrying out the mission of piracy on your own person." He straightened up and pulled out his revolver for what felt like the dozenth time that evening. "If so, there is but one of him and four of us. Our strength in numbers should help us overcome whatever cunning deviltry he might have concocted for us."

Dracula, Mina and I all nodded our agreement and turned to make our way back to Baker Street.

"We shall enter through other means than the stairs," Dracula said as we drew close. Holmes nodded and the two vampires, Dracula and Mina, both disappeared back into the alley shadows, leaving Holmes and I alone.

"Miss Winter will be very cross with us," I said suddenly, surprising myself with the somewhat unexpected thought.

Holmes raised his eyebrows at me, a wordless question.

"She sent us onward under the quite reasonable theory that it would take a great deal of detective work, work that only you could perform, to track down Moriarty's whereabouts. Had she but known that he waited back here at Baker Street, she would most certainly have left the supervision of clean-up and burials to someone else in order to accompany us."

"It is just as well that she did not," Holmes said, speaking low, but with a smile playing about his lips. "For I am not at all confident that our personal possessions, such as they are, would withstand the whirlwind. That woman is a fury."

I could not suppress a wry chuckle at our feeble attempt at humour and it was all we could do for each of us to keep the other from bursting out into laughter. Then, banishing this most inappropriate flood of frivolity, we mastered ourselves again, and opened the door to Baker Street.

Mrs Hudson came down the hallway. "Look at the two of you," she said. "Did you roll around in the dirty street to track such an abominable amount of dirt into my house?"

Holmes caught my eye and then looked up at the second floor, making it clear he did not want to say anything, even to Mrs Hudson, about our intruder lest vampire ears should hear our comments and so be prepared. As logical as that measure was, it took nearly every ounce of my nerve to let Mrs Hudson take my coat and bear with her running dialogue of commentary and criticism on the streets of London. I felt the warnings bubbling up inside of me as if they might burst out of my throat at any moment. It was a wonder she didn't notice, for my eyes must have been bulging in their sockets.

Holmes started slowly up the steps and I followed, both of us lingering while Mrs Hudson disappeared back into her rooms. Only then did we exchange looks and draw out our pistols. Our home at Baker Street, with its comfortable chairs and warm fireplace, always represented shelter from theft, from intrigue, from the murderous and outré, even when I hadn't lived there. This was the place where we heard stories about dangerous persons and terrible acts, but it was also the place where such fantastic tales were unravelled and explained. It was a place where problems found their solutions, owing entirely to the singular gifts and drive of Mr Sherlock Holmes. To be entering into this refuge with danger waiting for us *inside* was a strange and unwelcome change and it made my blood run cold. (That is, in so much as vampire blood *does* run cold, for I have found our blood – and flesh – *does* operate at cooler temperatures to our uninfected, that is, fully human, counterparts. As much as ten degrees cooler, I have found, though recent feeding can bring both of them temporarily up to more normal conditions.)

Holmes pushed open the door with his foot. It creaked open slowly, ominously. We entered, guns at the ready. I shiver now to think of it, that slow, tedious and terrifying prowl through our own rooms. After we passed through and nothing untoward happened, Holmes closed the door to the hallway behind us, locking it.

"To keep Mrs Hudson out," he mouthed when I looked a question at him.

Finding nothing in the sitting room, Holmes led the way into his bedroom, leaving the stairs to my own room as our next logical step.

Holmes had taken only two steps into his own room before my hackles rose. The scent of other vampires is minimal, but I could clearly detect it here, despite the window being open a crack. Holmes silently looked at me and darted a glance at the window. Clearly, *he* hadn't left it open.

The attack came from behind the door and *above*, where the man had evidently been clinging like a spider. So ferocious and so swift was it that the man battered Holmes on the back of his head and shoulders and dropped him to the floor before I had any chance to act. He was enormous, grizzled, with a full beard and a scarred face.

I aimed my revolver but a backhanded blow from our assailant knocked it out of my hand. The man was like a wounded bear. I'd never laid eyes on Moriarty before this apart from that brief glance at a distance all those years ago, but Holmes had described an aged and sinister academic, not this towering monster. And this fiend was a different breed than the many fledgling vampires we had dispatched underneath the warehouse in Gravesend, and it was as much as I could do to grapple with him before he flung me to one side and turned to Holmes.

Holmes had gotten up on one knee and when our attacker bore down on him, caught each of his hands in his own. They hovered there, immobile, poised in opposition, the vampire towering over the crouching Holmes, applying all of his supernatural force and power into overwhelming Holmes and depriving him of life.

But Holmes was no weakling, and while he abhorred exercise for its own sake, somehow managed to keep himself fighting fit regardless. An act, I'm sure, of pure will. The vampire gave a guttural, wordless grunt of surprise as his intended victim stood and forced him back.

Then a darkness reared up behind the vampire and a blow hard enough to fell a rhinoceros landed with bone-crushing force on the man's neck. He crumpled into a lifeless heap on the floor.

"I was starting to wonder," Holmes said, "if you'd been detained."

"It seemed best to let your intruder reveal himself before taking action," Dracula said imperturbably. I looked at Holmes's bedroom window, which overlooked the rear yard and now stood open a bit more than it had previously. Somehow, Dracula – and Mina, too, I now observed standing next to the Count – had entered unheard, unseen, and very rapidly, which must have involved some serious athletics as there is no terrace outside that window. I found myself actually somewhat relieved that the window had moved at all so that I could, at least, discount the wild stories the penny dreadfuls had told of vampires dissolving into a night's fog or turning into a flying bat. Dracula's powers, while formidable, at least could be explained by science, if only just barely in my mind.

"The Doctor may come and confirm my opinion," Holmes said, "but I believe this man is… rather dead." He made a distasteful face and lifted the man's shoulders so that the head lolled about sickeningly, then cavalierly let shoulders and head fall with a thump. There could be no doubt that the man's neck had been broken by Dracula's single, terrible blow.

"Mr Holmes? Dr Watson?" Mrs Hudson's voice called from the hallway, clearly responding to the noises from our brief but ferocious battle. The door handle that Holmes had locked rattled in place. "Mr Holmes? Dr Watson?"

Dracula had, quite surprisingly, gone to the door to answer her. He unlocked it and opened it a small crack.

"All is well," he said curtly. "Mr Holmes and Dr Watson are both well and have no need of your services at the moment." He went to close the door in her face but the stout woman stopped him by putting her hand on the door.

"I'll hear that from Mr Holmes or the Doctor themselves, I think," she said firmly, not at all daunted by the glowering countenance of Count Dracula.

I rushed to the door. "It's quite all right, Mrs Hudson, everything's fine."

"Hmm," she said, still glaring up at Dracula, who towered over her. "If you say so, Doctor. But if you need me… or the *constabulary*…" Here she redoubled her glare. "Remember we're but a shout away."

"It's quite all right, Mrs Hudson," I repeated.

She finally tore her gaze away from Count Dracula's. "Be careful, Doctor," she whispered. "I don't like the look of that one!"

"I quite agree, Mrs Hudson," I said, with more heartfelt feeling than was strictly diplomatic.

She favoured the Count with one more glare before allowing me to close the door.

The Count gave me a considering look before he turned to return to the room with the man he had just killed, but, as always, his face was unreadable.

Holmes and Mina were carrying the unfortunate man back into the sitting room, that being a presumably more appropriate place to examine the body. I wondered at the things we had become used to. Mina looked very unconcerned with their charge, and let it fall onto the carpet with another thump that had me wondering if we'd get Mrs Hudson back at the door again.

"Careful, Countess," Holmes said, catching my eye with a macabre flash of a smile, "or Mrs Hudson will come and run us all in."

"Mina, please," she reminded him. "The other names, as I've explained to you, simply do not suit."

"As you wish," Holmes said. "We will, of course, have to summon the police eventually, but it would be beneficial for all involved, including Scotland Yard, if they were a little bit further behind on this case. Further than they usually are, that is."

Holmes started inspecting the body, rifling pockets and examining the face and limbs, then the shoes. The dead man had been a large customer, with rough-cut black hair and a hard, weathered face, even now.

"I need hardly tell you," Holmes said as he worked, "that this man is not Professor Moriarty."

"He is not?" Mina said.

"We assumed," Dracula said, "incorrectly, it seems. We have never actually seen him before."

"Me either," I admitted.

"Oh," Mina said. "That's right. You won't have seen him clearly at Reichenbach."

"Quite right," I said, still a little disconcerted by the idea that Mina, and the Count himself, if I were to believe his words, had both read my accounts of our adventures.

"Look at the hands!" Holmes said with impatience. "The man bears a lifetime of scars from handling rope at sea. Moriarty may have been at sea recently, but it would take far more time to develop this much scarring. Ah…" So saying, he pulled a ticket out of the man's coat pocket, but he took one glance at it and then flicked it away as if it were something distasteful, then took a long snuffle at the man's coat for all the world as if he were an eager bloodhound.

Curious, I retrieved the ticket off the floor. "Holmes," I said, "this is a ticket for a steamer leaving tonight! This is Moriarty's escape! Did he not tell you in the letter that he would quit England and take a steamer?"

"Oh yes," Holmes said. "He did."

Count Dracula took the ticket from my hand. "*The Hecate*? We shall have to move quickly if we are to intercept this before its departure." He took a step toward the door, but Mina caught his arm and shook her head. She was looking curiously and with some indecision at Holmes, like a woman trying to solve a difficult problem.

"Is it possible that even now, you do not see?" Holmes said, still on his knees with the body. "This ticket was clearly a gambit, and not one Moriarty could have expected to work particularly well. Likely it was meant to fool this piteous underling with any possibility of it derailing us as a possible bonus. Yet you have all taken it for gospel. Moriarty has no intention of leaving England. Searching out this steamer would grant him valuable time by side-tracking our investigation."

"How do you know this?" Mina said.

"Smell the coat!" Holmes said, holding up a fistful of the offending woollen material.

Mina did so, a sight more delicately than Holmes had. "Salt from the sea," she said.

"And?" Holmes said.

"Soot, possibly from a train."

"Do you not smell the machine oil used in locomotives, as well?" Holmes asked. "The tickets are a fairy tale, a ruse, possibly one that this sea captain believed, as well."

"Sea captain?" I said.

"When a man has that much scarring on his hands," Holmes said, "but little recent scarring, but still smells that much of the open sea, it is an even bet that he is still a sailor, but has a position that requires less of the manual labour – that makes a man very high up in the ship's hierarchy the most likely, you see? Captain, I should say, or first mate. I should be very surprised if the man does not hail from the same ship that tried to sink your ship, Count. At least, I have that hope."

The Count furrowed his brow. "Why do you hope this?"

"It would mean that he is running low on resources," Holmes said, standing up. "Certainly Moriarty's gambits are getting more and more desperate and the ruses more and more transparent. I do not believe everything in Moriarty's letter…"

Dracula looked surprised. "Letter, you say?"

Holmes whipped out the letter in question and unfurled it with a snap of his wrist so that the Count could take it. He then sketched a very brief account of our recent excursion.

"I don't believe Moriarty intends to cede London, or England, at all," Holmes continued. "But I *do* believe that the horde underneath the warehouse represented a mutinous element that Moriarty needed to be rid of. There, he had little to lose, few precious resources to expend, for if we died and they lived, he would still have lost one group of enemies and reduced another. As it turned out, much the same happened even when we survived, for his mutineers are removed from the board and we are reduced."

I closed my eyes briefly, seeing again poor Somersby dying and Kitty Winter's stricken face. I could hear a touch of that pain in Holmes's tone, as well, for all that he talked now like the pure, cold logician. Reduced was, indeed, the correct word.

"I have put certain forces into play to make certain that the ship that sank the *King's Ransom* will, in turn, be sunk," Holmes said. "Another gambit that Moriarty used resources on extravagantly and it is my hope, as I said, that he is running low. However, the scent of soot is an oversight. I had already formed a few theories as to Moriarty's next action and considered a train escape out into one of the counties surrounding London to be a high probability. A falling back to regroup, but not yet conceding the game, which is, of course, England."

"If you deem that the most likely," Dracula said, "what do you propose?"

"We strike while the iron is hot!" Holmes said. "Your arrival has changed much, for Moriarty has to expect if not our deaths, at least an injury severe enough to take us out of commission for a few days, or possibly an exposure of Watson's vampire nature, both of which we shall neatly avoid. We shall head to the train station, I think, to see what traces we can locate there of our quarry, if you are up for it."

"Of course we are with you," I said.

"Good old Watson," Holmes said, with gratitude. He looked at the others.

Dracula and Mina exchanged a glance, then both nodded.

"We owe you a debt," Dracula said. "If you believe this to be the correct next step, you shall have all our powers at your disposal."

"Excellent!" Holmes said. "Now it only remains to give Mrs Hudson specific and direct instructions so she does not stumble onto a body, and we shall be off!"

Chapter 20

THE CHASE

We had a hasty word with Mrs Hudson and then Holmes had us into a four-wheeler carriage in short order and we were bouncing our way toward Kings Cross train station. This was a far cry from our previous trip which felt mired in defeat and Holmes was animated, practically quivering with pent-up energy. He had gone into his rooms before our departure and come out with a Gladstone bag, but would not reveal to any of us what was in it. He bore that bag with him into the carriage.

"I should like to drop Mina and Watson off on the platform together," Holmes said. "For I believe that while Dracula and I would be spotted at once by any agents Moriarty has keeping watch, Mina would be an unknown to them, and Watson, being slightly more nondescript, should be harder to spot, particularly in the company of a woman."

Certainly, both Holmes and Dracula, each with their height and lean, aquiline features, would both stick out severely. Still, I thought to object to Holmes's plan, partly because they might very well be on the lookout for Kitty Winter. While Mina certainly didn't have any of Miss Winter's wildness, she was still a woman to attract attention, with her long black mane, striking looks, and pale, pale skin. Also, while I did not quite possess Holmes's aquiline features, certainly being in his company for as long as I had would make me almost as likely to be spotted as he was. Still, Holmes often had reasons beyond the stated ones for his actions and something about the gleam in his eye as he made this request made me hold my tongue.

"I have no objection," I said.

"Nor I," Mina said.

"Will it be dangerous?" Dracula asked, his gaze slipping to Mina.

"I am not a wilting gardenia, my dear husband," Mina said mildly. Her tone was calm, but I could see that this comment touched on some other argument they had had previously, for there was a slight current of tension between the two of them. Mina's expression did not change and she continued to watch Holmes.

"We are battling Moriarty," Holmes said. "There will be danger the moment any of us step out of this carriage. There is danger if we let Moriarty work unfettered. We are encompassed all round with danger."

"I am not a wilting gardenia," Mina repeated firmly and Dracula nodded his reluctant acquiescence.

"But shall we not need you to pare down our choices of which trains to search?" I asked Holmes.

"He might attempt to go in stealth, hiding alone among the public crowd on any of the trains," Holmes said, "but that would be a great exposure to him, should he be discovered. It is my opinion that he shall engage a special, private train, peopled with what remains of his forces who are themselves likely to be his most loyal and stalwart vampire henchmen. This is suggested by these proceedings happening at night. It is my guess that he is relying on speed and plans to be gone by the time we would have followed his red herring to the docks and discovered our mistake. Look for anyone out of place, very likely in a railway uniform. While you are doing this, Dracula and I shall pursue our own line of investigation."

"Your logic seems sound," Dracula said, "but it is not, by any means, the only possible answer."

"Let us say the balance of probability," Mina said, interrupting my friend before he could answer. "This is where our literary studies give us our instructions, my dear, for it is very clear to me that Holmes has additional plans that he is reluctant to tell us." She looked at me with a dark twinkle in her eye, as if something about all this amused her. "It falls to us, Doctor, to play both the hounds in Holmes's plan, does it not? Flushing out Holmes's quarry while he and my husband circle in from the rear?"

"Madam…" Holmes said, sounding a trifle uncomfortable.

"Still," she said, "we all know enough from the Doctor's stories not to question your methods, don't we? I am quite sure there will be enough danger, as you said, for all concerned. I hope the Doctor and I can play our parts to the final denouement – and here we are."

The carriage had drawn up to the outside of the station as she spoke. She put a pale hand briefly on her husband's face. "Be careful, my love." Then, without waiting for the driver to come around and open the door, she opened it herself and stepped out into the street.

"Let us away, Doctor," she said, smiling.

A short bark of a laugh burst out of Holmes and he sat looking both a little chagrined and very amused by Mina's statement. "Is she always like this?" he asked the Count.

"Yes," Dracula said. His face was a stony mask and not one that invited comment or question, but I thought a slight shadow of a proud smile played at his lips when he thought we weren't looking.

"Very curious," I said to Holmes as I climbed out. "That is usually the question that everyone asks me about you."

Holmes laughed and called out to the driver to circle around to the other side of the station and the four-wheeler pulled away.

"Come along, Doctor," Mina said, holding out her arm for me to take. I was a little taken aback by this gesture, too, wondering what the Count might say, but she would not take no for an answer and certainly it would make us harder to spot, as Moriarty's lookouts would not be on the lookout for any kind of couple. Mina's outfit was sombre, mainly of dark red with a grey shawl, but certainly nothing seemed untoward about us as a couple or suggested anything unearthly. She even drew the shawl up a little around her face, which would not hide her identity from close inspection, but would certainly hide her exceptional beauty from the casual passer-by.

The station was busy, as it always was of an evening, with

several trains standing, steaming idly, while another pulled into the station. People of all class and character milled around in wait.

It was no trouble for Mina and I to wander the station and observe the doings without ourselves attracting attention. We had done this for only a dozen minutes or so before Mina pointed at one of the black engines backing slowly up to five train cars so as to link them all together. A red light hung in the engineer's compartment that seemed dull in the brightly lit station, but would undoubtably throw a hellish pall over everything once it moved into the darkness. The cars were painted red, too, gleaming dully.

"Holmes's special!" I said, speaking low. Then I saw what had tipped her off, in addition to the small number of railway cars. A pale man in an ill-fitting railway uniform. He had his cap pulled down, but he was almost certainly a vampire.

"May Mr Holmes's guesses always be right," Mina breathed and we started in that direction.

We'd gotten within a dozen strides when the man stepped off the back end of the rear carriage, heading in our direction.

"'Ere now," he said. "This is a private coach and not for the likes of…"

He bore down on us so quickly that it was child's play to raise the silver tip of my cane and jab it into the man's throat, so swiftly that I hoped no one would notice. To my absolute relief, the move worked astonishingly well and the man dropped at our feet, the silver reaction making a bubbling wreck of his throat. He shuddered once on the platform and went still.

As to my attempt to avoid any kind of outcry, laughable as

that was, that portion of my intentions became an appalling failure when Mina hailed a passing constable.

"Oh!" she cried out fretfully. "He just fell over! Please, sir, come help!"

"What are you doing?" I whispered.

She ignored me and waved the constable over. He came, along with a certain number of bystanders, drawn by the sudden curiosity. Mina, meanwhile, drew out of the now-forming crowd and led me up the stairs that our conductor friend had just quitted. I let myself be led and closed the train door behind me. We found ourselves without ceremony and fuss in a well-appointed train car with rich upholstery, heavy curtains, and a small bar set off to one side.

No sooner had we stepped into the compartment than four persons stepped into the same compartment through a door located on the other end. There was no doubt that we had the right train now, for these creatures were even more clearly vampires than the conductor had been, all of them bearing the train guard uniforms and caps with which any purveyor of the railways is familiar.

In that instant during which we all eyed each other, a slightly distant steam cry wailed out from the front of the train. Then came the rumbling of wheels underneath us as our train lurched into motion. Our train was underway. Whatever gambit Holmes had imagined employing, he and Dracula had missed their opportunity. I could see the glimmering lights from the platform fall away as we moved, leaving the station and entering the London night. Mina and I were on our own now.

Mina leapt at the attendants, a snarl issuing from her throat. She moved so fast she was almost a blur. If I had thought that the monsters under the warehouse or Miss Kitty Winter had fought with an alarming ferocity and speed, they were all of them nothing compared to Mina Dracula. She leapt the distance and used a clawed hand to rip out the nearest vampire's throat before I had raised my pistol. The other attendants gathered around Mina immediately so that I was afraid to fire for fear of hitting Mina. I had a moment's half-blurred remembrance of the implacable fury that Dracula would hold for anyone that caused her harm and did not want to generate a new enemy for England in this fashion, but I was also cognizant of a newly born respect and admiration for this strong-willed woman.

I moved in and used my cane on the nearest vampire grappling with Mina. The heavy silver end landed with a satisfying thump and my opponent fell. Mina had already dispatched a second vampire. The last spun and attempted to disembowel me with heavy claws, but I was able to bat his arms out of the way and then cudgel him down to the floor. I realized at that moment that the vampire I'd just knocked into unconsciousness was actually a woman, and felt an entirely inappropriate regret for having treated any woman so, regardless of the disease and her savage attack on my person. The man in the conductor's uniform outside on the platform had spoken, however briefly, and had clearly passed through the animal stage of the vampire transformation. He might be a criminal in Moriarty's employ, but he was not a monster. I had to assume that these four might be the same. Three of them, including the man I had just felled, were unconscious, but alive. The fourth person was alive too, but just barely, bleeding even as I watched from the terrible wound to the throat that Mina had inflicted.

"Doctor," Mina said. "Time is pressing."

"This will take but a moment," I said, tearing the man's shirt to make a quick bandage. If it were bound, with the vampire's ability to heal, it was very likely the man would recover.

"They would not perform the same service for you," Mina said.

"All the more reason for me to do so," I said. "Or else what kind of world are we fighting for?"

"It is not a fight, Dr Watson," Mina said. "This is a war."

"If it is war and we wish to fight for the angels," I said, "it would be well for us to act as if we deserve victory. There, it is done."

"If they are to remain alive, we should at least ensure they are bound," Mina said, bending over and suiting action to word. I agreed to this clear necessity and performed the same on our next incapacitated prisoner.

Mina stood up when we had finished with a curious look on her face as she regarded me with her marvellous dark gaze. "Stout British morality. I had almost forgotten it and there are things you miss out in the wilderness of Transylvania. I see now why Holmes has kept your company all these years. Your value as a moral compass far surpasses your value as a chronographer." I looked to see if she spoke in mockery, but her tone was clearly wistful and her expression serious. She put a hand on my shoulder and opened the car door so that we might penetrate further into the train.

The air was brisk as we went between cars, whipping by quickly, for we had already picked up enough speed to be going at least twenty miles per hour and were accelerating still. I thought we headed west, but was by no means certain of that prognosis.

The next car had been outfitted to hold a king, it seemed, so sumptuous were the surroundings. Mahogany tables and stuffed brown leather divans and armchairs all crowded in together, the latter two littered with scarlet cushions. Rich curtains covered the windows on the right side, but the left was covered completely with bookshelves fitted with carved rosettes, corner blocks, medallions, and plinths, as well as decorative guardrails to hold the books in place. The books themselves seemed to cover, at a brief glance, a wide variety of topics, though I noticed mathematical subjects dominated. Several small brass chandeliers hung from the railcar ceiling, and glittered opulently as they swayed slightly to the movement of the train. The carpet was rich and soundless, a deep and dark chocolate colour. There must have been further soundproofing custom-built into the room as well, for the sounds of the rails and the engine were soft and distant. Even the motion of the car seemed subdued, and I had to wonder if some kind of shock reduction had been engineered into the wheels and undercarriage. Never in any visit to the train station before had I experienced the like.

At the far end was a brass ladder that led to a trapdoor in the railcar ceiling and a man was poised several rungs up with his hand reaching high.

He wore a black suit, cut in the continental style, with plain buttons that somehow did not quite fit the magnificent room around us. He was mostly bald, with a grey-haired fringe remaining, neatly cut, but a cranium of portentous proportions. I had no doubt whatsoever about who he was. He glanced briefly down at us with cold, reptilian eyes that held no warmth in them at all, and flicked dismissively away from us in the same motion. His hand finished the motion we'd interrupted with our entrance and pushed back the trapdoor in the ceiling. It fell open with a thump and a sudden rush of air and noise.

I lifted my revolver as an explicit threat, but Moriarty – for I was filled with certainty it must be he – gave us one more dismissive glance and leapt, in one shockingly swift motion, out of sight and onto the roof of the car. I never even had a chance to aim. He certainly did not move like an elderly person. If I had needed any reminder of the supernatural nature of our quarry, that sudden, swift motion confirmed it completely.

"He's on the roof!" I said, somewhat needlessly. Mina and I gave immediate chase.

I was first to the ladder and went up it as quickly as I could, Mina right behind. Again, I chafed at the unfortunate circumstances that had left Holmes and Dracula behind. I dearly yearned for my friend's cool and decisive manner in times of action. The motion of climbing the ladder with a drawn pistol was, by necessity, a slightly awkward one that did not leave me a free hand, and so I lost my bowler hat the moment I poked my head up into the cool night air.

The moon was out, a pale lantern in the city sky, and the dark shadows of buildings and open fields were sliding by on either side. We were going fast now, and clearly out of the city proper.

I crouched on the rounded roof, still awkwardly holding onto the pistol while I braced myself with my other three limbs. Not seeing anything toward the rear of the train, I craned my neck around to view the cars in front of us, and saw the figure of Moriarty scuttling on all fours with inhuman alacrity along the top of the train toward the engine. Mina joined me and I inclined my head in Moriarty's direction and we stood, swaying, and gave chase.

Before Moriarty had taken another dozen rapid steps, he froze, then stood up, slowly backing away from the gap between the second and third railway cars, which he had been about to reach. Moriarty's figure blocked our view, so it took half an instant for me to realize that he had stopped because someone climbing up the outside ladder had thrust a pistol into his face.

Moriarty continued to back away, very slowly, from the figure that moved, somewhat unsteadily on account of the train, to stand in front of him. The figure had to struggle with his top hat, too, lest it suffer the same fate as my bowler. The train's engine spewed gouts of smoke and soot into the air which made visibility poor and brought a great reek to my nose and throat. I found that even with my slightly heightened vampire reflexes, it took some concentration to adjust myself to the motion of the train, as well as to the slippery roof of the train car, for there was now some slight rain flying into my face and the surface made for a very slippery one.

Holmes! He hadn't missed the train at all, but had somehow managed to infiltrate it before it had left the station. I still hadn't seen any sign of Dracula, however, and wondered if they'd separated.

Mina and I reached the same rooftop as Moriarty and Holmes now, though they were on the far side. Moriarty between Holmes and us, with his back in our direction.

"You have won, Mr Sherlock Holmes," Moriarty said, lifting his voice to carry over the ramshackle rhythm of the train. "Will you kill me in cold blood?"

Holmes moved in a slight crouch, stepping away from the ladder, and gestured to it for Moriarty to descend.

Then the train made a slight shift, perhaps crossing the points, which jolted us slightly. Holmes stumbled, which was all the opportunity Moriarty needed.

Moving with that blinding speed I had seen him demonstrate before, Professor Moriarty slapped the pistol easily out of Holmes's hand. They were still a dozen yards away and I cried out, but it was no use. Moriarty had Holmes by the neck and twisted him around so as to present him to us as a human shield. A great swath of dirty smoke billowed around them, making them briefly indistinct, before clearing away. Holmes's hat, dislodged by the Professor's sudden manoeuvre, flew into the wind and was gone. Holmes gasped, soundlessly, as the Professor held him.

"Not so fast, Doctor!" Moriarty cried out. "You wouldn't want to risk hitting your friend. What would the world do without its greatest detective and the second-most powerful intellect in all of England?" His voice dripped scorn and derision. "You wouldn't want that, now would you?" He had one hand around Holmes's neck and held him fast with an iron grip, but my view of them continued to be intermittently blocked by the billows of sooty smoke. I had reason to know that Holmes's grip was no slight thing, but it was nothing now to Moriarty's, and I could see that Holmes's fingers pried frantically, but uselessly, at Moriarty's immobile fingers while he continued to gasp for breath.

"Unhand him, monster!" I shouted, but Moriarty presented too small a target, hiding as he was behind Holmes, for me to risk a shot on the roof of a moving train. Holmes seemed helpless in his grasp, losing the struggle to get air.

"It won't be like Reichenbach Falls," Moriarty gloated, shouting into the detective's hair. "That's far enough, madam. Unless you want me to snap his neck?" This last was to Mina, who had inched forward slightly. I put a restraining hand on her elbow, though I kept my revolver aimed, hoping for an opportunity.

"I had just come into my powers then," Moriarty raved. He was seemingly focused entirely on his helpless prisoner, but the instant I moved my weight to take a step his gaze snapped on me and he moved his free hand to seize Holmes by the hair, bending my friend backward, against all his strength. Moriarty positioned his arms so as to snap my friend's neck in an instant. I froze and my heart quailed.

"Foolish to try and apprehend me with your weak link presented in the forefront," Moriarty said. "The weak, *human* link, Holmes, but I knew you would never see yourself in that light. Your ego would not permit it and this is a blind spot, so easy to exploit. You do not understand, Holmes, the profound and powerful combination of a superior intellect that drives an enduring, potent vampire body. You yourself had the opportunity to seize it, I understand, but were too weak to embrace it. Fool! You value your resources, your friendships, which is your ultimate weakness." He shook Holmes like a ragdoll without releasing his grip and I feared for my friend's life, but never had the chance to get a clear shot and dared not advance. Moriarty had lost all reason. His hair was wild, his eyes blazing, and spittle hung from his lips.

He regarded Mina, standing frozen next to me. "You are alive, I see. Unexpected, but not entirely unimaginable. Your husband must have survived, too, I wager."

No one answered him and he glared down at Holmes. "Resources sometimes fulfil their ultimate potential when they are expended, and you never saw that? Friendships are a weakness, Holmes. I would think that you, of all people, would understand that. There is no room for friendships in the mind and heart of the true ruler. Only someone that has lived with power for countless centuries. Isn't that correct, Count Dracula?"

He shouted the last two words of this speech. I was astonished at the uncontrolled display of fury. I had never met Moriarty before this, but Holmes's descriptions had prepared me for a malevolent force, to be sure, but one of controlled malice, not this snarling, spitting, furious monster of a man. Moriarty's schemes had all contained plans within plans, and when Holmes had portrayed him as a spider in the centre of an enormous web, it had been a testament to his patience and cunning. This man was a fury of passion and I saw now why Holmes had had his doubts about it being the same man behind the machinations all this time. Vampirism had changed Moriarty, making him far more reckless and perhaps even more dangerous to everyone and everything around him.

"Dracula!" Moriarty shouted again. "I know you must be here. Holmes would not be so foolish as to come without you. Reveal yourself, or he dies!"

The train whistle blew and a cloud of steam and soot and smoke washed over our heads, but no other answer came. Or so I thought at first.

Then the cloud cleared completely and I saw the figure astride the roof of the engine. There was no mistaking the proud silhouette of the Wallachian nobleman, tall and stern, with the grand sweep of his black mane and the cloak billowing around him.

"You see?" Moriarty said. "You see now, at last, how little friendships matter to one who is immortal? With your intellect gone, there is no one who can sit across the board from me as an equal. Even now, I have agents, both human and vampire, in places that you cannot, Count, possibly ferret out without the help of the world's... greatest... detective..." Here he shook Holmes again, punctuating every word with an angry, bone-rattling motion. "They can find you, Dracula, find you and your lovely bride, and end you. For I have set into motion a world that will know all the important details of you, your bride, and your kind. They will know the vampire, not as a tale to frighten, but as a world-ending plague that needs to be eradicated for the human race to continue. Imagine the frightful forces that could be raised against you once the world knows everything? Do you think you can stand against all the nations of the world? How long would it take agents of the same to find you during daylight? How much will they sacrifice to end you once they realize that their very existence is on the line?"

He turned slightly so that he could face the Count behind him, while still holding Holmes as a shield against my pistol.

"So what say you?" said Moriarty. "You could attempt to benefit with your association to Mr *Sherlock Holmes*, who offers you little, or you could come into an accord with me, who offers the world. Who could stand against the two of us, with Sherlock Holmes gone?"

"No, my love, please no," Mina breathed, but she looked more frightened than I had thought possible. Suddenly, much about the Count and Mina became clear to me. I could hear, in that brief prayer, and see in her worried expression, that she indeed feared for her husband's eternal soul, and perhaps her own. Vampires they were, yes, but only as victims of a rare blood disease, not as the monsters that Stoker portrayed. Yet Count Dracula had lived many years, many centuries if even half of what I had heard was true. Living so long as other humans died around you would make it supremely difficult to maintain the clear precept that human life had value, as clear a demarcation for morality as any I'd ever known. It was also clear that in Mina's mind, she and her husband were on a moral precipice and in very real danger of falling over into a Dantean abyss, from which there would be no recovery. That moral fall, her very own Reichenbach, held more terror for her than death ever could.

Dracula said nothing, did nothing, and a cold, cold terror rose up inside of me.

Then he lifted his arm, very quickly, revealing, of all things, a pistol. At the same time, Holmes, revealing a strength I would not have given him credit for, broke Moriarty's iron grip and pushed him out at arm's length.

Dracula's pistol fired, twice. The reports of the pistol cracked and were then whipped away by the wind.

Moriarty stumbled, hit. I fired my own pistol, putting another silver bullet into Moriarty's chest.

Holmes pulled Moriarty into his own clutches. Then, my mind felt nearly rent asunder as Holmes, my lifelong companion of many years, *buried his teeth in Moriarty's throat*, tearing for all the world like a lupine predator, spattering a fountain of blood into the night air that dispersed into a scarlet mist as the train rushed heedlessly on.

I have campaigned in foreign wars and seen, in Holmes's company, some of the most appalling crimes ever perpetuated on man, most of them very recently in Gravesend, and yet it is the sight of Moriarty's throat being torn out on top of a moving train that still haunts my daylight slumber.

Holmes, blood dripping from his lips, still had a grip on Moriarty's coat so as to prevent the mortally injured man from falling overboard, but it was Dracula who rushed forward, still holding the pistol, and put yet one more silver bullet into Moriarty's head, ending the man completely and finally.

Then Holmes – for it was Holmes, *not* Dracula who had appeared on top of the engine – dragged off his unruly black wig that had lent him Dracula's appearance and lowered his pistol. Dracula, who had torn out Moriarty's throat, now dropped the body without ceremony onto the roof of the train car. He shook out his hair, which had been slicked back to provide, along with Holmes's overcoat and scarf, the appearance of London's consulting detective.

"That worked far more admirably than I expected," Dracula said. "The scent of your clothes I now wear would not have stood the test of close proximity."

"The top of a train in the rushing wind did thoroughly suit our purposes in terms of disguising scent and providing poor visibility," Holmes said. "We have Moriarty to thank for that. I had hoped for a second or two's grace from our ruse in order to grant us a decisive advantage in our coming battle. I had hoped that this advantage, plus the addition of Mina and yourself, who I did not think Moriarty expected in the first place, would tip the scales in our favour."

"It worked wonderfully," I said.

Mina had gone over to her husband and into his arms, an open display of affection I found both touching and strangely out of place on top of a moving train.

"You look strange in another man's clothes," she said, gazing fondly up at him. "How did he ever convince you to perform such an act?"

He looked down fondly at her, his dark, hooded eyes soft. "He promised it would make things less dangerous for you and shift much of the greatest risk onto myself."

"You take too many chances," she said.

"Could we possibly take this conversation out of the wind?" Holmes said. "None of you feel the bite of the wind, but I assure you it is quite intolerable!"

"There is one more thing to accomplish," Count Dracula said, brushing a stray lock out of Mina's eye before he released her and turned to the body of Professor Moriarty. The train was visibly slowing now, but still moved at twenty miles an hour or so, I hazarded. We chugged out onto a bridge running over a heavily forested area, including a small tributary of the Thames, though I was too ignorant of our current geographical location to guess which one.

Dracula lifted his foot and shifted his weight in order to give the body a push with his booted foot, but Holmes lifted his hand and quickly knelt to search the body. His eyes glittered with pleasure as he pulled a small booklet from Moriarty's coat pocket.

Dracula, seeing Holmes had searched to his satisfaction, kicked the body off and Moriarty's corpse slid off the roof of the train and disappeared into the forested darkness.

"An exceptional waste," Holmes said, looking down. "A mind of the first order. He might have done so much had he taken a different path."

"Indeed," I said.

"Come!" Holmes said. "I am quite losing the feeling in my hands and would very much prefer to be in my own clothes."

Chapter 21

DENOUEMENT

"As I commented on the train, the plan would hardly have worked as well in a stuffy parlour," Holmes said back at Baker Street. He stretched his long legs toward the fire and lit his pipe. "I had actually envisioned rather a long chase. I thought that Moriarty would have an escape route planned and that our plan would necessitate following. So I had resolved to attempt to spring my own trap in the out of doors, or else our little ruse could hardly be expected to last very long. The scent, you see, and Dracula has little compared to your average Londoner. I thought him wearing the clothes I had worn previously and thus carrying my scent would buy us a little time, but I had hardly expected the good fortune of having our encounter on the top of a moving train. We were quite fortunate that the smoke from the train occluded both sight and scent, too."

"Good fortune," I snorted. "On top of a moving train! Hardly my idea of ideal circumstances."

"Yet it was ideal for us nonetheless," Holmes said with a smile playing about his lips.

"It was a matter of making surest use of our advantages," Dracula said. "We would lose any element of surprise from my appearance the moment that Moriarty saw you with the good doctor and so measures were needed to preserve it." He was restored to his usual mode of dress in his sombre suit and cape and sat now with Mina on the settee, as unnaturally immobile as only the ancient vampire could be. Mina seemed deeply amused by the night's harrowing adventure. Her dark eyes shone with excitement and she looked perfectly at home. For my part, I could not take quite the same view, suffering as I had on many occasions Holmes's need for secrecy and dramatic effect, but I did have to admit to being very gratified as to the results.

"You two may find this of interest," Holmes said, handing them a new article folded so as to present the section indicated. "The Royal Navy has found and sunk Moriarty's vessel, the one that sank the *King's Ransom* and very nearly you two with it."

"It is truly over then," I said with great relief. "Moriarty is dead and all his machinations fallen with him."

"Yes," Holmes said. "I believe we can safely say that."

"You have been of great service to me," Dracula said formally and pulled a small leather satchel out of his coat pocket. "There is some gold here, and silver, and even some English pound notes. I hope the amount is sufficient?"

I half-expected Holmes to refuse payment, for he had a long and mercurial history in this regard, but Holmes reached out a long arm and took the satchel, dropping it unexamined with a heavy clink on the table next to him. "More than sufficient, I am sure, which is just as well, since I have already committed a portion of it to a new endeavour that may interest you."

"Oh?" Dracula said. There was a note of forced casualness, and a certain mischievous gleam in Holmes's eye that made the rest of us lean forward slightly.

"I believe it may be useful and necessary for us to confer from time to time and as such, I thought to procure a suitable place for your stay should you have need to travel to London again. It will not be unfamiliar to you, I think."

Dracula leaned back, looking more than a little shocked. "I see. This is unexpected. In fact, I expected... something different. A warning against my return to London, perhaps?"

Holmes waved a hand in dismissal. "Not a bit of it. You have proven yourself a valuable ally against the darkness, despite your reputation. It is important for the logician to view things as they *are*, not as they appear, and London owes you a great debt for your assistance. Besides, this is Mina's home, is it not? It would be very uncouth of me to attempt to prevent her from visiting it."

Mina smiled. "You said the place would be familiar to us?"

"More to the Count, I believe, than yourself. In fact, he used to own it some years ago. Carfax Estate is the place I mean and solicitors are already at work preparing the paperwork for my ownership."

"Carfax Estate!" I said, stunned, thinking of the horrors that had passed there; some distant, if even the smallest part of Stoker's tale was to be believed, and some of them very recently. "Holmes, sometimes your sense of what is appropriate is… somewhat lacking in taste. Carfax Estate, indeed!"

"It is a wonderful name, is it not?" Holmes said. "Carfax, Carfax. It rolls off the tongue. I suggest, my dear fellow, that the next time you are looking for a nom de plume to populate one of your stories, a technique I know you scrupulously use to protect the actual identities of our clients, you should try Carfax on for size. I think that Lady Carfax has a rather nice ring to it, don't you?"

I threw my hands up in the air in defeat. Holmes was in fine spirits with the successful conclusion of this affair and was very likely to be completely insufferable for days.

"I will, of course, leave the tending of the house to your care," Holmes said to Dracula. "You still have agents in the city, do you not?"

Dracula looked surprised yet again. "I do, but how did you know?"

Holmes reached over and hefted the satchel again. "There is certainly some metal in here, but I detect quite a bit of paper and you made a reference to English pounds. You have been here before and owned several properties before, which would have required a great many agents. You having retained some of these, despite being repelled from London previously, is the simplest explanation that would account for this sum."

Dracula nodded. "You are quite right."

"There is one other matter," Holmes said. He reached over and picked up the small notebook he had liberated from Moriarty's body. "I have been spending some time with this remarkable little book. Moriarty, even as a vampire, was a careful man, and his notes are purposefully cryptic and sparse to a degree that it is nearly an exercise in cryptography to decipher them. However, it has provided some information and I believe I can shed light on a few things. At the beginning of the case, you had come to the conclusion that our adversary was an 'elder' vampire, to use your term, giving us the impression that we were dealing with someone who had been a vampire for decades, if not centuries. But this was clearly incorrect. If Moriarty had acquired vampirism just before our encounter at Reichenbach, which is what an entry in this book suggests to me, then Moriarty had only twelve years as a vampire. This is an astonishingly short period of time in which he seems to have both understood the transformation far better than we have and also acquired a number of the powers that you have ascribed to 'elder' vampires."

"I do not follow," I said.

"You, yourself are the proof of that," Holmes said. "You were lured out into the street through a feat of mental manipulation that I suspect Dracula would be hard-pressed to emulate." He looked pointedly at the Count, who nodded in curt agreement.

Holmes continued. "Mary showed no sign of these powers when we encountered her later. Who else but Moriarty could have provided the assistance?"

Both Dracula and Mina looked, in degrees, disbelieving, astonished, and finally, soberly thoughtful as the implications of Holmes's words sunk in.

"The first point is this," Holmes said. "We must continue the good professor's work. We must come to a better, more scientific understanding of vampirism. Its disease and its powers, bereft of superstition. Who better equipped, I ask you, but the persons in this room?"

Dracula and Mina shared another glance.

Finally, Dracula inclined his head. "Yes, there is great wisdom in what you say. I see now that I have allowed… the situation to wrongfully dissuade me from pursuing, as you say, a scientific approach. I shall not make that mistake again."

"Capital," Holmes said. "The second point is this…" He paused, looking dramatically at each of us. When he finally spoke, his voice was so quiet that all of us, even with our vampiric hearing, had to lean forward to catch it.

"Who infected Moriarty?"

Dracula and Mina and I all sat backwards, collectively stunned. I certainly had not considered this incredibly profound and important detail and I could tell from the expressions on the others' faces that they had not either.

Holmes took a long drag on his pipe, his eyes glittering, and I could see that he was privately pleased by the stir that his question had caused. "Consider this: if it was an 'elder' vampire, as you deem them, then there is still a significant threat out there."

"You disturb me, Mr Holmes," Dracula said.

"It is a disturbing thought," Holmes agreed.

"You have given us much to think upon," Dracula said, standing and smoothing his waistcoat, "but if there is nothing else, I believe the time has come for us to depart. Again, you have my thanks." He took Mina's hand as she stood up to join him.

"We should perhaps view the estate grounds before departing England," Mina said. "With your permission, Mr Holmes?"

"I was about to make the same suggestion," Holmes said. "It will, however, be a few days before the solicitors bring over the keys and paperwork, but a few gates and barred windows are not likely to be much of an obstacle in the meantime for either of you, I believe."

"We might as well take over Moriarty's empire," I said ruefully, "for we are well on our way to forming our own criminal enterprise at this rate." But I couldn't keep a smile from tugging at my lips.

"All for the good of London, I am sure," Mina said with a brilliant smile. She reached for my hand and I gave it to her. "You are a good man, Dr Watson, for all your reservations and despite your misleading narratives."

"Misleading, madam?" I said. "I assure you that Holmes is every bit as remarkable as I have portrayed him. Exaggeration on that front has never been necessary. Surely you have seen that for yourself?"

"Oh yes," she said. "It is *yourself* you misrepresent. Your stories, dare I say, present you as a trifle slow, while I have found you perceptive and quick, in addition to being compassionate and honourable."

"Beware Watsonian deception," Holmes said with a laugh. "There is no use knocking on that particular door, dear Mina. I have been trying for years with absolutely no success. The good doctor's compulsion to romanticize and embellish for dramatic effect is, I'm afraid, irredeemable."

"How very fortunate," Mina said, "that you are, yourself, above such dramatic gestures." Her face was a perfect mask of polite seriousness.

"A touch, my dear," Holmes cried. "A distinct touch!"

"Count Dracula," I said, extending my hand.

"This is a night filled with surprises," Dracula said, but took my hand in his strong, ancient grip. "Let me also offer my deepest condolences for your loss. I was not able to before, but wish to now. I know," and his glance strayed to Mina, "how much the loved ones in our life can keep us whole."

"Thank you," I said sombrely. "That is very kind."

The two of them departed as I watched out the window, waiting carefully until the four-wheeler with the Draculas in it had left our kerb, clattered down the street, and then turned the corner.

"Carfax indeed!" I said, turning to Holmes.

"I will admit to some reservations about the Count Dracula," Holmes said. He had seated himself again, lit his pipe while I had been at the window, and now blew blue smoke rings into the air.

"Reservations?" I said. "While he was certainly instrumental in stopping Moriarty, there is no doubt that the man has a deeply homicidal past!"

"The man has been at war," Holmes said. "He was a king and soldier, first against aggressors in his land of Romania, and then, after his transformation, against all of humanity."

"You believe that part of the story?" I asked, incredulous. "We have only his word for that."

"We have a little more than that," Holmes said. "He has the stride of a soldier, even after these many years. There are other signs that incline me to take his claim of nobility at face value, not the least of which is his scrupulous adherence to honour and the truth. Also, there is Mina to consider. With Mina in play, I see our Count Dracula as becoming, perhaps, a potent and powerful force for light."

"Surely you must be joking."

"Not a bit," Holmes said. "Consider carefully his deportment in London during this last case. I saw every evidence that he was fastidious about his methods and harmed no living person during his stay here. He has committed no crime against the decent London citizenry and really it is beyond my purview, I think, to enforce crimes in another country and from another century."

He reached out his long arm and grabbed a sheaf of letters off the table, then thrust them at me. "I see you remain unconvinced, but let me see if I can perhaps put this into perspective. These are some of the letters that I have received and been, as yet, unable to answer due to the focus on the Moriarty affair. Do me a favour and give me your opinion on which one best deserves our attention next."

I frowned at this transparent attempt to change the subject, but rifled through the papers anyway, then found myself suddenly paying more serious attention to what they said.

"This first one seems to be about the Whitechapel murders," I said. "They think that they are starting up again."

"Yes," Holmes said. "Not without interest. And the next?"

"This one claims… Holmes, this is preposterous! They claim to have been burglarized by a lion that walks like a man." I rifled through the rest. "The next appears to be from a woman whose employer can disappear in plain sight? Where has this ridiculous collection of fairy tales come from?"

"In the case of the last one you mention, Sussex," Holmes said lazily. "I have been sifting through my correspondence to locate the most outré for you, but this last bundle rather outdoes itself. We have tales of disappearing men and talking animals, cadaverous monsters and magical portraits. You have, as usual, dredged up the most appropriate term imaginable when you say 'fairy tales', haven't you?"

"You can't take any of this seriously?" I said.

Holmes waved a hand. "A year ago, I did not take stories of vampires seriously and now we both know very much better, do we not? In the past year we have encountered not only vampires, but mysterious cults that call on inhuman sea gods and get answers. Monstrosities of the sea both large and small. Mark my words, Watson, humanity is expanding its level of knowledge in all the scientific fields and finding that a multitude of impossible things are out there waiting for us, now that we have become advanced enough to see them. You read that bundle of letters and call them fairy tales, but we already organize and fund a clandestine organization to police the morgues and cemeteries for creatures of the dead. What other dangers might require an organized response? I would be very much surprised if we do not encounter all of your fairy tales, and more, in the coming year. In such a light, would it not be better to keep Dracula as an ally?"

"I suppose you are right," I said.

The next day found us in the dappled sunshine of Highgate Cemetery. As many funerals as I have attended over the years, circumstances invariably unfold during these occasions to provide weather fitting to the occasion so that the proceedings are filled with a dreary and cold rain, while the mourners are always a tangled mass of slick ulsters and black umbrellas. If, by chance, the sun ever shone during such a solemn occasion, there was always a sense of bleak irony about the scene. Today, however, there was nothing ironic about the blazing sun overhead as they lowered Nigel Somersby's closed casket into the earth. The sun was an oppression to me, entirely fitting for the saddest of occasions, with nothing of the bright cheer that I had once looked upon the sun with. The night and the darkness was home now to those of us with the vampire affliction.

Somersby's mother had become a vampire and Somersby had had to stake her himself in order to save the rest of the family. The circumstances left Somersby's father and sister with the impression that he'd been quite mad. As such, they did not attend the funeral. Somersby's work on the Midnight Watch had further estranged him from daytime friendships so there were no mourners except for Holmes, Miss Winter and myself, and half a dozen others from the Midnight Watch, because Miss Winter would not hear of engaging a funeral director or professional mourners. Holmes demurred completely, admitting to me in private that it was probably just as well to invite fewer participants and fewer questions.

Miss Kitty Winter, bedecked appropriately enough in black dress and veil, with her vibrant fire-red hair held back and hidden in black lace and a large black umbrella held up against the sun, did not cry or openly lament, but merely stood with a dour expression that might have been carved from stone. I noticed that the rest of the Midnight Watch, none of them vampires and all of them men in Holmes's employ, did not attempt to converse with Miss Winter, though I had the impression that it was respect, deference and not a little fear that held the men back, rather than any intended slight. She stood alone and her stiff-backed stance did not invite approach. Even Holmes and I, when we offered our condolences, received only the barest of nods. In our relatively short acquaintance, I had seen Kitty Winter suffer great loss with Somersby, Shinwell Johnson, and even Baron Adelbert Gruner, for all that he had been a mortal enemy to her before that. The poets and religious texts have said that every life is encompassed round with death, but while this may be true for every man, woman and child, it is more true for some than for others.

She came to us under the shade of an enormous elm after the clergy had finished saying their words and the caretakers had started working. The constant scrape of shovels biting into the earth were a backdrop to our conversation.

"The Midnight Watch is needed more than ever," she said without greeting or preamble. "I'm more determined to see it through than ever now, in case you're wondering. Might be the only thing that's worth doing anymore. I'll be keeping watch over the graves long after you are dead and buried, Mr Sherlock Holmes. See if I don't."

"Thank you, Miss Winter," Holmes said simply, "and… I am very sorry. Somersby was a good man."

"He was," Miss Winter said. "Thank you." She turned to me. "I know your own wife passed some months ago, though I won't pretend to know the details. I can see in your eyes that her being gone weighs on you just as my losses weigh on me. I never offered my condolences before, but I'll offer them now."

"Thank you, Miss Winter," I said. "I am very sorry for your loss, too."

"We'll have more in common every passing year, won't we?" she said. Her gaze slid momentarily to Holmes and I could see she was thinking about how our lives, hers and mine, would very likely stretch for years after all our companions, such as Sherlock Holmes, had long since passed.

"Yes," I said to her, "it is very likely that we shall."

She nodded in stark satisfaction. "Well, gentlemen, if you need me, you know where I'll be." She swept her gaze around, taking in the cemetery along with the worn granite gravestones and monuments and those interred beneath, then shouldered her black umbrella and left us.

"I believe that we had best return to Baker Street," Holmes said. "I have many letters of interest to view and, I suspect, you have your own literary work ahead of you. At least the next few weeks, if not months, are not likely to be dull." He spoke casually, but I could see the gleam in his eye that told me his mind was already cataloguing his next steps.

"It seems," I said, "very unlikely."

For more fantastic fiction, author events,
exclusive excerpts, competitions, limited editions and more

VISIT OUR WEBSITE
titanbooks.com

LIKE US ON FACEBOOK
facebook.com/titanbooks

FOLLOW US ON TWITTER AND INSTAGRAM
@TitanBooks

EMAIL US
readerfeedback@titanemail.com

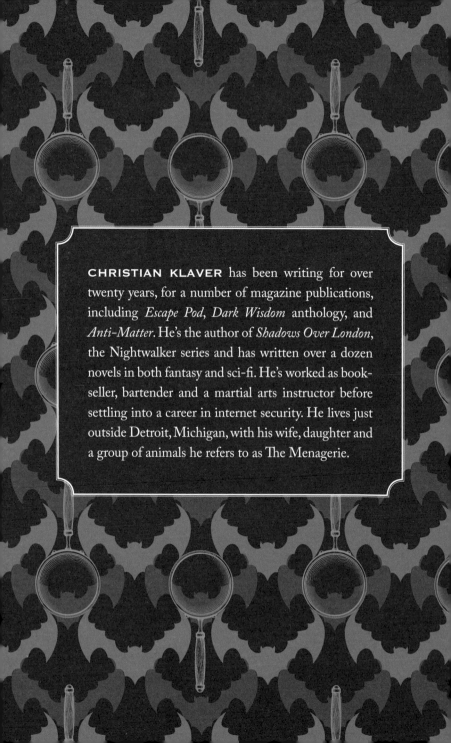

CHRISTIAN KLAVER has been writing for over twenty years, for a number of magazine publications, including *Escape Pod*, *Dark Wisdom* anthology, and *Anti-Matter*. He's the author of *Shadows Over London*, the Nightwalker series and has written over a dozen novels in both fantasy and sci-fi. He's worked as book-seller, bartender and a martial arts instructor before settling into a career in internet security. He lives just outside Detroit, Michigan, with his wife, daughter and a group of animals he refers to as The Menagerie.